ROASTMASTER
A Coffee Novel

JANICE LIERZ

BEAR PAGE PRESS

This is a work of fiction. Names, characters, places, and incidents are either the product of the author's imagination or are used fictitiously, and any resemblance to actual persons, living or dead, business establishments, events, or locales is entirely coincidental. The publication/use of trademarks is not authorized, associated with, or sponsored by the trademark owners.

Copyright © 2014 by Janice Lierz.
All rights reserved.

No part of this book may be reproduced, scanned, or distributed in any form without express written permission of the publisher.

Published by Bear Page Press, Asheville.

Bear Page Press and the Bear Page Press logo are trademarks of Zreil Global Marketing, Inc. or its affiliates.

ISBN-13: 978-0-9840584-1-9
ISBN-10: 0-9840584-1-9

For my father—
the greatest coffee man who ever lived.

1

Seven Sisters

Before the blue stars brighten or the gunpowder scent of the moon penetrates the sky, the air percolates with a strong brew. Scents can come in pairs, prodding some to choose. The daughter breathes in, while the mother breathes out. Capri's boyfriend gave her a ring. Her mother plans to take it away.

Two weeks ago, on her seventeenth birthday, Capri dyed her hair the color of a barn. It was as if her great-grandfather had handed her his old farmer's bucket full of his homemade concoction. A recipe of flaxseed oil and the blood of a recent slaughter, his secret ingredient was a dollop of milk to give the tincture that burnt-orange red.

Capri had all the signs.

The next day, she ran away with her boyfriend.

Now, she faces her mother with chopped and kinked hair and eyes that refuse to accept any possibility of grave consequences. Her hair has faded to pink, a shade that would look better on a lady's slipper or some small garden miracle still blooming in her mother's backyard. But her mother thrives on solving treatable problems, like coffee stains on carpets, snags that can be cured with the right consumer products and diligent scrubbing. If all else fails, she knows how to hide blemishes with end tables and makeup.

She does not know how to speak with her teenager about love.

Everyone hopes this will all fade, just like Capri's hair and Mexican tan. Hopefully, her experiments will run their courses. But her mother needs reassurances. She needs to see a safer path for her daughter. Her mother knows how love can cause life to veer off in dangerous directions—like Aunt John Mallory's did.

Capri's story has always been tangled in her aunt's death.

That is why they sit in the office that overlooks the garden at Rainbow Boulevard, near Kansas City, where seven sisters once lived, and why her mother drums her fingers on Granddaddy's old walnut desk with her hoop earrings rocking to the rhythm on what will be a full moon night.

Capri inherited this weakness for men from her mother, Trinka. She has heard stories about her mother's torrid affairs, not from her mother's lips but from her aunts'. Trinka, too, had once been a temptress of obsessive young love, addicted to short-breathed escapades with unsuitable lovers up rickety stairs. She ran just ahead of the bulls herself. Dressed in red.

Trinka is desperately trying to convince Capri that she knows a thing or two. How, in her day, many men loved her. Some wanted to possess her and lock her away, like a prize in their trunk, a baseball card or coin in mint condition, but she didn't let them.

The illusion of control can be a wicked taskmaster.

The mother has always chosen to raise Capri differently, not like her parents raised her, with commands and reprimands. She wants her daughter to make her own choices. So she guides her with gentle nudges down open hallways, with less focus on what she wants as a mother and more on what Capri desires.

Problem is, Capri desires Mac. Maybe she'll marry him.

That is why Capri finds herself brooding with her mother, with her five aunts pressing their ears to the door (failing to suppress their giggles), with her granddaddy resting miles away, and with her boyfriend waiting for her call.

The mother's eyes are dark droopy clouds that rest on the stone on her daughter's finger. Capri looks out the window. Her life is heading towards an array of games and gadgets—computers, phones, connectivity but unreachability when she chooses. Still, she has inherited her dead aunt's sprightliest sense of smell. She can detect fleeting scents in the spring breeze. With one whiff, Capri can identify the brew in her mother's coffee cup.

Ironically, it's a Mexican blend.

Her mother opens the drawer and pulls out a photo she's hidden in the back. "At the very least, you have to understand why I'm worried," she says as she hands her the black and white. "It seems like a lifetime ago. Years ago and today."

Capri cups the picture by the edges.

It is a snapshot of her dead aunt John Mallory.

"What does she have to do with me going out with Mac?"

"I'm going to tell you, young lady," her mother says, then sighs. "You remind me of her in so many ways. You're brainy, but your head's in the clouds. Full of life and headed straight for the cliffs."

Granddaddy says she reminds him of John Mallory, too. On some moon-filled nights, he takes the same photo out of his wallet and shows it to her, as if his seventh daughter was a story he cannot stop telling. Charms dangle from her bracelet as she points to the sky, as if a bird were going to come and land on her wrist. Her hair flows over her shoulders. Sun-drenched, he calls her. She's barefoot, near coffee trees, not much older than Capri, and at the foot of a mountain.

Granddaddy says Capri's laugh is like hers, and she has her lips. Her eyes aren't the same shape, but they're the same color, the color of the sea. They change and deepen depending on how she feels and what color she wears. Mood eyes, he calls them. And she has John Mallory's nose. "That nose," he says, looking at it with a tortured look on his face, as if he'd like to cover it so Capri can't smell, but he knows it would mean she'd quit breathing.

He always looks so sad then, and he slips into one of his blue moods, staring into space. That's when her mom and aunts start looking at the sky, dancing outside all hours of the night, and everything gets crazy, like the air is electrified. That's when her granddaddy always goes away.

Lately, Capri has started thinking John Mallory was her real mom. The way they go on and on about her, how she had that uncanny sense of smell, then they look at Capri. After all, Capri hasn't ever seen a picture of her mom when she was pregnant, and Trinka's never talked about any before or afterglow. Her mom claims motherhood is the cause of her cankles. Like she's been banned from a Victoria's Secret life because of Capri.

Her mother's hair is pinned up tight in a ball, like an egg sack on a spider's web. Capri is determined not to let family strings bind her. "I think John Mallory looks happy. And free."

Her mother swallows. "Granddaddy's gone. Let's stay in and play cards tonight. We could do our Mother Bean dance." She smiles and starts to stand.

"No," Capri says, narrowing her eyes. She drops the picture on the desk and concentrates on peeling her dried cuticles. She wonders if her mom has let the air out of her tires like she threatened. "I'm going out with Mac."

Her mother takes a deep breath, then closes her eyes. "Far away," she says, "we are in the land of coffee with the migrant Panama Indians. Listen closely, and you can hear the flute and drum calling in the distance—"

"That's probably the toilet running."

Her mom looks at her as if she knows nothing about Capri's species. She moves to the window and hugs herself. Capri knows her mother is with her dead sister in her mind because Capri begins to smell unfamiliar scents in the room, fruits of a foreign land, plantains and wild animals. It's as if scents are reaching to her through the wind, forcing her to relive memories she doesn't have.

Lately, the fragrances have been growing stronger. They make Capri restless. She's afraid to tell anyone, unsure if she can re-cork them if she gives them life with her words. So she holds her breath, resisting the odd scents that are trying to penetrate her body.

"I've got to go," she says, finally exhaling. "Mac's waiting."

Her mother's jaw tightens as she opens her eyes. "Let me tell you the story of the blue stars, of the Pleiades," she says. "Of the Seven Sisters."

"Really, Mom," Capri says with her hands on the armrest. "I'm too old for fairy tales. Anyway, I don't have time."

"Time," she says. "It's a funny thing we know nothing about." She shakes her head and reaches for a tissue, as if she were hoping paper could bring her tenderness.

Capri's mother has been telling her stories since she could remember. Trinka claims life as a sentient being with a heightened sense of smell brings magic or ruin. However, Trinka has a history of distorting tales, too. Like when Capri was seven and her mother convinced her to sharpen her mysterious powers and become more like Cinderella by misting grime with white vinegar and hydrogen peroxide. She convinced Capri to clean the attic with a magical potion of lemon juice and olive oil.

Capri looks at the clock, then lets her body relax. Her hands are back in her lap, but she raises her eyebrows as if that will speed along her mother.

"Once, there were seven sisters who loved to dance," her mother begins. "Some say her death was Sun's fault. He never should have tried to keep his youngest daughter for himself. But others claim it was a man. He was a robber." She sighs. "They both loved the seventh daughter too much."

"Mom, please."

"It's more than a myth. That's what I'm trying to tell you. About the Pleiades. It's why we're this way. Why we do what we do. You said you felt lost, and I'm trying to help."

Capri sniffs, concerned about the odd mixture of ocean and coffee she smells in the room. She tries to pretend she's not that interested in what her mother's saying, but she is a bit curious, because she knows her family is different. No one else's granddaddy fed them coffee in their baby bottles. But doesn't every kid think their family is packed with circus freaks?

"Your granddaddy has always been intrigued by the blue stars," her mother says and points to the window with the tip of her chin, "for obvious reasons. The Seven Sisters. I think it makes him feel heavenly, kingly even. Hot blue stars. The brightest ones."

Her granddaddy loves to point them out, the Seven Sisters in the sky with their hazy rings. He's shown them to Capri a thousand times.

Capri squeezes the end of her nose and releases it. It's becoming more difficult to ignore the stench. It's seeping under the door and through the windows. She keeps her eyes on her mother and sips the coffee. It is old, and the earthy undertones have turned bitter. It sat on the burner for far too long.

"Right after John Mallory left us, an article appeared in *The Kansas City Star*. It said that the Pleiades would only survive another 250 million years, then they would disappear." Her mother rubs her arms. "Well, Granddaddy panicked. It was almost as if they had said we would disappear. Tomorrow. Looking back, I think it was the first time he questioned his own mortality. That's when he started to get lost in time. He became obsessed with fairytales about the blue stars, about seven sisters. He checked out books at the library, collected stories."

Capri picks at a pimple on her face and stares past her mother. The sky is colored like sapphires, so deep that she could be a tiny dolphin lost in its ocean of smells. She tries to focus on more familiar scents. She remembers dancing with her mother under the golden light of the moon, both of them barefoot, twirling under the stars. They dipped salted crackers in honey and drank raspberry tea. Then Granddaddy would join them, twirling Capri under his arm. Her mother has always had an eerie fascination with the night sky, just like Granddaddy does. But he always goes away, like the moon, and her mother dances with her sisters, like some Celtic ritual that Sister Mary Joseph would certainly disapprove of.

Foreign fragrances begin to crowd Capri's senses again. She stands up. "I've got to go."

"Hear me out. If you do, I'll let you go," her mother says.

"With Mac?"

Her mother glares, as if Capri is two years old and has just asked to be left alone with paints on her white carpet.

"It's happening again," her mother says. "Not long after John Mallory arrived in Costa Rica, she stopped calling. Then her letters turned into postcards, and soon they stopped coming. My father never told us then, but we know now. Your granddaddy knew that his seventh daughter was in danger—she had fallen in love—and that would alter her life compass. We would all be cursed."

"Cursed? Come on, Mom."

"We are the Seven Sisters. We're the blue stars. It's as if we came from the sky in a basket. A man is in the bushes watching us dance. He falls in love with the youngest—"

"Mom, I hate to break it to you, but you and your sisters are not the incarnation of the Pleiades." She fakes a laugh and plops back into her chair. "And Mr. Wilson always watches you from the bushes, I've told you that a hundred times—"

"Listen, you may not believe me, but we're not like everyone else. History repeats. Right now, always." Her mother sits down and picks up the photo. "I'm trying to make you see. I see how you're changing. We all do. And you and John Mallory, you're connected, you're magical, you've always been—"

"Listen, I'm not magical. I wish I were," Capri says, "but none of us are. Frankly, right now I'm feeling a bit cursed." She holds out her palms.

"But you are magical," her mother says, taking her hand. She sweeps to her daughter and holds her cheeks. She leans so close Capri can smell the peppermint underneath her coffee. Her eyes shimmer, like fancy green diamonds. Capri knows her mother's trying to hypnotize her with the lull of her voice, the songbird of storytellers. Trinka cups Capri's face, spinning her fairy-tale with her mumbo-jumbo. She says, "Magic can be found in the bean of a fruit."

It's as if a larger mind knows Capri, her circumstances, her thoughts and needs. It knows that falling in love too young cannot be fanned away, like swirling blue smoke. It arranges events in the physical world, blinking lights at the mother-daughter crossroad.

"Imagine," her mother says, looking deep into her daughter's eyes, "if John Mallory had never gone. I never would have either. Then everything would have stayed the same. We would have her, and him, how we knew him, and there would be no sorrow or shame. But you see, Capri, a piece of each of us died in Costa Rica. We are of Sun and Moon, the Seven Sisters, and each one of us lost a chunk of our soul in the sky. John Mallory lives..."

Capri's lungs open, and her head begins to spin. In the sprinkle of moonlight, she breathes deeply below the canopy of kapok trees. In the cool cloud forest, wild monkeys swing from branches. Sweet bananas and plantains hang in bunches. Brilliant-orange flowers bloom on the vine before turning to pomegranate. Birds stir from their nests in the shade. Clusters of red and golden cherries rouse on the coffee trees.

Capri always felt like she had lost a part of herself somewhere between heaven and earth before she had ever started living. Her mother unspools the story because stories never really die. It's as if it's being whispered by the coffee cherries, somewhere in lands far away, where John Mallory walks, where they say she is a river, her breath the rise and flood, the fertilizer for the soil of her beloved coffee.

JANICE LIERZ

And Sun says to Seventh Daughter:
To fly, you say,
you must soar through
the sky, your skin the blush
of coffee cherries.
You leave only
your popsicle toes
to hold—the tail
of your kite; You
take wing
into the wrinkled sky,
crowded with stars, yearning
to taste the moon. I want
to release but am
afraid to fall
in sleepy eyes.
Under ray of black,
I tighten my grip.
For to lose you in the sky
means blackness forever.
Days and nights without
Love

2

Baby Dolls

John was downstairs drinking his third cup of coffee, staring at the large vinyl head of a Cabbage Patch doll. He couldn't stop admiring the marketing genius behind this must-have toy, now toddling its way into mass-production. But the grandfather clock had chimed too many bells. He sighed. Hours ago, before she had left for the Nelson Art Gallery where she volunteered, Barbara had given him his marching orders. Oh, how he missed the days when his wife adored him and waited on him hand and foot. Back before she knew her way around the city. When she didn't wear lipstick or paint her nails. When she wore pennies in her shoes and bobby socks on her ankles. Even before she put on her sunglasses, Barbara said, "Wake up Lady John and tell her it's time. Do it today!" Then she turned on her spiky heel and slammed the back door.

He eased his heavy boots up the steps. Normally, he would have called out, "It's morning, sunshine! Time to start your day, John Mallory," but this morning he wanted to catch her before she rubbed her eyes.

At the top of the stairs, he stood at the edge of her room while the sun reflected cherry-red in her dark hair. In her bed, she sighed from her cotton sheets, her lips curled like tulips. Still his Little Girl, he knew she had a scar on her thumb where she used to suck it. She had promised when she grew up she'd live next door and have him over for dinner every night. Blinded by his love, he couldn't see that the rest of her room looked like the aftermath of a wrecking ball—tossed books and clothes on the floor, a Jane Fonda workout tape underneath a tipped over coffee cup—his eyes were on the fresh lavender she had arranged in a vase.

The sound of her breathing made him realize how vulnerable he felt. He had to help her find a more orderly life.

Just yesterday, they had taken a walk. After she buttoned her jacket, he wrapped a scarf around her neck. In fur-lined boots they walked arm-in-arm and he tried to bring it up.

"You need a path," he said, "preferably one with benefits and security." She kept her eyes focused on the snowy sidewalk. "You graduated early because you said you wanted to get started on life, but you haven't. Come work for me. It's your destiny, John Mallory. Coffee can be your way of life too."

But she waved him away with a mitten.

"You're funny. When I read books on Saturday nights, you tell me to enjoy life more. But when I do, you tell me to find a job. You say don't grow up too fast, take my time, but then you're anxious for me to figure it out."

He shook his head and swallowed. "But it's been months. I don't think your future was prepared to wait so long."

"Don't you mean my mother?" She winked at him.

He slowed down, careful to avoid the icy patches. His favorite boots were warm but not invincible.

"I'm following my bliss," she said.

"Well your bliss appears to be dragging its feet."

She tossed back her head in laughter. "Daddy, you just don't understand. We don't all know what we want to do with our lives. I know you worry about my future, but I want to find something that ignites me. It'll come to me. I promise. I'm attracting it."

Half the time, he didn't understand her. All she seemed to be attracting was fruit flies and her mother's wrath. Besides, he thought he had attracted many riches. After all, he had made several modest fortunes in his lifetime. His father never gave him the luxury of lazing around contemplating what made him feel good. But just when he was about to argue with her, even press her, she started humming and grabbed his elbow at the edge of the street.

His namesake knew how to do things he had never thought about: how to sit still in a room, silently saying OM as she emptied her mind; how to cure the sniffles with Echinacea and his tennis elbow with the touch of her hands. She could solve a Rubik's Cube in less than two minutes and read books about mythology for hours. She ate raw fish rolled in seaweed and rice. At night, she entertained him with songs on her hammered dulcimer. He had expected her to be a mini-clone of himself (albeit the other gender) given that she bore his name, but in many ways they were worlds apart. The biggest surprise about her, though, and possibly the most magical, was that from birth his daughter detected every juicy drip of life. With the sprightliest sense of smell, no aroma ever swept by his daughter's nose without her flaring her nostrils.

That was how he knew she was destined for greatness.

He had intended to tell her that morning—she had to get a job—but she had been humming and he had so enjoyed her voice that his mind got sidetracked. Instead, he had called hello to Mrs. Potts.

"Did you ever notice how Mrs. Potts smells like McClain's Chocolate Cup Cookies?" John Mallory whispered. "Every Friday she wears that same white pantsuit and has that smirk on her face. Likes she has a secret treasure stashed in her kitchen. Old Mr. Miller smells like cookies on Saturdays."

It could be true, though he hadn't noticed. "You're so observant," he said.

"Now I'm dying for a cookie. Let's go to McLain's. My treat."

"Well, if it's your treat," he said, laughing. She took his hand and twirled under his arm. As they danced in the driveway, he forgot his thoughts. Instead, he whirled her around shallow puddles, so she wouldn't slip.

But this morning, as he stood at the foot of her bed, he furrowed his brows. His knees creaked even though he didn't bend. He couldn't keep her under a glass dome forever. He knew that. And, he supposed, he should stop trying to spook the neighbors so they'd move and she could live next door. He told Barbara he had no idea why Marge Johnson would install flood lights and start locking her doors. A Peeping Tom? In this neighborhood?

He must let her go, he knew now as he gazed at her so deeply satisfied in sleep. But she kept him spellbound, as if her freckles really were kisses from angels. Her eyes were in the shape of crescent moons. Just knowing when she woke he'd hear the magical flute of her laugh made him smile.

"Wake up, sunshine," he said at the foot of her bed. "That job isn't going to find you." But John Mallory just rolled over, looked at the clock, and shut her eyes again.

She called herself a bohemian and had consider lots of professions. Maybe she'd be a teacher or librarian. She had even thought about being a foot or hair model. Her sister had mailed a picture of her to the Long 'N Silky folks for a contest. She talked about being a nurse but couldn't stand the smells of antiseptics. She tried selling shoes at The Jones Store but hated the stench of leather. Her mother brought home a flyer for a pizza delivery job at Papa's, but John Mallory said she could never be locked in a car with cardboard and pizza. Even house-sitting for neighbors turned into a three dog night. She got dizzy scooping poop, and he ended up feeding the dogs on his way to and from work.

Ah, it seemed like just yesterday when seven pairs of legs dangled from checkered skirts at the kitchen table. Peter Pan collars were lightly pressed. Delicate socks covered thin ankles. Each girl's shoes repeated her sisters', laced and polished in oxblood (regardless of their original color). Long, combed hair had been swept into barrettes, away from scrubbed faces. Barbara broiled nine pieces of bread on a cookie sheet in the oven. Buttery smells filled the air. Every morning, John would have two slices of toast, and each of the girls would have one. Barbara would stand by the sink and nibble the crusts left by the girls. As always, John sprinkled sugar on the girls' toast. He handed out spoons, and the girls stirred their coffee, swirled with whole milk and sugar, and they dropped splashes of it onto the sugared toast. After each bite, rings of sparkles hooped their mouths.

After faces were swiped with a dish towel, it all became a flurry of sack lunches, each soggy bag marked with the first initial of each daughter. Then their mother loaded them into the station wagon and rumbled down Rainbow Boulevard towards Bishop Miege, then Curé of Ars. That's when John would leave for work.

He would have kept that life, his big job, mounting stocks in the family-owned coffee company, his assortment of girls frozen in time. But the sands had shifted underneath his feet. First, it was the buyout by the mega-conglomerate. Then his friends, one by one, lost their jobs. When he refused to relocate to the new company headquarters, he was forced out. Him! The innovator and instigator of the mega coffee trends. By then, though, his stock was worth a king's ransom, and he could afford to buy his own little coffee business. Yes, early on, it had been a struggle. But his crown had never dulled, and he wisely bought the rights to innovative vending machines. Hot coffee for a quarter! And he owned the inventory. Money, he knew, bought bluebirds of happiness.

Maybe he should have spent more time with his family, kept a closer eye on his daughters. Over the years, the girls had ventured away from Rainbow Boulevard and left empty chairs, smaller cans of coffee in the pantry. Their identical coffee mugs waited, neglected and longing in the cupboard. He wished he could do it all again. Eager to keep them, he had paid for private schools, offered them loans for down payments on houses, even credit for used cars. He swung his pocket watch in front of their eyes and bribed them with treasures and titles.

He leaned over John Mallory and nudged her. She groaned but didn't open her eyes.

"The Big Girls want to see you about a job," he said. He and Barbara referred to their three eldest daughters as the Big Girls. The Little Girls were the youngest four.

She pretended to be asleep.

It had been his wife's idea to name their children in alphabetical order: Abigail, Bess and Celia. She and he—or was it just he?—had wanted an ark full of kids. Yet, after Diana's birth, Barbara's ship had kind of sunk. By the time the fifth girl popped out, still without the desired male apparatus, she had given up and named her after her best friend and bridesmaid, Lolly. No one knows why, but she named her sixth daughter after their dead dog, Princess Katrinka of Leawood. He was horrified to find the name Trinka on his daughter's birth certificate. Barbara delivered her bladder along with their seventh daughter, so she really didn't care when John named her after himself. By the time his wife woke up, the doctor had stuffed the organ back into the traffic of her womb, tied her tubes, and zipped her shut. John knew that somewhere in their adventure she had lost her enthusiasm for birthing a tribe.

John, however, still had every intention of creating a brand. "Get up," he said to his youngest.

"I am up."

"Up means out of bed."

No answer.

A good father created boundaries. It took courage. And if he were lucky, his daughters would turn out okay, in spite of any unintentional mistakes. John did not think, however, he had this one in the bag. So far, four of his daughters had accepted his offers of employment at Early Mountain Coffee. Unfortunately, Diana had flown the coup and gotten away with her husband to California. He had funded Lolly's venture into gourmet dog cooking—her store next to Laura's Fudge Shoppe made pastries for the pampered pets of Mission Hills—but he knew she'd give in when she got sick of the clientele peeing on her linoleum.

He couldn't bear to give up on John Mallory, even when she insisted on trying out shape-shifting. She was his last one, his baby. All parents had moments in their life when their kids tested and investigated. He just needed to confine the parameters of her wild-eyed experiments.

It had taken him weeks to devise his plan. After countless phone calls in his broken Spanish, calling in favors and making promises, he had found a lit path for John Mallory. After all, he still had hopes—and it had been he who had encouraged her to take her time. "Dream big," he had said. Now, every time his wife stomped into the room, he found himself squeezing his eyes shut and praying big.

He called to her again. "Get up, John Mallory." She didn't stir. Still, he loved saying her name. "You don't want life to pass you by," he said a little louder.

"It wouldn't dare. Not with you standing guard," she said, smiling without opening her eyes. "Let's declare it a holiday."

He sighed. He knew what that meant. She would spend another day watching *Fraggle Rock* cartoons. Already eighteen, it was time for her to think about leaving Rainbow Boulevard—but his heart ached. That's why he had called upon his friends, people who could help her. Today was the day to break the news to his daughter.

"It's Saturday," he said. "Let's do the shopping." She didn't open her eyes. "I'll take you to the florist afterwards. You can smell the orchids." Now she smiled and tossed off the covers.

"Finally. Good morning," he said. "I'll go make a list." Before she could change her mind, he rushed downstairs to compile one.

On Saturdays, John always did the grocery shopping. He loved the smells of frozen goods and fresh produce, the bright lights, the polished linoleum floors. Whenever possible, he took John Mallory along. When she was little, he loved to say his seventh daughter's name aloud and called it out at every opportunity. "John Mallory, look both ways. Stay closer. You're too far ahead. Alright, go ahead. No, don't. Well, I'm tired too, you need to walk. Okay, I'll carry you."

John Mallory began an early apprenticeship. Right away, she demonstrated an interest in his profession. He'd plop her in the grocery cart and wheel her up and down the aisles. She stared at the shiny cans, the boxes of cereal, and pointed. He admired her critical thinking skills. Even then she had an eye for detail. She knew what jumped from the shelf, even if she didn't know why.

He taught her the importance of shelf positioning—eye-level being the most desired—and how shelf-spread built a billboard effect. After lessons on the value of rotating inventory, they discussed which packages made the most powerful impacts. Crisp paper, fine print, gold tops all communicated to Mrs. Shopper. At twelve, it was John Mallory Jr. who had suggested a crown could be added to a package to add nobility to the product. She had mentioned it to him one Sunday morning as they filed out of their pew. He encouraged her with a loud proclamation of, "You're gifted, John Mallory!" But now he was sure that someone in the parish had overheard them—and had stolen her brilliant idea and sold it to the Imperial margarine people.

As always, on the top of his list he wrote C-O-F-F-E-E-!

He liked to see his own brand ring through the cash register.

Overhead, he heard the shower running, so he put down the pen and quickly helped himself to a bowl of sugary cereal. He sighed. He mustn't have her wandering along the rosy paths of a fig garden all her life. From the beginning, she was destined to be a Coffee Queen. Her brilliant nose was a sign. Yes, maybe he had spoiled her a bit, but if it were he who had forsaken her, then it would be he who would redeem her. In his heart, he knew that crops that had made him rich and famous could be sowed again in fertile soil.

She must go to Costa Rica.

But a surprising (and disappointing) lesson he learned in life was that his daughters would have minds of their own. No matter how much he stomped his red cowboy boots or snapped his fingers, they did as they pleased. As an enterprising man, however, John learned that if he brought them his ideas, delicately placed on a golden platter, sometimes he could make them believe that they had spawned such brilliance from their own imagination. All men should learn this clever trick! After all, sometimes his daughters believed he had magical powers.

Just as soon as he washed his bowl and hid it back in the cupboard, John Mallory walked into the kitchen. She wore a long, lacy shirt with tattered ribbons hanging from the ends. Her jeans had holes and fringes around her shoes. Must she wear rags like Oliver Twist? "It's such a pretty day for a nice wool skirt," he said. She raised her eyebrows, then on her tiptoes reached into the cupboard for a mug. "Do you need money for clothes?"

"I'm fine," she said and poured her coffee. She sniffed the air, then plopped down across from him and blew into her cup. "Been eating that tootie-fruitie cereal again?"

He blushed. "Sunshine, I've been thinking about your future."

"Oh, a Cabbage Patch doll! For me?" She swept it up and broke out in dimples. A bell hung in the crevice of her collarbone, and it jingled while she laughed. Unlike his slicked hair, hers had been haphazardly tied at the top of her head with clips and bands. Long strands drooped around her face. He had meticulously trained her to appreciate fine things—crystal, jewelry, oriental rugs—how could she have missed his lessons on artful grooming?

"You're too old for dolls," he said, but when her smile faded, he sighed. "Okay, take it. Sure, it's yours. But, honey, I need your opinion. William is ready to retire next year. I need a replacement. Any ideas?"

She placed the doll pigeon-toed at her plate, then sniffed the coffee and turned up her nose. "None come to mind."

"Well, you know, being a Roastmaster is a very important job. The backbone of the company actually. It takes a brilliant nose." He stared at hers, noting how delicate and dainty it looked. "How's that coffee?"

"A little bitter. How old is this can?" She popped open the coffee lid and whiffed.

"See! You have that," he said. "It's a gift. That's what I mean. You have the nose."

She sipped the coffee again, and then got up. He kept talking as she took cinnamon from the cupboard and sprinkled it in her mug.

"I need someone with a brilliant nose, a nose like yours actually, someone who wants to learn our trade. It's a job reserved for only the cleverest of coffee connoisseurs. This person must be wise and diligent." He immediately regretted using that description when she sat down and began flipping through a *People* magazine. "It would be an apprenticeship. He or *she* would be highly respected," he said.

"Is William?" She looked up, the glossy page frozen in mid-air.

"Is William what? Of course he is." He looked down at his coffee cup and frowned. "Well, he isn't a particularly gifted Roastmaster. He doesn't have a nose. And he doesn't have any vested interest in the long-term health of our company. He admits he doesn't have the dedication." He could tell by the way she cocked her head, with just one ear turned towards him that he had lost her. He had better backpedal. "It wasn't his fault though. He wasn't educated properly, like someone else could be. Someone who has learned the craft. Someone with a nose. It's an art, you know, being a Roastmaster. It's best to learn the trade secrets from a mentor, an experienced Roastmaster, a master of the bean. If only I knew someone who could fit that bill," he said and propped his elbows on the table. She hadn't perked up one bit. She sat twirling her hair and pointing at pictures of movie stars that wore ill-fitting dresses. "We've been looking for months, there's no one," he said.

"Have you placed an ad in the paper?"

"For a Roastmaster?" He cleared his throat. "We need someone inside. But whom? If only someone we trusted were interested. Someone willing to take the time to learn the nuance of the business. It's a big job, and not just anyone is worthy to apprentice with a Roastmaster. And a woman would be unheard of! Why, think of that. The first woman Roastmaster. Someone must go to Costa Rica. Study under a master. It'd help me out, too. It would be rewarding for both of us. It's so cold here in January," he said and blew into his hands.

"Costa Rica?" she said. "Who's going to Costa Rica? One of the Big Girls?"

"They already have their hands full," he said, even though he knew none of his daughters ever worked very hard. Maybe he had spoiled them, like Barbara kept telling him. Whenever he went into the office, it seemed like his daughters were chatting on the phone, their feet propped on the desk, or just getting back from lunch, or just going to lunch. Most years, the roasting side of the coffee company earned a slim profit. Yet, roasting and selling coffee was more than a profit-seeking venture. Royalties, dividends, it did a man's heart good to indulge in his passion. He never got the hang of golf or cared for fishing, and he didn't like watching sports. He was a doer. His joy came from packaging and marketing the world's second largest commodity (second only to oil). Despite his best efforts, however, he worried that he was failing at his fiduciary duty to make sure that his daughters were independent earners. Deep down, he knew they weren't.

John Mallory didn't even appear to be listening. She had taken to scrubbing the belly of her arms and behind her knees with the inside of a perfume ad.

"Maybe I'll send Trinka to Costa Rica," he said. "She loves sunshine." They both knew Trinka wouldn't go. She'd never leave her boyfriends. Number six daughter sold coffee through a drive-through window from the parking lot of the Hen House grocery store. The coffee hut had been another one of John's big ideas: coffee on every corner, but Starbucks would later prove that they had more time, money, and energy than John.

"Trinka to Costa Rica?" she said. "I thought you said one of the Big Girls was going."

Just a few weeks ago, as they shared a blanket on the divan, watching an old Doris Day movie, John Mallory had made a comment that bothered him: "Do you notice how the little kids in a big family never have any speaking parts in movies? They just sit there and act cute or unruly, while the older kids have all the lines. Always bossed around." He hadn't noticed any unwritten rules in their house with the Big Girls, but since then he had tried to be more perceptive. At dinner last Sunday, he realized that the Little Girls scrambled for every crumb: the last seats at the dinner table, the empty bowl of mashed potatoes. They were bossed around and left staring into the distance while their older sisters recounted over-told stories. Even though all the Little Girls were well on their way to adulthood, the seesaw of power still slanted in one direction.

As always, it took the ever-perceptive John Mallory—she had always been so observant—to help him right any wrongs. He owed it to the Little Girls, at least to John Mallory, to make her follow her destiny.

"I'd like to send one of you Little Girls. What do you think about Trinka? Her going to Costa Rica and studying with an internationally famous Roastmaster? Lorenzo Domingo. You may have heard of him." He got up and dropped a piece of white bread into the toaster. "He's agreed to work with someone from our family. Someone, he says, who demonstrates passion for the coffee cherry, someone with a long line, a history of working with the bean. That's us. Family. You know how Costa Ricans are about family, so dedicated and loyal. It'd be more like a vacation really. I've arranged for a nun from the local church to watch over whoever goes. What do you think about Trinka? There are beaches and the rainforest. Did I mention that? Can't you smell them?"

John Mallory began nibbling her lip, her eyes fixed on a corner of the kitchen.

"Of course, she, or whoever took advantage of this opportunity, would need a new wardrobe. Maybe you could help. I wouldn't want her looking like a pauper. More like coffee royalty." He thought he noticed a discernable change in the color of her eyes. With the only blue eyes of his daughters', they changed from sky blue to navy based on her moods. "Certainly, a new wardrobe comes with the job." He forced the buttons on the toaster to release the bread, then buttered the dry toast.

"How long? I mean if Trinka were going."

"It'll probably take a while. Maybe two or three months." He tried not to wince. "But that's not long when you're talking about a lifetime." He placed the toast on a plate in front of her. "Of course, we'll need someone to take over the coffee hut while she's learning her new trade. Hey, here's an idea. You can do that!" He saw her flinch. "Eat up, let's get going. I'll talk to Trinka before we go to the Hen House. We'd better go!"

As soon as he started up the Lincoln and pulled out of the driveway, with her in her pea coat, fiddling with the radio, and him in his tailored jacket, he launched another balloon. "I'm not sure, though, if Trinka will go. Leave all her things." He avoided using the word *boyfriends* with all his daughters. "I need to think about this. I need your advice. It's an important position. The person we choose will have a tremendous amount of power in the company. Practically be in charge. Maybe you should talk to her."

"Me?"

"Sure. Feel her out. And if you think she can handle the job, you can go shopping with her and help her spend her budget. Unless you're interested. That's a thought." He looked at her with his eyes and mouth opened wide, as if the thought had just occurred to him. He tried not to look as eager as the bobblehead dog on his dashboard.

John Mallory stared over his shoulder and looked out the window. Her eyes were dark blue, matching the skeletons of the trees. He worried about her, always growing blue when the Kansas City skies turned winter gray. He shivered and turned up the heat.

"Long time 'til spring," he said. "If I had the chance, if I were just a few years younger, I'd go myself. Beaches. Rainforests. The warm glow of sunshine. Ah, the smell of fresh bananas in paradise. Guava! I bet you've never smelled anything like that before. It's a once-in-a-lifetime opportunity, don't you think?"

By the time he pulled into the Hen House parking lot, he was sure she was mulling it over. Her eyes were fixed on the coffee hut, squinting.

"It could be a good opportunity," she said and opened the door. "Don't worry, I'll talk to her."

If he were just a common man, his plans would require nothing more than putting thoughts to paper, then wishing on stars. But John Mallory Sr. was not a common man. He was a marketer and a father. He was used to painting images of ladders that led to the sky, and nudging little feet up into clouds. He was used to calling on a higher order, *mano a mano*.

"Thanks, John Mallory. I knew I could count on you." Then he shouted after her, "Look both ways!"

3

Time Out

Capri was born on Mother's Day, a pleaser or a teaser, depending on who's telling the tale. Radio station KUDL FM 98 was giving away ninety-eight dollars to any baby born nine pounds eight ounces. While Capri tried to consume just the right amount of nutrients in the womb, her mother, so certain she'd win, kept her eyes on the red lacy number wrapped in tissue beside her bed. She'd pre-spent the winnings on lingerie she planned to squeeze into before leaving the hospital. Capri's granddaddy and aunts drank coffee and played Seven-card Stud in the waiting room, not letting anyone touch the dial on the radio. And, miracle upon miracle, Capri John Mallory slid into this world exactly nine pounds eight ounces. But when Aunt Bess called to collect, they said the promotion had ended last week. Last week! Ever since, Capri swears, they've considered her a bad bet, a near miss, just touching the hem of the robe. But, Capri knows, if she'd been able to talk, clutch that phone in her curled newborn fingers, she would have collected. Seventeen years ago and Capri still finds it hard to shake the feeling that she started out life being bamboozled. She certainly won't listen to KUDL, not until they pay her. She knows the smell of a rat.

"Just out of curiosity," Capri says, linking her fingers and resting them in her lap, "do we have any supernatural powers?

Besides flying in baskets, of course." She tosses a paper clip at her mother's coffee mug and it clinks into its side. "Darn it. No precision or cat-like reflexes. But, hey, that must be a magic potion you're drinking, because I smell a lot more than coffee in this room."

"What do you mean you smell a lot more? Like what?" Trinka says.

Capri shrugs.

"That's what I mean," her mother says, pushing back stray hairs and leaning back. "You've stopped talking to me. I want to talk, like an adult, but you close up."

Capri flares her nostrils. Her mother and aunts are always whispering, keeping secrets, dancing in the backyard, staring at the moon, as if they could conjure up baskets in the sky or raise the dead. She wasn't about to let her mother know her life has become a potpourri of jungle scents. Next thing she'd know, her mother would have Capri floating in a sensory deprivation tank again. Astronauts may lose their sense of smell in space, but Capri knows her weightlessness only ignites hers.

Her mother leans forward and stares at her shoulder. "Is that my blue bra strap sliding out of your blouse?"

Capri feels her face flush. "Maybe."

"You took my boots to Mexico." Capri rolls her eyes. "Why won't you stop taking my things? My bras are too small for you, and now it'll be stretched out."

"I thought we shared."

"No, we do not share, because sharing with you really means you taking what's mine."

"Well," Capri says, "maybe you should have told me sooner. I've had it for two months. You weren't wearing it, and now I have a date." She shakes her head.

Her mother exhales. "We have not agreed that you have a date."

"Fine," Capri says and reaches around her back and unhooks the bra, then wiggles her arms so she can pull it out of her sleeve. "Here," she says and drops the bra on top of a stack of papers. Her mother's eyes don't leave the faux diamond on her daughter's ring finger. "You're right, I shouldn't take your things, but I am going out with Mac." She starts for the door.

"Wait," her mother says. "I'll give you back my credit card." She pulls it out of the top drawer. "But you have to stay. I just want a little more time. Talk to me."

Capri tries not to act surprised and stomps over, then slips the credit card in her back pocket. "Okay, but time is money," she says, using one of her granddaddy's favorite expressions. She looks at the clock and sits down. Neither one of them wants her to leave in huff, or without the bra.

Her mother swallows and Capri can tell that her heart is beating fast because when she picks up the photo of John Mallory again, her hand is shaking.

"It was her," she says. "She made me so scared, and you were always more like her, even when you were little. How you loved to dance in your tutu under the moon, smelling wildflowers and putting them in your hair. You've always run wild, whiffing the world. It's always scared us."

"Till you started stuffing a coffee bean up my nose every time I did."

Her mother chuckled. "Doc Simpson said it would keep you from smelling too much. Letting smells overpower you. It works."

"He meant if I was getting a migraine. I asked him."

"Yeah, well, old Doc Simpson doesn't need to know everything. That's what I mean. It's because of her. You know, sometimes I hate her, making me so afraid, and sometimes I cry myself to sleep, missing her." She keeps staring at the picture, making a wrinkle between her eyes.

"I don't know why we're talking about her anyway," Capri says, briefly locking eyes with her mother before inspecting her cuticles again.

Capri, however, cannot ignore the link she feels with her aunt. Smells are connected to memories, she knows, she's read all about it. The olfactory bulbs, how they're part of the limbic system, but these smells aren't her memories. She wishes her aunt were alive so she could ask her how she handled it. No one else she knows can smell things the way she does. She wonders, too, if John Mallory would have been disappointed in her. Capri hates feeling not good enough, and with the odd musky smells overpowering her in the room, she actually feels like finding a coffee bean for her nose. "Listen, Mom, I'm going."

"Why'd you have to do that to your hair?" she asks, dropping the photo. "You had such beautiful hair."

"My head, my hair," Capri says.

"My house, my rules," her mother says, then touches her throat, blushing.

"It's Granddaddy's house," Capri says. She regrets the words almost immediately. She can tell from her mother's eyes that she's hurt her. Capri touches her hair and tilts her head. "Don't worry. Hair grows, I can wear scarves. Maybe I'll start a new trend."

She had been going for an edgy and pretty combo, but even when she looks in the mirror, Capri hates to admit, she only sees pretty darn edgy. She flattens her bangs on her forehead.

Her mother's face softens, like she wants to lean over and wipe milk from her daughter's lips. Suddenly, Capri feels tiny and innocent. She can smell the darkness of a jungle night seeping into the room. The air is thick and musty.

"Who knowingly lets their child disappear into the wild?" her mother says. "It's why your granddaddy goes away—but none of it would have happened if he had never sent *her* away in the first place."

Capri sighs.

Her mother tends to point fingers. She blames Capri's behavior on everyone, her boyfriend, her friends with too much freedom, movies with too much violence. Capri plays too many video games, she says. But what she doesn't know is that when Mac's parents separated, he got so depressed, she couldn't abandon him. He needed her. She didn't plan on going to Mexico. It was a dumb, crazy thing. They planned on relaxing in the Ozarks, lounging around on rafts. Capri said she was spending spring break at Tracy's lake house. Mac said he was spending it at Maloney's fishing cabin. They just wanted to escape for a couple of days, be adventurous. But Mac's friends were going to Mexico, and he thought it'd be fun. She thought, why not? Maybe she hadn't been thinking. Maybe not.

Her mother called her thoughtless and reckless and dishonest.

Honestly, she just didn't think she'd ever get caught. Worst part, she came home with a nasty case of Montezuma's Revenge.

In Capri's mind, John Mallory was the only one in this family who ever broke ranks. She took chances, just like Capri wants to. So Capri says with what she thinks would have been John Mallory attitude, "I am allowed to explore how I feel about this material society."

"Material society?" Her mother snorts. "Like the one that's been paying your way? So your fantasies can become my nightmares." She laughs. "Correct me if I'm wrong, but wasn't it *my* credit card that bought your and your boyfriend's plane tickets to Cancun?"

Capri can't think of a good comeback, but she's glad she already has the credit card back in her pocket.

Since Mexico, her home has become a Mexican prison. Picked up from school every day by one of her aunts whenever her mom can't be there, tonight will be her first date with Mac since Mexico. Even Granddaddy has turned a deaf ear.

Last night, when Capri sat with Granddaddy at the kitchen table with their cups of coffee, he had said, "What parent wouldn't react that way? You could have been killed. She could have lost her baby girl." He stared out the kitchen window as if they weren't talking about Capri and her mom anymore.

"But I'm fine," she said, rubbing his arm. "I can't be locked away in a tower, like Rapunzel."

His eyes were frozen. He acted as if he hadn't heard her, mumbling, "You remind me of her. That way." He didn't finish his coffee before he headed for the door. Without turning around, he said, "Gone away. Lost in the sky..."

Sometimes he talks about John Mallory as if she's away on a trip, and she'll walk through the door any minute with her arms full of wildflowers. Then, this morning, her granddaddy flew the coup. Took one of his business trips. Seems he's been going away a lot more lately.

"Sister Mariella said she'd be happy to chat with you," her mother says. "You always love Sister Mariella."

At any moment, Capri expects her mother to pull out her fourth grade recorder from underneath the desk and ask Capri to play her some tunes. Sometimes she thinks her mom still sees her as a little girl in a checkered uniform. Her mother will always be inspecting her skirt for lint, her face for crumbs. But a black belt with a blue recorder hadn't taken more than mastering some silly songs, with Capri working her way up from *Hot Cross Buns* to *Ode to Joy*.

Mac's the only one who understands her. He lets her cry on his shoulder. When Capri backed into the garage, he painted the door. When she changed her hair, Mac was the only one that said it looked sexy. Mac's the kind of guy who doesn't think it's odd when she plugs her nose or complains about being over-sensitized by smells in a room. He fans the air. So when Mac got depressed and said, "Baby, let's go to Mexico," Capri felt like they were two flatlanders venturing out to breathe in the ocean. She thought she was going crazy, with college applications, worrying she'd never measure up, feeling so disconnected and weird smells getting stronger and stronger. Even the high school cafeteria smells like fumes from a tomb. And with her mother always mad at her, and her granddaddy always giving her that disappointed look, and now her aunts following her around the house tsk-tsking her to death, she might as well bury her head in a beach.

"Capri, young love is dangerous. Please. Listen. It's not a myth. You don't understand—"

"This family is glued together by myths," she says. "And it smells like beans and rice in here. Have you been eating Mexican?"

Her mother glares, but they both jump at the knock on the door.

"Who is it?"

"Let's use our laser vision," Capri whispers.

Her mother frowns and shakes her head. "Come in."

Aunt Abigail storms in. One hundred percent intense, she masters the grim reaper look with clunky block heels, always reeking of smoke and fire. Capri has accused her of getting her fashion tips from old Sister Claire. She's tried to convince her aunt she'd look ravishing in red. But Abigail means business, sister, and she means business all the time. She doesn't even crack a smile when toasting her champagne glass with everyone else when she reports record coffee sales at the dinner table.

"Do you come in peace?" Capri asks, bowing her head and folding her hands in prayer.

"Is she doing drugs? Are you doing drugs, young lady? You should be ashamed of yourself, scaring us half to death. Mexico," Abigail says, with a snort. "I'd never let you see that boy again."

"I'm trying to be reflective, Aunt Abigail. Peace be with you," Capri says, blessing the air.

"Trinka, I'm telling you, you should get her tested." Abigail does her best to ignore Capri by slightly turning her back and placing her hands on her hips. "The code is 8333."

"Code?" Capri says. "For our decoder rings?"

"I've looked up drug testing centers," Abigail says with her thumb over her shoulder. "There's one just down Mission Road."

Her mother gives Capri a look like she'd better not dare, and her aunt gives her one like she wishes she would, but Capri notices that her mom doesn't jot down the number. Since it's the last four numbers of their phone number, Capri guesses she doesn't need to.

"We did it. It's a smart decision. You'll see. We'll be waiting for you," Abigail says. They make eyes at each other, like they're using their telepathic powers, and then Abigail storms out.

"What did they do?" Capri asks.

"Nothing."

"What's that code for?"

"Nothing, Capri. It doesn't concern you."

Capri sighs. "See. That's what it's like, living with you guys. Some kind of secret world. I'm stuck in Sisterhood of the Round Table, but they forgot to tell you—make room for involuntary recruits."

Her mother has the nerve to chuckle. "Kind of," she says. Then she turns away and keeps her eyes focused on the window. She wrings her hands. "I cannot bear to lose you," she says. "I don't want to be left. Not again."

Capri looks at the ring on her finger. It even sparkles like it's real. She loves Mac, but will she marry him? Maybe, but probably not. The ring's just a knockoff from a Mexican vendor. But he was so proud, showing it off to all his buddies.

Her nostrils widen. Suddenly, salty smells fill the air, but it's not the ocean she remembers from Mexico. The aroma is misty, raw and green, but sweet too. Capri stands.

Her mother jumps up. There's fear in her eyes, as if she were being hunted by a wild animal. Her tall, curvy body has that need-to-run and itchy look. With black circles under her eyes, she looks like she could use a hundred-year nap. She is thirty-eight, healthy, fit, beautiful, and, apparently, her teenager is trapping her.

"Every woman," her mother says, "is one bad boyfriend away from disaster." She glances at the door. "Young love is dangerous," she says, as if Capri doesn't know about love, just because she's seventeen. "It can kill you," she says. And then she stops and holds her throat. Her hair is falling from her bun. "Oh, my god," her mother says, flapping her hands, as if she could shake off scalding coffee. "We *are* one of those families. It's happening again!"

"Mom, you're overreacting—"

"You don't understand," she says. "We aren't like other people! We're different. You think you know it all, but you don't know how dangerous the world can be. You don't know about love or time. But I can protect you."

She's tugs on her daughter's shirt, and Capri feels panic rise in her own chest. Scents wash over her, pushing her down, rushing water, dark and suffocating. She starts to feel dizzy.

"Stop." Capri pries her mother's fingers from her sleeve.

"Stay," she says. "Don't go." Suddenly, her mother lets go and straightens her shoulders. She has a faraway look in her eyes and reaches for her cold cup of coffee. "Here, drink this," she says, holding it out to Capri, "and you'll feel better."

"I don't want coffee," Capri says, louder than she means to, and pushes it away. Coffee splashes onto her mother's blouse, and she gasps.

Capri closes her eyes and pinches the top of her nose, trying to suffocate the scent-drenched emotions in the room. Jungle vapors fill her nose and throat. She breathes in and out through her mouth. Unmoving, she shrinks in silence, hoping none of the odors will brush up against her.

"No, it's okay," her mother says. She rests her hand on Capri's fingers and tucks her hair behind her ear. "I'm just fidgety," she says, petting her, "but we'll both be fine." Capri moves away. Her mother sips her coffee, never taking her eyes off her daughter. "Maybe my sisters were right. I have to stop this," she says as if they were talking about Capri borrowing her Lexus.

"You can't keep me here." Capri's head throbs. "This is my life."

"Now I understand how Daddy felt," Trinka says, shaking her head. "It's up to me to keep you from making the biggest mistake of your life. I will not let my daughter make the same mistakes. It's all happening again," she says. "You don't understand enough about love."

"I know a lot more than you give me credit for."

Her mother looks sad, and then her face lightens, as if she discovered something locked in her mind.

"It's set then." She looks out the window, up to the sky. "We've suffered so much. Cursed by our sister's death. Mother's cancer, driven to an early grave. Daddy, poor Daddy...You being marked. From birth. You have that look in your eyes, like you're somewhere far away. And that nose. It's a curse. Daddy always said you're her reincarnation. And it always makes us so uneasy when he goes away. We pretend no one knows, but they do. They know. We feel their stares. We hear their whispers. People can be so cruel. But some people are just born into stories," she says.

"I don't know what you're talking about," Capri says. She doesn't know what to think. Her temples throb and the room fills with scents from other worlds.

Then, in a calm voice, her mother says, "We are of the sky, of Sun and Moon, but we are also of Earth." She looks at Capri. "They're right. Come with me. You need to come."

Her mother glides across the room and opens the door. She leaves without looking back.

Capri tries to catch her breath. She looks around. She feels so tired, with her senses overloaded, so she mindlessly follows the scent of her mother.

The house is deserted, and her mother is headed up the stairs. Capri walks past the front door. Outside it's dull and gloomy. The trees are towering shadows of moss. She can smell the dampness of the flag that hangs against the pole in the yard. Her legs feel like they weigh two hundred pounds as she climbs. The wood feels soft but sounds hollow. Pictures slant on the wall. Everything smells damp, swollen, forgotten, and rotting.

Her mother turns and goes into Capri's bedroom. She follows her.

"Sit," she tells Capri, and she does.

When her mother turns to leave, she closes the door, and Capri watches her until she is no more than one eye in the crack, a click, and then nothing.

Capri sees the shiny new deadbolts before she hears the snaps, before she can reach the doorknob. "No!" she says.

"Yes, ma'am," her mother says as if she's suddenly Mrs. Butterworth and Capri just asked for another stack of pancakes.

"You can't do this!" Capri scratches the brass, as if she can stop it, but she hears a succession of three more locks, like a jail cell closing for the night.

"Consider yourself in Leavenworth," her mother says, with the floorboards squeaking as she jumps up and down, clapping in victory. One of her aunts calls to Trinka. Now Capri smells popcorn and salt, sweet and sour voices coming from the kitchen. A blender grinds. Her mom answers her sisters' calls. "I'm coming, I'm coming," she says. "Deal me in! Fill the bowls and make me a whopping margarita!"

4

Mapmaker of Smell

As she approached the Early Mountain Coffee hut—before she heard children crying from the back of a station wagon, the clatter of a discarded shopping cart, or even the twitters from the robin—John Mallory smelled coffee. Most people would not be able to discern the rich aroma through the haze of middle class smells: teenagers smoking cigarettes, dirty roads plowed of snow, Kentucky Fried Chicken in the air, but growing up with coffee had heightened John Mallory's third sense. At home, while her sisters would complain about the Johnson's poodle barking in the backyard, or giggle on the telephone, John Mallory's senses were being finely tuned to distinctive smells, faint and fleeting, all around her. John Mallory could always smell her sister Lolly's butter croissants before she ever crossed the yard with her crowded plate, and the wafting smells from upstairs when her mother spritzed her neck with Youth Dew perfume before a night of bridge club. She could always smell a fresh pot of coffee brewing before she woke.

Even closer, she could smell the orange sprig of her sister's shampoo through the drive-through window. When she held out a paper cup to the driver, John Mallory thought she detected the dark embers of a French roast. However, it could have been a dark Columbian brew.

Her sister Trinka appeared to be flirting with a man in a convertible Porsche, tossing her hair and leaning down so her ample breasts swung at his bulging eye level. The cliché of falling in love with a rich man—or a much older one—had been lost on John Mallory, but Trinka haunted every caviar-serving whistle stop. She often told John Mallory she should follow her pedicured footsteps. "Don't spend your own cash," she said. "Not when you can snatch a solid gold ring from the nostril of any horny bull."

Trinka groomed herself with a meticulous comb and fell in love with swelling income statements. Then, just as her lover grew attached to her wild ways, she cast him aside like a disposable summer dress.

Some say it was the Mallory girls' hour-glass figures and their long hair that made men itch for just one touch—they were all able to hypnotize men with just a flip of their curls—but John Mallory always thought what made Trinka most appealing to men was the fact that she just didn't care that much. To her sister, life was an endless buffet of succulent men. Her plight in life was to taste each one before she spat him out.

On the other hand, men appeared to be intimidated by John Mallory, always stumbling on their words, dropping glasses, tripping over nothing. She was the girl in high school every girl waved to but hated. Tall and full-figured, more unusual looking than a beauty, she had deep questioning eyes that begged to be explained to. Often, men looked at her and said, "What?" as if she had said something. Her hair grew long and swingy, too, and wavy as the rough seas of the Caribbean.

Since the first day of kindergarten, when they met, when he had chased her around the duck-duck-goose circle trying to steal a kiss, John Mallory had been the stabilizing tail to Bobby Simpson's kite. She kept him from rolling and diving. Her father and sisters called him a drag—he cussed, he strutted, he pretended to be a celebrity. She ignored the whispers about his wandering eyes. He couldn't break her heart because she wasn't in love with him. Frankly, she stayed with him simply because she didn't have the drive to replace him.

Now, however, she would no sooner hang up the phone with Bobby before she could smell the petulance of her sisters' smoke rings, the burning incense coming from her father's library, and the drum call of the secret meeting of the clan. When she peeked through the keyhole, she caught them huddled in their skirts, mounds of hair parted and bobbing, and her father in the middle, an inferno of war paint blazing across his cheeks.

They constantly dipped their toes in her love life. For the past six months, every time Bobby called, or asked her out on a date, her sisters followed up by dragging a potential new beau to her feet, some inflated man with an interest-bearing bank account.

First, her sister Celia showed up for Sunday dinner with a guy in huarache shoes. James called himself a human resource visionary, though John Mallory had to hold her breath to ignore his numerous evolutionary shortfalls—his massive head and long forehead and that he smelled like mildewed towels. The entire dinner he rambled, adding emphasis by waving a bread stick. He gave her pointers on how to make direct eye contact, told her not to slouch, and then proceeded to pitch an expensive training program to Celia. Even after sticking her nose into a freshly brewed pot of coffee, John Mallory couldn't clear her senses.

Then along came her sister Abigail with Bill. He owned seven cars and introduced himself as a lubricant engineer (with a wink). He wore t-shirts and spandex pants. She couldn't get past the slick smell of metal he wore around his neck. Abigail said, "You have to look past fingernails. He's really quite funny." Abigail forgot to mention that Bill had already driven one wife to the brink of hysterics, leaving a dirty trail with three children still in diapers. No amount of polish and scrubbing could cover up the smell of recycled engine oil.

The final straw was Lolly, with Keith, the trust fund baby and Afghan dog breeder. She looked past the fact that he wore makeup and women's blouses and high-heeled boots. She liked his raw scent of domesticated animals. She thought maybe canines could be a career. So she spent an afternoon helping bathe the dogs in mango shampoo and blow drying their hair. She brushed their teeth and snipped their nails with baby clippers. With all the glamour pooches tied in silk ribbons, she innocently used his grooming shears to trim her split ends. He just about wet the carpet. "Those cost a thousand dollars!" he said and ripped them out of her hand, then swatted her on the head with a rolled up newspaper.

So yesterday, when Trinka had begged John Mallory to let her fix her up with a rich poet (as if there were such a thing) named Stewart, John Mallory wasn't hypnotized by her dancing hands. She yawned at her descriptions of his rippled chest and sea-blue eyes. Trinka explained. "He's too old for me," and then added, "and dull." As if that weren't enough, she told her he would consider her disheveled appearance a condition of her over-processed intellect. "He's a poet," she said. "He thinks cracks in the wall add character."

That's why John Mallory slowed down as she came closer to the coffee hut. She noticed the beautiful couples sitting under the umbrellas, their smiling faces, hands locked on the table tops. It appeared everyone had sniffed out their mate while she had wasted time exploring scents in the sky with Peter Pan. She had always suffered from a serious case of feeling like she never fit in. She had considered college, but more closeted schooling didn't appeal to her senses. She struggled to pinpoint what she wanted to do—and that worried her. Shouldn't people know by now?

She slid into a chair and waited for her sister. Trinka had decided to put tables on the concrete slab in the parking lot so she could sit outside and sun herself when business slowed down, or pose when she saw a sassy car drive by. At first, their father had resisted the idea. "They pull up, they get their coffee, they leave. Don't let them amble around." But Trinka, like John Mallory, appreciated amblers. Now, sometimes when they didn't have anything else to do, John Mallory and her father would read the newspaper under the Early Mountain umbrellas and fill in crossword puzzles. She liked sampling scents of passersby, smiling with their cups of coffee.

"I'm so glad you're here," Trinka said as she came out of the hut. She held a newspaper in her hand. It was the weekly *Coffee Klatch*. "I'm meeting my support group. Would you man the booth? My part-timer called in sick."

John Mallory hated sitting in the hut. The four tiny walls and the low ceiling ignited tortuous smells of claustrophobia. Certainly that's when she developed her reaction to ragweed, haunted by fits of sneezing. "What kind of support group?"

"Good idea. Let's just close the hut," said Trinka. "It's Saturday, the sun is shining, and I want you to meet this great guy."

"Not the poet."

"No, no. This guy's better."

John Mallory sighed.

"Come on, it's a support group for children of the rich and almost famous." Trinka handed her the paper, then tapped to the circled advertisement in the personals sections. "It's right under the one for the Conscious Introverts."

John Mallory glanced through the advertisements. "Let's go see how the Conscious Introverts unite. Probably alone and in their own homes." She laughed, but Trinka was already lowering the metal shades of the hut and locking them.

The guy in the Porsche sailed by and blew her a kiss. Trinka's eyes widened as she faked shyness, saying, "Tuesday!"

"I told Daddy I'd go grocery shopping," John Mallory said.

"He'll be fine. He's probably already delirious, cross-merchandising a coffee display next to the bagels."

So while Trinka waited in her convertible Saab, John Mallory ran into the Hen House. Sure enough, she found her father in the bagel aisle, assembling a cardboard display, dusting coffee cans and pricing them. He cocked his price gun at the makeshift masterpiece.

"Did you figure out Costa Rica?" he said. "Not only can you take over the hut while your sister's in Central America, but you can help me set up displays. Every day. Won't that be fun? How about the dairy aisle? Mitchell said he'd give us a sweet spot in front of the eggs."

The four tiny walls of the coffee hut started closing in. John Mallory could bear meditating on the hard stool inside the hut for hours, even handle the honking horns, and the impenetrable cold of the open window, but she almost fainted when she thought about the smells—poisonous exhaust from the idling cars, dirty snow, mold, the skunky rotten smells of winter. To top it off, she'd add the frigid smell of freezer burn at the Hen House? Why not breathe deeply, fresh fish of the salted seas, the pulpy green juice of a rainforest? Maybe what she needed was a lung full of chocolates of a new land.

She hadn't completely made up her mind by the time she and her sister pulled up to the low brick building a few blocks away. It wasn't until after they walked in and she met her intended.

"Hey, Trinka, who's your buddy?" a man from the corner asked.

"Oh, her dad owns a coffee company."

"A coffee lady? He the one with all those coffee machines?"

"That's the one."

"Rotten luck," he said.

"Come along, John Mallory. Don't trip over chairs."

"If I'm the coffee lady, who do they think you are?"

"Oh, I don't know," she said, waving her hand. John Mallory tripped over the metal legs.

"There he is," Trinka said as a bronzed blond in a muscle shirt slipped in the door and took a chair. "His grandfather was Mr. Universe in 1923. He's third generation. Worth a fortune. They hold patents. And he's developing a prototype for some juice machine. It'll squeeze the pulp out of oranges. Can you imagine? Priceless!" Trinka scooted a metal chair next to him and flipped her hair in his direction.

John Mallory realized that her sister did not intend Mr. Juicer for her. So she took a seat on the other side of Trinka. A thin man (nothing but skin pulled over a skeleton) sat down across from her and crossed his legs. He propped his elbow on his knee and placed a finger alongside his nose. Trinka smiled and nodded until John Mallory raised her eyebrows.

She thought he looked wise and kind of handsome in that library book kind of way. She tried to catch a scent on him but thought she smelled compost and birdseed.

"We've got a newbie here tonight," he said. A man in control, he appeared to run the support group. "I hear your father introduced freeze dried coffee."

John Mallory stared back at the faces in the circle. She tilted her head and waited for questions.

"You must have tremendous guilt about the way massive coffee companies are putting the small farmers out of business and not paying fair market value. Much less the fact that they're destroying the natural habitats of birds."

"Excuse me?"

"No, he's nice," Trinka whispered. "He is. His name's James," she said. "Direct descendant of John James Audubon. The bird guy? And I can assure you that he's hopelessly single."

A wooden swing dangled from tarnished chains on the front porch of the house on Rainbow Boulevard. It faced away from the bedroom that the Little Girls once shared. The cushion sagged in two places where girls' bottoms had worn holes in the flowered fabric. Long ago, John had hung the swing with the help of the Little Girls. They had crowded below him in matching nylon dresses. They held his hammer, nails and hooks. Over the years, he remembered soles of bare feet swinging next to near-summer white legs of older sisters. The little feet were later replaced with the hairy thighs of gentlemen callers who kissed his girls under the stars. He hated that.

Usually now, the swing only swayed with the help of a gentle wind, hungry for one more angelic song, another giggle, or a wish whispered while looking at the sky. He was used to seeing it empty, so when John pulled up in his Lincoln, he wondered who could be outside on such a bone-chilling night. A closer look and his heart knotted.

Ever since she budded when she was twelve, John Mallory had attracted looks from doe-eyed strangers. Men that were much too old for his little girl put out cigarettes when she sauntered by, sucked in their gut, and tried to make small talk about the weather. Because of her height and the way she could hold their eyes in hers—or maybe it was the way she swung her hair and held back her shoulders—they mistook John Mallory for a woman. He knew that her long waist and hair, her bedroom eyes made them think of silky sheets and crumpled clothes at the foot of the bed. But just one dirty look from him, with his fists balled, and they would back off, their open palms thrust in the air, apologizing without saying a word.

He got out of the car, sucked in his gut, and hiked up his pants.

She and the Simpson boy were pushed too close on the swing. John heard her laugh in the winter air—that enchanted flute. It made him trip as he picked up his pace.

But as he approached, he lowered his glasses on his nose. His Little Girl wore an off the shoulder sweater. The boy was giving her a long, deep kiss. John resisted the urge to punch him in the nose. Instead he cleared his throat and stood at the edge of the porch and cleaned out his nails with the tip of his pocketknife.

"Oh, Daddy," she said, the color in her face matched her top, "we didn't hear you. Bobby came for a visit."

John closed the knife and slipped it into his breast pocket. He patted the bulge on his chest. "Hello, Robert," he said.

"Hello, Mr. Mallory," Bobby said, holding out a strong hand.

Just then, Barbara Mallory came out the door, leaking pot roast and potatoes in the air.

"Why, he*llo*, Bobby. Are you here?" She went on, talking fast, waving a pot holder. "Stay! Stay for dinner! Silly me. Seems I've made too much again. This one"—she said, shaking the pot holder at her daughter, "is always watching her figure. And that one," she said, squeezing her eyes shut at John, "loves his meat. Such a carnivore. You must stay and help us."

"I probably shouldn't," Bobby said.

"Oh, I know. You college boys are always so busy. But I know bachelors, never cooking for yourself." She shook the pot holder at him. Then she took his hand and pulled him to his feet. "But it seems I've made too much."

"Barbara," John said, "the man doesn't want to stay."

"Sure he does." She locked his arm with hers. "Besides, I need your strong fingers to open a jar of peaches. John doesn't have the same grip he used to." She looked over her shoulder in a playful manner.

"Be happy to help, Mrs. Mallory." He said, "I do love your cooking."

"Oh, you angel." She giggled. "How are you?" she said, tapping his arm. "John Mallory can't stop talking about you.

It's always Bobby this, Bobby that. I've been reading about you in the papers. You and that football team. Rock Chalk, Jayhawk! I've always loved that mascot. Did you know our dear friend Hal Sandy drew it? Look at you! I know how busy you must be. And no one can expect you to eat all by your little 'ol self." She laughed and pulled him inside.

John watched the door shut, then looked at his daughter.

"Daddy, you could at least pretend to like him." John Mallory said, getting up and straightening her jeans. "Be nice or I'll tell Mother you've been stopping at Baskin-Robbins again."

John resisted the urge to check his breath with his hand. "He's a cad," he said.

She sighed. "I don't know what you want from me." She sounded more concerned than annoyed.

"What any good father wants. For you to be happy," he said. He held open the door. "Pity he's so chubby."

"Chubby? Those are muscles. You're terrible. He's fine."

"You're probably too stunned by his big nose to notice he's gotten fat."

John Mallory shook her head and stepped inside.

John knew. Everything was wrong with Bobby Simpson. Couldn't she see? Liar. He even cheated at cards. And nobody, nobody loved Barbara's dry meat.

In the kitchen, his wife leaned against the sink. As he reached for a water glass, John snapped his fingers in front of her eyes. She swatted him away but kept talking.

"You don't say? That just doesn't seem fair. I mean, why is it that people are so quick to judge? Always suing each other. And doctors. They're just trying to do their jobs. Sure, they're going to make mistakes. They're human, aren't they? Can't imagine being given such a hard time. Tell your daddy we thank the Lord he's there to defend the poor souls."

She was mesmerized. For years now, while John labored at work, she coerced Bobby Simpson into cleaning out gutters. He changed light bulbs too tall for her to reach without a ladder. Sure, he opened jars. Anyone can do that. More than once, he heard him tell Barbara, "I can see where John Mallory gets her drop-dead looks," and his wife would pretend to wilt onto the kitchen counter.

John knew his type, running from dorm room to bedroom faster than the neighbor's gossip. And Bobby was smart, purring around his Little Girl and his wife. What woman could ignore his hairless, barrel chest when he pranced around the yard? Or the spiral of baby-blond curls that bounced around his eyes? Bobby made a middle-aged woman think of poodle skirts and Sock Hops.

Problem was, John secretly feared him, like any good father would, any former pulsing teenage boy. He was certain that Bobby had been sent by God to repay him for all the times he had callously discarded women's hearts, been thoughtless to someone else's Little Girl. Even worse, Bobby Simpson drove a custom van. Tinted windows meant John couldn't peer in to see if there was a mattress.

John took his seat at the table so he could keep an eye on him. John Mallory settled next to her father. He patted her hand.

Little did he know that after she got home from her sister's support group, John Mallory had called Bobby. She could no longer bear tossed leftovers. After all, at least Bobby appeared to want her. Maybe a near miss, but he was also possibly her best shot for a secure future.

"Sit, sit," her mother said to Bobby, pulling out his chair. "John Mallory's been dolling herself up for hours while I melted over the stove." Barbara gasped, as if she realized she was vandalizing her own ruse. She started chattering about her daughter's purported blessings. "Of course she looks nice. Doesn't she smell good, too?"

"Mother."

"Well, she does. Doesn't she," Barbara said.

"She does smell good," Bobby said.

After all, John Mallory had shaved her legs and spritzed her hair and skin with lavender water. She had dabbed honey behind her ears and on the back of her knees. She had slipped into lacy underwear she'd bought at the Plaza and tucked a red rose in her hair. She hardly said a word while her mother chattered because she knew ordinary people could not smell some scents, like sugar. They needed to be tasted. Instead, she softly rocked, leaning forward to pass bowls around the table. She hummed from her chair as she smelled steamy words spill from Bobby's sugary lips.

"Sure, I'd like to be married someday. Of course I would," Bobby said.

"What's the hurry?" her father said, dropping a spoonful of roast on his white shirt. "Damn!" He swiped at the stain with a napkin. "Barbara?" he said, but she didn't move.

"You're quite a catch, Bobby," Barbara said. "Can't imagine those college girls aren't trying to snatch you up left and right." She looked at her daughter and then stood to refill Bobby's plate, briefly stopping to rest her hand on his back. "John Mallory, too. Had plenty of offers," she said ladling over the steaming pot. "But she's saving herself. Aren't you, darling? As any fine lady should. A man with an appetite is so appealing," she said, setting the plate back in front of him. "Don't you think, darling?"

"No need to rush," John said.

"I wasn't talking to you," Barbara hissed. "John Mallory?"

"Honk, honk," her father said under his breath, cupping his nose.

John Mallory shook her head and smirked.

"I should say it's tough at college," Bobby said. "Even steaks on silver platters in the athlete's mess hall can't compare to your home cooking. A lucky man finds a cook like you, Mrs. Mallory."

"Oh, John Mallory can cook. Can't you, darling?"

"Can't boil water," said her father.

"Hush up, John!"

"Oh, cooking isn't everything," Bobby said and glanced at John Mallory. "I like a woman with a good head on her shoulders too."

"Good head you say?" John said.

"John Mallory's a brain. She got the president's award in both the seventh and eighth grade. No one has ever done that. Not before and not since. None of our other girls," her mother said.

"Is that right?" Bobby said and winked at John Mallory.

"Humph," said John.

Underneath the table, Bobby's fingers drew imaginary circles on John Mallory's thigh. She arched her back and pulled away, banging into her chair. Her father frowned. She struggled not to breathe too deeply. But the thick smells of Bobby Simpson were potent, his gamey musk. Her nostrils flared, every nerve tingled, even the muscles in her nose twitched. It took all of her power to resist the urge to bury her nose in his hair. Sitting next to him, she couldn't ignore the power of his scent. He had always worn the heavy aroma of a wild animal. No, she didn't love him, but she craved to be wild with desire. She wanted something to make her want to run through the woods and dance around fires.

"Sure, you could marry anyone," Barbara said, sinking into her chair with dreamy, faraway eyes. "Have your pick."

"What's all this talk of marriage?" John said.

"Truly," said Barbara. "It's critical if you want children. I never liked children much, but John. Well, you know. Catholics. Litters of them. That's what we women do. Make sacrifices. I assumed I'd like them once they got here. But there are so many of them..."

"Oh, that's funny, Mrs. Mallory," Bobby said, but her eyes stayed fixed on some distant place and time.

"Children, a nice home. Security," Barbara said. "Seems like that's all a girl needs. Doesn't it? But she needs more. Love, companionship. A smile every now and then. Someone to open jars. Make a fuss over her pot roast. Makes life worth living, don't you think?"

"It is wonderful pot roast," Bobby said, spooning a large bite of potatoes in his mouth.

"There isn't much you can do," Barbara said, "to change things once they're done."

"I am hungry," Bobby said, holding his plate out for thirds. He dropped his hand to his lap for just a brief moment before it was back on John Mallory's thigh.

Her father made a pig face with his napkin and snorted, then honked, cupping his nose again, trying to catch his daughter's attention.

John Mallory tried to focus on other smells: the sweetness of milk in her glass, the gummy mildew of the spider's web in the corner, the raw black dirt on the bottom of her shoes. Every savory scent led back to Bobby. He overpowered her. She could almost taste him, his curls like lemon popsicles. A bundle of smoldering grinds, his smell suffocated her, even in her mother's kitchen. While his husky voice spoke of nothing, he teased her, ran his fingers up her thigh. It exhausted her to fight him. His scents busted open her sweetest seeds of memories.

She couldn't deny the animal magnetism. She couldn't.

By the time she realized that they had stopped talking—noticed his slow smile, his pink tongue moistening his lips—she was kicking off her shoes. She wanted him to catch a glimpse of her red toenail polish. She stood to clear the table. She flipped her hair and threw back her shoulders, hoping her lustful scent would tumble through the air.

Suddenly, Bobby looked up like he tasted something sugary. His speech came in sputters. His boasting stories dried up. John Mallory gave him that come-hither look and smiled. While she nibbled her lip, she glided closer with a full bowl of steaming potatoes.

Neither one could feel the chilling bite of Jack Frost from the end of the table.

"We always read from the Bible after supper," John said, pushing away his plate. "Lead us not into temptation."

This boy worked for the devil. More than ever, John knew this trip to Costa Rica could be his Little Girl's salvation from the ill fate of a putrid marriage.

5

Shade of Smell

In Bobby's car, with the windows frosted from their steamy breath, the smells defeated her. Even fruit flies were confused and were nose-diving at the empty McDonald's sacks. There were crushed beer cans on the floor, and the seats smelled liked Ben-Gay. A massive stereo system blasted a Dolly Parton tune. John Mallory offered to massage his skin with a blend of orange blossom and sweet almond oils. With her gentle touch, rolling and pressing, she told him about her life, as if it were a distant relative that she pitied.

"It's not that I don't have dreams, you know. I do."

He winced. "More shoulders. You mind? They're so tight."

She kneaded his back. All the while, she circled and roamed his skin, she released her heart. Without reservation, she told him how deeply she yearned for a bigger life. "It's just that pursuit makes me more confused. I can't find any hints in books. Seems like I should know what I want to do with the rest of my life, but then again, that's a long time."

She pressed his shoulder blades, probing and rubbing.

"Right there. Ah, that's good."

"Don't you have dreams?"

He said, "I'm living them, babe."

She knew men found her sexy. She saw it in their puppy dog eyes. And she had tried to be a good companion, but she couldn't get over the nagging feeling that there was something else she was supposed to be doing. Sweet scents had begun calling to her, ripening fruits and others exotic aromas, unfamiliar but warm.

"My father can be rather nerve-racking," she said. By now she knew he was sitting in his leather chair watching Johnny Carson. His feet would be crossed as he balanced a bowl of popcorn in his lap. He'd probably get up and peek out the blinds.

"Oh, he seems like a good enough fellah."

She covered her mouth. No one had ever dared call her father a fellah. Of course he was good enough.

"Beer?" he asked and popped the top of a can.

She shook her head. Maybe if she knew every inch of his body, like an old wife, she'd love him. She smoothed Bobby with her hands while he drank deeply. Before long, the empty beer can was on the floor. She recognized the puffed rhythm of his sleep, so she focused on the sky. She had the eerie feeling that she was being watched. A tree branch scraped the glass. At any moment, she expected a face to appear in the window.

Under a bulging lemony moon, John Mallory looked at her reflection in the rearview mirror. Her heavy lids and empty eyes frightened her. She wiped away the smudged mascara below her lashes. She smelled insects, probably ground deep in the carpet. She leaned down and saw a large bug but muffled her scream. Lifeless, she scooped it up. Mint green, its back was smooth and unbroken. Looking closely, she was sure it was a scarab beetle. She had seen a picture of one. To the Egyptians, they symbolized transformation, a messenger of the sun god when the earth crossed over the moon. Egyptian women tattooed scarabs on their shoulders or the nape of their necks. They were etched into tombstones and monuments. Considered a holy animal, it was a prevalent symbol among the Egyptians, as widespread as the crucifix to the Christians. She knew Egyptians made amulets with the sign of the scarab to attract luck, or ward off evil. John Mallory studied the chalky etchings on its back. She smelled it. Dryness, raw land, a hint of cocoa.

"Jeez. Don't smell that thing. Kill it," Bobby said.

"It's a sign, it's sacred—"

"Don't be so dumb," he said, rolling his eyes.

Her mouth fell open. She thought she'd cry, but then she realized her father was standing in the window, leaning over, looking in.

"Daddy, please." He frowned and then looked at his watch.

"I've got to go." Bobby said. "Thanks for dinner, Mr. Mallory!" He gave him a toothy smile. "See ya," he said to her, then patted her shoulder. "Thank your mom again."

She clutched the beetle and started to get out.

"Seriously?" he whispered. "Get rid of it. It's dead."

"It's a sign," she said. But he rolled his eyes. Before she could shut the door, he had revved the engine and then he took off with a jerk.

She stomped past her father, carrying the beetle. In the kitchen, she delicately placed it on the ledge in the pass-through. Its black eyes were petrified and dull. Not only a beast of transformation, it was a symbol of immortality. Its presence puzzled her.

If the beetle was a sign, what did it mean? She obviously needed a charm to ward off demons. She knew she couldn't spend her Sundays avoiding contemptuous looks from her family, or Bobby. But college didn't ignite her senses. Though he put on an act for her parents, mostly Bobby bragged about being a king at quarters. She'd never fit in, chugging beers at frat parties. She had no idea what she wanted to be, much less who. Suddenly, John Mallory's thoughts were consumed by stench. She threw open the windows in the kitchen. Anything that could fit, she ground down the garbage disposal, leftover pot roast, potatoes, gristle. Even the cilantro and basil in pots on the windowsill couldn't cover up the frightening smell of a bed already made. No soap, no loud humming could drown out the sensory overload—blaring television, horrific molds, grime. Her father glanced up from the TV. She knew he had watched Bobby's taillights until they'd disappeared. For some reason, even that made her want to plug her nose and cry.

She trudged to her room and threw herself on her bed. She tried to meditate but everything reeked of yesterday's socks. No matter where she went, ugly aromas chased her. Even the coffee in her cup was cold, old and bitter.

"Young lady," her father said from the doorway, "we need to talk."

"No, we don't," she said. "I've nothing to say." They both knew he'd talk anyway. "I need to make my own decisions, for my own life. You can't come tapping on the window every time I'm with a boy, a man."

"A proper lady—"

"A proper lady? A proper lady sits under umbrellas and sips sassafras tea. Look at me! Nobody comes running when I ring a bell. I have nothing."

"You have me."

"You don't get it," she said, but even when the words left her mouth they felt sharp and cutting.

She felt the air move from the doorway and could smell the emptiness of where he used to stand.

The next day, her father didn't say a word, punishing her with his silence. In the kitchen, early in the morning, when she playfully bumped hips with him at the counter, he didn't bump her back. He looked out the window while he poured his third cup of coffee. When he started to leave for work, she walked him to the car. He paused underneath the weeping willow. But he never stretched his arms around her. Even when she smelled the early frost and predicted snowfall by midnight, he stayed mute. He just stared at the wedge of frozen water in the birdbath.

"Don't be mad at me," she said. "You know I can't stand it. I know I'm a disappointment."

He sighed. His eyes were sad, but he didn't dispute her. Behind the coffee, she could smell the sugar on his breath. Finally, he looked away.

"You're not taking care of your diabetes—"

"Your mother says there's an awful smell coming from your bathroom. And mud all over your shower curtain. She says she can't get it out. She's tried ammonia. Thinks she'll have to bleach them."

"It's henna. I was practicing henna art. Don't worry. It's temporary."

He shook his head. "Not on the shower curtains. Do not give yourself another pedicure in the middle of the day."

"What's this about, Daddy?" she asked. "My dreams aren't big enough?"

"Dreams? Not long ago, you were reading *What Color is My Parachute*," he said. "What about junior college? You told me you were going be a coffee queen. Run the company. Remember? But it seems you have no ambition, no dreams. What a waste. You're refusing to grow up."

She kicked a clump of ice on the sidewalk. "It's murder being a Little Girl," she whispered.

"I feel betrayed for believing in you. I thought you were special."

"You don't think I am?" She gathered her sweater around her throat. "Well, I certainly don't have the power to control your thoughts," she said, turning towards the front door, "or anyone's for that matter." She looked at the ground. "I do well to keep myself in-line. Frankly, being the underachiever that everyone obviously thinks I am, it's no wonder pleasing everyone else isn't on my agenda."

"Well, you could have saved both of us a lot of heartache, if you'd been forthright." He stomped his feet as if he needed to unravel his pants from his boots. "John Mallory, you wear the label underachiever like a merit badge. Underachievers are lazy, that's all there is to it. They're people who don't achieve."

"There's a lot, a lot to think about. Making life decisions, not knowing where I'm headed. There are too many balls to juggle—"

"You dropped the ball."

She blinked.

He looked at the sky and shivered, and she followed his gaze.

"You're just depressed, that's all," she said. "You always get blue in winter. That's what this is all about. Who can blame you?"

"Don't confuse our emotional states. If you're unfulfilled and depressed..." He shook his head.

His eyes were small and red. She thought she smelled regret. Then his voice softened, a sweet syrupy voice. He opened the door to the Lincoln. With one boot inside, she smelled the yolk of his disappointment. "Listen, honey, I'm not discounting what you do, but maybe you doubt yourself. John Mallory," he whispered, "find your position in society. Don't spend too much time roaming around with your thoughts." He tapped his temple. Once his briefcase was in the car and his coffee cup on the roof, he held his hands over his heart. His eyes were soft blue. "Come to me. Let me give you choices."

She didn't move.

He snatched his cup and tossed the coffee onto the frozen ivy, then held out the mug for her. She paused before she took it, then trudged back inside.

All day she moved from room to room, dusted with lemon polish, and vacuumed the carpet. She even combed the fringe on the oriental rugs. Her mother nodded, but they never exchanged a word. When her father came home, she was scrubbing the half bath with Comet. Without so much as a hello, he moved to the living room to smoke his pipe. Blue smoke circled his head. Stale tobacco mixed heavily with the chemicals. Open drapes had not leaked a peek of yellow into Rainbow Boulevard, and now it was time to turn on the lights.

Each of her sisters had called, asking what had happened. Her father had been in a foul mood all day. Some even followed him home, coaxing him as if he was a bunny under the porch, and they held bright orange carrots. Lolly came by with sugar-free chocolate croissants, Trinka with sugarless ice cream sprinkled with coffee. He said he was watching his weight. Even Abigail couldn't get him to indulge in a root beer float. Her father stayed mum. Puffs of pipe smoke hit the air like a bomb in the distance.

John Mallory didn't know what to do. But she knew she didn't want to spend the rest of her life waiting for her mother and sisters to drag men to her feet. They were giving her the wrong advice.

"Fine," she said, after her sisters had left. "You win. I'll do it. Whatever you say. I can't stand this silence. It's deafening."

Her father put down the newspaper long enough to look her in the eye. "I want you to become a Roastmaster."

"Okay," she said.

"Thank you. It'll be good, you'll see. Tomorrow, we'll go to the office. Your sisters are expecting you. The Big Girls will brief you on your training." He stood up. The pipe smoldered in the ashtray. His white shirt had spaghetti stains, and his pants were baggy. A pillow on his chair fluffed back out, relieved to no longer be burdened by his crushing weight. The owl that usually sat in the weeping willow tree had just woken up, but its eyes were still heavy. "First thing in the morning," he said. "Eight o'clock," and after a moment's hesitation he added, "sharp."

He touched her arm as he passed. As his feet crossed from the oriental to the hardwood, his knees creaked. He turned off the lights and lumbered up the stairs. Only the tobacco lingered behind.

She bowed her head. If only she could please her father—since she couldn't please herself—at least she would feel some sense of accomplishment. Intuitively, she knew she should be thankful for his direction. She should find a place for herself in the world. Set goals. But John Mallory had never really thought about taking care of herself. After all, there had always been Daddy—and her sisters and Mother. She had never been required to think beyond books. She tried to be independent, but when she wasn't at Rainbow Boulevard she felt lost in the big world. Traffic lights blinked too rapidly, horns honked too loudly, and people jostled her on the sidewalk. It took all of her mental capacity to focus on singular smells: snow on a warming sidewalk, fallen nuts from a tree. John Mallory felt like a tiny digit in a rapid-fire world. Without her father's love and approval, she was no one.

In the darkness, she stared at her feet. She felt as neglected as her toes in the winter. The red polish had started to chip. Her heels were dry and cracked. Still, she waited for the song bird to sing from the vacant trees, or the fairies of the night to lead her to secret doors where she could laugh and play. She wanted to dance in eternal moonlight.

As soon as she entered the building of Early Mountain Coffee the next morning, John Mallory smelled trouble. The strong, native odors of Sumatra coffee hung in the air with the scent of rotting flesh. The earthy, wild brew could never hide the sickening smell of the bunga bunga flower. The corpse flower was an eye-watering stink that only attracted sweat bees and carrion beetles.

Ever so faintly, she detected the hint of bug spray in corners and freshly lacquered wood. Someone had dripped coffee onto a burner, for just a second, and had wiped it up, but she could still smell the acrid black. Certainly, everyone acted like it was any other day: Janette, the barista, was waiting on customers at the counter; soft music pumped through the speakers; and the Roasters, Ricardo and Steven, waved from behind the plated glass. Her father hadn't made idle chit-chat as he drove her to the building. He deposited her at the door of the conference room and didn't look back as he headed down the slender hallway to his own office.

She knew the Big Girls were waiting inside.

The three Big Girls took weighty positions in the company: Abigail led operations, Bess was in charge of finance and Celia human resources. When John Mallory opened the door, three bushy heads glared at her from underneath the willow of their furrowed brows. Impatience scalded the air. In shades of smoke and white, Abigail couldn't keep the militant tone out of her voice.

"Father says you'll be going to Costa Rica as an apprentice to Lorenzo Domingo." She issued a statement rather than a question. John Mallory swallowed. "This is an incredible opportunity, a gift. Don't squander it." Abigail took off her glasses and rubbed her eyes. "Lorenzo, as you probably know, should know, is a world-renowned Roastmaster. To my knowledge he has never taken on an apprentice from the United States. I don't know of a single woman Roastmaster. You should be honored. I know I would be. If I weren't running this pony show every day…Well, I'd love to have the opportunity."

She nodded at Bess, number two, all shoulder pads and blazer, who slid an envelope across the table. "Your airline tickets, traveler's checks and a credit card to purchase clothes and sundries before you go. Your budget is generous, but don't be greedy." Her sisters grunted in agreement. "Spend wisely."

John Mallory could smell the solvent ink on the paper.

"And don't forget that while you're there," said her sister Celia, her cheeks pink with cherry blush, "you represent us, and all Americans—you are a steward of Early Mountain Coffee, the Mallory name, and the United States of America. We expect you to make us proud."

"And you represent all women, too," Abigail added. They all nodded enthusiastically.

Her sisters' stares bore into her. The perfume of their simmering moods made John Mallory feel dizzy. She knew she was looking back at them—she didn't even blink—but she couldn't see, and no words formed on her lips. Instead, she absorbed their commands, as a flower absorbs the rain. One by one, she heard her sisters push back their chairs. She smelled the air cool as they breezed past her.

John Mallory wanted to rise. She wanted to follow them, but her legs wouldn't allow her to stand. Instead she sat hypnotized, mesmerized by a tiny black spot in the middle of the wall. Closing her eyes, she tried to smell cheesecake, or peanut butter cookies. All she could smell was old coffee, a banana, and the smell of a bunga bunga corpse flower.

6

Seeing Stars

Capri, like her mother, like her granddaddy, like her dead aunt John Mallory, was born of farmers. Even thirty miles away they're never more than one step from the vapors of a plowed crop. Farmers can never completely scrub the soil from underneath their fingernails. And they're not afraid to use excrement if it will enrich their output. In their world, there is no plowing around tree stumps. They dig them up. To reap a rich harvest, like the waving wheat of the Kansas flatlands, there must be the right soil and sunshine, nutrients and just the right amount of rain. For the richest red cherries on a coffee tree, there also must be mountains.

Capri is locked in her room, pissed off but practical. She tastes the metal of her shackles but tries being pitifully sweet. "Mom," she says over the intercom, leaving off the Mommy Dearest moniker that's dying to ooze out from underneath her breath, "I need you. Can you please come here so I can have a word with you?"

"I *can*," her mother says, "I'm certainly able. But *will* I?" Her aunts giggle in the background, offering a round of approval with her mother's grammatical correction.

Capri hears clinking ice cubes and crinkling bags of tortilla chips. By now they're knee-deep in guacamole dip, pleased to include Capri in the fat content that doesn't count because it's "the good kind." Even from her room, she can smell the avocadoes and tequila. They're always more gutsy when Jose Cuervo is involved.

"*May I* have a word with you?" Capri says.

"After this hand. *May*-be," her mother answers in a singsong voice.

"Come on, I really need you bad," Capri says, trying to sound desperate. "Right now."

"Never fear, we are bad," Aunt Celia says, singing too. "You need her bad*ly*."

Just what Capri needs, all of them grammar hammered.

"Mom! Please. Please! This is child abuse."

"Yes," Trinka says, "my child has been abusing me." Then she and her sisters break out in a round of belly laughs.

"Bartender," Capri hears Aunt Bess say, "another round."

"Dibs on the sofa bed," another one says.

Where is Child Services when she needs them?

"Mom, I'm serious. Really. Please. I beg you. Just give me a minute. Just one minute."

Through the intercom, she can hear them whispering. They sound like they're playing rock-paper-scissors. Finally, a chair skids away from the table and she hears steps on the stairs. Her mother doesn't say a word, but Capri can smell her perfume on the other side of the door, an expensive floral blend of plums and orchids.

She could smell her mother a mile away.

Capri drips her voice with sticky honey. "You said you wanted to talk. I do too. We can talk about Aunt John Mallory. I'll listen. Tell me the story."

"Just as soon as you show me a little respect, young lady," her mother says from the other side. "You will not leave this house until I'm certain your head is screwed on straight. Leroy said I don't have to let you out until you're eighteen, not if I don't want to, maybe not even then. You're in for the night, maybe the rest of your tweens."

Typically, her sense of smell is precise, but Capri smells something indescribably foul seeping under the door. It's disturbing, like a flower that smells of rotting flesh. She can only attribute it to Leroy. It infuriates her. "You're listening to Leroy now? Come on, Mom. That guy's a land shark."

"He's been a prince through all this."

Capri can detect his pheromones on her mother's skin.

"Leroy steals little old ladies' life savings for a living. He hasn't even passed the bar. Isn't it illegal for him to be giving legal advice when he's not a lawyer?" She can still smell her mother's perfume, but Capri knows how two scents can create deadly explosives. "Come on. You've got to be kidding. That guy's a toad. Maybe we both need to talk about our romantic options."

Her mother snorts. "He may not be pretty but he's rich and smart," she says, "and reliable. He'd never lie to his mother."

"He smells like his old Cadillac. That heap of primer spots he calls a classic."

She gives a humph and Capri hears the creak of the floorboards as her mother stomps down the stairs.

Too late, she realizes it would've been smarter to hold her tongue. Her mother has gone back to casino night with her sisters. Capri resorts to beating the door with the heel of her favorite cowboy boots. They make welts but can't break through. She smells lemon polish and looks around, but the windows are nailed shut.

Leroy is obviously handy with a hammer, too.

Capri tries the intercom again, saying, "Listen, I'm sorry. Mom? Are you there?" but she hears Aunt Lolly's voice answering with, "Joe's Bar and Grill," then laughter.

Capri huffs. She expects better things from a woman who rescues stray cats.

She can't even call Mac, and he's probably stewing because she's hours late. So she stands in her closet staring at her linens and cottons trying to decide what to do. Finally, she resorts to old tricks. She sprinkles baby powder under her door and uses her hair dryer to blow it through. Coughing and gagging, she dumps the entire twenty-two ounce bottle down the hornet's tunnel of the vents.

It's not long before her mother appears in the doorway. The room is flooded with baby powder smoke. Her mother's hair, face, and clothes are coated. Betty Crocker has risen from the kitchen, and she's cussing up a storm tunnel, spitting up flour.

"You drop that right now," her mother says, pointing at Capri's hair dryer like it's a semi-automatic weapon. "Do you know how exhausting you are? You make me want to pull out my hair."

"Dibs on the Dior scarves."

Her mother looks at the ceiling and closes her eyes. "You have no idea how much stress it puts us under. And then you—"

"You're under stress? I'm the one who's locked up."

"You're locked up? Now that's funny." Then she puts her fists on her hips. "I guess I might as well tell you. Then maybe you'll understand." She eyes Capri like she's sizing her up for a coffin. "Do you know why Granddaddy goes away?"

"Business trips," Capri says, but she gets the impression that her mother wants to pin it on her. "I don't know. Who cares? What? You're going to pretend it's me? Maybe you should stop ratting me out. Fine, go call him. Tattle away, I've got my side. Get him on the phone. We'll see." She figures she'll have a much better chance with Granddaddy than her mother and her aunts when they're drinking margaritas, thinking everything they do is hi*lar*-i-ous.

"He goes to the hospital," her mother says, like she was spitting it out.

"Hospital?" Capri's heart sinks. She feels the blood drain from her face. She runs around the room, flapping her arms, collecting clothes. "Well, let's go. Why didn't you tell me?

Where is he? What's wrong? Is he dying? Oh, God, don't tell me he's dying."

"Capri, honey," she says. She reaches out and tries to calm her daughter by tucking her hair behind her ear. "Everyone dies, but he's not dying, not like that."

"Then like what? Dead is dead," Capri says because it seems that too many important people in her life have already died.

"Seems we're always dancing around death's stage door. Our scripts are well rehearsed."

Capri hates it when her mother talks that way, whenever she drinks tequila and lights candles and starts reading poetry. When she and her sisters dance in the backyard, Capri turns up her music. Sometimes she watches them from the window, but most of the time she closes the shades and leaves the house. She loves to dance, but not with her mom and aunts on the lawn, not with candles and sparklers and chanting. She just wants to be in a normal family. She wants to travel, but her mom hasn't flown in a plane since her sister's death in the 80s. Capri has only flown once, with Mac, and traveled a couple of times with her granddaddy. They drove to the Ozarks, Branson and Silver Dollar City, and Oklahoma for a boat show. She begs him to take her on his business trips, but he never does, and she misses him so much when he's gone, leaving her to travel in her books. Play cards with the crazy sisters. And be home by nine.

"Don't worry," her mother says, "your granddaddy's a survivor." Then she stands up straighter and says, "You come from hearty stock," as if Capri is nothing more than a can of soup with tenderloin chunks.

"What's wrong with him?"

"He goes to a hospital, honey, but it's not a regular hospital. He's different." She stops and raises one eyebrow. "He goes to Research, Capri," she says with a sigh, as if she's just cut off her own ankle bracelet.

"To research what?" Capri says, sniffing. Her sinuses are filled with baby powder. "Don't tell me he's studying with some kooky scientists." Her mother shakes her head. "Please don't tell me it has to do with the Pleiades. With the Blue Stars? He thinks you're the Seven Sisters. And what? That makes him the sun or the moon?"

"Well, yes, kind of. No, but you pretty much hit it on the head."

"Hit what on the head?" Capri feels like she's banging her thumb with a hammer and her mother keeps saying, "Good job."

"He thinks he's the sun. We're the Pleiades. I told you."

"You haven't told me anything." Capri gives her mother a puckered look. "Fine, okay," she says, not even trying to hide her disgust for the putrid smells in the room, "you've all lost it."

She heads for the door.

"Research Psychiatric, honey," her mother says. "It's a psychiatric center."

Capri's hand freezes. She stares at the doorknob. Her mother lays her hands on Capri's shoulders, and she can feel her mother's breath on her neck. But Trinka's smell is too close, a stomach churning mixture of perfume, baby powder and tequila.

"I wish we could go see him now," she says. "He always loves to dance with you. Sometimes it brings him back. Sometimes he wakes when we dance."

"Bring him back? What are you talking about?"

Her mother looks out the window while Capri tries to catch her breath. "Your fates have always been intertwined," she says. "I've always felt that."

The baby powder has settled on her dresser and bed. Her room looks like a crime scene. Capri closes her eyes and pretends it's snow on a summer day, and she's ready to board a plane, but it's no good. The sun has melted and shadows creep into her room. She smells the oddest scent of a rotting flower.

"Maybe you should go with me," her mother says. "Seeing you would do him good. If you dance for him, I know he'd come back, I know he would. It works. It works sometimes. That's what we do, and he always loves to dance with you. You're just like her. Your eyes and lips…"

She reaches out to touch Capri's nose, her skin pasty from the powder. Sweat has formed on her upper lip. She smells like a ghost raised from the dead. Capri moves away.

"She didn't die," her mother says, "because you look so much like her, and the way you carry yourself. You have all her mannerisms, even her rhythm. You dance like her. You've always reminded me of her so much, ever since you were born. I should've told you."

Capri turns around. "I knew it. You lied. You're the one who's nuts!" And then her eyes fill with tears. "Dance for Granddaddy in a psych ward?" It's the dumbest idea she's ever heard. She can feel her eyes darkening. Stiff, raw and empty, she feels like a petrified beetle.

"I know it sounds crazy, but it works. Sometimes. You'll see."

"I will *not* see because I'm not going."

"It's not like we want to, but it's just that…" Her mother shakes her head. "He gets the idea that he's the sun, and he starts seeing John Mallory, and sometimes when we dance, it makes him come back. Sometimes, it works. When he thinks we're the Seven Sisters. He sees the seven stars in the sky…"

"I'm surprised you haven't resorted to swooping down in a basket from the weeping willow tree. Well, I'm not taking any part in feeding him your crazy myth. It's all lies—"

"You know, Capri, someday you'll learn. Sometimes you do things you wouldn't do. When it helps someone you love. I know it sounds crazy, but…" She rubs powder from her cheek and touches her hair. "Pink face, pink hair. You look like an orchid waiting for a drop of rain."

Capri twists her head so it's out of her mother's reach. "How could you keep this from me? Why would you lie?" Her breath comes in chokes. Her sinuses are blocked. She is not a girl in pigtails.

"We thought we were protecting you. For years—"

"You thought it was better to lie? Is that what you said?"

"But if we told you…It was better, we thought. But when he's gone, he's there. He's with her. He has to be."

"So it's okay for you to lie."

"I'm trying to tell you now. He's not on business trips, Capri. He's always been at Research." Her body tightens. She closes her eyes as if that will give her strength, but Capri can smell the plums and orchards of her mother seeping from the room. "We thought it was best. To shield you and your cousins. So you wouldn't get hurt. We can all see you're just like her."

"I knew it. You aren't my mother," she says. "My mother's dead."

Trinka looks at her as if her heart is breaking. "Your mother isn't dead. I'm right here."

"Granddaddy's crazy. My entire family is crazy."

Trinka's head snaps as if she's been stung.

"My sisters and I always use the word loosely," she says. "We say, 'He's crazy, don't listen to him. Don't pay attention, he's crazy. Must be the crazy fool in him.' We laugh, because it's the only thing that keeps us sane. We make jokes no one else can possibly understand. That's what it's like. But if anyone else heard, they'd think we were being mean, but they can't know. When your daddy is stuck in time, it's the only way. Laughing is the only thing that keeps you from crying. We say crazy," she says, her bottom lip trembling, "but when it comes from someone else's lips, it's wrong. It's harsh and thoughtless." Her voice breaks. "It's cruel. You're being cruel, Capri."

"I'm being cruel? You're a liar. He's crazy, you're crazy, you're all crazy!"

"Watch your tongue, young lady, or I'll wash your mouth out with soap."

Now Capri feels the sting of fury rushing into her eyes. "You think you can control me with a bar of Ivory?"

She pushes past Trinka and runs down the stairs. Mac is standing in the doorway with Aunt Lolly, looking like he's seven feet tall. She rushes into his arms, sobbing.

"Get me out of here, take me back to Mexico," she says, and he cradles her head. He kisses her hair and says, "Baby, baby. What's wrong, baby?"

"You will not leave this house!" Trinka shouts, clomping down the stairs in her clogs. She's covered in baby powder. "You think you tasted Montezuma's Revenge? You'll only wish you had cramping and diarrhea!"

Capri's eyes widen, horrified because she's told Mac about her watery stools. "How could you?" she says, screaming.

She paws at Mac as if he can stop her. Her aunts come running, and Mac reaches for the door. When Capri snatches her purse from the front table, Trinka shouts, "You can't leave me, I juiced lemons for your enemas!"

Capri screams until the windows rattle, until Mac flings open the door and pushes her out. Trinka stays on the front porch but yells so all of Johnson County can hear her. "You cannot take my little girl! You cannot!"

"What was that all about?" Mac says when they're a few blocks away. His car rumbles and tires screech as he takes corners on two wheels. Capri always tells him he should stop annoying the neighbors and spring for a new muffler. His Mustang smells like French fries and beer, but Capri doesn't care. She just wants away from the madhouse. She leans against the cool window. Her stomach is in knots. She doesn't know when she ate last, but if she had eaten she'd be throwing it up.

"What was she talking about?" he says, chortling. "Enemas?"

She scratches her neck. She wants to crawl into the McDonald's bag and die. She kicks it and doesn't say a word, but Mac won't drop it.

"Aye-yi-yi," he says and laughs. "Is that what she said? Jesus. Enemas?" He wiggles in his seat. "Isn't that where you squirt stuff up your ass? That's crazy."

Mac is getting on her nerves, and Capri is not crazy.

"Enemas aren't crazy," she says. "They flush out your colon. And coffee stimulates the liver and gallbladder. It releases toxins. There are spas, you know. People use them to cure major illnesses, you know."

"Jesus. You didn't? First the old man puts coffee in your baby bottle, now your mom's convincing you to put it in your ass? Man, I've heard everything." He laughs.

"First of all, I don't know what Jesus had to do with all of this. And stop cussing. It makes you sound illiterate." She shakes her head and closes her eyes, realizing she has just parroted her mother. "Listen, it's a way to communicate with your soul, the sacred. It's important to see your body as a sacred vessel. It's the only thing on this earth that was created just for you." She realizes that she has begun paraphrasing John Mallory, like Granddaddy does, and she doesn't know why, but she can't stop herself. John Mallory must be her mother, because she's in her head, her blood and bones. She even smells coffee, though there's not a drop in the car.

"Sounds like some crazy shit. Man that's crazy."

"It is not crazy," Capri says. He has no idea what crazy is.

"Well, I sure as hell can promise you I wouldn't do anything as crazy as that. Shoving lemons and coffee up my ass...Doesn't sound holy to me. Holy shit! Get it?" He laughs. "Are you wearing baby powder?"

"I didn't say holy, I said sacred! Shut up, Mac!" Capri screams and throws things, anything close, beer cans, trash, a smelly tennis shoe. "Shut up, shut up, shut up!"

"Calm down," he says, and pulls into the parking lot of a 7-Eleven, then slams on the brakes. Her head almost hits the dashboard.

She plugs her nose and breathes through her mouth. They sit in silence, staring out the window as people pass by them to pay for gas.

"Listen, I'm sorry. But you know I hate it when you cuss," she says, trying to catch her breath. She pushes back her hair. Her head pounds. His eyes are wide. The look on his face is somewhere halfway between confused and pissed. She has to tell him.

"I think my mother just told me that she's not my real mother."

"Fu—" he starts to say but then stops himself. "That is some crazy shit."

"Please," she says, completely composed, "stop using the word crazy. And shit."

He looks from side to side, which always kind of makes him look like an owl on a cuckoo-cuckoo clock. That's when she thinks about her granddaddy, confined to a bed, guys with white jackets poking him with needles. She can smell the incarceration of four walls closing in on him, moldy and dirty. Somewhere her granddaddy's alone and scared. The thought makes her want to throw up.

Trinka and her aunts did this to him.

"I need some coffee," she says, knowing that a cup of coffee can calm her, bring her closer to him. She digs through her purse for her wallet. She runs a brush through her hair, then gets out and dusts off her shirt and slaps baby powder out of her jeans. "Want anything?"

He leans over and says, "Yeah, buy a six pack, will ya?" but she closes the door.

Even if they were old enough, which they aren't, Capri would not buy Mac a six pack. She follows the smell of coffee to the back of the store. It doesn't smell bad for a gas station. She gets an extra-large cup and fills it with coffee, cream and sugar. Nothing else smells appetizing. She wonders whether she should take Granddaddy some, so she pours another cup but leaves it black, like he likes.

"Do you know what this is?" she asks the guy behind the cash register.

"Coffee?" he says.

"Yeah, it's coffee, but what kind? I don't mean to insult you, but it smells like robusta. And if you could, look on the bag. See whether it's French Roast. Columbian, maybe? I know it's not Sumatra," she says with a laugh.

He gives her a blank stare.

"It's plain old coffee," he says and rings it up. "Anything else?"

She sighs, looking through her wallet.

"Hey, you got a phone book?" He rolls his eyes but pulls one out from under the counter.

She finds it in the Yellow Pages. Unbelievable, but she finds it in the Yellow Pages. It's under Psychiatric Clinics, as if it has been there all along, just waiting for her. Research Psychiatric Center it says, bigger than life.

"You know how to get here?" She shows the guy the address and he tells her, "63rd and Prospect, follow the hospital signs," then tells her how, as if he knows, too, as if everyone in Kansas City knows where this place is, and they all probably know that her granddaddy is a gold star member there, in a mental institute.

She walks away, trying not to let the fumes of the parking lot overwhelm her. She slides back into the car with her two cups of coffee.

"Not for you," she says when Mac eyes her granddaddy's coffee. "I need you to take me somewhere." She gives Mac the directions the guy in 7-Eleven gave her.

"What's at 63rd and Prospect?" Mac starts the car. It's on the side of town where they rarely go. "Isn't that near the zoo?"

"Yeah," she says and spits out a laugh. The irony is too much, even for her. "Hey, you ever heard the myth about the goddess? When she's the creator? Her body is the universe."

"Babes and their magic bodies," he says, but he isn't really listening because he's trying to find a song he likes on the radio.

"The goddess swallows the sun," she says. "She swallows it in the west and gives birth to it in the east. The sun passes through her body. Because she's the goddess, and she's the dominant mythic form."

"Save Mother Earth," he says. "Cheer up, babe. I've got you covered." He winks then turns up the music.

Capri looks out the window. The Kansas City sky is turning red and orange. The sun is low in the sky. The evening's chill is coming from the north. To the west, there are miles and miles of corn and wheat, where her great granddaddy worked the land, like his daddy did before him. To the south, there are mountainsides of coffee trees that live and breathe. John Mallory walks the land in the cool cloud forest. She is the red coffee cherry, the dark blue bird, the green seasons and seas.

Capri can sense her. Her story is Capri's as much as coffee is in her blood.

Still, Capri knows the sun rises in the east, and so she must go there. She must find her granddaddy and bring him back. It's the only way. Oddly enough, the only thing she's thinking about is how she knows she lives in the sky of stars, but her sky always includes her granddaddy.

7

El Río del Tiempo

With the sun low in the sky and green mountains crayoned on the canvas, John Mallory touched down in San Jose, Costa Rica with her old suitcases, hot, tired, thirsty, and more than a little jittery. She stepped off the plane to warm air and peppy music. Dirt and fresh blooms filled the air. A boy no older than sixteen held a handmade sign with her name.

She waved to him and he smiled. With dark slicked-back hair, he smelled like earth and the slightest hint of pickled eggs. He didn't speak a lick of English except to say, "John Mallory?" which he pronounced Yawn Mah-yee, and then pointed to himself, saying, "Carlos."

He led her to where they could find her luggage. Happy they had sent someone, she looked around for anyone else. Her father had told her to expect one of the nuns from the church. Sister Somebody would be her charge and keep an eye on her. There were locals and a few tourists connecting with their rides, but she didn't see anyone in a long black robe or a woman with searching eyes. Her father said he had arranged it with the Roastmaster. She didn't know the word for nun in Spanish and could only remember the word for sister, so she asked him, "*¿Hermana?*"

He burst out laughing and pointed to himself. "*¿Hermana? ¡No hermana! Me llamo Carlos.*"

"Right," she said. She could feel her face flush. He kept looking at her, trying not to laugh. He reminded her of a young Mr. Armstrong, natural, preoccupied with the earth, a science teacher she remembered fondly at her elementary school, always smiling and joking, with his rough elbows poking out of a checkered short-sleeved shirt, his skin the color of golden tobacco.

She would give anything to go to the bathroom, but she waited for her bags. When they were thrown onto the dusty floor, Carlos gladly picked them up, hoisting one on each shoulder. She struggled to remember the word for bathroom and didn't want to make a fool of herself again, so she tried using English.

"Could you point me to the ladies room?" When he looked at her with a puzzled expression, she said, "Bathroom?" He didn't understand, so she said, "No problem," and he repeated, "*¡No problema!*" obviously excited they had connected. She signaled she would be going away and went to search for a lavatory.

When she came out, he was gone.

She panicked, wondering if she'd made a mistake, or if he'd misunderstood. Maybe she should have waited for Sister Somebody. She ran in circles, searching the baggage area and strangers' eyes. She looked for someone in a uniform, then ran outside. She found Carlos directly in front of the door, leaning against a two-toned Sedan, dented and full of scratches. Her bags were already in the back seat. He opened her door. She blushed and got in. Then he ran around to the other side, jumped in, and turned the ignition. The car gave a high-pitched shriek, like air being let out of a balloon, and they took off, squealing down the road.

She tried to make conversation, fanning herself and asking him questions about himself, but he only smiled. "Any chance you have air-conditioning in *su coche*?"

He cocked his eyebrows. To demonstrate, she waved her hand in front of her face, puffed up her cheeks, and blew hard.

"*¡Ah, sí!*" he said. From his back pocket, he pulled out a piece of candy.

"No," she said, "not my breath. Do you have any air? Cold wind? *Frio*...I'm hot. *Yo soy caliente*," she said, beaming because her years of high school Spanish were finally paying off. She remembered the word for cold and for hot.

"*¡Sí, sí!*" He smiled, nodded, then leaned over, trying not to touch her while he rolled down her window. She caught a strong whiff of his sweaty underarms. Even though she had always been an excellent student, her Spanish was failing her. She realized she would have to change her expectations, which made her stomach flutter but also made her feel proud and adventurous.

They left the big city with its urban bustle, passing homes with curled barbed wire along the top of fences. Men held long guns outside of buildings. Their eyes were steady, faces expressionless, as if they were soldiers guarding palaces.

At the edge of town, he traveled along back roads. She noticed there were no markers or street signs. The roads were narrow and dusty. She tried not to tense up, or feed her ugly thoughts about being dumped on the road, or her concerns that she would be forced to take a month-long walkabout without food, hot showers, or even a glass of water. Carlos kept eyeing her, smiling. He seemed harmless, but she pinned up her hair and buttoned up her shirt, then crowded into the corner gripping the door handle, trying to conjure up scents from home, like her father's blue smoke.

Along the way, they passed coffee farms, and blackberry farms, and rows of broad-leafed plantain and banana trees. Coffee trees clung to the mountainside like houses in a seaside village. Birds flapped and twittered from tree branch to bush, free of telephone lines in the air. Up ahead, Carlos pointed to a fork in a fig tree, something sitting in the branches. At first she thought it was a chicken. But then its enormous boat-shaped beak turned towards her: a large yellow, black and red bird. She squealed and shouted, "Unbelievable!" She had only seen a toucan on the front of a cereal box.

"*Dios te de*," Carlos said as he leaned out the window, slowing the car until it idled. She struggled to interpret. It delighted her when the bird echoed back, as if its call repeated his: "*Dios te de, dios te de.*" May God be with you, May God be with you.

Suddenly, another toucan flew across the wooded area, in front of the car. Its top-heavy beak forced it into a nosedive position. It landed on a low branch in the same fig tree. Then another, and another, until there were seven or eight toucans in the tree, hopping up to higher branches. The first toucan paused, looking back as if it were counting inventory. Then it hopped to the highest branch, and dove, building speed in flight. The others sat with their heads cocked, waiting. This time, the call sounded farther away. One by one, each dove from the highest branch, with tidbits of time lapsing between each launch, summoned to the field by the sound of a whistle.

Carlos smiled at her, then slowly accelerated, until they became tiny ribbons of stripes behind them.

"How can they possibly fly? They're Jimmy Durante with wings." She tried to catch their scent on the wind. She looked at him. "Of course, you don't know what I'm saying. You'd be a great best friend. You're such a patient listener." She smiled. "Since you don't understand me anyway, I guess it wouldn't be rude if I asked you how you got that scar on your cheek. I imagine your life is very different than mine. I have a scar on my chin from trying to do spins while ice skating. I can assure you I'm no Dorothy Hamill. Want to see? Great," she said, "a few hours in the jungle and I'm jabbering away. You must think I'm rude. Do you? Don't answer that."

He grinned but kept his eyes on the road and his face close to the steering wheel. She wondered just how long he had been driving a car. She thought she smelled the ocean, wet sand and salt. She couldn't wait to walk along the shore, barefoot to the rhythm of the crashing waves. She looked forward to digging her toes into the sand. "To the beach please, *amigo*," she said, and laughed. He laughed too.

The sun faded behind them. Once she got used to it, the temperature was ideal, not a drop above 23 Celsius, and she was glad he couldn't understand her because she may have complained about the lumpy seats and every bump along the way. Given the chance, she knew she would have whined like an ignored kitten clamoring out of a cardboard box. Instead, she sat and listened and smelled the deep raw earth in this exotic land, misty, green, lush.

They followed a muddy road up into the clouds. Carlos pointed outside.

"*Cerro de la Muerte*," he said. The road had become windy and narrow and steep.

Her Spanish was limited, but she recognized one word. She said, "Death?"

With a heavy accent, he said, "Mountain of death," and smiled, showing her his crowded teeth. His hands gripped the steering wheel tighter.

From then on, she kept her eyes glued to the road. Pushed up against the dashboard, she pointed out eroded sides of the mountain and yelled as he sped around hairpin turns. She tried to help him see the edges, even though he gave her no indication he needed help driving. Never had she felt so close to the brink, her sinuses filled, her nose so close to the breath of the grim reaper.

Around dusk, they stopped for the night. She could barely breathe, frazzled and spent as a grasshopper that had clung to a blade of grass during a tornado. A woman in a muumuu greeted them, her face open and splotchy. Her long toes hung over the front of her sandals. It was a makeshift hotel with small rooms that opened to a courtyard and a cantina with a stone floor. With only a small sink and a stove for heat at night, the tiny woman laughed and chatted with Carlos in Spanish.

"*¡Fantastico, Carlos! No, no*," she said.

"*¡Sí, sí! Es verdad*," he said.

John Mallory smiled and folded into a wooden chair. The woman reached out and patted her hand, then gave her a bowl of beans and rice. John Mallory understood only bits of their Spanish. She knew they had laughed about her grammatical hiccups, and her screaming, but they seemed happy and harmless. Still, she declined the sugary dessert. Instead, she pretended to study the stars. She breathed in the dirt of Costa Rica, trying to inhale the life in front of her.

The mood of the sky matched her mixed emotions: expansive darkness with a twinkling of faraway lights. She searched for the poetry in its dark gaps. She felt completely unfit for this wilderness. She had no idea where she was, except deep in the rainforest—she really could have been abducted by Carlos and his accomplice. In the woods and thick brush she imagined wild, hungry animals. Damp and gamey, she heard shrill cries and whistling birds, and then the thump of the webbed feet of a brightly-colored frog that hopped along the path. She recognized the giant kapok tree from pictures in books. Tall, with its straight trunks cylindrical, smooth and gray, it was majestic and powerful. She wished it would bend from the sky and fold her in its arms.

The woman blew out the candle and nodded, signaling it was time to sleep. In her room, John Mallory dragged a chair over and propped it against the door. Two hours later, her eyes stayed open as she lay on top of the white sheets of her tiny bed. She thought of her father and the look on her mother's and sisters' faces when she left. She already missed the smell of her own tribe.

"What an experience you're in for. You'll see. You'll thank me," her father had said, but she felt the anxiety in his grip. "You'll come back a different girl, and I'll be here, waiting. You're excited, aren't you? You always said you wanted to be a foreign exchange student. Well, this is better! You don't regret it, do you?" She could smell his fear, as if he knew a snake was hiding in the bushes.

"It's exactly what I needed," she had said, lying, but she had no interest in watching her father writhe from the pain of his doubt. She folded her arms around him, breathing deeply into his bristly neck of Old Spice aftershave and the hint of ocean spray detergent in his collar. She touched his hair, so her fingertips would smell like the oil he used to sleek it back.

Her mother and sisters, stiff and pressed, gave her pecks on the cheek, all spicy beauty chemicals and Agree shampoo.

"Don't eat the vegetables," her mother said. "They're washed in dirty water, and it's full of parasites. Stay away from the meat. They eat goats and rats. But don't swim in the rivers, either. They're loaded with piranhas."

Her mother stood with her pink lips pursed, her pocket book dangling in the crook of her arm. Her sisters were lined up by age, all bushy eyebrows and forests of hair. Her father wiped the corner of his eye with the back of his finger.

"Back by spring," John Mallory said, and then trying to convince herself, "No worries."

"Another thing to look forward to," he said. "You and the spring flowers."

"And popsicles," she said with a laugh. "When I get back, it'll be warm, and we'll dance under the stars like we always do."

He held her hand and she twirled under his arm. She laughed, and he smiled. His lips paused on her forehead. She felt them trembling.

From the end of the line, Trinka stepped away and stuffed a frilly package into her carry-on bag. She whispered, "Don't open it on the plane," and then louder, "Bring me back a native!"

"Don't forget to make us proud," said Abigail.

"I won't," John Mallory said, but she didn't know if she really meant it. She tried standing a little more erect, like a bronzed statue, and tucked one hand into her pea jacket, between the buttons, as if she had just taken a hill or conquered a city. She pretended to be courtly, hoping to pull off confident, which was hard to do with her teeth chattering.

She remembered lumbering her way with the sea of people, headed to the airplane gate, and glancing back. Her mother and sisters were already walking away. Her mother turned around then, like a sea turtle taking a final look over her shoulder to the mound of sand where she had buried her eggs. But John Mallory never knew if the sea turtle glanced back with pride or relief. They disappeared and John Mallory rounded the corner, but her father remained. Motionless, with his hat in his hand, he stayed behind the imaginary line that had separated them.

In her small room in Costa Rica, John Mallory gulped and pulled the sheets up to her nose. She knew full well that the most palatable way for her to demonstrate pride would be to swallow it. She trembled, feeling the vapors rise from the earth, making her nose quiver with doubt.

She remembered the package from Trinka and jumped from her bed to get it. Inside, she found a ten dollar bill and a little piece of folded tissue paper. Something hard was hidden. She delicately unwrapped it and hooted. Her petrified beetle. Trinka had laughed at her when she explained its symbolism. But she could smell the clear fingernail polish Trinka had used to shellac it. Its minty body gleamed like a varnished floor.

The black eyes were hard and shiny as marbles. She had used pink nail polish to paint on tiny lips. And there was a tiny note, written with her sister's pen. It said, "I'll always believe in you." It gave her goose bumps. She breathed it in, and underneath the cocoa, she could detect the slightest hint of her sister's baby powder. John Mallory set her only Costa Rican friend on her pillow and fell fast asleep.

In the morning, there was a tap on the door. A bowl of melon and cream waited on the table outside. Still in the same muumuu, the woman boiled unnaturally red-colored beans to brew something thick and dark. She placed a cup in front of John Mallory.

"Thank you. What's this?" she said, looking at the cup and then the woman. Her dark eyes stared at John Mallory with a blank expression. "Coffee?"

"¡Sí! ¡Café!" the woman said, with enthusiasm.

John Mallory shrugged, then took a sip and almost gagged. Later, she would learn that all the coffee bought by local merchants and roasters were dyed an unnatural reddish color. It was a requirement by the government, a precaution against illegal imports. Locals were sold the inferior beans, old cherries that had fallen from the trees, and young green cherries. (It wouldn't be the worst coffee John Mallory would taste in Costa Rica, not by a long shot.) She swallowed but held her breathe. She gave the woman a thumbs up, and the woman giggled and mimicked John Mallory. But as soon as she turned her back, John Mallory tossed the pungent brew on a banana tree.

In the United States, the cities would have been called tri-cities: Santa Maria, San Pablo and San Marcos. Three cities of saints. She sighed. At least there was a straggle of buildings and what appeared to be a couple of tourists. Through the window she saw a rainbow of fruits, bright yellow, orange, and flame-scarlet, strange heart-shaped ones and ornamental leaves. A pungent aroma drenched the air, fresh, sweet and juicy. The market was thick with guava, mango, papaya and avocadoes. Locals gathered outside for gossip at that time of the day, with tipped back hats, talking coffee prices and fruit conditions. If John Mallory had stopped, they would have gladly informed her of the reputations of the cities.

"Live in Santa Maria with its large Catholic church and the park across the way," they would say. "Invest your money in San Marcos where they're more progressive and have banks. And have fun in San Pablo where there's nightlife." Because everyone knew that the people in Santa Maria stuffed all their money under mattresses, while the people in San Marcos grew fat watching their investments grow, and the people in San Pablo spent every last penny they ever made having fun and dancing.

But Carlos didn't stop, even though John Mallory pointed to a boxy building with windows, what appeared to be a restaurant, and then to her mouth.

"Eat," she said. "Hungry." She rubbed her stomach.

Carlos chuckled. She feared the daredevil she smelled inside of him. Outside of town, he took an unpaved road deeper into the shrubs and tussocks of grass. By then, she had learned to tighten her shoulders when her head hit the ceiling and grip the seat with her buttocks. She had never been on African safari, but she imagined she could match their adventurous stories.

Hours later, and over a bridge, they finally slowed down. They wound up a long street and then drove slowly past gates with a wooden sign that read *EL CIELO VERDE*. By then, her hair tumbled around her shoulders, half pinned to the top of her head, the rest sticking to her cheeks. She slapped at bugs that buzzed around the dusty car, and wiped her neck with the tail of her shirt. They stopped in front of a small building. Before she could pull her bags out of the car, a man approached with a wide grin.

"Hel-*lo*, little lady. Bill McCracken." He was American and tall, well over six feet, with a hearty handshake and muddy eyes. "Welcome to *El Cielo Verde*. Our Green Heaven." His hands were rough, his body like a feeder river that had forced its way across wild terrain just itching for a chance to arm wrestle the ocean. Though his mustache and beard were scraggly, he appeared healthy and young. His cologne was the scent of a man in charge, a faint mixture of soap, hair tonic and sweat.

"I'm so glad you're expecting me. You can't imagine. And to hear someone speak English. Flash cards in Spanish class can't really prepare someone for the real thing, can they?" she said, laughing. "I am *so* happy to see you. I expected Sister to meet me, so I can't tell you how happy I am to see you—"

"Glad you made it," he said, tipping back his hat, studying her. "We're always short on hands around here. So you're the offspring of the notorious John Mallory. Good man, good man." Before she could ask questions, he belted instructions in Spanish to Carlos. Then he yelled to a man passing on foot, waved his hat and trotted to join him.

On tiptoes, she called after him, "Of course! We'll catch up later. After I've settled in and rested!" He never told her where she'd find her guardian nun. She watched him until he disappeared over a hill, never glancing back. She smoothed back her hair and looked around. Already halfway up a stone walkway, Carlos signaled for her to follow him.

"You don't think he wanted me to follow him, do you?" she asked Carlos. "I'm sure he'll catch up to me later." That's when she would relay her story, her panic, the bumpy trip by widening her eyes and touching her throat. She would use her high voice. Bill McCracken would lean forward, his hands on his knees, completely captivated by her courage and her ability to spin such whimsical tails. It made her laugh already.

At the top of the walk, Carlos smiled, gave a slight bow and said, "*Aquí*, Yawn Mah-yee," urging her to stay put, and then he left her, too.

The outdoor porch could easily seat a hundred people, with a ruddy stone floor and hand-crafted, lacquered beams. She inhaled. Coffee brewed nearby. Good coffee. But there were other odors that she couldn't identify. They were raw yet earthy. In the background, she detected wild animals, maybe the scat of a large cat, and a tumbled whiff of something swingy and dirty.

She was drawn to the far side by the perfume of open space and sunshine. As she approached, a mural view unfolded a masterpiece. Mist haloed a green kaleidoscope of mountains. Pink clouds rolled into shapes. Though she was nowhere near Kansas, she was reminded of home. She breathed deeply and held the railing. Her eyes drifted and her mind wandered back to Kansas and her family. Her father would be reading the paper with swirling steam coming from his cup of black coffee. Frank Sinatra would be singing about love on the radio. Snowflakes flittered down and clustered, making rounded peaks on the patio furniture. He would take pictures for Mother, and she would mail the best ones to anchorman Larry Moore at KMBC, Channel 9. Daddy would head to the office, but John Mallory couldn't bear to follow him to Early Mountain Coffee. Her heart ached. So she followed the trail of her mother to the Nelson Art Gallery. In her Youth Dew and high heels, she teetered across the marble floors. John Mallory breathed in the antique smells as Mother led a group of third-graders through the section of Italian paintings. Her mother's favorite, *Saint John the Baptist in the Wilderness,* by Caravaggio, would be spotlighted up ahead, like a favorite lazy cat napping on a window sill. Mother would purr, trying to convey the richness and depth of the master, stressing the importance of the works from the 16th to 18th centuries. When a boy reached out to touch it, Mother pounced on him, like an enraged panther, hissing, "Hands to yourself!" A few miles away, Trinka counted change, with a phone balanced on her shoulder as she flirted with her latest boyfriend. She'd pretend to giggle, all licorice and cinnamon sticks, saying, "You shouldn't say those things over the phone." Back at Early Mountain, John Mallory could smell roasting coffee. Abigail and Bess would be crowded into Celia's office arguing about what they could write off from the tragedy last week. One of the roasting machines had caught fire—Ricardo felt bad, he had been distracted by Angela and forgotten about the batch of beans—now the machine lay soaked like an old lady drenched at the beauty parlor, so much mess from the water, more than from the fire. Down to one machine and working three eight-hour shifts, they wondered what to do. Celia would pretend to be listening while she read her mail, but she was really shopping in a glossy catalogue. Her heart skipped a beat as she studied a picture of a woman in a draped coat with droopy jeweled earrings. She must have them and added them to her mental shopping cart.

John Mallory leaned her hands on the flat, cool stone and started to hum. She jumped, startled by a pair of huge eyes staring back. It was a fuzzy moth, a leaf-like creature with wing spots that resembled eyes. A small beast doing its best to frighten away predators, it fluttered away.

Her stomach growled. When would she eat? She craved a piece of bread or a hunk of meat. She knew she looked mangy. She sneezed and shook. The smell of stray dog invaded her senses, wandering down back alleys, begging at restaurant doors, hoping a grumbling cook would toss her a scrap.

In a sea of flowers and fruits, a mecca of scents, she must force herself to focus her nose, as if she were an alchemist. So she smelled coffee.

Everything reeked of wild, curvy and tall, expansive. The mountains were alive. They must have smelled her hunger, too, because it was as if they were shifting their feet, trying to stop her stomach from aching. And the coffee trees emitted the most erotic scent, soulful beings pregnant with life, lavish, bursting and full. Beneath the peaceful giants, they were red stoops that trumpeted about life's possibilities. A gust of wind blew, rustling their branches, as if they were greeting her. She breathed in and then spoke to them.

"Hello, my luscious coffee trees. I'm finally here. We've known each other a thousand years, and we'll know each other a thousand more, and I'm finally here." The wind blew again, and she looked at the sky.

The sun was lowering. Her family roots stretched to the north. But here, she must find her own direction. Quiet and abundant, the coffee trees would never question if they were good enough. They would never doubt if nature would bring them dishes. Even if the wind chapped their skin, or too much water fell from the heavens, even if the sun drenched them with too many kisses, they would not be disbelieving. They would be thankful. She decided, right there, she would no longer complain, to the nun, to the American, to anyone she met. She would learn from her ancient sisters, the grounded, centered, rooted, sentient beings. She would be thankful, like a coffee tree for its magical beans.

Here, she stood on grounds where her future would be her present.

Everything whispered, showering, spritzing, sprinkling her with dizzying scents. Her senses opened up. She could smell the river next to the old trail where, years ago, they drove corn-fed pigs to market. Later, she would be told it was called Pig River by the locals, *Rio de los Chanchos*. She could see the footpath. She would follow it downstream, to the top of the waterfall, where the hurried paddled across the river for a shortcut to Santa Maria. On tiptoes, she could see the longer path, past jagged rocks to the safer one, a footfall, where the drive across the river was slower, where she had snaked around. The walk to town took a few more steps, and a baby's breath away was a home she would come to love.

She detected the singsong of sherbet in the air. Above, there were double rainbows. They had been shimmering and wriggling in backbends, trying to attract her with their heavenly scents. Their feet were pressed into the grassy green, with tailbones pointed to the sky. Touched down on the banks near the shade trees, their power blossomed in her lungs.

Her nostrils dilated to the scent of a wild animal. She looked around. A stone's throw away, a spider monkey swung from a tree. She tried not to scream with joy! A gymnast with a bloated truck driver's belly, it stopped and stared. Its long fingers curled around twigs, and its black toenails pigeon-toed in the air. A black and furry head, it had chocolate eyes that sunk into its skin, the color of silver dollars. It puckered its lips, wetted with curiosity. She laughed. Then it scurried down the trunk, as if determined to sniff her. Uncomfortable with its toes on the ground, it soon scampered back up the tree, to safety.

The hills were carpeted with coffee trees. She was engulfed in faint and potent perfumes. They made her nose wiggle. Invigorated and alert, she felt less lonely, less scared, more relaxed. Inexplicable but true, in their layers, she had found home. Aromas tethered her memories of another time, another place, maybe even another lifetime, to being there, right then. Maybe it was their fertility, their glossy green leaves, bursting with cherries, emitting the rich aroma of a lustful reproduction—sun-drenched fruits—a motherland of life, flesh and beans.

Endlessly interlacing, breathing in, then out, it was as if they were capturing each other's fragrances in the crystal bottles of their bodies.

"I wish Daddy could see you," she said. "You are magical. Maybe with you I will be, too."

Here, everything smelled like coffee—and coffee comforted her, like her father's arms. Coffee had been in her blood since her baby bottle. A powerful bean, it would help her claim respect and freedom, her right to her destiny. Father would swell with pride. Mother would invite her to play bridge and eat finger sandwiches. The Big Girls would come to her for advice and decisions.

"You are sweet nectar," she said, then singing in the wind, "Hear me queen mother of *el grano de oro*,"—the golden bean—"coffee of Costa Rica, you are the chocolate of the earth. Let me be your Roastmaster! *Sin café no hay mañana*," she said, dancing with her arms in the air. "*Sin café no hay mañana.*" Without coffee there is no tomorrow.

"John Mallory," a deep voice said.

When she turned around, she noticed the wooden tables on the other side. A small, dark man beckoned her with his finger. He hunched over and poured a steamy liquid into cups. His black hair hung forward and covered his eyes. He wore a long-sleeved shirt and worn, brown shoes. Friends, she would learn, described him as steady and slow, a tortoise, and she would tease him that it was because of his hard shell. He rarely smiled. She couldn't catch a scent on him, either, beyond coffee.

A dozen cups were evenly spaced on the two tables.

As she approached, he said, "I am Lorenzo Domingo," with the slightest roll of his *r*. He pointed to the first cup. "Let us discover what you know."

"*Señor* Domingo, hello. And you know English, thank my lucky stars. Yes, I'm pleased to meet you, too. I've heard so much about you. You're a legend where I come from," she said, rubbing her hands on her pants. "I am so pleased to meet you. Lorenzo Domingo, the Roastmaster. Should I call you *Señor* or Lorenzo? Your reputation precedes you. I admit," she said, feeling herself blush, "I'm rather intimidated." She reached out her hand, and then decided to curtsy.

"I am Lorenzo. Please, cup," he said and pointed to the table, then stepped back and clasped his hands behind his back.

It is a fact that the first taste to ever cross John Mallory's lips—all of the Mallory girls' lips—was that of warm milky coffee. Her father believed it held magical properties. Pink and wriggling, she had sucked from the nipple of a baby bottle, underneath the ginger-red of hospital lights. Nursed by coffee, it was as necessary to her as breathing and blood. Yet, she had never taken part in a formal cupping. Many times she had heard William page his team members over the intercom at Early Mountain Coffee, calling them to the cupping room. Once, when she was eleven, she wandered down, hoping to discover their secret rituals. She hid in the shadows while William slurped and pondered, and then he spat. She tried not to gasp. At parochial schools, young girls were forbidden to spit. The process struck her as barbaric. The other men followed William down the line of coffee cups, like cowboys spewing their chew. Yet she also recognized the honesty in practicing this vulgarity. So John Mallory had stepped into the room and asked if she could try. Their faces lifted, but William shook his head. He said it wasn't proper. He'd never allow her, or any girl, to be part of the ceremony. No girls were allowed in the cupping room, and he shooed her away.

Beyond saying yes to her father, she had not thought about what it meant to be a Roastmaster. Now, here she stood, in a jungle of smells, with a man who wore no other scent than coffee. He demanded she spit. It would be like asking a man to wear lipstick. Call her naïve and ignorant, but her father had prepared her for beaches and rainforests, not for snapping on the suspenders of a man's trousers.

She could feel her face grow long with fear. What if she failed or disappointed them?

"*Señor* Domingo, I mean Lorenzo," she said, blushing, "if you don't mind, I'd like to watch. You see, I'm better at observing. I'll follow you around. See what I can take back from your people. I'm a good learner, a good student. Then, when you're really sure I'm ready, let's talk about it."

"Watch?" he said, disgusted, as if she had asked to watch him take a shower. "You cannot learn about coffee only with your eyes."

She knew he was right. But if she spat with this man, she risked damaging her credibility before she got started. She was being asked to enter a personal contract, a boys' club, and she felt unprepared. It felt too personal, too soon. It would be better to ease in, break bread first around the family table.

"Maybe we could have lunch," she said. She also had no desire to test out another rotten coffee before another mealtime.

"You cup. Now," he said, opening his arm to the tables. "Show what you know of Mother Bean. The queen you called her?"

"Mother Bean? Oh, that. You were listening? That was just me being silly. Don't pay attention to the madman behind the curtain," she said, laughing. When his eyes widened, she said, "No, sorry, don't be scared. I'm just a bit jittery. Doubt another cup of coffee would be a good idea before a little snack."

"Cup," he said again.

She sniffed. "I hate to disappoint you, but it's just that I have these pesky allergies, you know." She wiped her nose. She definitely smelled something rotting in one of those cups. "Maybe you should go ahead without me. I'd hate to waste all of this."

She would rather study him, to make sure she could follow the ritualistic order of his process.

Lorenzo's eyes narrowed. He picked up a spoon and leaned over the first cup of coffee. He broke the puffy brown crust, and it caved like marshmallows. Dipping in his spoon, he brought up a thick liquid, then slurped loudly. He held it in his mouth, then spat quickly into another cup. He waved her over.

"Yes, I see," she said, giving a small laugh.

He handed her a spoon and pointed to another cup. "Tell me what Mother Bean speaks to you."

She smiled. "Okay then, talk to me, Mother Bean," she said in what she thought was a playful tone. But instead of leaning over with the spoon as Lorenzo had done, she set it on the table, bent over the cup and whiffed. Yes, she could smell the fresh earth, the fine chocolates of the land. She even detected the slightest hint of cocoa and avocados.

"This cup comes from a fine sample of local, fresh beans. About three days old?" she said, smiling at him with an air of confidence. "Good job. Nicely roasted, not too dark, not too light."

He shook his head, then slapped his ear with the palm of his hand, as if he were trying to release water.

"You must taste her *aquí*," he said, holding his hands over his heart, just like her father would do. Then he nodded to the spoon with his chin. She could tell by his creased look that she had disappointed him. The pock marks on his face had deepened. A waft of wind carried dust to her nose. She tried lifting the cup to her lips, but he pushed it back to the table. Drops of coffee sloshed over the sides. "You must taste her," he said, louder.

"That's what I'm trying to do."

She blinked.

Lorenzo frowned, grabbed the spoon again, held her wrist, and then slapped the silver into her palm. Her face flushed. He reminded her of Sister Mary Theresa and her wicked ways with rulers. Even if he was being rough, she knew the best protection would be to display no emotion, not crumble, so she leaned over the cup, dipped the spoon, and silently sipped. After she swallowed, she wiped the foam from her lips, saying, "Yes, good," and attempted to hand him back the spoon.

He rolled his eyes. "You must spit."

She shrugged.

"Cup," he said, "and Mother Bean speaks. She must tell you her story. *De su corazón.* Of her heart. To your tongue, *entonces probablemente* to your heart. Not before. It is her life she gives to you. Her story, the mountains where she lives, the people she loves. We are circles, the soil under her feet, the sunshine," he said, waving at the sky. "The skies feed her. It drops the rain. To you, she must whisper her secrets. Of her land. She must give you her heart. You see, hear, smell, taste, touch, and feel her," he said, covering his heart again. "Then you know her story."

"And she told me," John Mallory said. "She whispered that she was from a fine sample of beans from a nearby mountain. About three days old. That next cup," she said, pointing and leaning over it so she could breathe deeply, "is older, about two weeks." She moved down the line to the next cup, leaning and breathing, and saying, "This one is younger than both of them, just a day. Beans absorb everything, such little sponges, and Costa Rican beans are very specific. There's the slightest hint of cocoa, and bananas, and blackberries. Definitely avocados too. Is that what you mean? And the fruits are so pungent. Are those plantains? Guava? We don't have them back home. You know, I smell the animals, too. Birds and monkeys. Is there a large cat around here? I smell one, and the beach. Or is that the rainforest? Lorenzo?" She picked up the last cup and whiffed again. "How far is the beach?"

He dropped his spoon and shrieked. He screamed words in Spanish, then waved his arms and shook his fist at the sky—she could only assume he was cussing. She wasn't sure if she should run for help, or if that would give him the idea to pounce on her like escaping prey. So she pinched her blouse at the tip of her throat and waited, holding her breath.

As suddenly as his outburst started, it stopped. He tilted his head and waved his hand, as if dismissing some unseen force. Then he bowed and cleared his throat. He approached the next table and another cup. Without another word, he leaned over, dipped his spoon, gave another atrocious slurp and then spat. He stepped back and bowed slightly for her to proceed. His face never betrayed what he tasted.

She smoothed her hair and approached the table. Even five feet away, her nose quivered. It throbbed with horrified expectancy. Air smoldered over the cup like houseflies over dung. It smelled of moldy cheese and bacteria.

"Maybe not this one," she said. "I think I'll just stick with the other beans."

"Continue," he said.

For several seconds, neither one moved.

"Fine, you win," she said. She leaned over the cup and whiffed. The offensive smell curdled her tongue. "It's awful. It's old and moldy." She backed away and gathered her shirt collar.

He thrust a new spoon into her hand. "Tell me what you know about acidity. Body. Aroma. Flavor of the bean. Suck! Mix the air with her. Spray her across the back of your tongue like a lover. Then you spit!"

She blushed, embarrassed by his callous use of the word lover.

He continued to stare at her, and she felt her nose twitch.

Under normal circumstances, she would have slunk away. She never would have been forced to obey such an absurd, crazed man. She wanted to pack a bag with crackers and cheese, some grapes, and go find the beach. Or explore the mountains, turn over the smooth rocks and study the bugs. She wanted to pick wildflowers. Maybe she could lunch underneath the coffee trees. She looked back at the massive green and the waving coffee branches. She could smell their strength. She tried to wrap the heady aroma of their native scents around her, like arms or shoulder pads. Wild animals waited for her, exotic birds, monkeys. Was that a jaguar she smelled?

She breathed in and out several times, then looked back at Lorenzo. He waited with narrowed eyes.

It had never occurred to her that her teacher would be a mad man who smelled like burned coffee. She swallowed the lump in her throat.

But being a smart young woman—and remembering the promise she had made to her family to make them proud, and, maybe even more importantly, the promise she had just made to herself—she held her breath, then leaned over, broke the crust with the new spoon, and brought it to her lips. Her hands were shaky, but she breathed and slurped. She let the acrid black bubble on her tongue.

Her eyes immediately rolled back in her head. She was certain that her mouth was dying! A bit of her soul had flown away! The sewage slipped down her throat. Her reaction was involuntary and violent. She projectile vomited, and coffee spattered across Lorenzo's face, on his lips and chest. Horrified, she opened her mouth to scream and the horrid coffee dribbled down her chin. She reeled and spun, unable to stop.

"I'm sorry. It's so repugnant! It's offensive!" she said, shouting, almost crying. She wiped her lips with the back of her hand. The coffee stung her tongue like a poison frog. She leaned over and tried spitting on the ground but started to gag. Dizzy and disorientated, she swung her arm and knocked over several cups. They shattered on the stone, and dark liquid pooled like blood. Appalled, she spun again and her foot caught the leg of the table and it collapsed. Porcelain slid into porcelain with a mighty clatter. Coffee dripped from the table. Broken pieces skidded across the porch. The air smelled like smoke and burning acid.

"Water. Please," she said, begging him with her eyes for something to wash it down.

"Ah!" Lorenzo Domingo screamed. With his thumbs pushed into the fleshy part of her shoulder, he held her. "She no talk to you! Mother Bean no talk to you!"

She ripped her arms away. "After that disgusting affront," she said, yelling at him, toe to toe, "*I'm* not talking to *her* either!" She bit down on the ends of her hair hoping for a reprieve of herbal essence, glaring at him and panting.

Neither one moved.

He kept his hands fisted. She kept her hair in her mouth. His dark eyes moved from her to the shattered cups on the floor. Her eyes followed his. Although his lips formed words, they caught in his throat. Exasperated, she squeezed shut her eyes and held her breath, as if her nose were being pulled away from her face.

Lorenzo began ranting in Spanish.

She couldn't understand him, and she didn't care. The winds blew hard through the cantina, as if trying to clear her air, willing her to breathe in sweeter perfumes. She opened one eye, and closed it. Then she opened both, afraid to take them off Lorenzo.

Finally, he combed his fingers through his hair and breathed deeply, as if gathering his thoughts. "The bean must speak," he said. "She must taste you. As you taste her."

She relaxed a bit. "Like quantum physics?" she asked, removing her mouthful of hair. Her interest was sincerely piqued by his theory. That would be a phenomenon she hadn't considered. She had always been fascinated by theories like quantum physics, how energy flowed, how simply being watched changed living organisms. She believed in all organisms being made of the same substances, and she suddenly had an affinity towards Mother Bean. Maybe he was on to something. "Do you agree with the butterfly flapping theory?"

His eye twitched. "It takes much time with Mother Bean, to know if she trusts you."

"That sounds good. Take time to get to know each other. Well, maybe not that last one," she said, pointing. She shuddered, then smiled weakly.

"*Lo siento*," he said, "I am sorry." He took out a handkerchief from his back pocket and wiped his mouth and then his hands. He shook his head. "You have no skill, she cannot trust you. You have a nose but…" He opened his mouth and gently caressed his long pink tongue with the hankie. "You do not taste. You cannot feel. You cannot be a Master of the Bean. Go home," he said, waving at her with his soiled cloth. "Go to America, to your dresses and dolls, *señorita*. You cannot be a Roastmaster. You have a nose, but you sniff, *como un perro*."

"I don't understand." Her lips tightened and she swallowed. "*Un perro?*"

He shook his head, then placed both hands on top of his head and stuck out his tongue. With his eyes bulging, he whimpered, and then he barked.

By the time she closed her mouth and could breathe, and her senses returned, he had disappeared down the stone steps.

He had called her a dog. Never had she been so violently insulted. He had told her to go home. It could not be possible. She simply could not fail before she even got started. She would not allow the possibility!

As she filled her lungs, her eyes turned a deep shade of blue, and then black. Two scents collided, steeping her outrage with audacity. Her olfactory perception widened. The evolution of her odors marched backwards. Watery emotions shifted over her membranes and transformed.

Instead of absorbing smells, John Mallory released them.

She had never felt the rage of her own humiliation. She breathed it in and blew it out, like fire on the wind. Instead of the fear of prey, of the rotting breath and foul smell of disease and defeat, she sizzled with provocation. She emitted the sweet aromatics of determination and grit.

She became an alchemist of rapture.

Some say it was then that her world turned upside down, with her first true taste of Costa Rica coffee splashed across the ten thousand taste buds on her tongue. With her heart ripped opened and crushed, out of its domain, the sun no longer could claim it was her only ruler. John Mallory sprouted new scents, like tendrils reaching to the sky. She released her pheromones to the wind. She invited the darkness along with the light. She commanded them to come to her.

John Mallory forced the seeds of her memories to break open new universes.

If anyone were watching, besides the mythical eyes of storytellers, they too would have smelled the sugary fruits that surrounded the seventh sister in mist. Pools formed around her feet so that her shoes remained rooted to the stones. The ends of her hair curled. Her nose turned pink and glistening. At the scream of her smell, birds cast into the sky like black opals.

The kaleidoscope mountains echoed her perfume. The waters of the singing river hushed. Even its silvery beard—the two hundred foot waterfall where, at the tip, Machu Domingo was whistling and bathing—quieted and drew in gulps of her aroma.

Machu cocked his head. He had never smelled the rumble of the mountains, or inhaled such abandonment mixed with fury. Wind howled and struck his face, urging him to hurry. Without thinking, or even putting on his clothes, he hopped out of the shallow pool and rushed down the path. Flowers bloomed as he climbed the steep side of the hill. Even the red and green cherries who had been sunning on the nearby coffee trees perked up and sprayed incense when he ran by.

He followed the whistles of birds in the sky. They led him closer and closer, until a flock of them gathered, in all shapes and sizes on the stone wall of the cantina. They began their song in perfect unison. It was a ballad of flute and harp.

Everyone knows when scents are used for mystical purposes, to invoke enchantment, they can make slaves of men.

Truth be known, it was the coffee cherries who cast the spell of magic. With each footfall, they sprinkled desire on the man with the large, round, moon face.

*Once upon a time, there was a man,
bathing as last rays of Sun
slanted
through coffee trees
while brown booby birds whistled
and glided through
the fog-bow arc,
chasing a wickerwork basket
descending from the sky
with seven
sisters.
In the shadows
he watched as they
touched down on lemon
grass
and the seven tall girls,
dressed in purest white,
linked hands and
began their
Dance*

8

El Novio

On the terrace, John Mallory wrestled and danced through the smoky perfume of her doubts. She could not be sent home. She could not return a failure. It would be better to not return at all. Her eyes had turned a metallic blue-green. They vibrated and shimmered. Her legs moved. She slowly spun around. Sweating, exhausted and confused, overwhelmed, she threw her hands in the air, as if releasing a thousand blue morpho butterflies. Stung into awakening, she cast her scents into the atmosphere while planting her heels on the stones, hoping her stems would take root.

In that window of time, many would have predicted she'd fall, rejected, stamped, and returned home within the week, like a package to her Kansas doorstep. Several of her sisters had already bet against her. And she did sway. She almost lost her footing.

Machu Domingo saw her. It was not a dance he had ever seen in his village, by anyone in his tribe. He picked up his pace. He raced towards her, drawn into and lifted by the nectar clouds. Monkeys howled in the forest. A flock of gray-neck wood-rails sang out, urging him with duets. Wet, naked, and dirty, with torn skin, he exploded through the bushes into her mist. By then, she was unsteady and slumping. Sense-drenched and dehydrated, he swooped, and she looked up.

His face was large and round. Without hesitating, it seemed the most natural thing to do, to sink into him, to let him give her balance, to allow him to shade her.

They were almost the same height, but he was stocky and wide. His black hair was curly and hung in soupy knots to his shoulders. He had hooded black eyes. They fluttered. His arms were long. He wrapped them around her and pulled her close. He held her upright and rocked, breathing her in. She breathed him in, too, while he calmed her with his deep voice. It hummed in his chest, like the murmur of a great seashell. "Hush," he said. "Don't worry. I'm here. I have you. We will stay for as long as you wish. We will hold each other."

It was if she had been ready, had always expected him. She hadn't seen him as he rushed through the forest, but she had smelled him on the wind. His fragrance was pure and unconditional, the essence of raw land. He was a potpourri of mountains and oceans, coffee trees and chocolate, of bird, of beast, of being born. He smelled otherworldly and magical. He used calming words, in perfect English, smooth, deep, and spoken slowly without a single rolling *r*. His unbroken English and deep voice soothed her. He pulled her closer, his hand lightly stroking her hair and down her back. She became intoxicated, spellbound by his smell.

Love has its doorways. No one knows when or where. It could be years or moments. Sometimes it sneaks in the back, through a window, while driving on the beach, or pressed into the wind on a bicycle. A convertible of aromas, it is sleek and quiet, taking tunnels through nasal passages. In hair, on skin, it mists soft and silky perfumes, concentrates, almond oil, sage, lavender and violet, rose waters. For some, it is the unexpected knock that provokes the most questions. How can it be? It is vanilla, so soon, undisguised, it must not be real. Many cannot believe in its magic. They are not wrong, but it is not meant for them, no more than fleeting fragrances are nonexistent simply because they go undetected. And it will not come to them, not this way. Because their questioning would force it to recoil from the light, slink back. It would be as unnatural to them as kissing a statue.

But the saddest ones of all are those who sense it, who taste it on their lips, who smell it, but then suffocate it in doubt. They chase it away with sticks, only to find themselves, later, shaking their heads, wondering why, why. Racked with fear, they live the rest of their days hidden behind heavy curtains or rocking on front porches, stepping out in the yard only to look back, with their hands held up, shielding their eyes from the sun. They hold their breath, bristling like cacti, doubting they will ever have another moonlit night with fragrant aromas or be awed by the blooms of foot-wide flowers.

Love is zesty, spicy, gentle and warm, an aroma difficult to recognize or accept. For those who can and do, it is undeniable. They know love can be instantaneous if they remain quiet, with their senses vulnerable and wide open.

"Should I fetch you some water?" he asked.

"No," she answered, whispering, her nose buried in his neck. "Thank you." She didn't want him to move. She wanted to keep breathing him in.

He had followed the hawk's flight and was winded. His heart thumped and drummed, and she listened to its rhythm. She felt comforted by his tight muscles. She could smell the salt water and coffee in his blood and on his skin.

"Are you injured?" he said, holding her tighter.

"I don't think so."

With his hands still locked behind her—he would never let her go—he leaned back and looked into her eyes. They were sparkling and the clearest blue. The fading sun reflected coffee-cherries in her dark curls and on her lips. He exhaled, then smiled, breathing in and out, his eyes warm and melting, as if he were seeing an angel walking on his land. His eyes roamed over her, looking for cuts, scratches and blood. Her clothes were not ripped. "Was it a man?"

"Yes," she said. "No, I mean. I'm not hurt."

"But it was a man?"

"It wasn't physical," she said, feeling her cheeks redden. "Nothing like that."

"Because if someone—" Considered a peaceful soul, at that moment Machu would have cocked his arms against any giant.

"He frightened me. That's all. It's nothing. He's just a mean man with a wicked tongue."

"He hurt you with his tongue?" Machu dared not mention the atrocities that he imagined in his mind.

"No," she said and shook her head. She chuckled. "It really has more to do with noses."

With her hands around his neck, she looked at the disaster across the room, the leaning table, the crushed glasses and puddles of coffee, a heap of devastation. He followed her eyes.

"Did you do that?"

She nodded.

He leaned back and laughed. She couldn't help but twitter, too. The musical song of her laughter made him laugh even more, and his muscles relaxed.

"It'll sound stupid if I tell you," she said. He nodded, furrowing his thick eyebrows. His eyes were so dark it was like looking deep into a wishing well. "It was about my nose. It's hard to explain. It's just…this means a lot to me. You see I'm here to become someone. Something more. An important man said I can't. He won't let me. He called me a dog."

Machu exhaled, shaking his head. He hugged her. "Then that man is an idiot. You can be whatever you choose. It is obvious to me. He is not important. He is blind. With the nose of a toucan."

He held her out by her shoulders and leaned back so she would look at him. He smiled. Then he cupped his nose and honked.

She inhaled and her eyes widened. Briefly she flew over the fields and to Kansas, to her family's dinner table, where she smelled pot roast and potatoes. It was as if she were an arm's length from her father as he covered his nose and honked, too. Yet she was in this man's arms, so she drank in his strong brew.

As she laughed, his grin spread. Each time he honked, she made the sweetest sound, such a magical flute, that he couldn't stop honking, just to hear her.

It was then, as they were unaware, holding each other, when Lorenzo Domingo climbed back up the stone stairs on the other side. He carried a tray with a bowl of beans and rice, and a glass of water. A broom was tucked under his arm. Tired and now huffing, he stopped at the top of the steps. He thought he heard the clucking of a white-throated crake and looked around. That was when he spotted two people locked in an embrace near the ledge. He turned around, not wanting to intrude or eavesdrop. He only made out a few words. Then he looked closer and rubbed his eyes. He almost choked. His heart almost stopped. He yelled at them, "What are you doing?"

John Mallory looked at Lorenzo. She signaled with her eyes. "There he is," she whispered. "That's him."

"That man?" Machu said, holding her hand and stepping in front of her. "Father, did you call this beautiful goddess a dog?"

Lorenzo could not breathe. The wind howled. He saw the taut skin around the neck and jaw of his son, his clenched fist, and how his lips quivered. His naked chest glistened; his body was bare. Lorenzo could see from his son's large eyes that he would never let this girl go.

He set down the tray and stumbled, then ran towards his son, shooing him with the broom. "Cover yourself!" he said.

"Are you crazy?" Machu said.

"You are *loco*. Naked. You have no clothes!"

Confused, John Mallory shook her head. Her eyes drifted down the man's chest, over his stomach and stopped. He leaned back, watching her. But she didn't gasp or recoil. Her eyes slowly traveled back up until they reached his. And then she laughed her magical flute, making the birds sing again. His lips curled and his eyes wrinkled into crescent moons. They both shook with laughter.

Lorenzo poked at his son's head with the broom and swatted his backside, trying to sweep him away. So Machu sprang for the wall. Standing on top of it, he spun around, almost losing his balance. His large moon face grinned at her. Then he covered his nose and honked. She held her stomach, leaning over with laughter. As Lorenzo beat at his feet with the broom, he danced and honked again, and then, like a mountain lion, he leapt for the bushes.

Even after he disappeared, she could still smell him. As he ran through the coffee trees, down the trail and next to the river, she could hear him singing about *amor*.

9

La Luna

There were many reasons why Lorenzo Domingo would not allow this love affair, and why he stomped across the mountains until he found his employer Bill McCracken, where he was working alongside the pickers on the far mountain. He counted the reasons on his fingers. First, there were the promises he had given to the American, a coffee man that his employer deeply respected, vows that his daughter would: *Come to no harm, Be protected from men, Go to church,* and *Never swim.* Then, of course, there was the inappropriateness of his apprentice being distracted by romance. He hoped she would soon be climbing back on the wings of the same vulture that had carried her to his land.

But, most of all, and he wasn't necessarily proud of this fact, he had promised his son's hand to Tulipán Navariz, or at least to her father, Gustavo Navariz, a rich man with connections in the coffee industry that far surpassed even those of Bill McCracken. These were complex ties. Over tequila many years ago, they had formulated their plan when Gustavo Navariz's only daughter was born. Like Lorenzo Domingo and his wife, Gustavo Navariz could have no more children, so there would be no sons. The matrimonial union, an arranged wedded bliss, would benefit all of them.

However, Tulipán was still too young, a girl of fifteen. So they waited. The years passed quickly and familial bridges would be built. Whenever they passed on the streets, Lorenzo

Domingo and Gustavo Navariz would greet each other with a slap on the back. They raised their drinks at dinner parties and winked across the table. They had grand plans for their only offspring, and no doe-eyed beauty with bewitching locks would crook her finger and destroy everything.

Lorenzo tripped. He wasn't listening to Mother Bean, stubborn as a mule across the hogback. Yet Mother Bean would not be ignored. The earth, the creatures, the rocks and water, called upon the coffee trees to stop Lorenzo Domingo—after all, the trees loved him the most, and could read his mind as much as he could theirs. They had been watching and listening. Their red hands tightened over their hearts, like a million red and golden silk flags. For even if they burst open in ripeness, gave themselves to him in one or a thousand, a dozen times over, they would never have enough for him. Even more, they could not allow his disruption of the Universal Plan.

So as he passed by, they pinched his ankles and nibbled his calves. Because, unlike Lorenzo Domingo, the beans held the power to see into the future and the past as if it were bundled into one. They knew that if Lorenzo Domingo lay down on the tracks of Father Time, that the sky would be altered, houses would fall, people would fall, and he would be destroyed.

They may all whither.

"*Señor* McCracken!" Lorenzo Domingo said, grabbing his throat to catch his breath. He would not use his native language, but his English always became choppier when distressed. "A strangler fig has crept into our forest! I must speak to you about the girl. The American girl. I know she is *importante* to you, her father is *importante*, but you see, she has no tongue. She has a good nose, a very good nose, *posiblemente* the finest nose I have known in my fifty-five years—does she smell the jaguar?—but you understand, *Señor*, without the help of the buds of the tongue, without the whisper of Mother Bean, she is no good. She cannot feel. She will suffocate us. She cannot apprentice as a Roastmaster. She wastes my time, *su tiempo,* and is *posiblemente* an *infinito* embarrassment to *El Cielo Verde*. From the beginning, you know *Señor* McCracken, I told you it would be *difícil,* difficult to teach anyone to be Master of the Bean. In so few moons. It takes time, *muchos años* to understand, to love our Mother Bean. And Mother Bean will not love her. A woman, she has disadvantages, too. Her softness makes her weak, less attractive to the bean. This girl you sent me, with her curves, her mountains of hair, her tiny nose, her whiffing nose. She is *un perro*. No! She is *una danta*. I know you understand, *Señor*, why I must recommend you send her away. Send her back. She is young, she is beautiful, there are many things, *muchas otras cosas* she can do. She has quickness in her eyes, a good nose, I cannot deny that, and her beauty. She can be in American picture shows. Yes! She should back among her people, people that understand her beauty, her bewitching ways, her power over the strongest souls. She smells of love. She lures men to rocks. Her hair ties up his heart like a strangler fig. The way she slips into the mind of a man. It is her perfume, but he is promised! No, *Señor*, it would not be fair to let her stay. Even the strongest man, even the moon in the sky could not resist that sorceress. I must ask you. No! Command you. You must send her away! Before it is too late. Before we are all maimed and crippled. Before the trees and mountains burst into flames. Before Mother Bean turns her face on her people in shame. She has a fine nose. Probably the finest nose I have known. Even Mother Bean told me that she admires her nose, that she loves her, too…"

He gasped.

That was when Lorenzo realized that Mother Bean had tried to speak to him. She had spoken to him about the woman as he crushed through their path. But his ears had been as tight as the jaw of a bushmaster snake, so the bean had altered his voice. Just now, he had not delivered an eloquent and convincing speech to his employer. Instead, had been singing like a honking ass! He had heard himself, the idiotic sing-song of children's lullabies, of mystical nonsense. And he could tell that *Señor* McCracken had been listening, too.

His employer propped against a tree and grinned at Lorenzo.

"Why, Lorenzo, old man," said Bill McCracken, "you're pink with joy. I've never heard you sing. And I never expected a serenade, not from you, my friend. Does my friend's daughter please you? I have to tell you, old man, I'm so glad. My father's friend was in such a state when he called. I couldn't turn him down. But I told him if any man could make a Roastmaster out of a woman, that man is you! A woman Roastmaster. Right, I almost forget, Sister Maria was called away to her sister's sickbed. Until she returns, you are responsible for our guest. Be good to her. What am I saying? I know you will be. You'll be good to her. I trust you with our future."

He looked at Lorenzo.

Lorenzo blinked. "*Sí, señor.*"

"It means much to our relationships with the United States' coffee industry, you know, and for our farmers."

"*Sí, señor. Gracias.*"

The workers had stopped picking. Their baskets were full of coffee cherries. He could see admiration shining in their eyes. They took off their hats and swiped sweat from their foreheads. They grinned and nodded at him.

Lorenzo Domingo smiled and then turned around.

He found a rock under a shade tree so that he could sit and rest, so he could gather his wits, so he could clear his nose, throat and ears.

John Mallory didn't know which way to turn. She considered following the man's scent through the bushes, but she didn't even know his name. She had never been so instantly attracted to anyone. Maybe it was because she was so far away from home, or because of the way he rushed to defend her, even against his own father. But just as suddenly as he had appeared, he had disappeared, like water easing down a crack. Gone, back into the brush, along with his heavenly smells, he disappeared back into the rainforest.

Alone, not knowing what to do, her heart should have raced, heavy with blood. Yet she felt nothing but silence, as if it weren't beating at all. Then it pounded too heavily as if a foot had stomped on it.

She turned away. At the top of the hill, she saw Lorenzo, a tidal wave as he swept towards the sun and over the mountains. Even if she had wanted to follow him, which she didn't, she never could have kept up, even though he hopped as he swatted at his ankles and raged towards the horizon.

Instead, she followed the winking lights in the distance. She smelled cooking. Down the stone path, along a sharp edge, she discovered that the smells belonged to the corrugated tin roof of a block house. She found comfort in its overflowing flower garden of friendly petal faces, full of sweet fragrances. She plopped on the porch, below the hanging potted plants. When she looked up, she saw the mist of sunlight stringing through the trees, and she thought of the man—unknown but knowable, unrecognized but familiar, as comfortable as her lavender-spritzed bedsheets. Her eyes closed as she untangled the tropical fruits by the scent of their skins—banana, mango, guava—and the nut trees, almond and cashew. A few patches of cilantro and rosemary grew along the wall. Everything in this world smelled like him.

Juanita Domingo, who had hobbled outside to beat a rug with a broom, discovered John Mallory there, with her eyes closed, on the porch whiffing the tiny bits of sunshine.

"*Señorita*?" Juanita Domingo said.

"Yes?" John Mallory answered. "Hello, ma'am."

Those were the only words Juanita needed to identify the American girl. She instantly took pity. Juanita's posture wilted like a thirsty flower. Her large face curled into smiles.

John Mallory should have been startled by the unbelievably round face, yellowy-white, doughy and dewy as a wet marshmallow. She looked like pictures of Grandmother Moon. But John Mallory was grateful and tired, and she didn't resist the motherly hands that gripped her elbow, pulled her up, and dragged her inside.

"My name is Juanita," the woman said, her fingers sticky.

John Mallory hiccupped, so the large-headed woman offered her cool water. She winced, and Juanita lifted her feet on a chair. As soon as she thought the girl had recovered from whatever ailed her, Juanita pranced around the room. It smelled sweet and earthy.

"This is the home of *Señor* McCracken. *El Casa Grande*. The Big House. I work for *Señor*."

"This is the Big House of Mr. McCracken?" she said. It smelled of prominence though only looked well-kept. To her relief, they had electricity, even running water. Juanita showed her the stove, identical to the Domingos' at home, she said.

"But I have a wooden stove at my house, too," said Juanita with her hand to her chest and added, "because we know things taste better with a wooden stove."

John Mallory smiled and nodded. She was particularly pleased with the indoor plumbing. Though the toilet was rudimentary with its small hole, it also had the tinny smell of a wishing well.

When Lorenzo finally made his way to the Big House, the modest four-room home of Bill McCracken where Mother Bean had told him he would find John Mallory, she sat with his wife in the kitchen. Juanita was fattening her up with blackberry pie and ice cream.

"Lorenzo!" she said, scolding him with a spoon as soon as his boots clamored across the threshold. "You never told me the American girl is here. And hungry! Look how skinny she is, and she loves my pie!"

Everyone loved Juanita's pies. Lorenzo tried to dip his index finger into the tin, but she slapped it away. Instead, he kissed her on the forehead.

A pear of a woman, Juanita Domingo had been cooking for *Señor* McCracken, the first *Señor* McCracken, the father of Bill, before she could peer over the kitchen counters, just like her mother had before her. Most of the time, Juanita could be found in the Big Kitchen in her apron, covered with flour, with hot liquid smells bubbling in pots and pans. Over the years, she had added to her culinary skills, along with her English, by learning from international travelers, whether it was the pastry chef from Bolivia, the baker from Italy, or the short-order cook from Louisiana. Guests raved about her chili rellenos, her spicy meats, and her crème brulee, that among other things, the French sous chef had taught her to make. He had stayed for months. Juanita loved hash-slingers, gourmet cooks, bakers and confectioners, but, mostly, she loved anyone who was hungry. She was certain beans and fried plantains would fix any ailment—or in extreme cases pork, chicken or potatoes with chilies folded into cornmeal and steamed in a banana leaf. She swooned over people who weren't afraid of thirds.

On the other hand, Lorenzo, like many men who claimed they weren't afraid of anyone, was mortally afraid of his wife. He loved her with all his heart, but he was smart enough to never cross her wide berth. "I see you met *mi esposa*," he said to John Mallory.

"Yes. *Doña* Juanita," she answered, adding the title of courtesy, making Juanita blush. John Mallory wiped the blackberry drippings from her chin with her napkin and waited for his reaction.

Juanita piled more ice cream on her plate and hugged her. "She is so hungry! Eat! Eat!"

From the corner of the kitchen, Lorenzo watched as his wife tucked John Mallory's hair behind her ear. Juanita winked at her husband with her wrinkled eye. Then she flung another spoonful onto the heaping plate. He trembled. He had only seen that hungry look in his wife's eyes when she fed their son Machu.

He sat on a stool. This girl was more trouble than over fermented cherries, more pungent than rotten fruit fallen from the tree. Not only did his employer have expectations, but somehow this girl had already hypnotized his son and his wife. Besides that, Mother Bean *had* spoken to him. She loved her, too!

However, he had devised an ingenious strategy. During his long walk to the Big House, Mother Bean had helped him formulate his plan for John Mallory's apprenticeship. He had his own motives; he didn't deny that. The sooner she became a Roastmaster, the sooner she could sail back to the United States. For these weeks or months—how long would she stay?—he must keep her hidden from his son. It would be no different than moving sugar cubes under cups. He would juggle one to one side and slide the other one over. No one could keep track of changing cups.

It would be a challenge to help her develop her tongue. The girl had no taste. Actually, it had been *Señor* McCracken who had inspired his idea, as he spoke with him when he picked alongside the migrant workers.

Lorenzo gripped his knees to push himself up. "*Mi amor,* she will live with us," he said.

"Sleep in our house?"

He nodded. His wife sighed, then wiped her eyes with the tip of her apron. Lorenzo had never allowed a visitor to stay in his house before, to be her guest. She fanned her face. Ever since Machu had moved into the cottage by the river, she had been so lonely. And, Juanita had always wanted a daughter—her husband knew that—even when her baby Machu had ripped open her womb with his over-sized head. It had taken the doctor thirty-three stitches to sew her up. Her body still looked like a ratty suitcase with a rusty zipper. Still, she never complained.

She grinned shyly at her husband while she stroked the long hair of the girl. She would take any daughter: black, white, purple, no matter. For many years, she had dreamt of a daughter with mountains of hair. In her dreams, Juanita would brush her daughter's hair with virgin oil, braid it with crystal beads, and tie it in silk ribbons with silver bells on the tips. But when God had decided to give her only one son—she made the sign of the cross and looked at the sky—a fine son, she never complained.

Now she knew why her thousands of lit candles had gone unanswered, why she hadn't been chosen again. As a gracious servant of God, she would be rewarded with a goddess to protect and nurture.

After a quick peck on her husband's cheek, Juanita tossed off her apron and pulled the girl to her feet. "I will show you our house," she said with sugar in her voice. Even with heavy work boots, she leapt to the door. "*Su casa.* It is your house, too, *hija.*"

John Mallory held the hand of Juanita Domingo, like the tip of a bird's tail, and they promenaded down the path from the Big House, across the mountain range, and under the rainbow. She pointed out the fruits and flowers along the way while John Mallory tied their sweet scents to her memory. They stopped at a berry patch at the doorstep of a scrubbed-up but run-down cottage, tucked inside the forest outside the village. It was just across the river from where Machu Domingo had slipped into his clothes and waited on the banks, shielding his eyes from the sun so he could watch the sky.

10

Casa Grande

Upon her arrival, no perfumed invitations arrived from the Big House. No hand-scratched notes. No bonanza gathering in her honor, no recounting colorful tales to Bill McCracken, and no grand entrances down a spiral staircase. There was no Big House. John Mallory packed away her expectations like the best china, along with her ball gown. Disappointment stunk of rotted eggs.

Still, she had vowed to be thankful. So she spent her first night in the Domingo's three-room, block home whiffing the foreign scents. Their home, too, had a corrugated tin roof and tile floor. But she could smell the dirt beneath the scrubbed surface. Juanita hurried around the house, proudly unveiling the refrigerator and her small appliances: a blender, an electric iron. There wouldn't be any television, but Juanita tugged John Mallory to the back of the house to show off the concession of a small washing machine. To John Mallory, it reeked of confinement, but Juanita tapped her chest with a closed fist and said, "Only a few of us have one."

"It looks efficient," she said. The proud look in Juanita's eyes made her smile and she found herself running her fingers along it lovingly.

In the kitchen, Juanita sharpened her knife. It glinted in what was left of the fading light. A chicken blissfully pecked its way around the yard. The Domingos ate meat about once a week, but that night Juanita would go to the chopping block in honor of her guest. She would prepare the daily staples of rice, beans, and fried plantains, too, while Lorenzo spoke with neighbors on the porch. She couldn't stop humming.

John Mallory snooped around.

Something foreign lingered in the air and pulled her to the largest room. An oil painting of the three members of the Domingo family hung on the farthest wall. It was the child, he was eight or nine, who captured her attention. With her nose close to the painting, she could smell the layer of dust on top of the oil. She studied each of them closely, trying not to let Lorenzo see her, though he kept peeking in through the windows. In the painting, Lorenzo looked like a political refugee, a man in exile, with his face determined, as if he might be ambushed any moment. Undoubtedly, he would be ready, his fingers curled around his wife's shoulder, the other arm across the back of the boy. Juanita sat in a chair in front of the two males, with her stocky hands folded in her lap. Her giant head titled at an angle, with her chin up, as if it were a globe stretching to show off the neck of Central America. She had a look on her face like she would prefer to be kneading bread, as if she feared her spirit were being suctioned from her body. She was resisting. The child stood in back, obviously standing on a box. He rose several inches above Lorenzo. His face was a smaller version of his mother's, not as large but spongy. His soft skin was not pocked like Lorenzo's, and he had the warmest eyes. Even then, John Mallory could smell the coffee in the family's blood.

She turned to look out the window, into the moonlit sky. Juanita resembled the moon, and the boy had that piece of her in him, too. She looked back at the portrait. His skin was buttery yellow. His eyes creased in smiles. Just like the moon, ever patient, he was content to watch the world unfold from the stairs of heaven. Without a whisper from his lips, she could smell a thousand sugary words flutter through the air, like silky caresses in the breeze. He would sing of love, the smell of rain and rainbows, and she could fall into the blackness of his eyes and never fear landing. He would teach her the nectars of the earth, of blackberries and stars. It had been an odd feeling, meeting him like that, him holding her. It was as if he, this place, these people, were her destiny. She wondered if she had fallen in love. Could she love a man she barely knew? If it was love, it was more than just in the cocoon, because she felt her heart flowering open. She felt like she was finally breathing freely.

"*Señora*, is this your son?" She didn't look in his mother's eyes. Maybe her young love should be hidden, like a chocolate in a cupboard.

"*Mi hijo?*" said Juanita, coming from the kitchen, wiping her hands on her blood-soaked apron. She smiled. "Yes. Our son Machu. He is a lovely man."

"Machu, yes," she said, "I met him. He is lovely. Very lovely. Magnificent."

"*Sí, sí.*" Juanita beamed at the picture. "You met Machu?"

"Yes, today. He was so warm, strong. He came out of nowhere when I needed him, almost surreal. I'm probably talking too much, but I've never..." She stopped. She smelled the wings of a bird as it flew towards the glass but changed course and veered into the sky.

"He is *magnífico*," Juanita said.

"Yes, *magnífico*. I suppose it's in his nature to be so kind. He must get that from his mother." Juanita pretended to blush and fanned her face. "Maybe it's being in a foreign land, the rainforest, the smell of coffee all around. And then I met you," she said and smiled at Juanita. "I've never felt so safe." She felt the warmth of the moon watching over her.

"Yes, you would like my son," Juanita said, smiling.

"I do like him. I like him very much. He's magical."

John Mallory blushed, but Juanita Domingo beamed.

"Where does he live?" she asked, hesitantly. "Near here?" She felt her neck redden. "Does he have a wife or children?"

"Children?" Juanita looked confused, then she laughed. "No, no. He is not married." She tilted her head, then she pulled John Mallory closer to the painting. Wrapping an arm around her, she patted her wide hips. "My son is very nice. He is a kind man. A very good man. And he is smart, too. He went to university." They both stared at the picture, Juanita in her blood-stained apron, John Mallory smelling the air. "My son wants a wife and children," she said. "Many, many children. Do you like children?"

"Yes, I do. I love children," John Mallory said, surprised but meaning it. She had never given much thought to having children of her own. "I've always loved children."

"Machu, too," she said, rubbing her back, touching her hair.

"He is *magnífico*."

John Mallory inhaled, trying to memorize every detail of his round, luminous face as if kissing him goodnight for the first time. Silently, she let his name spray across the back of her tongue and down her throat, just like the finest coffee.

11

Lasting Treasures

The sun drops in the sky and the evening's chill pushes through the window. Capri shivers. By the time they come close to the address of Research Psychiatric, she feels numb, smelling nothing but the coffee. They drive around the block a dozen times but can't find the building. She tells Mac to pull into the hospital parking lot.

"What're we looking for?" he asks.

"Who knows?"

Mac leans over and holds her hand, looking at the ring he gave her. She knows it makes him feel proud even though it's nothing more than tin with a cubic zirconium. He moves towards her. Conscious of the fact that she left her bra on her mother's desk, she lays his hand on her belly, sucking in her stomach just a bit. His palm feels warm.

"Someday, we'll have little Mac in there."

She freezes but tries to force a smile. Seventeen is far too young to be a mama.

Girls swoon for Mac. He's that kind of guy, sweet, ripped, a Romeo with penetrating brown eyes that make girls want to melt into his arms. He has a smile that makes Capri want to do things she wouldn't normally do. He can always make her laugh. But she doubts she'll be playing house anytime soon. The smells of Mac attract and repel her at the same time, piney and a little dirty. He's the sweat that attracts queen bees, but Capri can't see herself buzzing around making a nest. Even though Mac is a tapestry of earthly smells, she is looking at the sky.

Her mind drifts back to a night when she sat on the flagstone in the backyard, with her mom and Granddaddy, watching Aunt Lolly dig in the dirt. Granddaddy drank a cup of a dark exotic blend, leaving silky chocolate and hazelnut in the air. Capri played with the litter of six-toed kittens, a half-dozen furry shades of blue and gray. Her mom was barefoot, letting her toenails dry from the coat of fresh peach polish she had given them. She was teaching herself to read Tarot cards, spreading them out and flipping through a book.

"You're the empress," she had told Capri. "Daughter of heaven and earth. See. Her crown has twelve stars. Look at the symbol on her shield."

Capri leaned over. It was the same one she'd seen in biology class to represent the female gender.

"It's the symbol of Venus. Lucky you," her mother said, "goddess of love. The second-closet planet to the sun. It says she's Earth's sister planet, the daybreak star, the last stage of life and wisdom."

Granddaddy chimed in. "Brightest star in the sky, except the moon," and then he looked Capri in the eye, saying, "but she never ventures far from the sun."

Capri looks at Mac and back at the sky.

She doesn't want moonlight to shine on her face tonight. Her coffee smells cold now, like the chill of a neglected brew. She feels betrayed, as if someone has blown wind into her throat and belly and blasted her to pieces. Nothing makes sense any more. Seems Granddaddy and her mom and aunts have always been telling tales around tables, and she's never even noticed. Her entire life has been built on a couple of well-told stories.

She smells birds she doesn't recognize, and she thinks she can smell the monkey from the zoo. Her stomach hurts, as if she had a belly full of ice cream. She just wants comfort and moves Mac's arm around her shoulders.

"Going commando," he says, running his fingers down her braless back, and then, "Yee-haw."

She moves his hand to his own lap.

"So what happened back there? You didn't call. Did I mess things up? I was worried. I knew something was going on. Come on, what's wrong, tell me, don't be moody, baby, tell me." When she doesn't respond, he says, "You really want to go to Mexico again? You said I should take you back. I'm game, baby. You and me together."

"I don't want to talk about it," she says. "It's driving me crazy thinking about it." It seems she can't stop using the word crazy, and that's driving her crazy, too. But smelling zoo animals as if they were lying in the car doesn't help her feel any better about her mental disposition, either. Maybe she is going crazy.

That's all she keeps thinking about—crazy, crazy, crazy. And the more she thinks about it, the more she smells weird aromas in the air, and the more she smells, the more afraid she gets. And the more afraid she gets, the madder she gets.

We are the blue stars, the Pleiades, her mother had said, as if that were a normal thing to say out loud. Were they all crazy? What gave them the right to keep secrets from her? When they impact *her* life. To hide her real mother. Is that what she said? Her granddaddy. No wonder they never had a house of their own, always living with Granddaddy. They made a deal. Once her mother died, Trinka would raise Capri as if she were her own, as if she were her daughter, and he would help, but he couldn't help, not all the time, because he's crazy.

They're all crazy. There she goes with that word again.

She looks up at the moonlit sky.

Granddaddy told her each of them is born for a reason. He said they have work to do on Earth, something specific. "There's more to life than school, jobs, or having boyfriends," he had told her. "Family, love, that's what's important. The soul has its own destiny, like a star in the sky. We all live in the light of the sun, even the moon."

Her mother said Granddaddy sounded more and more like John Mallory every year. They'd all pass around books about mythology, gods and goddesses, books that had soul in the title, weird stuff no one else's family reads. Another embarrassing oddity somewhat explained.

Capri just wants to see him, talk to her granddaddy. *Well, Granddaddy, the moon is full in the sky tonight. But there aren't any stars. No northern star to direct me. No blue stars in sight. Not six, not seven. There is only me, sitting in a car, below the emptiness of a deep dark sky, looking up at nothing.*

The vapors of zoo animals and sweet-smelling fruits crowd into the Mustang. She opens the door so she can get some fresher air. Lilac mixes with the smell of the paved parking lot, cigarettes and fried chicken. People go inside the hospital, some with sad and worried looks on their faces. Nurses and doctors cluster outside the door, smoking cigarettes in their green and white cotton. They are in front of blooming magnolia trees. The summer drought has tricked them into blooming early, along with crab apple trees and pear trees, like the ones her Aunt Lolly tends. Granddaddy and her mom make fun of Lolly, always fussing over plants and animals, but they all love to sit in the garden, smell the sweet scents and chew cinnamon basil straight from the vine.

She wonders if she should call her cousins about Granddaddy. Jenna and Charlie? They'd want to know, but they're busy with college. Not Maggie, she can't handle stress, and if she tells Jenna, Jenna will tell Maggie. Maggie is better off not knowing, just sticking to her glass beads, how she spins them on a mandrel, mixing red and gold from cylinders of glass, like making stars for the sky.

The sky is nothing but lemony moon.

It's all so crazy, just crazy.

"I'll be back," she tells Mac. "Wait here."

She follows the blue smoke and tobacco smells and heads over to one of the nurses. She is slumping on a stone wall, blowing smoke rings and poking her finger through them.

"You know where Research is?" Capri asks.

She stares at Capri with tired eyes. The nurse is wearing purple Crocs with daisy buttons. She points over her shoulder with her thumb. "Research Medical, just like it says."

"The psychiatric unit," Capri says. "In there?"

Then the nurse blows out a puff of smoke and steps on the cigarette with her Croc. She picks it up, holding the crushed cigarette in her hand. The smell of tobacco is almost overpowering. The nurse points over Capri's shoulder, across the parking lot.

"Right there," she says.

Mac is staring through the windshield looking for Capri. She slides back in the car and tells him where to drive, and they cut through the parking lot, almost clipping a blue Camaro. It honks and Mac lays on his horn. They come to a low brick building, separated from the hospital by an open field. The sign is small but it's there.

"Research Psychiatric Center?" Mac says with that you've-got-to-be-kidding-me voice. He raises his eyebrows.

"Yes," she says and points to a Visitors' parking spot. "My granddaddy's in there." Now she can smell the germicides, needles and bleach. He's in there, maybe in a padded cell, maybe wearing a straitjacket, maybe crying out for help, maybe even calling her name.

"Your grandfather's in there?" Mac says.

"He's in there."

"Wow. That's some heavy shit."

"It's crazy," Capri says and gets out with her and her granddaddy's cups of coffee.

The Camaro that Mac had honked at pulls up in front of them, blocking them. Capri's heart sinks. That's all she needs, a rumble in the parking lot. Then Capri sees her friend Tracy behind the wheel, waving and laughing.

Capri and Mac walk over.

"Hey, guys! What're you doing up here?" She's toothy, a big blonde who always looks like she just came from a Neiman Marcus makeover. Her backseat is loaded down with shopping bags with little white rope handles. Tiffany is in the passenger seat, a snotty soccer player that's always flirting with Mac. She has her bare feet up on the dash board. Her toenails are painted blue.

"Didn't you see me? I honked," Tracy says.

Mac laughs. "Didn't know it was you. Sorry, gorgeous."

Capri can't believe they didn't notice Tracy, but she's never seen the car before. Mac circles it, his hands in his pockets, catcalling. He buffs her door with his elbow and leans in.

"Whose ride?"

"Mine," Tracy says, all grins. "My dad just bought it in St. Louis."

"Is that right," Mac says. "Saint Louie." He smiles.

Tiffany leans over. "Why don't you jump in, Big Mac. We'll take you for a ride," she says, winking at him.

She's had her eye on Mac since before he and Capri started dating, since before the earth began turning on its axis.

He looks at Capri and smiles, then shakes his head. "Nah, we're just driving around. We're going to the zoo."

"Tiffany and I went shopping at the Plaza. We just stopped by her grandmother's. Are you guys coming to Tommy's? He's having that costume party. You said you might come, Mac." Capri looks at him, and he shrugs. He never mentioned any party. "Come on. Go! Everyone's going and wearing costumes. We bought cowgirl boots and cap guns. Tiffany's going to do her floozy dance. I meant to call you, Capri. I know you've been locked up, but you guys should come."

"Maybe," Capri says, knowing she's in no mood to go to any party, particularly one where Tiffany will get drunk and floozy all over her boyfriend.

"Look what I got, Capri," Tracy says. She leans over the back seat and grabs a bag. She yanks out a pair of white boots and gives a holler. "Wait. There's more."

She pulls out a white suede jacket with fringe. A piece of string falls in her lap. Mac picks it up and stares at the thong underwear.

"Who's wearing the dental floss?" he says, laughing.

"Oops," Tracy says, blushing. "I know, but Tiffany talked me into it."

Mac doesn't say anything, but Capri smells exotic perfumes in the air. She smells wild animals, as if the zoo were next door. Suddenly, Capri feels dizzy. It's as if everything is whispering, showering, spritzing, sprinkling her with dizzying scents. Her senses open up. She's overcome with sensual smells, and it makes her feel uneasy.

She snatches the thong from Mac and hands it back to Tracy.

"Hey, don't blame me," he says, shrugging.

Capri shakes her head.

"I got a pair, too, Big Mac," Tiffany says. "Mine are baby blue." She winks at him.

"To match your blue mascara?" Capri says. "You do make a good floozy."

They give each other snotty looks. Tiffany's the kind of girl who thinks every guy is fair game. She's blind to guys' reactions, thinking it's just a matter of her batting her eyelashes and spritzing her pheromones in the air.

Tracy says, "So what're you guys doing here?"

"Like I said," Mac says, "going to the zoo."

"The zoo's closed," Tiffany says, then leans forward and squints to read the sign. "Did you know you're parked at the nut house?" She looks at Capri and says, "Checking in?"

"We thought you might appreciate a visitor," Capri says.

They give each other fake laughs.

Tiffany hops out of the car. "Hand me the camera," she says and snaps her fingers at Tracy, then points to something on the floor. Tracy sighs, then leans over and picks up a disposable camera. She looks at Capri, kind of embarrassed. Tracy starts taking pictures. She takes one of the sign. She points it at Mac. She gets a close-up of Capri, one Capri is sure is nothing more than her nose from an odd angle. "These are going to be priceless. Hey, you guys, pose. In front of the building. Act like you're crazy and going in. Come on." She nods to Tracy.

"Come on, Tiffany, let's go," Tracy says.

Tiffany snaps her finger at Tracy, and she groans, then gets out of the car. Capri says no but Tracy leads her by the elbow closer to the front door. She's still holding her granddaddy's cup of coffee. Mac shakes his head then follows her.

"Okay, now give me a look like you're trapped, like you're behind bars, screaming," Tiffany says.

Tracy contorts her lips and puts her hands in the air as if she's a mime pressed up against a window. Then she screams, raising her arms. Mac stands with his hands in his pocket, looking at Capri. She stands there, unmoving while the camera flashes and goes dark, flashes, dark, flashes, dark.

"Have some fun, Mac," Tiffany says and gives him pouty lips.

"Let's go, baby," he says to Capri.

"Okay, now make goofy faces," Tiffany says. "Roll your eyes. Drool."

Tracy lets her tongue hang to the side. She makes gurgling sounds. Then she laughs and pretends to be a monkey, howling and jumping up and down with her arms curled.

Capri doesn't move a muscle.

"Come on, Capri," Tiffany says, "make crazy," she says to her. Tiffany is calculated. The camera is on Capri, zeroed in. Tiffany's painted smile twists and stretches to a smirk. Her face is smooth and creamy, with a perfect little nose and sculpted cheek bones, and big eyes, like an expensive doll. Capri wants to bust her face with her fist. "You can do it, Capri, I know you can. Make crazy," she says.

Mac strides towards Tiffany, trying to shoo her away.

"Why don't you guys give me that address," he says, opening the door to his Mustang. "Maybe we'll head over there, too." He looks back at Capri.

Tiffany takes another picture, this one of Capri by herself.

"Are you going to give me the address, Tiffany?" he says.

"Oh, I'll give it to you, Big Mac," Tiffany says, strutting towards him. "We're just having some fun." Her lips are fat and pouty. "Do you promise me you'll come to the party?" She pretends to pout again and puts her hands on her hips.

"Why don't you, Capri?" Tracy says. "Come to Tommy's. Everyone's going."

Tiffany is writing down the address in a pink Sharpie on the back of a receipt.

"We're wearing braids," Tiffany says. "Oops, sorry, I forgot. You don't have any hair," she says, looking at Capri's pixy.

"Shut up, Tiffany," Mac says.

Tracy walks over to Capri and twists her finger in her hair. "I think it's cute. We can put glitter in it. You'd be a perfect goddess."

"I'm not much in the goddess mood," Capri says, "but thanks."

"Be Bonnie and Clyde then," Tracy says. "You can have our guns." Tiffany frowns, but Tracy holds hers up. "It'd be so cute."

Capri shakes her head.

"Oh, come on. You've been in such a bad mood ever since you gave yourself that haircut." Tracy digs through her bags and pulls out a red silky shirt with sequins and holds it in front of Capri. "You're a natural. You look like a diamond or a star. Lucy in the sky with diamonds."

Capri can smell the coffee, the spring night, and it makes her think of Granddaddy. Her mind drifts back to the time he took her panning for precious stones at Silver Dollar City when she was ten. He bought two of the big buckets. Perched on stools in front of a wooden water alley, they dumped their loot into wire screens and sorted sand and rocks through clear water in search of diamonds. They tossed worthless stones against the backboard that fell into the pile beneath their feet. When they found a keeper, they lined it up in front of them.

There were dozens of greens, mostly aventurine and a tiny emerald, clear quartz and tourmaline, a couple of garnets they almost tossed away. Granddaddy said they looked like petrified dinosaur poop until the guy working there told them they were valuable. Capri found a topaz even though she didn't know what it was. She liked that it was smooth and wheat-yellow. Everything smelled like rich caramel soil. Gemstones, treasures that would last forever, like the sign had said.

Granddaddy didn't think she saw him, but every time he found a big one, a gorgeous ruby in the rough or a purple amethyst, he tossed it in Capri's bucket. She'd roll it out and act surprised. He always turned down her offer to share. So she'd keep it. At one point, a big black rock caught her eye and she put it in her to-keep pile, admiring it every few minutes, showing it off to Granddaddy.

"Look how big it is," she had said.

The guy who patrolled the mine came up behind them and pointed to it. "That one's no good," he said. He held Capri's big black rock up to the light and looked at it with one eye closed. Then he handed it back to her. "No good."

"You sure?" her granddaddy said.

Capri inspected it closely, because she'd already grown partial to it, even named it Beauty in her mind.

"Been doing this for thirty years," he said, but Granddaddy wouldn't believe him.

"It's got to be something," Granddaddy said.

"Yeah, it's something," he said and took it back, glaring at Granddaddy. "It's a leaverite," he said.

Capri knew it; she knew it. Beauty was a diamond.

"A leaverite," she said back to the man.

"Leave her right *there*," he said, flinging the black rock hard against the backboard.

Capri must have had a horrified look on her face because before she could say a word, Granddaddy scrambled under the water alley and came back up with her big black rock in his hand. Still on his knees, he held it out to her.

"Why, you don't say?" Granddaddy said, blowing it off. "A leaverite. Haven't seen one of those in years. Valuable, very valuable," he said to Capri. "Thank your lucky stars, honey. A leaverite."

The guy sighed and walked away with his hands in his pockets.

"That's their racket," Granddaddy whispered, keeping one eye focused on the space behind Capri's back. "Tell everyone the biggies are worthless. Tossing them away and collecting them later for themselves. But you didn't let him fool you." He winked. "You knew better."

Later, when they sorted through their piles with a guy with a magnifying glass, Granddaddy told her to save the black rock and keep it on her night stand. It was too special. The guy shrugged. Her granddaddy paid to have her topaz cut and made into a necklace, one Capri still wears sometimes. The gem cutter had said when some topaz are heated they turn reddish-pink. Hers would turn almost white, like the moon.

Capri touches her throat, wishing she had it on right now. She wonders what ever happened to her leaverite.

Mac and Tiffany talk in low voices. He's trying to guide her back into the car, but she's trying to tickle him.

"Lighten up," Tiffany says. "You have such a worried look on your face. Like you're going in. Pictures of you guys outside the loony bin. Classic." She swats at him. "Oh, my God, look. Capri's scowling at me like she's crazy. What's up with the coffees?" she calls to her.

He turns to look at Capri and frowns. He waves at Tracy, then shoves his hands in his pockets before coming back to Capri.

"You coming?" Tracy says. "Come on! It'll be fun."

Mac looks at Capri and then Tracy. "Probably not. We might drive around."

"Your life's a real page turner," Tiffany says to Mac but looks at Capri.

"Epic novel," Capri says. "A fairy tale."

"Fine," Tracy says and starts up the car. "Suit yourself, party poopers. Let's get out of here. This place is creepy," she says, looking at the building. "Isn't it?"

Capri doesn't say anything to let her think otherwise.

"Loaded with freaks in straitjackets." Tiffany says. As they pull away, Capri thinks she hears Tiffany say, "Say hello to Granddaddy."

As soon as they get out of sight, Capri turns to Mac. "You told her!"

"I did not."

"Then how'd she know?"

"I don't know. She doesn't—she doesn't," he stutters.

"You'd better not be lying," Capri says. "I don't like liars. I don't even care. You can tell her, you know. Tell anyone you'd like, I have nothing to hide. I'm not embarrassed."

"I didn't say you should be."

"You can go to the party. Why don't you go? I'll be fine. Go. I'll take a cab. I'm going in, and if you don't want to go, then that's fine. I can go by myself."

"Oh, come on, baby. I'm not leaving you here. Come on. Don't. Let's not fight." Then he gives her his puppy-dog eyes. "Let's get out of here. Something smells good. Are you wearing baby powder?" He leans over and buries his nose in her neck. She wants to stay mad at him, but instead she starts crying.

"What, baby," he says. "Don't cry. You know I hate it when you cry. Baby, please."

But Capri can't help herself. She wants what every teenage girl she knows wants. Nothing but happiness, shopping and lunches, parties and cameras, laughing. She wants creamy skin that never has zits. She wants to be a straight-A student without even trying, to be a superstar at something. She wants a car that is inappropriately-expensive and a dad who buys her one. She wants a mom who whips up cookies from scratch. She wants long blonde hair and blue toenails and lingerie bags with twisted white ropes. She wants boys to want her. She wants the moon to be more than the color of necklaces.

She wouldn't mind being a blue star.

But more than anything, she wants her granddaddy.

"Let's go," she says and jiggles her granddaddy's cup of coffee as if it might have evaporated.

"Seriously? We're going in?" Mac glances at his feet.

"What? Why are you looking down? Then go, leave. But I'm going in."

She doesn't wait for him because she knows better now, just like she did then, and she's certain. While she walks away, she says to the sky and earth, to the moon and stars, to anyone and anything within ear shot. It comes roaring out of her like floodwaters bursting through a minefield. "My granddaddy is no leaverite. My granddaddy is no leaverite!"

Mac doesn't say a word, but she's got to give him credit because she smells him. His musky footsteps are right behind her.

12

Café Con Leche

As a child, John Mallory wanted to be a weather girl. Then she could masquerade. She desperately wanted to wave her arms in front of the blue screen without seeing anything at all. Flutter her eyelashes at the thought of sunshine, frown with disappointment at rain, and hold rigid with a sense of urgency at ice, floods and tornadoes. She had the bone structure of a weather girl, the personal presence on stage, and she was certainly articulate. Surely she could prepare the public for any natural disaster that would befall the Midwest.

Yet, as the baby and seventh daughter, she had been milk-nursed like a boneless orchid. She lived in a sandy pot. Since a baby, her father had slathered her in white lotions so she wouldn't burn. Going to parties was discouraged like dry rot. He preferred she only wander outside with friends when she became bone dry with loneliness. Her father fertilized her education by encouraging her to listen and watch. Trips to the coffee plant, with its air thick with burned grinds, and she would watch the cans waddle down the production line like distant relatives. She'd watch films and slide shows in shafts with dusty light, about coffee cultures she had no plans to visit. She'd study commercials starring Mrs. Olson or Juan Valdez. She didn't dare *do* anything. However, her father ignored the fact that even a growing orchid would have to be repotted.

In Costa Rica, the Domingo household raced the sun and awoke before it stretched its weary arms. Juanita shook John Mallory out of her dreams in the wee hours.

"Come," she said with the voice of a twittering robin.

In her foggy condition, John Mallory raced to the door, assuming there must be a fire and her nose had betrayed her. "What is it? Let me grab my suitcase," she said, ready to race for her bags. Juanita petted her.

"*Desayunar*," she said.

"Breakfast? In the middle of the night?"

Juanita giggled.

No emergency, it was just the beginning of daily chores. They prepared breakfast: *agua dulce* (hot water mixed with milk and unrefined brown sugar), *gallo pinto* (rice and beans) and bread. Then Juanita left for the Big House to prepare the same meal for *Señor* McCracken.

John Mallory dressed in her coffee royalty best, fresh for an invigorating and titillating day at a plantation—all white—a sleeveless silk blouse, zippered culottes, and beaded sandals. Juanita insisted on braiding her hair and swirling it around the top of her head, which made her feel a bit like Swiss Miss. But John Mallory bit her tongue. For a short time, she would no longer suds up in a long, hot shower. Instead, it would be short baths, icing down with a bucket, like a cult member trying to beat back her sensual desires as if they were demons. Juanita treated her so kindly that it didn't seem appropriate to repay her motherly overtures with a constant, frantic search for any open door.

When John Mallory woke that morning, the name of Machu Domingo still lingered on her breath like an erotic dream. She thought she smelled his musky rhythm floating in the air, imbedded in the old sheets. Was it only *desire* she felt for Machu? Or love? She hardly knew him. Still, something had altered inside her, and it was more than smelling lush new lands. She had never felt this way before. Frankly, she surprised herself. Even in her most egoless days, she had never expected to fall for a man who was—she hated to say it—so foreign. Yet she found him intoxicatingly exotic.

It was almost as if Lorenzo could read her thoughts that morning.

"How can you appreciate our beauty?" said Lorenzo as he picked up his pace. "Do you listen?"

"I am listening," she said, but in her mind she had already left for a few days at the beach with Machu. Fresh fish and citrus in the air, sand between their toes, drinking coconut beverages with tiny umbrellas. "How far is it to the beach? I'd love to see it."

Lorenzo tried not to look at the strange girl. She had been whiffing and sniffing since they left, so he cocked his ear to listen for guidance from Mother Bean, to see if she, too, had noticed the oddness of this girl. At any moment, he expected to hear their bean choir of mocking laughter. But Mother Bean only whispered in delight at the girl.

"The coffee bean is patient. She is never anxious," said Lorenzo.

She thought he had a one-track mind. Lorenzo acted as if coffee lived and breathed. She knew all the semantics: what elevation it grew best in, how the beans were picked, processed, roasted and brewed. She could discern the regions of the bean with just one whiff. Graduated with honors from her father's academic rigors, she had studied the business aspects of buying, supply and demand, of inventory control, of balancing the books. She knew about marketing, of package design, consumer messaging, and telling the story. After all, she had watched films. She had been studying shelf space and brand positioning since she could walk.

"How old are these coffee trees?"

"Many of them over a hundred years."

"And the mountains?"

"*Siempre*," he said, then cleared his throat. "Always."

The mountains in Costa Rica were different from the Rocky Mountains of Colorado, where she'd been with her father one winter. She sighed. Mountains awed her. She felt more comfortable nestled underneath them. A flatlander (even though Kansas City was a land of hills), she knew she belonged in the mountains. Sharp steeples of rock, the Rocky Mountains were for gawking, for conquering, skiing or staring at through a picture window in a chalet while her father sipped coffee with brandy. She drank hot chocolate, with her socked feet propped in front of a crackling fire. To the timberline, the Rockies were blanketed in powdered snow, with ruddy spruce pines and poplars, all height and power. The Cordillera de Talamanca—these glorious mountains!—were quiet and gentle. Ripples of green, smaller yet peaceful, with majestic shade trees and oaks, they were ancient giants watching over her in the valley.

As she hurried to keep up with Lorenzo, she took in deep gulps of air. She smelled sweet mineral syrups—fresh sprigs of growth, rich soil, the promise of summer rains. The spring rains, of course, smelled much sweeter than summer rains with thirsty flowers, banana and plantains on the vine, a patch of wild onions somewhere nearby, avocados. Now that she knew them, she smelled the toucan, fur and animals, monkeys.

"Don't you smell a cat?" She had been to the zoo; she recognized the wet and wild, the gamy scent of a hunter. "Not small sandbox nonsense, a real cat. A cougar? A jaguar?"

Lorenzo shuddered.

Some people would have misinterpreted his shuddering for fear, but that would have been inaccurate. Yes, he wanted more land. He craved more land—for the jaguar. The thought kept him awake at night, forced him to work too hard. He walked the land until his toes cramped in his boots. Lorenzo owned less than 3.5 *hectares* (about 8.5 acres), which was about average for the average man in Costa Rica. All of his life, he and his family had worked their hectares, which used to be triple that amount. But his father, Flavio Domingo, always a gambler, had lost most of the farm in the 1930s, during the

Great Depression. He borrowed too much, and when the price of the bean fell, he relinquished most of his farm to Esteban Navariz, the father of Gustavo Navariz. Lady Luck continued to shun his father. For years, he labored on his farm, and the farm of Esteban Navariz in exchange for credit, but like a limping dog chasing a mechanical rabbit at the race track, he could never catch up. When the market rebounded and climbed to new heights, Flavio Domingo's land had become a distant, unreachable dream. No longer able to buy back his farm at the new price, without any hope, he had died, napping by the river. Barely a man himself, Lorenzo had found his father, had dragged him underneath the coffee trees, and positioned his body so that it looked like he had died working, working the land, harvesting the coffee, just like he had always done. Sometimes, Lorenzo still thought he saw his father down near the river. The ghost of Flavio Domingo always had his hand cupped over his eyes, overlooking the crop, with a longing look still on his face.

The Navariz family owned the majority of the land since then, wealthy overnight. Like a Monopoly game, they had invested in trucks, bought more tracts of land, set up *haciendas* and banked in cattle. They had sewn up most of the valley. However, Lorenzo didn't want the land back because of revenge—he held no resentment for the Navariz family, who were better businessmen. He never felt the need to avenge his father's death, or his family's loss. His father had been a hopeless dreamer. Lorenzo wanted the land back to reestablish his family name, leave something for his son, and his son's sons. He couldn't deny the loss he felt, the stolen childhood, a time when he romped through the unencumbered woods, his father telling him stories of the wild animals, smelling the beasts that used to roam the land. "One day it will all be yours," he had told him.

Lorenzo yearned for a return of natural wildlife, flora and fauna that had disappeared in front of his very eyes, driven to extinction, like his father. He wanted back the jaguar.

She had been talking about what (little) she knew about coffee.

"And they are all children of the same mother, an Ethiopian shrub," John Mallory said. "They are heaven..."

He noticed how the beans plumped up as she passed. Even Mother Bean couldn't resist such blatant flattering. The girl whiffed again.

"It's the smells that change their taste," she said. "They absorb the richness of this soil, of these mountains, of the birds in the sky and the monkeys swinging in the trees. But I smell people, too. Are there people close by?"

The girl was a great Noticer. If she weren't a Noticer, she would have stepped on the branches of the low bean tree and squished the fruit. Then the bean would have been angry. But without being warned, the girl had delicately tiptoed over twigs, around limbs, and never so much as nudged the shiny leaves. Lorenzo knew that the bean believed her to be one of the children of the land, one of their children, and as much as Lorenzo didn't want to listen, he couldn't ignore their insistence for him to tell her their stories.

They came to a clearing, and she heard singing. She wasn't sure who sang, but she heard the happy chirps of a Spanish song. Then she saw people, men and women in between trees, some stooping, some standing and reaching. None of the trees were very tall, but they still hid the people. There were dozens and dozens of people.

The women wore long dresses, in turquoise and gold, and the men were in t-shirts and pants. There were children with dark hair and scrubbed faces working alongside their mothers, singing. Each person wore a *cajuela* basket tied around the waist. Even the smallest, about eight, had a basket hanging down to his knees. While they sang, they picked berries with both hands, and quickly dropped the fruit in the basket's mouth.

"Children are working?"

"Yes," he said.

"Isn't that immoral?"

"Coffee is our way of life," he said. "Here, we work together. Families. Your ways are different in the United States."

Though the children seemed happy, it was hard not to judge.

"Today you pick," said Lorenzo. He lifted a rope and slipped it over her head, then fitted it around her waist. He secured a basket inside the rope so that it hung in front of her. "You pick with the people."

But all her life, John Mallory had avoided the nose of hard labor—sweaty arms, mildewed socks, blisters and pus. Her whole body was soft, her hands, her feet, her back. Her only strength came from practicing yoga. Often, she watched men and women working on the production line at the plant. Packaging coffee at a small roaster required a great amount of physical labor—lifting heavy sacks of green beans, wheeling roasted beans from one side to another, hand-packing inventory.

The singing had stopped.

"Shouldn't the children be in school?"

Lorenzo said, "For now, they pick coffee. School comes later. After the season passes."

He pointed her to the closest coffee tree, more of a shrub. She trudged over.

John Mallory smiled at the woman next to her. A baby slept in a sling on her back. Her eyes were large and dark brown. Her cheeks were wide and creased. Deep lines cut across her face making her appear older than her supple body suggested. She smiled at John Mallory and revealed large, white teeth that she tried to hide behind her lips. Her eyes didn't linger but moved quickly back to the branches. Her hands were unforgettable. They were calloused, stained inky black, with thick fingers and dark nails. Yet they moved fast, delicately, bypassing the green cherries for the firm pulpy red, a musician who worked the branches with the brilliance of a concert pianist. John Mallory struggled to keep up the same rhythm.

Between her spotty Spanish and some of the pickers' spotty English, she learned that they were Panama Indians, migrant workers. They wandered with the coffee crop, with their families during harvest season. For many years now, they had come back to the same cluster of wooden houses provided by *El Cielo Verde*. They had no work in their country. And since computers and air-conditioning, few Costa Ricans wanted to labor in the fields. Many of the coffee farmers could work their own small patch of land, but for those who needed help, those whose farms were larger, the competition for labor was fierce. So they created symbiotic relationships—the Panama Indians, even Nicaraguan families, with the American Bill McCracken, with Lorenzo Domingo, who treated them with dignity. They offered them a repaired home, good water and firewood, and sometimes rice and beans that Juanita lovingly prepared.

It didn't take long for Lorenzo to stop John Mallory. She hadn't even filled one basket. He peered in and sighed. Then he held out a limb.

"Pick as the tree grows," he said. She furrowed her brows, but he didn't wait for her to speak. "Coffee trees grow from the ground. This is the new growth." He pointed to the growth on the branches, starting with the green closest to the trunk. Then he worked his callused hands out the branch, towards the end. "The bud of *el año que viene*, next year, the bud of this year." The oldest growth was at the tip. "This part no longer produces. We will trim it back. Pick down instead of up. Protect the buds." He demonstrated. Comparing firmness and color, he said, "Pick the ripe red and golden cherries. Pass those that are not ripe. It is not their time."

"When will they be picked?"

"Before the end of harvest in March. We pass these trees *muchas veces,* many times. Before we pick *todo,* all the coffee. We pick only ripe cherries. Each time we pass."

"I never knew how much work—"

"You must learn. You must first pick the cherry, then you begin to understand the bean," he said. "One basket makes two pots of coffee," he said and walked away.

Her spirits sagged. She wished the singing would start again.

She studied the berries, delicately passing those that were too hard or young. She watched the woman next to her, who smiled. John Mallory tried to mimic her. She used both hands. After ten or fifteen minutes, she became more adept, but it took her almost forty minutes to fill just half the basket. By then, sweat beaded around her face and soaked her silk blouse, creating wet shadows under her arms. She arched her aching back. Her legs throbbed. Her hands had cramped into balls. The basket of the woman next to her swelled with the red fruit, and she had returned with an empty basket to fill another. It became painfully apparent to John Mallory that her efforts couldn't even satisfy her family's daily brewing. She had no idea that a cup of coffee required so much intensive labor. Picking coffee was like recovering a thousand beads that had bounced across a concrete floor, or like picking up toothpicks for eternity.

She asked the woman, "When do we lie down and rest?" But she only smiled. After another hour, John Mallory decided to take a break.

She moved into the shade, trying to hide from the sun under a plantain tree. She laid there for fifteen minutes, unraveling her hair. Her thoughts were back home. Maybe being a Roastmaster was too hard for her. She twirled a fig branch and tickled her nose with its sweeping rosy fragrance.

"*Señorita,* do you need help?"

When she heard the boy's voice, she moved the leaves and squinted. The first thing she saw was a pair of short cowboy boots. The toes were scuffed and chalky gray. They belonged to a boy with dusty pants. He squatted and held out his hand and clucked, as if he were trying to coax a fox out of a hole. His hands were black, not as black as the woman's, but as if in a few years they would be indistinguishable, as if they all wore the same hands, just different sizes. His hair hung like a canopy around his face, small dark features, open brown eyes that were deep as coffee. The thin, striped shirt he wore, even though soiled, appeared in good condition.

"Hello," she said. "*Hola.*" She shook her head. "It's just so hot. I'm not used to the heat."

In a swoop, he pulled a baseball cap from his back pocket and handed it to her.

"For you," he said. "*Por favor.*" He mimicked wiping his face with his own hands.

She didn't try to get up. Instead, she took the baseball cap and mopped her face. A few minutes ago, she had tried to use leaves that she had pulled from the plantain tree but they scratched her and didn't absorb a thing. So she smiled at the boy, then lifted her hair and rubbed the back of her neck with the cap.

"If you find us two tall glasses of iced tea, I'll pay you ten bucks." Her sister's cash would come in handy after all.

The boy stared questionably at her. "You are an American?"

"Yes. All the way from the good ol' U.S. of A."

"My name is Paco," said the boy, slowly. Then he grinned. John Mallory was surprised by his straight teeth. "You Dodger or Yankee?"

Raised by a mother who had grown up in the south, a mother who still considered herself a Southerner, John Mallory didn't flinch at the question. She sat up a little straighter, not expecting such an accusation to come from a ten-year-old boy in Costa Rica. "I don't consider myself a Yankee. I'm American. My name is John Mallory."

"You know Fernando Valenzuela? Dodger? Yankee?"

John Mallory looked at him with droopy eyes. "Listen, we don't call ourselves Yankees. I wish you wouldn't call me that. And I haven't dodged anything that didn't deserve being dodged. Fernando who? No, I don't know him. But the United States is a big place."

"Fernando Valenzuela? In Los Angeles?"

"No, I don't know Fernando. I'm from the middle of the country, smack in the middle. Kansas City. Well, Kansas really. Los Angeles is in the west—hours away—and it's a big city."

The boy pointed to the wadded baseball cap in her hands. It was royal blue like his shirt and had an LA emblem on it. The blue had been drenched into a dark navy. He said, "He is a pitcher. A Dodger."

"You mean," she said, "a baseball player!" With that, she tucked her legs and tried to gracefully roll out from under the tree. Her toes were covered with dirt, her manicure destroyed, and she could barely stand with the cramps in her legs. But the boy had the warmest voice she had heard all day, more of a chirp. She didn't realize how much she missed chatting about nothing. She mopped her forehead one more time with the cap. Then, somewhat embarrassed, she tried to brush it off. When that didn't work, she twisted it in an effort to wring it out. "I'm afraid I may have ruined your cap. Maybe I can send you a new one."

"Nopes." The boy took back the baseball cap and slipped it on his head. "I am going to the United States to see Fernando Valenzuela play baseball," he said. "Someday."

"Good for you," she said, and smiled.

With a sigh, she leaned over and peered into her basket of coffee cherries. Unfortunately, while she rested, none of them had procreated like she had urged them to do. Her back ached. She didn't try to settle the rope around her waist again but held the basket in front of her, as if it were a large bowl of dressing and she was off to stuff a big bird. Carefully, she plucked the twigs and leaves that were on top and tossed them away.

"I will go to the United States," he said again, still grinning at her.

"Are you saving for a trip abroad? That'll set you back a pretty penny."

The boy frowned.

"You have money? *Dinero*?"

"Nopes. I guard money," he said.

"You mean save money?"

"*¡Sí!* Save! *Mi abuela* will take me. She will take me to the United States to see Fernando Valenzuela play baseball. When I get big. I am a Dodger."

"Of course. A Dodger fan." John Mallory nodded her head slowly. "I went to a baseball game last year, the season opener. I love George Brett. Do you know the Royals? No? Well, we were near third base. Everyone stood up whenever a guy smacked a ball. I can still smell the popcorn and peanuts. Cotton candy and hot dogs. Some big burly guy kept raising his hairy arms and screaming. And we did the wave!"

"Wave?" he said, grinning, his eyes wide.

"Let me teach you!" She placed the basket on the ground and demonstrated by raising her arms and bending her knees. She urged the boy to try. "It works better in a crowd. You get caught up in the excitement. Those little ittty bitty balls, flying all over the place. One ball smacked right at us. My sister dove for it. I didn't move. I was afraid our father would see us on national television. I was *supposed to be* at a job interview. Anyway, all I needed was that camera on me. If my father saw me at a baseball game when I was supposed to be somewhere else..."

The boy shook his head as if he understood.

"You don't know who George Brett is?" she said. "We followed his limo all the way from Mission Hills to some barbeque restaurant on State Line once. We saw him get out. I love baseball, too."

The boy smiled and licked his lips. His eyes shined. "I will go to a baseball game in the United States someday!"

"Better be saving those pretty pennies then."

"Pretty pennies," he said.

She looked at her basket again and sighed. She scratched her dry and caked toes with her foot. A piece of red toenail polish flaked off. She leaned down to pluck it off, then tossed it at the trunk of the tree. At that exact moment, Lorenzo reappeared, stomping towards her.

"What did you throw?" He looked at the tree but luckily couldn't see her toenail polish. "Why are you here, not there?" He pointed at the pickers.

"We were talking baseball," she said.

John Mallory looked at the boy for confirmation. She picked up her basket to shield her.

Lorenzo stomped towards her and peered in the basket. "How many have you picked?"

"How many cherries?" She looked down, horrified by the thought of counting them.

"Baskets. How many baskets?"

She began to open her mouth—she had planned to say, "You mean I was supposed to pick more than one?" She wrinkled her nose and twisted her head to the side. Up ahead, she saw the pickers pouring basket of cherries into a burlap sack. As the bag filled, a man opened another, ready for the next basket from the next picker. She felt panic rise up her throat. She looked down at the ground as if she couldn't raise her nose and eyes to meet the naked honesty of a hard day's work. "I was resting."

"¿Qué?" Lorenzo ran his hands through his hair, looked at the ground, then back at the tree. She thought he might march over there and search for her discarded nail polish, as if to prove she had personally poisoned the earth with chemicals. When she turned back again, he was stomping away. Somehow, she knew he'd return.

Where was her paladin knight now? She needed a cup of coffee, a whiff of something strong and silent.

"I can help you," said the boy. He led her by the hand, back to the trees.

By late morning, she felt dizzy. The basket weighed a hundred tons. The small of her back bent and quivered with fatigue. Her hands—no longer her own—had grown numb and unfamiliar, as if a serpent had taken possession of her limbs. Her fingers had turned black with soil. Her fingernails had split and cracked. By the time the animal came over the hill, she thought she was seeing a mirage. Maybe it was the moon, beaming and white, rising above the hills signaling them that it was time to rest. Nightfall would be there soon.

"John Mallory, John Mallory," she heard the moon say, its lips full and pink. As it grew larger, she saw that the moon wore a full blue dress that billowed in the breeze; an apron spread across its berth like a mighty sail; her eyes twinkled in the light. The unfamiliar beast flashed its buck teeth and brayed.

"*Doña* Juanita," John Mallory said and collapsed at the woman's feet.

"*Hija*," she said, moving away the donkey. She leaned down to gather her in her arms.

The donkey carried lunch. The aroma of beans and rice spilled over the hills. Juanita held a cup of water to John Mallory's dry lips. After gulping the meal, she rested under a shade tree with her head propped in Juanita's lap. The giant woman brushed back the hair from her face as she hummed a tune John Mallory had never heard before. She sniffed leaves from the eucalyptus tree while the boy whittled a piece of wood with an old Swiss Army knife.

"*El árbol*," John Mallory repeated after Paco, trying to roll her *r*'s. Tree. "Why is it that tree, bush, coffee—they're all *masculine* words in Spanish? El *árbol,* el *arbusto,* el *café.* Spanish is so sexist. Where are the girl words? Feminine ones?"

Juanita dismissed her with a giggle. "Language, it is music with a thousand notes. Many songs. *Mucho silencio.*" She looked at her, sympathy cushioned between the wrinkles in her soft face—not because she pitied John Mallory, or was insulted by her ignorance, but because Juanita could tell that she had been taught so little about life. She was like a baby bird that had never been nudged to the edge of the nest. Her eyes were still closed, her feathers wet. "Many words are female. The land, the mountain—she is not male. *La tierra, la montaña.*"

John Mallory picked up a coffee cherry and rolled it between her fingers.

In Costa Rica, men lusted for land. They coaxed it like a hesitant lover. They gave offerings. Their fingers caressed its skin and fed it sweat, dining it with hard work and love songs. Short-sleeved men in straw hats talked coffee: the cost of labor, the price of beans, how much land they had harvested, who they could trust, who would give them a fair price. They talked time. But she was used to creamy bubbles of men in white shirts, with cuff links and sharpened pencils. They talked time and money. Immeasurable valuables, ones she hadn't yet understood, were swapped at The Exchange. They all lusted for money, but for different reasons. They came at it from different angles.

Above her, the sky still hazed with sunshine and the birds still twittered in the trees. She could smell the river. Lying underneath the painted green and pink bark of the eucalyptus tree, in front of the mountains, her horizon suddenly darkened. She opened one eye. Above her, Lorenzo cut a spear in her shady slice of heaven.

"*Aquí,*" he said. He held out her rope and basket. "Now you pick."

She sat up. "I will pick when I am ready," she said, with a bit too much sass.

It's hard to say why certain visions pass through a mind, without questioning the thoughts, but when John Mallory succeeded in being rude to a man she should have shown respect to, she cracked open a silver nut of near-miss dangers—when a snake slithered into the lemony sunshine to sun on a rock but fell and rolled and rolled and rolled onto the green grass, and she had picked it up only to have her father toss it down and sever its head with a shovel; when she went riding and the horse jumped, and she fell to the ground, feeling the cool mint breeze of its hoof just inches from her skull; when, as a child, she slipped open her mother's drawer, the one with the nose-sized bottle of rosemary and lilac, bathing in it, only to be slapped across the face and forced to stand in the corner, how her father came home and the pink mark still mocked her cheek, and he told her he would rope the moon for her.

She stood up and snatched the rope and basket from Lorenzo. "Fine, I'm ready now!"

He grimaced, but she hadn't noticed. The air reeked of freedom, and it felt good to have some. She knew Juanita bristled, but she also detected the slightest smile flash across her face.

Juanita used both her hands to push her heavy load off the ground. She brushed away the dryness. "Come home soon," she said to John Mallory and smiled. "*Sí*, Lorenzo?"

"*Sí, sí,*" he said.

After they packed the mule, and Juanita grew smaller and smaller, John Mallory could still hear her magical tune keeping perfect rhythm with the bray of the donkey. She sang of love.

At the trees, John Mallory plucked coffee cherries with diligence and vengeance, like at home with her mother when they separated rocks from lima beans: the unfit were segregated and ignored. To trained muzzles, unripe cherries smelled hard, bitter, tart as an immature apple. Ripe cherries were lush, sweet pea and violet, a school girl ready to graduate, with gloves on, books in hand, and a pursed look on her face. Even angry, she could not ignore the noble puffery of a ready cherry. She tucked them into her basket, like a best friend, as if they knew her every secret but would never tell.

Paco flanked one side of her while the woman with the kind smile was on the other. They shifted positions and pinched their ears. Paco and the woman couldn't listen to the birds or the happy Spanish songs, because John Mallory dominated the conversation.

Fiery scents flared from her nostrils. Words tripped from her tongue. She didn't care how much English her friends knew. Matter of fact, she was pretty sure the woman didn't know more than a few words. Like inflicting her demands on a tired department store beautician, twisting every tube of lipstick, John Mallory insisted on smearing on every shade and color.

"I've always been muted senseless. Monitored to death. I'm sick of it. You know? Sick, sick, sick!" She started to hyperventilate. "In my family, I'm always an echo, just someone rumbling around at the end of the road. Controlled by my father, ignored by my mother, bossed around by an endless brood of sisters"—or had her mother abandoned her and her sisters ignored her?—"Now I've been forced overseas for hard labor. I've never even been out on my own. The only reason I was sent here was to avoid embarrassing them. I'm pulled around like a dog on a leash. No wonder Lorenzo barked at me. My mother was dragging a ladder under my window so she could unload me to a no-good boyfriend, while my father built a Chinese wall around me. I've never even been allowed the dignity to truly fail on my own. I've been too scared. I was raised on coffee! That's all we know is coffee! What am I doing here?"

"Play baseball later?" Paco asked when he thought he had spotted a soft landing in the conversation. But the dam had broken and the flood waters couldn't be stopped.

Did she even notice Machu watching her from the trees? Would she have even cared?

"And that's another thing. My family never took us to baseball games. It was always piano lessons, coffee, if we were lucky Macy's at the Plaza. We always pretended to be high society—" She was still gentle with the cherries. "I was not taught to pick coffee. I can hardly handle an electric buffer on the linoleum floors. Those things have more power than me. You know, if I had learned how to spit, I wouldn't be in this bind!"

"John Mallory, I can teach you to spit," said Paco. His hands flew like hummingbirds, with his basket swelling in front of his belly.

"That's the problem, Paco," she said, exasperated. "I don't want to spit. I gargle. I dab. Sandalwood, lavender, peppermint. Essential oils. My lips weren't trained for spitting."

Finally, with everyone else folding up their burlap bags and carrying them away, Paco brought her to her senses. "My mother and father, they *muerto*. I live with *mi abuela*," he said. "You are lucky to have a big family."

She stopped cold in her tracks. Chunks of blue ice melted from her heart. Embarrassed, she realized she had been acting completely self-absorbed. "Your parents are dead? I'm sorry," she said. "I didn't know." Then she folded the top part of her sack and averted her eyes. "That must make you sad."

"Uh-huh, but *mi abuela* she take good care of me." He yanked on his own heavy bag and flung it over his shoulders. He had the grace of a swan, with arms no bigger than the swimming bird's neck. "We go to the United States, see baseball. You go with me, John Mallory. I can take you to a baseball game."

She looked down at her sack. A small miserable example, doubled over in shame, it was only half full. "You bet, Paco. Thank you. You're a good friend. You, your grandmother and me, that's what we'll do. We'll go to a baseball game. You're so generous."

He smiled and reached for her hand, skipping as they headed towards the others.

It was the end of the day, and they carted their cherries to the dump truck owned by *El Cielo Verde*. The other pickers had multiple, bulging, burlap bags. Only a few pickers owned a mule or a wheelbarrow, so most carried them on their shoulders. Like the other pickers, John Mallory poured her harvested cherries into a plastic basket. Eager to collect her payment for her, Paco ran with the basket to the dump truck. He handed the brimming container up to a supervisor who squatted on top of the truck. The man dumped the cherries into the truck's belly, pitched a coin into the basket, and then tossed it back down to be refilled. Paco raced back to her.

"*Aquí, aquí*," he said as if he had struck oil. He held out the gold token.

"We're rich," she said.

It didn't take John Mallory long to calculate payment for a basket of coffee cherries. They were being paid pennies on the pound.

Twice, John Mallory poured her sack into the plastic basket, and Paco ran it to the truck. Grateful she could fill two containers, her third didn't quite make it. Instead of embarrassing Paco, she said, "I'll take it to the supervisor. See if I can sweet-talk a coin."

She trudged towards the truck with her thighs stiff from her hard day of standing, squatting and stretching. If she had tilted up her chin, followed the usual airborne path, she could have nested in smells, the bold earthy balms. Or maybe she would have detected burning candles, the universal repellant for temptation. As she lifted her basket over her head, three-quarters full, strong and capable hands leaned down to take it. She felt the heavy energy of a stare. But her nasal passages were clogged. Instead of looking up, she stared at her toes.

After several awkward seconds, she finally heard the welcomed rush of hard coffee cherries being tossed onto the pile—and the kind thunk of a coin in the bottom of her basket. She realized she had been holding her breath.

When she looked up to retrieve the basket, a large face peered down at her.

It was *him*. His handsome face smiled, dimpled and dark. He honked and then grinned. His warm smells cooled and excited her, as if she'd discovered air-conditioning. He smelled of heaven—cocoa, coffee, ripe and golden—she would always swear, as she made the sign of the cross, that Machu Domingo was supernaturally spellbinding. It was as if he had unlocked her hidden diary and read every secret, and discovered he was her greatest love. Suddenly, she was nothing without the sweet perfume of Machu Domingo.

Her lungs filled as she fluttered her lashes. She stood on her tiptoes and forced herself to quit trembling as she reached for the basket. She smiled, delicately touching his fingers.

Suddenly, out of nowhere, the basket snapped out of her hands. She heard him before she could see him. He was a piercing cry in the middle of the night. His scent gave him away. He was scalded coffee, screaming with a savage raven pitch.

"Machu? What are you doing here? I sent you to town. She does not get a coin! No coin! Her basket is not full!" Lorenzo hunched over the basket, looming over it like a buzzard over a dying carcass. His pointy hands plucked the coin out. His eyes squeezed shut. A ping echoed, and for a brief moment she saw the ray beams of the golden coin as it turned and spun before it hit Machu in the chest.

Stench hung in the air. John Mallory covered her shame with the collar of her shirt.

Machu swung down from the top of the truck and landed in front of her. He spun around and stood toe to toe with his father, his hands clenched, forcing him to back up. His muscles were hard and tightening.

She smelled the rage of an uncontrollable forest fire.

"No, don't," she said, touching his shoulder. "I'm fine. He can keep his dumb coin," she said. But her eyes betrayed her. They had grown large, and she nervously twisted a strand of hair. Something sweet and shameful had filled her mouth and made her skin sticky. Her shoulders slumped.

Lorenzo darted around his son so he could stand between him and the girl.

"Father, I gave it to her!" Machu's voice boomed, but Lorenzo had blocked her view. She could only smell his tight lips.

She wanted to slink away. Conflicting emotions hung heavy in the air, making her dizzy. She yearned for a feather bed, then became enraged, a hungry animal digging in the dirt.

"Fine," she said, "I'm going."

They both turned to watch her. She smiled, then plucked the two coins from the safekeeping of her cleavage. In mockery, she held them up in the sun, as if she were seeing if they were real. She bit one. The taste of metal stung her mouth. She spat on the ground. It was a foreign gesture but felt spicy and right. It was as if she had been spitting her entire life.

She looked at Lorenzo and shrugged, as if his game and coins were child's play and worthless. She handed the coins to Paco. She didn't wait to breathe in Lorenzo's scorn. She could smell her own heat. Even the gentle breath of the coffee cherries couldn't cool her.

Machu stood gawking at the girl. Lorenzo sighed and coughed, hoping to distract him. He tried to stand in front of him, but Machu moved him aside. His eyes followed John Mallory as she sauntered away.

He was still staring at her when she reached the border of trees. She quivered. Her hands strayed over her familiar curves. Tiny drops of sweetness dripped in her cleavage. She leaned down and rolled up the bottom of her culottes. She tied the ends of her shirt into a knot above her belly button. She ripped a heavy vine from a tree, and bound her hair on top of her head. With her chin up, she threw back her shoulders and thrust out her chest while she rhythmically moved away from the fading sun, letting her arms swing loosely while her wide hips swiveled from side-to-side.

She wasn't consciously flirting. She didn't even notice that the men had taken to lying on the ground, fanning themselves with banana leaves, muttering Spanish poems out of the sides of their mouths. Even the women blew down their shirts to cool off their breasts. They had kicked off their shoes and fanned out their toes as they watched her.

In the last breath of sunshine, John Mallory walked boldly down the aisle, like a virgin in a white dress in the middle of the rainforest. Pink crystals fell from the canopy of kapok trees and stuck to her hair and eyelashes. As she passed the wild vines, the sun-soaked flowers bloomed and turned to pomegranate. *Hush*. The lips of the coffee cherries swelled and separated.

Even the skeptics knew. John Mallory reeked of the hot-blooded scent of lust.

13

Baile de la Diosa

After dinner of beans and rice, fried plantains, and an interesting form of baked rigatoni, men gathered on the porch of Lorenzo Domingo. Hours ago, the pickers had retreated to their homes and rolled into their beds with soft moans of bone tired but ready. It wasn't unusual for the farmers, men and women, to gossip about their days. But what was unusual was that the neighbors all tried to crowd onto the small porch of Lorenzo Domingo.

It seemed that a thousand noses had tickled in that fertile season.

Men held their hats. Their eyes were timid boys at the door. Moments before, they had splashed their faces and chests with cypress oils, black pepper and cocoa. Slipped out of their simple frocks, the women had transformed into rouged ladies. They had dabbed rosewood waters on the napes of their neck, between their breasts, and in the sweet spot behind their ears. Their long hair had been brushed smooth, swept to the side, and clasped in gemstones. They wandered along the pebbled path to the Domingos', like creatures in search of a Pied Piper.

Lopez played love songs on his guitar. Jugs of wine passed from hand to hand. Lorenzo stuffed his hands into his pockets, his conversations diverted: *Would Roberto allow Julio to farm a small parcel of the family's land? No, he didn't smell anything sweet,* he said. *Had there been any word about the coffee contracts? No, Juanita wasn't cooking anything special,* he assured them. *Have the beetles continued to spread? No, Juanita was not making any hot Italian dishes with noodles. Julio would go to the United States. He would be forced to. Did he want that? No! Nothing baking! Nothing sugary! Nothing cooking!*

Juanita watched from her window. A church-going woman, like most of the gatherers on her porch, she avoided temptation by burning tall candles. She looked at the bumpy white glass of the Virgin Mary, then fanned her face. Rosary beads dangled from her fingers. Words from the Bible crossed her lips while her fingers pressed the onion-skin.

"Don't go," she said. At the door, she held John Mallory by the elbow. "The red-eyed tree frog comes with the first rain. But I already hear the mating call."

John Mallory looked out the window. "I don't hear anything."

"They hide. Hundreds of them. In the leaves with their red eyes. The males hang from the branches. They wrestle upside down. Their purple bellies lock, their eyes fill with lust. Deeper than blood. They fight. For females."

"Where? I don't see them."

"The females, they are much bigger. He looks like a child on her back. But still they climb the trees with their long fingers." She spread her fingers on the glass of the window and peered out. "Pink fingers creeping with suction cups."

"They're not there, *Doña* Juanita. I would smell them."

"They should not be here until May," Juanita said. "But they are here."

John Mallory had slipped into a dress, a sheer, clingy, impractical black-blue silk that whispered: I have smooth skin, warm blood, and the deadly power of a tropical wandering spider.

Juanita squeezed her shoulder. "The men have savage on their breath."

John Mallory bent her head and said softly, "I know."

"It's almost dark. There's no moon."

John Mallory smiled and shook her head as if she already knew. "The moon is full. There's plenty of light."

Juanita shook her head. She knew that John Mallory had been given to her to protect, an heirloom pressed into her palm with final words uttered from lips that only *she* had heard. Only *she* could keep her safe. She feared the energy she felt outside: men slapping the rear ends of the women, taking long swigs out of a tequila bottle, the women raising their dresses to scratch their knees. They wiped their lips with the back of their hands. Luis Alvarez had raised a hoe to the venomous fer-de-lance and now swung the snake over his head. They all laughed too loudly.

"I am sorry," Juanita said and pulled her hand off John Mallory as if she were burning her. "I don't know why I am saying these things."

"You're frightened."

"*Sí*, but I do not know why."

John Mallory pretended to study the flowers in the garden. Their sweet smiles teased her with sugars and ginger spices, lacy pinks and red deep with cleavage. The men were preoccupied with the women—and the women were busy positioning their contentment like garter belts.

No one noticed John Mallory.

There was singing. One man fell off the stoop into a heap in the garden. He may have seen her then, but his hand reached for an ankle on the porch, begging, "Rosa, Rosa!"

Only interested in her own trapdoor escape, John Mallory followed Lorenzo. He had slipped behind the house with a man she hadn't met. The man was a tidy package. He reminded her of a lion tamer, but wealthier, with a small hat, a pocket vest, pressed pants, and a long moustache. With each word, Lorenzo inched forward. His intentions were sharp and growing in pitch. But the mustached man beat him back with the whip and chair of his closed lips. He never dropped his gaze. It all left Lorenzo pawing with the fiery eyes of a lion weighing his options.

John Mallory listened. She caught a few bits and pieces of their conversation.

"*La tierra*," Lorenzo kept saying, pawing at the air. She only knew enough to know that he talked of the land.

So she patted her stomach, coddling her unappeased hunger, and looked up in the sky. If she concentrated hard enough she thought she might conjure up Machu, like a ring of fire. She could feel his temperature nearby but she couldn't smell him.

She inched her way out into the yard and straddled a chair made of branches. Memories opened like the flap on the Big Tent: giggling on top of her father's shoulders, her knees pressing his ears pink; the world scurrying by like ants on a checkered tablecloth; riding up and down on a jeweled horse, the reins tight in her fist as the merry-go-round played tinker-top music; eating cotton candy from a paper cone. She dreamed of flying over the clouds. Up the stairway of heaven, she tried to imagine the scent of onion blooms and peach ice cream, even the hot sweat of roasted pig. She could smell crab apples and pear trees, as if she were back in unexpected blooms of an early Kansas City springtime.

There were no gusts of Machu Domingo.

"No," she heard Lorenzo say. His chest puffed out. But the lion tamer had paraded away. Lorenzo had forgotten all about John Mallory as he stomped behind him.

The final embrace of the fading sun slipped behind the mountains. John Mallory yearned to lie down in the cool grass and look at the blue stars. She craved a lilac bubble bath, and thought she even smelled it. But all she could see was the pale yellow light and feel the warmth of moonlight kisses.

She felt the tall perfumes of the rainforest tug her nose, so she followed the shadows with all their hocus-pocus.

At dusk the forest filled with golden eyes. Predators lay in wait in the bushes. Preoccupied, John Mallory didn't smell the foul breath of danger. To avoid detection, she traveled close to the trees. But the eyes watched her as she followed the trail to the river. At a fork, she came upon a worn path. The wild smells of the river called to her.

With each raised shoe, her footprints were fresher than the rest.

When she came to a clearing, she almost stepped into the opening. But the smell of something large and gamy crowded the air. Up ahead, an enormous, pig-shaped body made shadows in the light. She didn't know what it was, but later she would learn: a mother Baird's tapir, *la danta*, more than seven hundred pounds. The animal watched over a spotted calf while it lowered its head and drank from the river. A mixture of horse and rhinoceros, the animal lifted her snout and sniffed. Nothing separated John Mallory from the beast but a few leaves and twigs, and her quiet breath. When a ripe banana plopped on the ground, the mother gobbled it with one bite. Her fangs were wicked and long. So much ivory made John Mallory tremble. She held perfectly still, begging her body to stop smelling like human.

Then, suddenly, as if called to synchronized swimming, the Baird's tapir waded into the river. She sank like a stone to the bottom of the clear pool. She blew bubbles in the water. The baby followed, paddling its three-toed hooves behind her. John Mallory stood on her tiptoes to watch. Small fish swam over and nibbled on the mother's thick and bulky hide, hungry for ticks and lice.

But John Mallory leaned too far and fell through the brush. Her knees buckled, and her hands and legs sank into the river. The forest ears could hear her panic, splashing and squealing, as she struggled to free herself from the mud. But she kept falling, sliding. By the time she found her balance, the tail end of the pig-shaped bodies had zigzagged into the thick jungle—and disappeared.

The eyes in the bushes expected her to run. She should have been petrified. Instead, she quietly panted and held her fingers against her neck. Her body, a silhouette against the green, began to move. With a roll of her head, she curled her back and looked around like a stretching cat. She smiled. Without even a modest glance—no embarrassed smile, no looks over her shoulder—John Mallory slid down the straps of her dress and stepped out of the silk. She slipped out of her underwear and dropped her bra. Her clothing blended away, nothing but a small swirl of blue melted into the colors of the mud.

Dirty, with the unapologetic frankness of a creature in the wild, she no longer blamed the stinging-hard work of her day for her aching muscles, and certainly not the coffee cherries for her black hands. A child used to waiting—at the end of a long line of sisters as they waited for a cooling hot bath, her hips leaning against the wall and her towel dragging the floor—she did not hesitate. She melted into the warm waters. Only the softest splash could be heard.

She didn't care if a horsy mammal had just been paddling around. She was used to dirty bath water. She didn't even think about the dangers. She swam, like a swan that had broken away from the ducks. Her fingers pointed as she American-crawled to the deepest part of the river. She plunged into the darkness. Only the rising bubbles betrayed her path. She came up to the light for a gulp of air, then back down to the darkness. She didn't worry, naïve and loose with stupidity, about swimming snakes, crocodiles, piranhas or parasites. She glided, crawled, and treaded. She skinny-dipped under the light of the moon.

From the bushes, a pair of eyes watched as she came to shore, dripping. Her hair lay against her skin like parchment on a coffee bean. Her breasts were full and heavy as she rinsed out her clothes. Her nipples were baby pink. Her body glowed, fleshy rose, with a tangled dark jungle between her legs. Her eyes fluttered, a cascading *azul*, like the blue morpho butterfly. She wiggled back into her dress. It clung to her, and she shuddered.

She closed her eyes and began a quiet dance.

Barefoot, she was in a field of coffee trees and *guaria moradas* orchids, red hues, and purple with diamond shimmers, fragrances of her yet unfulfilled dreams. Away from the scrub and crabgrass of hungry men as they straddled chairs, groping their shot glasses, she relished being alone with the night. She flowed, waving in the breeze, tall as a reed of Kansas wheat. She closed her eyes, allowing herself to feel her bouquet of earthly emotions—sadness, loneliness, thankfulness, fear, celebration, longing and creative joy. Breathing forcefully, she emitted an inner-fire. She breathed in and out. Her legs rocked from side-to-side as her lips parted. She lifted her hands to the sky, while her heart beat to invisible drums.

At first, she didn't feel him. But the energy of his stare made her open her eyes. She looked up. A man had climbed the enormous buttress roots of a chilamate tree that curled out of the ground. The roots extended from his legs, coiling towards her like snakes from his ankles. Dressed in a plain white t-shirt and dusty white trousers, he appeared luminescent as a spirit, a stone outcrop, a road map to another world. He smelled of the land and sky. The heat of his stare made her afraid of the moon.

"Machu," she said.

She thought he whispered, "John Mallory." Even softer, the lips of the wind were saying, *Watch out or he will take you for his wife.*

It was a clear, cloudless night, and he slid down the tree as if he were guided by sunlight. He stopped at the riverbank and held out a piece of fruit.

"Are you hungry?" It was a small fruit from the chilamate tree, a wildlife relish. But it didn't seem trite, or not enough, not even wrong, as if the apple had lured Eve to Adam just as much as Adam to Eve, or the apple to the tree.

Still, she kept him back with her eyes, as if she were pressing the heel of her hand against his chest. She tried to harness her emotions. Her eyes begged him, but her mind wasn't sure.

He said, "I am sorry. Desire is like the jabillo tree. It makes you blind." He lowered his eyes. "It can make you crazy and turn you into a madman." His face, big, round and white, looked as if it were melting.

She held up her chin. A cold breeze chilled her and she looked at him. "Did you see me naked?"

"I'm sorry," he whispered, but then looked at her and slowly smiled. "Now we both know."

She blushed. Something stirred inside her. "Machu, I don't know what this is—"

"Can it be love?"

They looked at each other, knowing quick love seemed impractical, best left for fairy tales and movies. But it had come, masked in the middle of the night, and kidnapped them, as if forcing them at gunpoint. There were usually signs—an open window, a ladder thrown up, whispers. There was the expectation of time. Improbable but not impossible, because they found themselves powerless to move, and they dared not fight it, afraid it would disappear altogether.

"Falling in love so easily can destroy—"

"Or nurture," he said. "You cannot choose when..."

She whispered, "If it's love, then not like this."

"Yes." He agreed, but his eyes had softened with longing.

"Your father disapproves."

"He cannot keep us apart. We are already bound to each other. If it is our destiny, then we cannot escape it. It is human, this quest for two people to make a whole."

She knew he spoke from his heart. He believed it to be true. "Your father's afraid."

"We are not beetles on his crop."

She found herself shaking her head, smiling. It was as if the idea—to fall in love—had not been hers. No more than a shade tree knew when it would attract a bird. But coffee needed the shade tree, necessary and right, just as the bird needed to nest.

He held out his hand, and she took it.

"Tonight, I will take you back to my father's. You must get dry and sleep." They walked, hand in hand. "Up there, there's a platform," he said and pointed. "Twenty-five meters above the forest floor, where I watch the birds. Come there."

"When?"

"You will know when, my love."

She nodded.

Away from the riverbank, with the eyes of the jungle watching, he led her under the canopy of the rainforest in silence. They reached the yard near the Domingos' porch, and she turned to him and touched his face. She held it and smiled before she slipped into the light.

14

Dance Moves

Inside Research, Capri tells the girl behind the desk, "I'm here to see John Mallory." The receptionist looks at her with a blank stare. Capri can tell her tan is artificial, more orange than bronze, but Capri smells the jungle. She also senses the chemicals on the receptionist's skin. She adds, "He's my grandfather, Mister John Mallory, Senior."

The receptionist studies her, looking down her nose at Capri and Mac as if they are perpetrators from the bushes. "You can't bring those in," she says, staring at the coffee cups.

"Why not?"

"All the patients will want some."

"Why can't they have some?"

"Company policy."

Now Capri is really worried about her granddaddy. A day without coffee would be torture for him, like anyone else being told they couldn't have a drink of water.

But there's coffee in the room because Capri smells it. She looks around the lobby. A television plays some rerun of a cop sitcom. Two people watch the screen, but their eyes are fixed far away. There's an old pot of coffee on a burner in the corner. A basket of artificial creamers and packets of sugar sit in a basket.

"What about that?" Capri points to the coffee.

"It's for visitors."

"Well, I'm a visitor."

"And you can drink your beverage in the lobby, but you cannot take it in."

She rolls her eyes, finds a trash can, and pitches their cups of coffee.

"Now," she says, peeved, "may I see my granddaddy? John Mallory."

"Code?" the receptionist says in a snippy tone.

Capri wants to smack her, sitting there in her white dress, all smug while her granddaddy rots inside in a padded room, afraid and crying, beating on the tiny window to his locked door.

"You can't get in without a code," the receptionist says.

Capri looks at the thick door that separates the waiting room from where they keep the patients. She puts her hands on her hips. Then it occurs to her. She knows the code. It's the last four digits of their phone number.

"8333," she says, raising her eyebrows.

The receptionist looks at her computer screen, finally saying, "Do you know where to go?"

"No, but I'd appreciate it if you'd tell me."

She blinks, then sighs. She tells her she must sign in, in a log. Capri is tempted to put down a fake name, but she's worried the receptionist will ask for an ID, and then she'll be able to keep her from her granddaddy. So she signs and hands the pen to Mac. He pauses but scribbles his name. The receptionist slips two plastic badges on the counter with the word Visitor. Finally, she gives them directions to the Adult Ward: through the door, past the cafeteria, down the hall, and to another door where they'll have to ring a buzzer and wait for a nurse.

The receptionist pushes the buzzer, holding it, with a look in her eyes like she's the sphinx and she's allowing them to pass into the tomb.

Capri looks at Mac and he exhales. She marches to the door and opens it, but Mac is frozen with a horrified look on his face.

"I think I'll wait here," he says, looking at the rows of chairs and the television.

"No, come with me," she says, begging him, realizing she's not that gutsy.

"I'm not dressed," he says.

"Dressed for what? It's a mental ward."

"I'd rather be dressed. Like in a suit or something."

"He won't care. Just go with me."

Mac groans but shadows her. They follow signs down white hallways. Everything reeks of antiseptics, bleach, and soiled sheets. Mac jumps at every face, like it just appeared in a darkened window. Someone screams.

"Come on, let's go," Mac says, as if they're in a haunted house and can just step out of line. Capri shakes her head.

The only signs of life are nurses and orderlies. They nod as they pass, but no one says a word. It's as if they all know why they're there, and they're sorry. Capri flinches at the cafeteria food smells coming from an open doorway. It smells like roasted pig. They come to another door with the sign for the Adult Ward. There's a buzzer on the wall, and Capri presses it. A nurse peeks around the corner. When she sees them she grabs the keys dangling from her belt loop. The nurse is head to toe electric blue, with boots that match her shirt and pants, a rhinestone cowgirl. Her hair is tight, like a Nerf ball. She looks happier than she should.

"Maybe she's on her way to Tommy's party," Capri says, trying to lighten the mood so Mac will close his mouth.

"Hi," she says with a big smile. "Who are you here to see?"

"John Mallory," Capri says and then adds, "Senior."

The nurse crinkles her nose and tells them to follow her. The door clicks behind them and heads bob up, like puppets pulled by strings. They pass a desk. A woman watches them from her computer. There is a small room with a TV blaring where six or seven people in gowns and robes slump in chairs. Some follow them with their eyes. A few stare into the distance, whispering memories. An old man folded over in a wheelchair grabs Capri's arm and she almost faints. His grip isn't tight, but his hand is gnarled. His fingernails are yellow and thick.

Capri can't move. She smells the quicksand of fear and decay, people trapped in their own minds.

"Please, call my wife," he says, pleading behind moist eyes. His nose is pitted and shines. A blue vein throbs at his temple. The nurse pulls his fingers away and puts them in his lap. She pats them.

"Now, Reverend, you wait right here. I called your wife. She's coming, she's coming. You be patient." A younger woman, probably twenty, wheels by, pushing a thick lump of blanket, a woman probably eighty. "Greta," the nurse says to her, "the reverend needs his pill and glasses. What'd you do with your glasses, Reverend? You seen them, Greta?"

The old woman calls from her wheelchair, "I need glasses, I need glasses."

"No," nurse Greta says, "you don't wear glasses, Mrs. Girshbaum. Reverend? What'd you do with your glasses?" she says louder than Capri thinks is necessary.

"My purse," Mrs. Girshbaum says. "Where's my purse?"

Capri follows the cowgirl nurse down the white linoleum, wondering if the old man even has a wife, and if he does, if she ever visits him. She wonders if he'll ever find his glasses, or if he's even a reverend. She wonders if Mrs. Girshbaum will ever see her purse again.

They stop at room eleven.

Her granddaddy is there.

The sight of him knocks the wind out of her.

Tucked under white sheets, his eyes are closed. His head rests on a white pillow. His wavy black hair curls around his ears. He needs a haircut. He'd never wear it that long. The skin on his face and neck is thick and sunburned, like he's been working on the farm with Great Granddaddy again, but he hasn't been on the farm in over fifty years, and he never would have been allowed to sleep so much. Her granddaddy is a slender stalk of wheat, plowed into the bed, tucked in so tight that his feet are flat against the mattress. He looks dead.

She looks at Mac. He looks like he's ready to find a rock so he can hammer a wooden cross into the ground next to Granddaddy.

It's cold in the room, and there's another man, in a bed against the wall. He has an afro and moans, begging the nurse for biscuits and gravy. The cowgirl pushes past Capri and Mac and raises the arm on the man's bed.

"You're fine, Mr. White," she says. "Breakfast. Next time you open your eyes."

The man closes his eyes and opens them. "Biscuits, gravy," he says.

"Tomorrow," the nurse says.

"Give me soap," he says, and she sighs but goes to the bathroom and comes back with a white bar. "I need something to carve with," he says.

"No, Mr. White. We've gone over this. No knives."

"I can't carve if I don't have a knife."

"That's right," the nurse says and pats him.

The room is like any other hospital room, except there's furniture, a dresser, a metal closet, and a night table. There's no television or windows, but there's a chair waiting by Granddaddy's bed. Capri wonders if the rooms across the hall have windows. She wonders if she could get Granddaddy moved, get him his own room, one with a window.

Pictures crowd the dresser. They have frames but no glass. There's one of Capri and her mom, a recent one, taken last Christmas, one of the six sisters lined up by age, and a big one of John Mallory, the same photo Capri and her mom were just looking at. John Mallory is still waiting for the bird to land on her wrist. Capri picks up a snapshot from when she was four. She's in the backyard holding a metal pooper scooper. Aunt Lolly and her mother stand behind her with their arms crossed, laughing. Capri's head is tilted back. Her face is bright red and her mouth is open. She's crying. *Just like them to make me do the dirty work*, Capri thinks, *and clean up after Aunt Lolly's stray dogs, while they're drinking iced coffees and eating Pepperidge Farm cookies.* She hides it behind a crayon drawing Capri had made for Granddaddy years ago. It's framed and propped up but still no glass. In it, they are stick figures next to the weeping willow. She and Granddaddy are as big as the tree. There's a swing too. She wishes they were there, with Granddaddy standing behind her, pushing her into the sky.

She opens a drawer. Inside, there's nothing but a comb. She knows it's Granddaddy's. At least she thinks it is; he has one just like it, small and black. He keeps it in his back pocket. She picks it up and smells it. It has his oil on it, his Dippety Do, he calls it. She places it on the dresser next to her picture.

She turns to watch Granddaddy breathe, in and out, in and out. When did he get so small?

"Well, I'll leave you alone," the nurse says. She's propped knife guy up in a wheelchair and he's fingering the soap, studying it as if he's trying to find a way to release the masterpiece hidden inside.

Mac follows the nurse to the door and stops. He pokes his head in the hallway, like he's counting tiles to the exit. He turns around but stays in the doorway, his hands clasped in front of him, like a fig leaf covering his genitals.

Granddaddy sleeps so soundly, Capri doesn't want to wake him. She wishes she had picked some lilac to put beside his bed. She wonders how people entertain themselves in a psych ward. Jigsaw puzzles, checkers, Gin Rummy? She should have brought a book. *The Sun Also Rises* would have been a good choice. She can't help but smile, then covers her mouth as if she had stabbed him in the heart.

"I've got to take a leak," Mac says.

"Use the bathroom."

"No way."

"Chicken," she says. "Fine, I will." She has to squeeze past knife guy and his wheelchair. "Excuse me." He's humming a tune Capri thinks she recognizes, "Mr. Bojangles," and his slippers make a scratching sound as they slide sideways on the floor. He's wearing baggy black pants and a rust-colored t-shirt. He smells like raw dirt and fresh leaves. "Just want to slip by," she says. "I need to use the ladies room."

"No ladies," he says without looking at Capri. "Just us chickens."

Capri looks at Mac and he mouths, "Scary."

"My granddaughter will be here soon. Bringing me chicken soup," the man says, still fingering the soap while he slides his feet.

"Good," Capri says. "That sounds good."

"Yes-siree bob," he says.

She tries to get by, but he won't move his knees. "I'm a dancer, you know."

"You're a dancer? Oh, great—"

"Am. Have my own Arthur Murray Dance School."

"Isn't that nice," Capri says. She doesn't want to push his knees, they're knobby, and his thighs are the size of a bird's neck. He points his toe in the air as if he's doing kick ball change moves. When she tries to pass him, he kicks at her and says, "Cha cha cha."

She looks back at Mac and he mouths, "Really scary."

"Just want to slide past," Capri says, even more determined to pass the dancing gatekeeper.

"Cha cha cha," he says, kicking the air every time she moves forward.

Capri sighs, not wanting to be rude and invade his personal space. It's as if she's back in the sixth grade, and Sister Carmella is standing there in her hula hoop, saying,

"This is my personal space. This is how much space I need. Please respect my personal needs."

Capri taps him but he doesn't look at her, kicking and chanting his cha cha cha.

She sighs loudly. Knife guy isn't getting that much hula hoop space. She seesaws her shoulders and shuffle towards him. "I do my dance moves, I do my dance moves," she says, swiveling her hips, then twirls past him and slips into the bathroom. "Cha cha cha," she says, safely inside.

She thinks she hears him snicker and peeks back at him. He never looks up, a tap-dancing drifter locked in his cell. She wonders if he's blind. She doesn't see any dark glasses by the bedside, but he doesn't blink. She shuts the door, but it doesn't have a lock.

The bathroom smells like the inside of a diaper pail. There's water on the floor but no shower, and the toilet has dark rings. Only cardboard is left on the toilet paper dispenser. She wonders where they bathe. On second thought, she decides she can wait.

Mac calls to her. "Capri, let's get out of here. God, this place is *cree*-py."

She darts by knife guy. He doesn't raise a toe.

There's no clock on the wall. She says, "Give Granddaddy a few minutes."

"For what? He's out. Nobody's home. Come on."

"Granddaddy?" she says, tiptoeing towards him, like they'll both fall through the floor if she speaks too loudly. "Granddaddy, it's me. It's Capri."

He smells like a pee-soaked mattress.

"That smell," she says to Mac. "That's no good."

Mac turns his head and lets out his breath.

"Granddaddy," she says again, louder, shaking his shoulder. "Please, wake up."

And then he does. His eyes open. They are coal, darker than she's ever seen them, and mist covers them in clouds.

He looks at Capri, but his eyebrows furrow. His adam's apple pumps.

"Granddaddy—"

"John Mallory? John Mallory!" There's desperation in his voice. His body tightens and wiggles, like he's ready to explode. His cheeks flutter and his lips tremble. "John Mallory..."

"No, Granddaddy, it's me. Capri."

"I knew you'd come back. I knew you wouldn't stay away forever. You're back, you're back. My dearest child. You didn't leave me. John Mallory, John Mallory..."

"No, Granddaddy. I'm not John Mallory. She died. A long time ago. Remember? She went away a long time ago. It's me. Capri. Not John Mallory. Capri. Remember, Granddaddy?" She stands over him so he can get a good look. "I'm Capri."

His body relaxes and his eyes moisten. They click shut. Then they flutter open. He looks at the wall and furrows his brow, as if he wishes he could remember, and then he frowns and snaps them shut, grimacing.

"I'm getting up, Mama," he says, whining. "I promise, I'm getting up. I remember the cows, Mama, I'm getting up." He rocks back and forth. "I remember..."

"No, Granddaddy. I'm not your mama. She's dead, too, a long long time ago. Before I was born. It's me. Capri. Granddaddy? Remember?"

He wiggles but can't budge, like he's cemented in. She tries to loosen his sheets but ends up fighting them. They're too tight, so she rips them off. His arms are pinned with bands, strapped to the metal arms of his bed. He's wearing his good robe. It's tied loosely and falling open. Underneath, gray hairs poke out of his stained undershirt. He's wearing boxers covered with red hearts. His shoulders are narrow, his knuckles bloody and scabbed. The skin on his hands is paper thin, and he has a band-aide on the backside of the right one.

Where's his wedding ring? And the heavy gold ring from Rome? Where's his watch? He never goes anywhere without his rings and watch.

"Why do they have you…" She unbuckles the straps. Her granddaddy is not in prison, and he is not going to be anyone's stuffed animal to wheel up and down the hallway.

"Maybe you shouldn't," Mac says from the doorway.

"Maybe I shouldn't what, Mac? Leave him here strapped-in and helpless? What?"

He looks up at the ceiling and says, "Just saying…"

"Well, I don't care. I'm breaking my granddaddy out of this loony bin."

"That's not a good idea."

She doesn't care what Mac thinks. Her fingers work fast, unpinning Granddaddy, figuring out how to lower the arms on the bed. She pulls him hard. He's a rag doll, a question mark with his curvy back. She can't hold him. He collapses back onto the pillow.

"Come on, Granddaddy," she says.

"Maybe you shouldn't, Capri."

"Shut up, Mac."

She is not gentle this time and yanks him up. While she holds his back, she swings his legs around to the side of the bed. They are thin and bare, and white, almost hairless. He has on black nylon socks and slippers.

"The sun is coming," he says, then makes low, eerie sounds: *woo—woo—wooo.*

"Come on, Granddaddy," she says, "we're getting you out of here." She looks at Mac and he shakes his head. She sees the metal closet. "His clothes must be in there. Look."

Mac doesn't move.

"Mac, look!"

He lowers his chin and raises his brows at her.

"Come hold him then," Capri says, knowing her granddaddy will flop back down if she lets go.

Mac hesitates, looking from her granddaddy to her, to the metal closet, and back to her granddaddy. Mac still doesn't move. He has that look on his face, like he may be more pasture horse than stallion, and he knows better than to jump fences when he can clearly see an electrical wire.

"Mac! Hold him while I find his clothes!"

Finally, he comes to her. He holds her granddaddy by the back of the neck with three fingers. When Granddaddy almost slips off the bed, he says, "Oh, shit," and reaches to grab him, and Capri doesn't even correct him for cussing. No way Granddaddy notices. He's far away, staring into distant lands.

Capri opens the closet. Inside, there's a crushed-velvet blanket and his toiletry bag. His shoes are in the bottom, so she grabs them. She runs to the dresser and digs through the drawers. She doesn't recognize any of the clothes, but she finds a shirt and some stretch pants that her granddaddy would never wear, but she hopes they'll fit him.

"Help me dress him," she says.

Mac holds him loosely, but he isn't helpful. She sighs and pushes him aside and pulls the robe off her granddaddy's shoulders.

"I knew you'd come back," Granddaddy says, reaching for Capri. His hand trembles as he touches her arm. He looks into her eyes. "I had to tell them. Tell everyone. You were gone…It was your mother's idea. Didn't want it," he says, swallowing and opening his mouth. His eyes widen. Something deep in his throat gurgles. He struggles for more words to come. "Your sisters…" He begs and pleads. "Won't let her go. Don't go. Not again." He tries to rub Capri's arm. "I knew you'd come back. My little girl…"

"Granddaddy, I'm not John Mallory. It's me, Capri. It's me! Capri!" Her voice escalates. "She's dead! I'm Capri!"

"Stay in the sky," he says. "Where I can watch over you…The sun is coming." He starts to make wooing sounds again.

"You are not the sun, Granddaddy. You hear me? You are not the sun! You are my Granddaddy! And I am not John Mallory! I'm Capri!"

"Knife! Knife!" the man in the next bed screams. He's not strapped in and is more mobile than Granddaddy. He moves like a dancer, still flexible, lean. He rushes towards Capri, more tackle than dance. She drops Granddaddy and grabs him, afraid she's going to have to wrestle knife guy to his bed. Granddaddy almost flops off the bed. She looks to Mac, but he's too freaked out to help.

"What are you doing?" It's the cowgirl nurse. She's at the door with a wild look, her hands out, ready to wrangle Capri, Mac, the knife guy, and anyone else that comes along.

The knife guy slips past Capri, grabs Granddaddy's comb from the dresser, and sticks it in his afro. The nurse moves aside and he shuffles out the door. Capri can hear him soft toe shoeing down the hallway.

"I'm getting my granddaddy out of here," Capri says, panting, trying to help Granddaddy up again so she can put on the pants.

"You can't do that," the nurse says and comes from the other side. "Now, now, Mr. Mallory, you just lie back down and rest." She gently helps him lean back.

"Oh, yeah," Capri says, "just watch me." She slaps the cowgirl's hands and yanks her granddaddy, hugging him to her. The nurse gasps and rushes out the door. Capri hears her cowboy boots clicking on the linoleum and her yelling, "Call security!"

In the hallway, the ward comes alive. Squeaky wheels stop and more footsteps clatter. Dinner trays clank. Capri can feel the undertow, shouting, banging, and metal keys. She smells the smoke of an uncontrollable fire.

She doesn't have much time.

"Jesus Christ!" Mac says. "Come on, Capri. Let's get out. Save ourselves!"

Before Capri can even pull Granddaddy's shirt over his head, a guy in a black uniform comes in and manhandles her.

"Leave me alone," Capri says, spitting the words. She doesn't let go of Granddaddy and clutches him tighter. Granddaddy begins to gurgle and moan. She stops and looks at him. His head bobbles and his eyes are popped. Horrified, her body shakes and she can't breathe. "Mac, don't just stand there," she says, but he does, and she looks at Granddaddy, with his open mouth and white face. "Granddaddy—"

He uses a voice she doesn't recognize. "Please, don't take her! Not again! Don't take her! Not my Little Girl!" He tries to get up, but the nurse is on top of him, pushing him down. Another nurse comes in and shoves Capri aside. She has a needle.

"Don't do that to him! Don't do it! Let him go!" Capri shouts, crying.

But she is no match for the guy in the uniform, and Mac is down the hallway.

"Granddaddy—" she yells as the uniform pulls her out of the room by her elbows, "I'll be back for you, don't worry, I'll be back!"

"John Mallory! Don't go!" Granddaddy is still trying to sit up, but they're already strapping him down. He's still shouting, "Don't go! Not to Costa Rica! Please! Stay in the sky! No! Not the baby!" The desperation in his voice dwindles but Capri can still hear him as she's drug down the hallway. "Come back! No! No!..."

"I'll be back," Capri shouts. "Don't you worry! I'll be back, Granddaddy! Don't worry! I won't leave you here! I won't leave you!"

15

Néctar de los Dioses

John Mallory was not that sort of woman. She could do all kinds of things—add curry to chicken, lace to linens, moral righteousness to a bridal party, but she could not play the role of Rapunzel in a locked tower. So the next morning when Lorenzo walked her to the fields and deposited her like an indentured servant with the pickers, with the secret syrup of a rendezvous with Machu still on her tongue, she just couldn't add okeydoke to her vocabulary.

That morning, she had created a makeshift do-rag from a paisley silk scarf. She wore leather hiking boots with socks and a sleeveless cotton shirt. But she had no intention of straining herself to the point of exhaustion again—her wrists and fingers, her forearms, her biceps, her shoulders, the meaty part of her legs, or the small of her back. Her body exploded with pain. Her mattress had been hard, unforgiving, and the row of bones along her spine had turned crimson and raw. Every nerve pinched like twisted wires. Even the muscles in the bottom of her feet ached, and her hair smelled like beans and rice, no matter how much she rinsed it.

She huffed and puffed, and dragged her cement feet. If she had wanted exercise, she fumed, she would have thrown down a rubber mat and practiced yoga.

As soon as Lorenzo sauntered away, John Mallory found Paco.

"There you are, my little friend," she said, with her toes turned in. Her finger crooked, and he plowed towards her like a puppy. "I have an idea. It'll be fun."

There were other ways to collect payment at *El Cielo Verde*. She would make it sound like a game instead of her begging him, but she knew she was whispering promises in his ear. "For every basket you pick for *me*, I will give *you* three coins." His eyebrows shot up. "I'll pick a basket, you pick one, and I'll pay you three coins."

"Three?"

"Yes, just a little extra for your piggy bank."

"Piggy bank?"

"A way to save," she said. "Your pretty pennies. It will be our little secret. Don't tell anyone. Not your grandmother. It will be *our* secret."

Paco had no way of knowing that when John Mallory added the word *fun* to *idea*, and then dropped in *secret*, she was brewing a troublesome stew. That's what she had told her best friend Julie Flanders when she convinced her to hide all the small swimsuits in her gym locker. Everyone, besides Julie and her, of course, would have to wear giant-sized swimwear during gym class. There they were, John Mallory and Julie, gliding in the water, doing their laps in slimming sizes, while all the other girls did frog legs clutching their straps so they wouldn't flash the boys. Coach Howard didn't find it funny, or a great idea, and stormed after Julie blowing her whistle at the side of the pool, yelling, "Get out, Flanders!" Why didn't she think John Mallory had anything to do with it? They always thought she was a goody two-shoes, with her head in books. Smart enough to outwit Coach Howard, she told Julie they couldn't prove a thing—Julie stayed mum—and they never did.

This would be the same kind of fun, but more enterprising. No one would be harmed. John Mallory told Paco, "It's my way of helping you earn those tickets to Los Angeles. It'll be a surprise. For your grandmother." She rubbed glossy leaves between her fingers. She squeezed her eyes into a smile. That was exactly the way she saw it—doing her part by playing Secret Santa. "Go Dodgers!" she said.

His eyes lit up. "*¡Gracias! ¡Sí, sí!*"

After she repositioned her do-rag and smoothed it down so it lay straight, she clarified their agreement. It was as harmless as a flashlight under the covers after bedtime.

"I will pick the first basket," she said, because that would be long enough to dirty her hands. "Then I will wait for you under the shade tree." A bit away from the others, who were chirping their Spanish songs, laughing again now that they were used to the American girl's presence. "After you pick the coffee, deliver the basket to me and I will pay you." Meanwhile, she would stay out of the sun. She'd close her eyes and mentally prepare to meet her *novio*. "Alrighty?" she said. She held out her hand. He gave her a puzzled look, so she took his wrist and slapped his palm against hers. "Alrighty."

He repeated, "Alrighty."

Besides fiscal lessons, she was teaching him American lingo and mannerisms. She had just taught him how to give five. She would try to think up more valuable lessons for the young man. This would be a fine experiment in multicultural relationships for both of them. She took her studies seriously.

"Let's get picking," she said and they raced towards the coffee trees.

After an hour, she found a soft spot to lie down. Broad leaves and branches kept the sun away like a Venetian blind. The wind blew fresh citrus and vanilla through the air. With her head pillowed against the trunk, John Mallory thought she'd practice her Spanish words, but the only ones she could recall were *amor* and *beso*. Love. Kiss. They rolled across her tongue with tenderness.

"John Mallory, I go see Fernando Valenzuela. Soon!"

Eager legs ran towards her. It took her a few seconds to remember where she was—the smell of earth and citrus, the mist of the rainforest, the smell of coffee cherries. Her boots had kept her from comfortably twisting her torso enough to feel rested. She stretched her arms. A few dried leaves fell from the tangles of her hair.

Before lunch, her burlap bag had miraculously filled with ripe red cherries. With just a peek inside, she turned them to gold. Balls and balls of red-hot achievement. Her skin blushed with satisfaction. After all, she and Paco were two enterprising entrepreneurs—a train going through the mountains, the first transatlantic flight across the ocean. She extended a hand to a deserving young man, someone who profited from her tutelage. Her father would be proud.

"Soon! I come to the United States. We see Fernando play baseball!"

"We're thriving business partners," she said as she rolled a cherry in the palm of her hand.

"A baseball game!" Paco reminded her, grinning. He held out his hand and waited for her to slap it. "God is good," he said.

Luckily, Juanita had willingly exchanged her American dollars for coins, and she had promised to convert more that afternoon. John Mallory dug into her pocket and handed him three more. Not ashamed, she didn't take his proclamation as a reminder to reflect on her sins, though she had certainly spent plenty of time inside a confessional. It was like dropping coins in the offering basket at church. She swelled with affection for the boy. "Paco, do you know where a girl can buy a new dress?"

"Dress?"

"Something with lace? Something pretty? *Bonita*. You know, where a girl can shop. I need to find a store. A dress store for *muchachas*."

He nodded. "Santa Pablo. In town."

"Can you tell me how to get there?"

She leaned closer while he drew a map in the dirt with a stick. It didn't look far. Maybe she could walk or hitch a ride. She'd be there and back before anyone noticed.

She heard Juanita's whistle. Lunch had arrived, and John Mallory was famished. With a little shade from the sun, and help from her friends, she could make her way in Costa Rica. It would be a wonderful story to tell, back home in Kansas City, at Sunday dinner. How she had started her own business. Her father would be proud that she knew how to delegate work that didn't require her personal attention.

As soon as she stood up and took Paco's hand, she erased the map with the toe of her boot, just in case no one else admired her business acumen. Another secret pushed into the land.

No happy smells puffed through the house when she snuck through the door—no chicken, no coffee, not even beans and rice. John Mallory's intentions were to grab her traveler's checks, change her shoes, and if Lorenzo or Juanita caught her, give them a good excuse why she needed to go to town. She'd already been in the field most of the day. Teaming up with Paco had proven to be a thriving and brilliant enterprise.

With each basket she carried to the truck, Machu had looked at her with his hungry eyes. Several times she thought he pointed to the forest with his chin.

"Will you be available at midnight?" he had asked her, finally, and winked.

"Maybe," she said, trying not to grin too big.

He leaned down and brushed her hand. "I won't be," he said, "because I will be watching the birds." He honked and covered his nose, then held the coin to his eye before dropping it in her basket. She laughed and plucked it out, tucking it into her cleavage.

But when John Mallory stumbled inside the Domingos' home, trying to look wounded from her day of picking, her emotional façade wilted. Lorenzo looked at her with tired, baggy eyes, but he didn't question her. He sat at the table with Bill McCracken and Juanita. So she excused herself for a moment to lie down and listened at the door of her bedroom. The crackerjack house left no room for surprises. She tried to interpret as best she could, even though they whispered.

"He sold the land," Lorenzo said. He didn't disguise the frustration in his voice, as if he'd been excluded from an important decision-making meeting. "He said he cannot undo it, there is nothing he can do. He said he needed money. *La cooperativa* is failing. It is management! Bad management! He should not have sugarcane at *beneficio*. If only he would give Machu *más* responsibility."

"It's a small slice of land," McCracken said.

"*¡Exactamente!* Small plus small equals big. Once it is gone to foreign hands, it is gone forever. I mean you no disrespect," Lorenzo said.

McCracken assured him he had not been offended. They discussed if he could get it back, if it would ever be possible. McCracken offered some ideas, including borrowing funds from him, but Lorenzo refused. His employer had been generous enough.

"It cannot be over," Lorenzo said, his voice full of frustration. "I worked hard, he promised. He breaks his word? Piece by piece. First my finger, next my legs. Then my eyes!" His voice shook.

"Lorenzo," Juanita said, "you cannot fault him if he needs money, because it is not good for you. You know he suffers. If it is done, it is done," she said. But she spoke with the preoccupation of a woman who wished she had something simmering on the stove. "*Pura vida*," she said.

"We cannot sell to him anymore. No more. We do not need *la cooperativa*. We sell to *beneficio*."

Juanita clucked her tongue. McCracken didn't make a sound.

John Mallory couldn't resist opening the door just a tiny crack. McCracken leaned again the wall, chewing on blade of something green. Lorenzo sat across from Juanita, his hat in his hands. He looked small, like a rag doll made of hay. His eyes were on the floor. Juanita looked placid, as certain as the moon rising in the fields.

McCracken said, "We already sell behind his back. He thinks we betray him. He knows. We must do what is right. Not because of spite. What is right."

"No! I won't!" Lorenzo's voice sounded more certain than the look in his eyes. He kept twirling his hat, a boy who had been pushed too many times by a bully. "This is right." He tapped on his heart.

"What about Machu? He suffers in the middle," Juanita said.

"*La tierra, la tierra.*" Lorenzo spoke of the land as if it were a lover. "I *must* stop the deforestation. It is my duty, what I promised to my father. I must."

Like so many words, John Mallory realized then that *la tierra* had many meanings here—land, ground, country, homeland, soil. Earth.

Lorenzo desperately wanted to save the earth.

Below the canopy, John Mallory walked among the crosshatch aromas of webs and shadows. Twigs and branches snapped beneath her sandals on the rainforest floor. A pair of coatis the size of raccoons tinkered ahead. Their bodies were loaves of cinnamon and brown. Their ringed tails stretched high in the air, flags that led to the riverbank.

The dial that night had been positioned just-right—not too many notches to the left, nowhere near the brittle bone-chills of a hard Kansas winter; nor flipped too many notches to the right and the blazing hiss-fire of a hot, humid summer. John Mallory turned around to make sure that no one had followed her. Even limber, it had taken considerable energy and muffled groans to wriggle through her tiny window. Turning back for the view at the end of her scope, she saw a scene by Grandma Moses—a little boxy cottage, big heady trees, the stars twinkling above, and a moon-filled night.

She shivered. Dressed in a thin long dress, the color of midnight, her hair was loose and woven with the scentless pink, purple, and magenta flowers of the bougainvillea vine. She smelled of lilac and honeysuckle, the faintest hint of heaven extracted from a vial she had tucked inside her suitcase.

With a tiny flashlight, she followed the darkness. She listened for sounds and sniffed the air. The toucan rustled, settled from the busyness of its day. Spider monkeys snuggled into balls. The spectacled owl's knocked notes rose and fell with a low *Whu—whu—whu-whu-whu,* until her step was underfoot, and then the threatened, low *Whoof-whoof, Whoof-whoof, Whoof-whoof-whoof* to warn the others. Night smells were different, with sharp tools in the air, the wakefulness of those invisible at daylight. With her head down, she hurried her pace, swinging her arms, making enough noise, she hoped, to frighten away the undesirables that might be watching.

She wound her way through the forest and came to the clearing where Machu had pointed. High above, she saw the platform. Endless stairs would take her up into the sky.

She hesitated, her foot on the bottom step. She knew he was there. Even surrounded by the pungent smells of the rainforest, his scent pulled her towards him.

"Come up," he said. He held a lantern. His head peeked over the lip of the platform. Then his full, round face came into view, encircled by the light of the moon.

It looked too high.

"Do you need help?"

"No," she said. She had spent her childhood climbing trees, mounting the weeping willow in her backyard at Rainbow Boulevard. She and her sisters were all climbers, but her eagle's nest had been the highest. Over the years, branches had been cut away, making it more difficult to scale. Near the end of her tomboy days, she had to shinny up the trunk. Even Trinka couldn't follow her then. John Mallory had always reached the top. Poked her head out of the bushy crown and watched the neighbors: Mrs. Johnson as she dangled beef jerky above her poodle's nose, desperately trying to teach the canine a worthy trick; Tim Brown as he washed his mother's station wagon; Mr. Newman, in knee-high black socks and slippers as he watered the lawn. She could see everything from the top of the tree.

"Come," he said.

His voice poked through the skin of her hesitation, pulling her up the stairs like a star into the sky.

"Just a little farther," he said, and then he helped her onto the platform. "I knew you'd come."

She whispered, "So did I."

The platform was large, the same size as their back porch at Rainbow Boulevard. Nothing but bare planks, it smelled musty and warm. Uncomfortable by the height, she stayed away from the edge.

"Look," he said, holding out the lantern, lighting up the open patches between the branches. A keyhole to the rainforest opened the night. "Look there."

A group of monkeys swung from the branches, chattering. No bigger than dachshunds, their limbs were slim and limber. Their tails curled and were as long as their bodies, each with a black spot. Mothers swung with babies on their backs. They had light brown fur, and John Mallory could see the outline of black triangles on their heads as they came closer. But as soon as they spotted her and Machu, their cream-colored faces contorted with expression, surprisingly human-like, screeching and grunting to one another. John Mallory stepped back.

Machu moved in front of her, blocking them from getting too close.

But she moved him aside, giving a nervous laugh. "I'm fine. It's just…" she hesitated, embarrassed to confess her limited life experience, "I'm used to seeing them in pillbox hats and little jackets. Dancing at carnivals."

He grinned. "They are white-faced capuchins. There are more babies, and fatter, healthier. That is good."

A brave monkey tiptoed along the handrail. Its tiny black hand held something. John Mallory forced herself to stand her ground. Close enough, the monkey launched a husky shell at them. She screamed as it landed at their feet, and the monkey scurried away.

Machu laughed and picked up the husk. "Here," he said, "a present."

She was thankful it wasn't dung. She brushed off her dress and then looked at him, puzzled. It was a pod, half-eaten. "I thought monkeys ate fruit and seeds. Maybe bugs." Her shoulders relaxed.

"They eat everything—lizards, eggs, flowers, even iguana. This is from a cacao tree. A small cluster growing nearby, by the river. More cacaos, more monkeys. That is good."

"Cacao?" she said, pronouncing it, *ca-cow*, like he did.

"You know cacao. It makes cocoa. Chocolate?"

"A chocolate tree!" Her eyebrows shot up. She grinned. "This *is* good! Take me to this cluster of chocolate trees."

He laughed, then mocked her with his eyebrows, shooting them up and down. Furrowed, his eyebrows formed a unibrow. John Mallory caught her gasp before it unmasked her panic. She couldn't help thinking about a line she remembered from a werewolf movie: *Beware of windfallen apples and of men whose eyebrows meet.*

Machu said, "Here inside." He showed her the broken center. "See. Monkeys break open the pods and eat the beans."

She sniffed the air. "Something wild and fowl. Their scents are raw and wet and I smell—"

"My father is right," he said, laughing. "You do have a special nose."

"Really? He said that? He probably meant like a dog." She blushed.

Machu comforted her by wrapping his arm around her waist. His chest reached her heart. Built strong, closer to the ground than her, their noses aligned if she bent one knee. In his arms she felt safe. His hands cupped the curve of her shoulder. His skin felt rough but warm and strong. She breathed deeply. This was his scent—the trees, the animals, the sky. He was the perfume above the canopy.

"The capuchin pees on its hands. Rubs its feet and fur to leave a scent. A trail. Even the babies. And if a baby is ever lost from its mother, the other monkeys bring it back. Using the baby's scent, following the trail. They eat the food of the gods."

"Chocolate is the food of the gods? I never knew God and I had similar tastes." She felt nervous and licked her lips.

"Chocolate was a drink before coffee." She shook her head; she hadn't known. "For Spanish royalty." He moved closer and squeezed her. "Like Cortez, I will introduce you to the *real* chocolate. Ground beans, with some chili peppers."

"Sugar and cinnamon," she said.

"*Theobroma* means food of the gods. Theo, God, and broma, food." He chuckled. "I am sorry, I don't mean to be conducting a history lesson." He lowered his arm. "I must be nervous, showing off. Would you like to see the trees?"

She smiled, taken back by his honesty. Most men would have rattled off facts with fiction, primarily interested in seeing how quickly they could strip her of her clothes. John

Mallory had expected a seduction, but Machu spoke of chocolate drinks.

"My father and I grow cacao for the monkeys, for the birds and mammals. So there are more. The forest used to be crowded with monkeys, birds, wild animals. So many species lost. Man took the land. Planted rice, corn, soybeans and other human food. Houses and hotels went up. The forest is disappearing..." He dropped the pod over the platform and they watched it fall to the forest floor. "Soon, the monkey took more energy to find food. Naturally they died out. Humans took less energy for food, and our population fattened. It has created imbalance in our planet."

They stood facing each other.

"The ozone hole," she said. "Temperature changes."

"Pollution, too." Machu nodded. "Diminishing rainforests."

"So the cacao helps?"

"To restore the natural forest. Conserve the ecosystem." He leaned over the platform again. "In a few days, that pod will rot. Maybe it will feed squirrel, paca or agouti. The capuchin will go to the ground and search the shell for fat, juicy maggots."

She couldn't help but notice the bulges in his arms. His passion for the rainforest was a potent aphrodisiac. Her legs began to shake. She smelled chocolate and could barely control herself.

"Your father used the word deforestation the other day. He spoke to a little man with a big mustache. They seemed to be arguing."

Machu frowned. Then he suddenly reached over and rubbed a lock of her hair between his fingers, as if he were sampling a fine bolt of fabric. Every fiber in her body tingled.

"My father is very committed."

She could see trust in his eyes. She watched them as they gazed out across the expanse of land and swept across the coffee trees and mountains.

"My grandfather owned many hectares of land, along the edge of the forest. Now the trees have been harvested. Sold for their wood. The animals have been chased away. My father's dream is to re-acquire the land. Re-create the forest. Populate it. Invite the animals to reclaim their home. He wants a corridor. Connect the land to larger tracts that have already been reclaimed as refuges. Save the wild animals, bring them back. Make this land an ecological haven."

Machu and his father made her feel unworthy. With their passion for saving the world, she suddenly felt like a foolish girl chasing pleasures between the sheets while others barred the door and beat back savages with swords and rocks.

"Why can't he just buy the land?"

He laughed. "No money. It doesn't spill from trees like mangos. My father owns land but not enough. For years we have been trying. Gustavo Navariz, I think he was the man you saw, he owns my grandfather's land. His father bought it years ago. But Gustavo Navariz is not savvy like his father. He bought *la cooperativa* without peeking inside. Snakes napped underneath rocks. He did not hire men with experience. That is why I went to University. Now, I am learning. I know the land. Coffee. But if Gustavo does not pay the farmers, he will lose them—he will go bankrupt."

"Is that why he sold the land?"

"Sold what land?" Machu wrinkled his forehead into a unibrow again.

"I think I heard them talking about someone selling land. You father was in the house with your mother and Bill McCracken. He seemed very upset. Something about someone buying his land."

"Possibly a foreigner..." Worry lines deepened on his face.

"Yes, that's what he said. Who?"

"I don't know," he said. "My father didn't tell me yet. Many foreigners come to Costa Rica. They buy land. To them it is cheap and rich." He scratched his head, as if searching for a seven-letter word for a crossword puzzle. "A bargain."

"I wish I could help." Suddenly, her dreams felt small, skipping through the rainforest, picking wildflowers, and sunning on the beach. Child's play. When had her sandbox become so littered? "How much do you need? Maybe I could speak with some people—"

"No, my father would not hear of it, nor would I. Even if you could, he is proud. We will find a way for his corridor. We will bring back the animals. The earth."

Monkeys, birds, the idea warmed her. She watched the primates again with newfound love. In a branch nearby, a mother cooed at her baby. Others nibbled leaves. She wanted to be someone who could protect them, too.

Cool winds hinted of other hideaways—a three-toed sloth nursed her young, ready for another nap; cattle egrets lurked in the leaves, like pale ghosts; an anteater fished out termites with a sticky tongue; a family of leaf-cutter ants carried crescent leaves on their shoulders.

"Baird's tapir, like the one you saw at the river, there used to be thousands of them, now only a handful. Hundreds of birds' shelters have been destroyed, their bloodlines lost. Insects, butterflies, a habitat for sloths, toucans, frogs and snakes. We need ecological resources."

"I wish I had such bold dreams, such passion." She bit her lip.

"Yes, passion," he said and stood so close she was afraid he would smell the longing on her breath. She smiled, and he tucked her hair behind her ear. Then she moved to the ledge. "My father, he dreams of the jaguar. He lures them here."

"Jaguars? Like the big cat?" John Mallory sucked in her breath. She knew then. That was what she had smelled—an enormous cat, a spotted feline, the hungry beast. Had their eyes seen her? A creature that could sniff the surface for the softness of a footprint, to them her soles must reek of wild game.

"Can we see your trees now?" she said, feeling a shiver go down her spine.

Before he could answer, she had started for the steps.

On the rainforest floor, hand in hand, he led her to the grove of wild cacao trees. At times, she felt he pulled her too hard. Other times, she almost ran over him, bumping him, her chest pressing into his shoulder blades. Just the touch of his back made her skin tingle, her body ache. She tried to fight her uncontrollable desire, but she felt as if she were drowning. Engulfed, she struggled for air. She became dizzy with the incense of after-midnight.

Bristled by the brush of their thighs, the coffee cherries grew shiny and slick. Monkeys swung high from the branches, following them. Shadows shifted, and the forest filled with shrieking cries. Succulence of balm left the slightest trace of vanilla raindrops in the air.

Through a grove of coffee trees, almost there, her dress caught on a branch. With his eyes focused, she knew he intended to release her quickly. He gave her dress a few gentle tugs. But it held, stubborn and tangled. He tugged a bit more, and his fingers brushed her skin like an unexpected caress. Faster, his fingers worked the fabric, until her dress lifted and gave way. Maybe it was the coffee cherries that blew the breeze between her legs, like cool sweet kisses. Her toes curled in her sandals. Freed, she meant to hold her breath but instead sighed.

Still stumbling along the roots and shadows, she knew that yearning had a mixed bouquet—cinnamon balls dropped in rich dark chocolate, a white rose in the bitter frost. But everything seemed surreal. Magnified. Her senses were overloaded. Had she fallen onto the pages of *National Geographic*, or wandered upon heaven? Nothing felt within her control. Her head screamed of danger, while the heart of her nose breathed scents of home.

"Here," he said. "See." He turned up the lantern.

Next to the river, they came to a cluster of cacao trees, sisters of the coffee.

"A healthy cacao tree has pods," he said as he pointed to the cushion on the trunk of the tree. "They come from the flower." Like coffee, turning from green to gold, the pods changed color as they ripened. The fruits were brownish-yellow and purple, the color of wheat and animal flesh. "In my country a cacao tree can flower and grow all year long," he said, avoiding her eyes.

"Evergreen," she said. "Flowering chocolate." She caught her breath and stepped closer. She touched the skin of the pod. Oval-shaped shells, they were about the size of her hand.

"Harvesting the cacao tree requires hand-picking." He touched the pod. "With sharp knives, machetes. The pods are split by hand and the beans removed."

In the distance, they could hear the chatter of the monkeys. Her senses were being overloaded. Her heart raced.

"How many seeds?" she asked, moving closer. She held the same pod that he held.

"Twenty to sixty."

She said, softly, rubbing his fingers, "Do you pick chocolate?"

His voice softened. He blinked slowly. "No. Sustainable cacao helps chocolate manufacturers. But it will also conserve the ecosystems of our tropical rainforest." His breath had become shallow. His fingers gripped the flesh of the pod. "Our small orchard is in the rainforest to allow pollination," he said and leaned in to her. His pupils had grown large. His breath smelled of chocolate, coming in short gasps of air. "Its purpose is for containment of diseases and insects without chemical fertilization." Then he whispered, "We have already reaped considerable harvests."

"So you do harvest chocolate," she said. She leaned forward so that her lips brushed his. They were soft and sweet. She tasted moonlight.

He could barely whisper, "We harvest little. Most is left to increase biodiversity."

She brushed his lips again, light and longing. She pressed into his shoulder. With the weight of his grip shifted to the pod, it tore from the branch.

"How clumsy," he said, suddenly bumbling and shy. He averted his eyes. "See the seeds." With some difficulty, he pulled it open, then bedded his fingers deep into the pulp. "Let me show you."

But she didn't wait. She cupped his hand, then pulled his fingers from the flesh. They were covered in pink. She held them to her lips and breathed deeply—the sweet pulp of earth, soil, cacao, coffee, and his skin.

"Twenty pods make twenty pounds of cocoa. No. Two pounds."

She still held his fingers. "Sweet and sour," she said.

"Juicy," he said, his chest rising, his eyes were half open. He cleared his throat and backed away, holding the pod tightly again. He forced open the husky shell, then plucked out the marshmallow nest and dropped the husk. He unwrapped it slowly to show her the bean.

"Ah, the bean," she said.

He delicately stripped the thin skin that touched the fruit, then let it flutter away. "No, this is the bean."

She nodded.

"They are fermented in a box," he whispered. His hands had moved to her hips. "And dried in the sun." His lips were trembling and his fingers twitched. Sweat beaded on his top lip.

"Then the beans are roasted?" she said. "Like coffee?"

"Yes," he said. "And the higher the temperature, the more bitter the chocolate." He watched her lips. "The roasted bean is ground to produce the powder and cocoa liquor." He nibbled her top lip, speaking softly. "Beans are pressed to extract the cocoa butter, for cosmetics and lotions, to make skin soft," he said, touching her cheek. As if unable to stop, his lips lightly moved down her neck. "They're pressed back in with the ground cocoa for chocolate."

She wrapped her fingers in his belt loops and smelled the darkness of the sky in his hair.

"Pure chocolate liquor is molded into blocks and sold as unsweetened baking chocolate. Sweeter chocolates have extra cocoa butter and sugar." He moved closely to her lips again.

"Milk and vanilla," she said.

"White chocolate."

Her head rolled back and her breath became uneven. A deep sound came from his throat, unbridled joy, as if the moon had just realized the brilliance of the stars.

A monkey screeched and he pulled back, then laughed.

"The capuchins have babies year-round now," he said. "Something all primates are capable of when they're healthy. But," he said and leaned over as if he held a secret, "we must watch the cacao trees for disease—black pod, witches' broom, frosty pod."

His fingers touched the thinness of her dress. She touched his chest. Heavy work had left bulges and cleavage. He smelled of pine, of dark rich chocolate, of danger hidden inside the rainforest.

"Tell me," she said, "how do you protect the trees?"

He looked in her eyes. "We remove diseased material, but mostly with shade and pruning."

Midnight fell like manna. Eyes opened wide from the bushes. A beam of light nestled on the river, a sparkling path for thirsty animals. A brief blue star had lit up the sky. *Come*, it said, *for a nice, long drink from the waters.*

"Shade," she whispered, pressing into him, breathing him in. "Yes, shade."

16

Amor

With his namesake in Costa Rica, John Mallory, Sr's days had become wintery and full of shadows. He even tried adding half and half to his black coffee, but he only succeeded in creating a milky broth of disillusionment, more water than cream. He set down his cup.

He was not in a grocery aisle watching Mrs. Shopper scramble for his goods for her grocery cart, or in the lobby of a big-box chain waiting to see the buyer. His corner office didn't have red lights blinking on his telephone. To his disgruntlement, his life had not led him to a seat on a velvety cushion in a theatre chair, the man with money behind the famous director of a big-hit movie. Matter of fact, his name would never be generated for the invite list for much of anything, except *Romancing the Stone*, a new film opening at the Glenwood Theatres. Always a bit closer to a cornfield than a coronation, he pitched the flyer for the opening at the trashcan—and missed. Then he scowled with petulance.

"Isn't there anything you need?" he asked.

"No," John Mallory answered. "I'm good." But the phone crackled.

His seventh daughter sounded galaxies away.

His leather chair squeaked as he pushed his elbows onto his desk. Crowded with papers, the nudge started a cacophony of collisions—coffee cup spilled, tape dispenser tipped to its side, notepad slapped to the ground. A black and white photo fluttered away like singe from a fire and landed in an open box of coffee stacked in the corner. Above, a map hung on the wall. A pincushion in a general's tent, it was crowded with little balls of strategy—green for current distribution, yellow for prospects, and red for competitor holds.

Abigail appeared in his doorway. "It's time, Daddy. The leadership meeting." Tucked into a crimson blouse, with her lips puckered and her elbow cocked to look at her watch, she looked like a sour coffee cherry dangling from a vine. He glanced sideways at her, then hugged the phone tighter and plugged his other ear with his finger.

For days, he had tried to reach John Mallory. Only the seventh time he had spoken to her since she left three weeks ago, his voice cracked with desperation.

"Nothing? There's nothing you need?" *Tell me, John Mallory. Do they keep you warm? Do you get enough to eat? Was I right to send you away?*

"Nopes. Can't think of anything off-hand," she said.

Unusual, she didn't complain about her useless hair dryer or the lack of fresh laundry. There were no shopping malls, not even a Macy's around the corner.

"Tell me what you're learning. How's it going with Lorenzo Domingo? I've heard he really knows his stuff."

"He does, he knows his stuff." She paused.

What did that mean?

"I'm still picking," she said, "in the fields a lot."

"Picking? With the workers?" For three weeks? He flipped open the jewelry box where he kept his gold pen. Then he fumbled with a notepad. Out of the corner of his eye, he noticed Abigail leaning against his doorframe. So he stood up, and kicked shut the door with his boot.

"Yes. Lorenzo thinks it will help me develop a better understanding of what it takes to make a cup of coffee. He thinks it'll make me a better Roastmaster. To work as a picker." She sniffled.

"Do you have a cold?"

"No, I feel good."

"Well, I suppose. But for how long?" He didn't pay all that money for her to be one of the employees, join the rank and file. In a foreign country no less. She was John Mallory! Before long, they'd have her washing the dishes, if there were any dishes. My God, they would have her steal a loaf of bread just to fill her belly. Incarcerated in Costa Rica! Slimy walls, probably no more than a spit for a window, nothing but dark holes. His ears rang, rattled by the clatter of tin cups dragged across bars. It almost made him wretch.

"I don't know, he doesn't say," she said.

He would have a word with Lorenzo Domingo. Shake that man like a dog shakes a rat. He scribbled Lorenzo's name on the pad. After all, how long did someone need to pick in the fields—like a common worker!—before she understood the labor it took to produce coffee? Pick, pick, pick. Yes, it was understood. Inherent even! John knew that much, even if he hadn't ever picked more than a few cherries one time when he vacationed in Hawaii. Third world countries were no place for people like his Little Girl. My God! What was he thinking? Sending his baby, his namesake, to a prison in a third world country.

Furiously, he drew crossbars over Lorenzo's name on the notepad. "Odd apprenticeship if you ask me."

"Lorenzo," she said, "thinks differently. I'm sure he knows best."

"You don't say." It was alarming to hear her question his authority as a businessman, much less his wisdom as a father. Lorenzo was nothing but a third world thinker. Dead beat. What did he know? Besides, John had slapped the tar out of bigger tigers. Just yesterday, the idiot from the Cadillac dealer, last week the driver that literally backed into the warehouse, and then the advertising guy who wasn't qualified to empty his trashcan. They all knew—all his girls knew—when they needed Big Guns, they called Daddy. "Don't worry, sugar, I'll handle it. I'll make a call."

"No, Daddy! I'm fine. Don't call." Her voice raised several octaves and then dropped to a whisper. "Please. I want to show you that I can take care of myself."

For all he knew, she could be shaking underneath a table. My God! She probably had to hide in some dirty closet just to speak with her father.

But her voice softened and pleaded. "It'll look like I can't handle things myself. And I'm doing fine." Then she added, "Just fine on my own." This time, he heard the scrape of indignity.

He dropped his pen and sighed. "I thought he'd show you the operations, help you develop your palette."

"We do that, we do." She sounded nervous now, a little too eager. "Every day I cup with Lorenzo in the cantina. After picking. I only pick in the mornings."

"And McCracken? How's he? You getting along?"

"Haven't seen him much. It's harvest and he's really busy—"

"Oh, honey." Another red flag, a perpetual snorting bull kicking up dust. "What about Sister…What's her name?"

"Juanita. Daddy, I'm fine." She almost cried. "Let me take care of myself."

A large slab of sun sliced through the wooden plats into his office. It separated, making prison bars on top of his desk. He rose to peer into the sky. Filled with brilliant orange and red, sprinkles of blue where the stars belonged, he couldn't help but notice the shredded clouds, like bloody bandages that hung in the emptiness where the sun was melting. Dusk slithered from the southern skies. Darkness fell upon the trees. The only constellation for miles was the newspaper, *The Kansas City Star* that lay crumbled on his floor. He watched the sky emptying in front of his eyes.

Tell me I was right, John Mallory. Tell me they treat you well. Tell me that you're becoming everything we dreamed of.

He said, "Let me send you blankets and a box of detergent. How about some of the new scented Kleenex? They have a bundle pack now."

"Daddy, it's hot here. I'm good, really, I'm good."

But he thought she sounded sad. Did she feel she couldn't confide in him? Did she need his help? Had he pushed her too hard? He heard a soft knock on his door but ignored it. He said, "It must feel like the end of the world there."

"It does," she said, "and I never knew." Her voice fluttered. "Truly, Daddy, this is one of the smartest things I've ever done. I'm glad you insisted."

No longer certain whether her voice was sincere or mocking, he couldn't help feeling conflicted. Earlier, those were the words he had hoped to hear—but now they sent tremors through his veins. Not a microwave oven in sight, no newspaper delivered to her door, no padded coat hangers for her clothes. Creatures lurked in every shadow.

"I know you don't need coffee," he said and tried to force a laugh. "Should I send candy? Maybe something from Laura's Fudge Shoppe?"

She laughed, sounding like she was at the brink of hysteria.

"What is it, honey? Are you all right?" He fumbled on his desk, jerky but quick, with his pen in hand, ready to write.

"Nothing," she said, her voice full of gasps. "Believe me, you do not need to send me chocolate."

But he could no longer tell if the shrill in her voice reflected glee or destitution. So he sat at the desk with his head in his hands. His eyes dug into space, frozen between the distant silence on the other end of the phone and the flat shadows on the wall. As his eyelids drooped, the darkening skies tap danced cherries and chocolate drops on the black side of his head.

17

Comprensión

For many weeks now, Lorenzo had intended to show John Mallory *la cooperativa*. However, it seemed impossible to avoid Machu, so he kept her in the fields. He had already reassigned another man to oversee the coins, much to Machu's resistance—his great lumbering way of contesting his father, making excuses why *he* should drive the truck—"Carlos has a lazy eye!"—why he should oversee payment of the coins—"Carlos is terrible at math!"

"He only needs to count to one," Lorenzo had told him.

"But the people don't respect Carlos," said Machu without making eye contact. This time they were on the docks at *la cooperativa*. They both kept their voices down so the farmers wouldn't hear.

"And that is why you must be at *la cooperativa*. They respect you." Besides that, Lorenzo had made a decision, and it was his custom to stick to it. "Tulipán will help him." He also hoped that if Tulipán Navariz laid her eyes on the American girl, then she would recognize the dangers of the competition. Certainly women had a primal instinct for that, even if she was only fifteen.

Again that evening, Lorenzo worked with John Mallory at the open cantina, cupping, teaching her. With a slight breeze, the sky darkened but the stars were brilliant blue, and the early moon bulged with orange like a wagon wheel that rolled across the heavens. Again, he sighed. Most of the time he couldn't help but treat John Mallory as if she were acid rain ready to drop on his rainforest. He had little faith that she would understand Mother Bean.

"Coffee is lovely," John Mallory said, standing at the table, staring at the cherries and beans he had laid out so he could show her the differences in their structures—too young, too old, moldy and diseased. Rows of roasted beans wobbled in front of red and golden cherries. Porcelain cups were filled with coffee, crusted and unbroken. Steam rose to the whittled ceiling and then spilled over the edge. A torrential bath of freshness filled the mountain air.

"Yes," he said, "please, *ahora,* pay attention." He picked up a bean still skinned in parchment. "You see the thick skin. It protects the bean. The parchment is one of four layers. It keeps the bean safe. Safe so it can develop. Much like our skin."

A motmot landed on the table. A blue morpho butterfly lay motionless upside down in its beak. Black masked, the bird's blue feathers were greased back in a hood. He tried not to acknowledge the creature's presence, but she reached for it as if she could save the butterfly. Lorenzo waited until the bird fluttered back into the shadows before he continued.

"As our skin keeps our bones, our blood inside—" he said.

"And our heart."

He nodded. "Yes, it keeps our heart, *también.* See. The skin is tough." He held up the bean and scratched at the skin.

"That's the outer skin that it shows the world."

"Yes. It helps create the bean," he said.

"It manifests?"

He cocked his head, unsure of the definition. "Ah, yes. It shows the desire of the bean."

"Desire. Of course. The desire to *be.* Yes, I see." She took the bean and rolled it in her fingers and then sniffed it.

"It's a co-creative dance, isn't it? The natural dance of attraction. Of desire. Of creation."

Her eyes were brilliant blue and offset her skin, which had turned bronze from the sunshine. More freckles had sprung up across her nose and cheeks. Still, her constant whiffing disturbed the placidity of his lecture from the pulpit. Annoyed, he snatched the bean from her.

He said, "After it is soaked, it is fermented. Then the bean is dried in the sun. The parchment goes away—"

"It sloughs off and there is another skin."

"Yes. Slough off, yes. Look at this," he said, trying to recover his composure. He held up another bean in the light. The silver skin flecked like mother of pearl. "Nothing but paper."

"Another barrier. It is paper-thin. Then, finally, the true bean. It's love," she said.

"Yes, the bean—" But he craned his neck, then popped his jaw.

"I do understand," she said. "I understand everything. Of course the bean is love. It's how we were created—whole! There are four layers of protection for the bean." She counted with her fingers. "The outer skin, the pulp, the parchment and the silver skin. The outer skin is only what we see—a longing, a feeling for desire. It's a penny tossed in a wishing well, a formal request. Passion manifests in many ways, but it's critical to pick the bean at the right time, or it may be too young, all romance, amour, but an empty craving, as if chocolate could satisfy hunger long-term. It can't." She laughed. "Or too old and withered, multiplications of random cells that inadvertently create cancer. You can't wait too long, either!"

He looked away, but she kept prattling on.

"It's not their fault," she said. "It's the manifestation of desire. The outer skin is only important in that it reflects the possible given temperament of the bean inside. The conditions upon which the bean reflects its truth. And that can be confusing."

"Color tells you," he said. "Shape and size—"

"For the bean," she said. "Unlike most things in the world that aren't so easy to quantify." Again she laughed. "Color, size, beauty. It's just skin deep."

"Yes, that is true." He wondered if they were still talking about coffee. They both studied the beans in silence for a time.

A rare scarlet macaw poked out of its nest hole. Restless toucans gathered in a tree above the tiny ruby orchids that sprouted from the ground. The sky bloomed with enough light so that from where they stood they could see the rows of coffee trees, plumbed and sculpted, like spit-groomed children, perky and ready for the coolness of midnight.

John Mallory said, "And then there is pulp, another protection. It reflects appetite, maybe lust, a sigh for *being*." She twirled a strand of her hair and scratched one foot with the other one. With her shoes kicked off, her feet were broad but bony, her toenails painted red, like coffee cherries sprouting from branches of bones. "I understand."

He had never thought of pulp that way. Unclear if he understood her, he brushed off the table.

He said, "*Todos*, everything to create the bean. When the bean soaks, the good beans are separated from the bad. Floaters are removed. *El mejor,* the best beans sink because they are denser." He narrowed his eyes on the strange girl. It would have been better to show her this process at *la cooperativa*. She may have been less distracted.

"Of course! That makes perfect sense!" She stared over his shoulder into the distance. "Don't the trees look lovely in their velvety dresses..."

He hated it when she gushed about Mother Bean.

Hoping to distract her, he picked up a silver spoon and dropped it on the table. Her head turned to follow the clanking. He didn't want her complimenting the beans.

Already they were ruffling their branches and fanning their faces, blushing like shameless hussies.

He said, "Worms feed on the drained *agua* of the pulped bean. After they are fermented. The worms digest the liquid. They process it. Their refuse is our compost." He thought the beans had somewhat deflated. His shoulders sank. He never meant to insult them.

"Worms? Where? May I see them?" she said. Her eyes glowed. "That's so ecological."

He sighed. "Yes," he said. "You will see the worms."

She jumped up and down, then hugged him.

Lorenzo lowered his head and pressed his broad hands on the table. The breeze from the mountains blew his hair over his eyes. He had to move it so he could see her. A silhouette in the moonlight, she appeared fuzzy and white against the background of darkening green. She looked like an angel. Smaller than he realized, her eyes were childlike, full of questions and light, and his heart suddenly skipped a beat with softness. He couldn't help but feel unexpected compassion for this girl so far from her home. She never cried. She was good to his wife. He had never seen Juanita and Machu so happy. Humbled, he turned away.

"And the beans? Where do they go next?" she asked.

"The beans dry in the sun," he said and picked up one. He cupped it in his palm and then held it to his heart. With his fist, he tapped his chest three times. Warmth moved inside him.

"Are they still in the parchment?"

"Yes. Until the drying."

"The parchment is true yearning. Desire. The tough layer of pining."

Unsure about what she meant, he said, "It is not *difícil* to slough off."

"Yes, so easily." She smiled. "And then the silver skin."

Her eyes fluttered with promise, the green of the coffee trees, the blue of the sky—and he was the motmot that fed on the butterfly. Ashamed, he lowered his eyes.

"So if parchment is desire," she said, "or pleasure derived from outside oneself, is the silver skin unconditional love? Or is it truth?"

He shook his head. She spoke too fast. "It is paper-thin."

A misty fog-bow arched over the cantina, a luster of frosty breath in the night. He began to clean up, stacking cups and tossing coffee beans onto a wooden platter.

"So desire can bury love—or release it. Tenderness, caress, lover and flame. Love is never empty,"—she laughed—"or it shouldn't be. I do understand! Certainly love can be based on sexual desire, but love is unselfish, loyal, unconditional. Love is more than passion, even devotion. And the skin—"

She seemed to have stopped in mid-thought, but he couldn't really tell. She rolled up the tablecloth. Her fingers and hands were as small as a child's.

"The bean..." He held up a perfectly-shaped coffee bean, intending to redirect her attention. But then he forgot what he had meant to say.

"Yes! The bean is derived from within. It is joy!" She had stopped, unable to roll the tablecloth any further with his tray of cups and beans blocking her path. "It's whole perfection!"

"It is as it is," he said and lifted the tray. "*Pura vida.*"

"*¡Pura vida!* Exactly!" Then she rolled up the linen into a tight cylinder, past the empty spot where his tray had laid, just as darkness swept through the sky and the owls hooted from the branches, and the edge of forest turned to black.

"I smell your jaguar," she said. "You must be excited. Honestly," she said, and blushed, her hand covering her mouth, "I'm overwhelmed by what you're trying to do, and honored to be associated with your efforts. Even if in the smallest way. Thank you for caring."

Lorenzo looked at her. Maybe he hadn't noticed before how delicate and round she was—yes, soft from lack of work and milk toast feedings. But he could see that muscles were forming, growing like slumbering turtles in her calves and biceps, and her fingers were polished with the stain of soil. Her white dress, completely inappropriate for picking, hung down to her ankles with smudges of brown and red from the juice of the cherries. Her thick hair had been gathered in sparse knots by combs on top of her head. He knew his wife had glued the stones to those combs for her last week and pushed them into her hair that morning while he ate his breakfast. Birdlike arms, but strong, bare to the shoulders, he could see they were getting stronger. She fumbled with the tablecloth, like a child rolling her siesta blanket. Her heart-shaped face had no creases and looked at him with openness. She saw everything as if she were seeing it for the first time.

Deep in her eyes, he saw innocence, delight for things he had taken for granted long ago. If she knew fear, she never showed it, and that may have caused him to pretend that it did not exist for her. Her life had completely changed, overnight, and still she smiled. Without complaint she had helped his wife at their home. And even though he had never admitted it, and pretended to be preoccupied with cleaning his boots or sharpening his knife, he rushed home, looking forward to her silly stories: about the pickers' lives, Julia and her lazy husband, about Paco and his love for American baseball, stories about her experiences of people in his county, even her stories about those crazy peacocks with eyes in their feathers.

Through her eyes, he saw his land, his people, and even himself through her kaleidoscope glass.

He turned away.

With a skip, she headed towards the stairs.

He hurried to follow, almost dropping the cups. With one hand, he gripped the railing, balancing the tray in the other. Her whiteness floated down the path like mist over the mountains. The cloth bounced over her shoulder. The hair his wife had so lovingly bound waterfalled down her back. She looked back and laughed, a magical sound, waving her hand for him to catch up.

He couldn't help but trot, following the haze of sugar in the air, knowing that dawn would not be lonely as she padded across the floor in his home. He knew he had lured more than the jaguar to his land.

18

Locked

Everything's white and chilly when the cowgirl nurse stomps towards Capri in her rhinestone boots, like she's ready to kick some butt. She reaches behind her belt like she might take out a whip or gun, but Capri doesn't back down.

"Where's my granddaddy?" she asks.

"You just saw him," the nurse answers, then pulls on her cluster of keys on the string. They jingle and jangle, a mess of gold and silver. She studies them and picks one.

"No, I mean *where is he?*"

The lock clicks and the nurse pulls open the door and signals for Capri to go. Mac appears out of nowhere, a rush of wind blowing past her. He darts out like a cat escaping from the house. He's down the hallway and around the corner before Capri can even step one foot outside the Adult Ward.

"That's not my granddaddy," Capri says. "That's not him. I'm telling you, that's not him." Her body trembles. It takes everything she has to not cry. "Where is he?"

The nurse sighs, then gives Capri a dewy look, like she wants to reach over and pet her. She pats her shoulder. "Go home, honey," she says.

Capri looks at her and the guy in the uniform shadowing behind her. His thumbs are tucked into his belt, and he leans in as if he's ready to grab Capri, but then his face softens, too, as if he might say something, like maybe he knows where her granddaddy is. She waits, but then he closes his mouth and gives her a little smile.

With a clogged nose, she can't read faces any more. It's cold in the hallway and she shivers, wishing she had a Kleenex with aloe vera lotion.

"Where does he go?" Capri tries to keep her lips and voice from giving her away. "Where does he go when his mind is gone?" she asks the nurse, as if this cowgirl holds the keys that unlocks all the doors. "Just please, tell me that."

The nurse's shoulders relax and her lips go slack. "I don't know, honey. I just don't know." Then she turns and calls to the woman at the counter, saying, "Elizabeth?" She stomps over to her in her cowgirl boots. She says something to Elizabeth that Capri can't hear, and she hands Cowgirl something across the desk. They're slips of paper. She comes back and hands some of them to Capri.

Capri figures they're business cards for social workers, maybe a phone number for a hotline. Join a support group. Be with others like her. She gets her message. *Let someone help you, get it out, don't hold it in. It's not good for you.*

The uniform still stands too close, but he has a sad look now.

Capri shuffles the slips of paper. They're all the same.

Coupons.

Seems they aren't even trying to throw her out of the psychiatric center, at least not any more. She looks at the nurse. Cowgirl gives her a look like she's seen it all, and she feels for her. She shoves a couple more coupons in her hand. Capri studies them. They're for complimentary meals in the cafeteria. Then she gently nudges Capri out the door. For the umpteenth time that night, Capri hears the click of locks and it makes her jump. She spins around and looks back through the window—she wants to ask to see him one more time, just for a little bit, she won't cause any more trouble—but they're gone.

A zombie, she trudges down the hallway and follows her nose.

She pokes her head in the room with the smells. It's a buffet, and she thinks she smells roasted pig. So she pretends she's back at Luby's Cafeteria, with Granddaddy, which makes her happy, then sad, because she knows she's not. Granddaddy really loves his coupons, especially when they mean a free lunch. It makes her laugh, but tears come to her eyes.

There are other people eating, so she takes a tray and starts gathering bowls and plates of food like there's no tomorrow, roast beef and mashed potatoes, Granddaddy's favorites. They have brown and white gravy. There are green beans and fruit cups. She takes three rolls and two tiny cartons of milk. There aren't any desserts, but she doesn't mind. Loaded down, she can't believe the cashier accepts the coupon, and Capri has a bunch more stashed in her pocket. Her granddaddy really would have gotten a kick out of that. So she gets two cups of coffee and wanders to a table, but as soon as she sits down, her lips start quivering and the only thing she can do is bury her face in her hands.

Before long, a guy sits next to her, and then a couple more across from her. They're Capri's age, and they have trays of food. They give each other sympathetic smiles.

No one should have to be here. None of them choose it. None of them know how to end this nightmare. Granddads, Grandmas, Moms and Dads locked up. People they love. It makes them feel handcuffed and helpless. She knows.

She takes a bite of mashed potatoes and smiles at her dinner mates.

Capri has no idea what to do next. Those nurses will never let her back into the ward, and she doubts she can break in. Maybe she can climb through a window. Maybe she can pull a fire alarm, and when they evacuate, she'll wrangle Granddaddy away from them. Those nurses don't look that strong, except Cowgirl with her superhuman strength. They probably won't even notice, not with dozens of patients to wheelchair and capture. They won't notice one tiny man missing from the firing line. If she's quick, they won't even have the chance to call in the uniforms.

Granddaddy looked so small, itsy-bitsy, broken in his bed.

Where did his mind go? Where does *he* go when he's not with it?

He didn't make a very convincing sun. She should have told him that.

Capri pounds the table and the guys startle. She gives them a weak smile.

What did he see with those dark eyes? He thought she was John Mallory? He knows. He knows Capri is her daughter. He said something about the baby. Now she knows for sure that she is John Mallory's baby. And he says she's not dead. What if she isn't? Didn't her mom say that, too? What if they took her from her real mother, but she's still alive? He says John Mallory's alive. Granddaddy says her mother is alive.

She was born in Costa Rica. That's why her mom had to get a new birth certificate. She made up that phony story about her dad leaving and St. Mary's hospital burning down. Capri's real mother and father are alive, in Costa Rica. She belongs in Costa Rica.

She looks up and sees Mac in the doorway, beating dust off his black jeans. His eyes dart around the room. His cuckoo clock expression makes him look like a patient. When he sees Capri, he pushes out his chest so everyone can see the Visitor badge, and then he swaggers over, like he's a business executive who wants to discuss her insurance needs, or more likely, her boss who wants to talk about her poor performance on the job. From the look on his face, she has a feeling she's already well into the high-risk zone and a thirty-day probation period.

"There you are," he says with an exasperated sigh. "This is ridiculous, Capri."

When she doesn't answer, he keeps going.

"There are a lot of creepy things behind doors in this joint." His knees jiggle like they do when he gets nervous.

She looks at him but doesn't say a word. Her head swims with questions, tick-tocks away, trying to solve the puzzle. She stares at her spoon, wondering if she can use it to break Granddaddy out of the psychiatric block.

"Let's get out of here," he says. "This place gives me the creeps." He runs his fingers through his hair and then looks at the guys at her table. "Shit," he says, and starts to back up slowly. "What happens, you see, is we leave real quiet. No, don't look. Don't make a move. No quick moves. Just stand up quietly and follow me."

"Just give me a minute."

"Listen," he says, leaning over to whisper in her ear, "if I don't put on a suit and tie the guys in white jackets may mistake me for one of them." He uses his chin to point to the guys Capri's sitting with.

She lifts her head and looks at them. Then she looks around. The room is full of teenagers, all in different stages of disarray, in pajamas and sweats, their hair unbrushed, some of them with eyes that are too bright. Some of them stare into space, some talk to themselves. Some of them look like they could be her friends. All of them look small and lost, like baby polar bears floating away from the shore on blocks of blue ice.

"I'm out of here," Mac says and makes a dash for the door.

Capri tries to follow him, but it's as if she's frozen. She keeps sitting there, going through what her granddaddy said, eating her mashed potatoes. Could John Mallory be alive? Is that another one of the big secrets? And if she's alive, and Capri's her daughter, why isn't she with her? She is *her* daughter! Then it sinks in. Her mother is alive! Her father may be alive! She should be living with them in Costa Rica. They've probably been wondering what's taken her so long.

But Capri can't move. She belongs here. She belongs at this table. If her granddaddy is staying, then she is, too.

The guy across from her dips his spoon in her mashed potatoes. He offers her some, but she shakes her head. He reminds Capri of a kid at her school, James something. The kid was always doing drugs. Half the time he fell asleep in class. But half the kids at her school were on something, either drinking or drugging. Too often she gagged on the smell of marijuana leaking from the locker rooms.

It is creepy; these kids are her age. Who put them here? And how do they get out?

She thinks about her granddaddy again. She'll break him out, and they'll go to Costa Rica. Together. He'll have his seventh daughter, and Capri will have her mother, her real mother.

She'll forgive him. Then she realizes that she's already forgiven Granddaddy. He didn't know what he was doing. No, he shouldn't have lied, none of them should have, but she can forgive her granddaddy. He can be controlling and bossy, but it's in his nature, his generation.

Her fake mother, Trinka, though, that's whole 'nother story. She has no excuse. She will never forgive her. Her betrayal makes them irreconcilable.

The guy across from Capri offers her his mashed potatoes by banging her tray with his and then nodding to his plate. She looks at him, then picks up his spoon. She doesn't even wipe it off. She dips it into his potatoes, creamy white with yellow pools of butter. Her stomach growls. She's starved and dying of thirst.

Suddenly, the room bursts alive. First, the guy across from her screams. Mashed potatoes slide down his chin. Every kid in the room shrieks.

They're screaming for help, pointing to the window. Agitated and twitching, they're looking around for someone in charge, or escape routes. "Spy! Robber! Freak!" they're saying.

Capri follows their eyes. She looks at the window and sees Mac. He's in the bushes, beating on the glass with his fists. His mouth is open and he's calling her name. He sounds far away, like he's under water. He does look creepy in his black t-shirt and black jeans. He could be a spy.

The security guy rushes in, sees Mac, and then uses a key to open the back door. Capri jumps up, realizing he's chasing Mac, and she tries to follow, but the door is locked.

The teenagers lose their minds. They hop up and down. A couple of them jump on tables. A few try to make a break for the door. The nurses dart around with their hands full.

"I'm sorry," Capri says, backing out. "I'm sorry, I'm sorry."

Before they sedate her with the crowd, she gets away. She runs down the hallway and tries every door, but they're all locked.

Capri follows the path that led her in.

The security guy leads Mac away from the building. The uniform stays calm, but Mac looks frantic, with his face white, his hair going in fifty directions, and he's cussing like a rapper. When he sees Capri, he almost bursts into tears, but she can see he's puffing up, heading for the Mustang.

"You two get out of here," the uniform says, scatting him away. "Go on. Get! Before I take you in!"

"Wouldn't you have to call the real cops?" Mac says, over his shoulder.

The guy runs over and pushes him from behind. The uniform is getting pissed. Blue veins pop from his temple. He balls his fists. They stare at each other without blinking, and she doesn't know what to do. Mac jumps up and down, then squats and bends his arms, like he's back on the wrestling mat, and he plans to pin this guy in a cradle. The guy squats, too. Now that she's looking, she realizes how stocky he is, thick and solid. His cocked arms are three times the size of Mac's. They start circling. She can almost hear the whistle start the match. Chances are the uniform probably wrestled in high school, too, but he was a State Champion.

She doesn't want to leave her granddaddy, but she can see the match may be uneven. The uniform may not have a gun, but he undoubtedly has a knife in his sock. She will have to come back later. They'll break Granddaddy out tomorrow, or the next day, when they've forgotten about them and their guard is down. They can wait until this muscle-pumping guy in a uniform gets off work.

"Can we go now?" she says to Mac, trying her best to act like a bored cheerleader. She tugs on his sleeve, like she's confident, knowing he can take the guy down.

"I'm going to teach this boy a lesson," Mac says.

The uniform laughs and keeps circling.

She runs around the car and clicks the handle, acting like she has to pee. She starts whining, calling his name, like she really wants to leave. He looks over and she begs him, saying, "Come on, baby. Let's go, baby. Remember Mexico? Baby!"

Finally, he sighs. "Yeah, sure," he says, looking at the guy as if he's lucky his girl wants to leave. He doesn't say it loud, but Capri can hear him saying, "You want a piece of me? Come and get it."

Mac snorts, then backs away and points his set of keys at him like he's firing a gun. The whole time, he keeps one eye on the security guy.

They could be Bonnie and Clyde, minus the machine gun and loot. She has a stale taste in her mouth from the 7-Eleven coffee. It's mixing with some rancid metal. Maybe it's butter, but her nose is still clogged. She has a mouthful of nerves, but she can't smell a thing.

"Come on, baby," she says to Mac. "Let's get out of here."

Mac gives the guy another stare like the referee just raised his arm. He struts to the car. Before he gets in, he spits, like he's taken a bit of the security guy's ear.

The uniform watches them drive away. Still on the sidewalk when they drive by the building, he looks like a trigger-happy cop that can pull a gun any second and take them down with one eye and a couple of shots through the window.

Mac doesn't say a word, and she nibbles the inside of her cheek, something she'd given up for Lent over three years ago.

When they're a couple of blocks away, he says, "That was too much. That was too damn much." He runs his hands through his hair and turns on the radio. He hits the steering wheel. "What were you doing? God, baby. You were becoming one of them. I had to save you. God, baby, you were slipping in."

She rubs his shoulder, and then tickles his ear. She doesn't even reprimand him for cussing. Her mind is on other things. Her mother is alive, maybe even her father, and her aunts and granddaddy didn't tell her. She can understand Granddaddy's reason. He's acting crazy, lost in time, but they have no reason, no reason at all. She deserved to be told the truth. She should be with John Mallory, her mother. They never should have taken her away from her mother.

"Where to, baby?" Mac asks. "Let's do something wild and crazy." He winces, using that word, but crazy seems to be the only word in their vocabulary tonight. "How 'bout that party?"

"No," Capri says.

He pulls onto the highway and heads north, away from Rainbow Boulevard. She imagines her mother and aunts drinking coffee around the kitchen table, talking about her as if she just has a bad case of sinusitis, and they're certain they can flush her clean with a netty pot and salt water.

She'll let the light burn on the front porch tonight.

As angry as she should be with all of them, she realizes she doesn't feel mad any more. It's amazing, her seesaw of emotions. Maybe she does come from goddess stock. Things don't get her down for long. She's strong, and she tightens her thighs and arms to prove it.

All of the women in her family seem to have some sort of primal strength, intuitive powers. They may not be blue stars, but she can't help believe. John Mallory is alive. What if her mom and aunts are earthly stars? What if her granddaddy is the sun? They sure act like they're beings from another world. She'll give them that. Trinka has scarred her for life with her lies and secrets, her stories. But Capri is starting to feel magical.

Mac is cooling off. His knuckles turn from white to pink as he loosens his grip.

Her story is incredible, even if she has to say so herself, unbelievable even. How could this be happening to her? Just a few hours ago, she was just another teenager. Sure, she causes a little bit of trouble, her moods wobble, and she can be difficult, but now she knows why. A part of her soul was lost years ago, thousands of miles away from here, and she's just locating it. No matter how hard she tried to fit in, she never did, and there's good reason. She is of another world, or at least another country.

"I'm starved," Mac says.

He constantly wants to stick his head in a nose-bag of food. She takes a deep breath and decides to spill it.

"My granddaddy said my mother's still alive. My mother is really my aunt, and my aunt John Mallory is really my mother."

"Huh?"

"My mother John Mallory had a baby in Costa Rica, and that baby is me."

"What?" he says, glancing over. "No way."

"Way."

Mac keeps driving as if she hasn't just announced the most earth-shattering news someone can get. Maybe he didn't hear. She isn't who he thinks she is. She isn't even who she thought she was.

"Yeah, that's what he said," Capri says. "Granddaddy told me. My mother lives in Costa Rica. She's still alive. It makes me wonder if my dad is. Maybe I have family there, brothers, and sisters, grandparents."

"That is messed up," he says and squeezes her hand.

She squeezes back, knowing he's trying not to cuss because of her and her sensitive ears.

She looks up at the sky. The moon is full in the sky tonight. Why aren't there stars? When she really needs them. They'd help her get to the bottom of things.

The song "Soak Up the Sun" comes on the radio, and she turns it up and sings along. And when it comes to the part about telling everyone to lighten up, she dances in her chair and belts it out like she's Sheryl Crow. Mac always likes when she chair dances, and he smiles at her. She shimmies. She does her dance moves, knowing he's watching.

She has no idea why her mood has lifted, but dancing and singing makes her feel heavenly, goddess-like. In the car with Mac, she feels protected and loved and powerful. She can feel her body move, and she likes how it feels. She wonders what kind of body her real mother has, if they're shaped alike. She spent nine months in her body. Inside John Mallory, she walked on the earth, where she walked, through coffee fields, by avocado trees. She danced in the light of the moon inside her mother.

It's exciting, and her nerves tingle. She thinks she can smell exotic fruits.

Now it makes sense. She has been receiving messages from her mother through a psychic connection, some kind of psychic cord. That's why she went to Mexico. Her mother's psychic pull yanked her south. She was just a little off. And her father, her Costa Rican daddy, he's calling her, too. That's why she always feels like howling at the moon when it's full. They've been calling her, trying to find a way to communicate with their baby girl. That explains all the weird smells, too. They're perfumes from her native homeland, of course.

Why, why did they ever let her go? Granddaddy said he lied. He probably made up one of his stories. He told them Capri had some rare disease that could only be cured in the United States. They let her go with him, for the cure, but they thought she'd come back. Then Granddaddy probably called her mama and daddy and told them she had died, something like that. Capri sees that kind of stuff all the time, on television, reads it in books. It's an old plot line.

Now she knows why she always feels this painful withdrawal, like someone that loves her is far away, like she's missing something. Because they miss her, too. It's like when someone tells her about something incredible, something she didn't know about but everyone else does, like when she discovered Moose Tracks ice cream, and she couldn't believe she didn't know about that chocolaty peanut butter heaven, swirled with caramel, but everyone else has been enjoying it for years. Where was she? Under a rock? She can even smell the chocolate, right now, as if it were in the car. Maybe that's her mother calling her.

She has a mother who lives in Costa Rica. That makes her exotic.

"Hey," she says as it dawns on her, "I'm biracial."

"Cool," Mac says and squeezes her thigh.

"Want to get ice cream?"

"Let's do something wild," he says.

"Like what?"

Truth is, Capri is wired, tired but wired. She doesn't know how that happened, but she feels exhilarated. Her world has baskets that land on Earth. If she saw one, she'd definitely jump in. She'd command it to take her to Costa Rica where there are fields of coffee, where bananas and plantains dangle from trees. Monkeys swing from branches, and men sing from bushes. Right after she swoops down for Granddaddy.

Drums and flutes come through the radio.

She loves Mac. She loves his strong forearms and the way his hair curls around his ears. She loves the way he blindly followed her into a mental ward. He didn't ask questions, he didn't make fun, he just went, like that. He has incredible eyes, good bone structure, and he has a semi-normal family. Maybe they will have beautiful children. Maybe he is the man she wants forever. He is her moon, her man in the bushes, and his light shines through her. He saves her.

They're far north on I-35 now. She has no idea where they're going, but she sees planes flying overhead, as if they have stars to catch, their red lights drifting into the clouds.

The sign for the airport is up ahead. Mac turns on his blinker and exits.

"Where are we going?" she says, chirpy.

Maybe they'll watch planes come and go. That sounds romantic. She lets her body sink deeper into the seat and rolls down the window a tad. The air is warm and the scent of cedar drifts through the crack. She presses her hand on her heart to quiet it. She has a mother in Costa Rica. She loves her and has been sending her psychic messages from an exotic foreign land. She is far south, where Capri belongs. She doesn't know if she's lovesick for Mac or John Mallory, but it feels good. It seems she has always been thinking about John Mallory, not just for a few hours, but all her life.

"Let's go to Mexico again, baby," Mac says.

She looks at him wondering if he found a closet of prescription drugs at the hospital.

His eyebrows cock.

"Come on, baby, let's go. Just you and me this time. I'll buy you a thong bikini."

"Passports?" she says, laughing, and moves closer to him, knowing he's kidding. "You know we don't need the hassle from Mexican Immigration."

"Your wish is my command," he says. "Look what I got." He reaches around to his back pocket, then tosses a passport on the dashboard. "You still have that credit card?"

"How'd you get this?" She fingers her passport and opens it. She shuffles the pages as if they were a stack of hundred-dollar bills. She fans her face with it.

"It was by the front door, on that table, so I took it."

The pit in her stomach only lasts a split-second as she dismisses the fact that Mac has stolen something from her house.

She looks at him, and he smiles, and she smiles. They can't stop smiling.

"Mac," she says, moving even closer, "you're brilliant."

"You just figure that out?"

She pulls out the credit card and shows it to him. "To the airport," she says, lost in her own agenda. Costa Rica, here she comes.

Already far away, Capri is in the land of kapok trees and red ripe cherries. She is on the leafy banks of Pig River underneath the southern skies.

19

Perdón

For weeks, John Mallory and Machu cloaked their desires in whispers, only speaking with their eyes as they passed. They arranged to meet behind bushes, or near the cantina, outside the kitchen of the Big House, even under the window where Lorenzo ate his beans and rice.

When can I see you again? Will you sneak away? Perhaps at lunch. Tonight. *Medianoche.* Midnight. Half night.

They took every possible opportunity to meet down on the leafy banks of Pig River. If they had been lovers back home, she never would have led him to a public park and made wild love to him in the bushes. In Costa Rica, everything was raw. They made a nest of leaves underneath a plantain tree. There were no blankets or pillows. No light except from the blue stars. Their music was the birds and the wind, their wine the mist from the rainforest.

Fearless of being caught, they bathed in the cool waters of the shallow pools, next to the bank where they had made their bed. Afterwards, Machu lit candles, and over the lighted flame they explored and explained every scar on their bodies.

"This one? On your knee," he said, his head hovering over her legs with the candle. His fingers butterflied across her kneecap.

"An uncontrollable ride down a steep hill. On a tandem bicycle with my sister Trinka. When I was ten years old." His eyebrow shot up, and she laughed, calling them furry caterpillars. "A tandem is a bicycle built for two."

"Yes! We should ride a tandem," he said, intentionally shooting his eyebrows up and down several more times, then honking, which always made her laugh. "Any more? Any more scars?"

She pointed to her chin. Like a miner, he roamed up her skin with the candle, past her belly, over her breasts, and stopped on her face.

"Where?" he said, feeling for the scar under her chin, then finding the tiny jagged zipper of skin. She twirled her hair while he pressed it with his index finger.

"It was a risky maneuver on the ice."

"You are an ice skater?"

"Hardly. Trying to be someone I wasn't."

"You are perfect the way you are."

His wounds were from coffee trees, and things of the earth, doing his part to manifest a cup of coffee. A rusty lever at the wet mill left a scar on his thigh. He had a deep scar on his calf from a machete, when he was eight. The one above his eye happened when an old mule butted him with its head. It had been dying, and he had been careless, he said.

Warm wax dripped and pooled on his stomach as she explored his belly button and his naked chest. They drank lemon water from an animal sack. At first, it was hard for her to understand his dedication to the fertile soil of his country, his devotion to a slow lifestyle devoid of any modern pleasures, but then she couldn't remember any other way.

Before long, she spoke of *madre* and *padre* as if that was how she had always referred to her parents. Staring at the stars, she told stories about her sisters and parents as if her tribe were a distant group of entertaining and colorful friends. Far away and tucked into their farmhouse in the city, they would be watching their *telenovelas* and sipping sassafras tea.

For the umpteenth consecutive day, the sun shone heavy in showering sprays and brought out the nutmeg in her hair. From her perch under the shade tree, she painted her nails candy-apple red. She had already buffed her feet with the banana leaves and painted her toenails. Then, out of nowhere, a whiff of fury caught the wind and rode it bareback to her nostrils.

What made her suddenly panic, made her rush around in a mad frenzy trying to look busy—hiding the bottle of nail polish in her bra, rubbing dirt on her dress, scraping her fingers on the bark of a rainforest tree like an ocelot sharpening its claws—was the vision of Lorenzo pulling two unhappy creatures over the hill, a donkey and Paco. At first, she thought it was a mirage. She was always parched, after all. As he puffed towards her, steam rose from his ears. He grumbled at the donkey and the boy, giving little regard for anyone's differential in size, legs, or disposition.

She could hear him all the way up the hill, and down, like a train over a mountain. Moments later when he halted in front of her, he breathed flames and puffed steam.

"Paco pays other boys to pick his coffee cherries," he said. He shook his finger at Paco. "Nine coins for eight baskets!" He jangled a tiny but bulging gunny sack in her direction.

If that were true, John Mallory quickly calculated, and she had paid him three coins for every basket, then Paco had made twenty-four coins for every eight baskets, which meant he had been pocketing fifteen coins without lifting a finger.

"Paco!" said John Mallory. "How could you?" She had not meant to shout and make Paco jump. Already he had greasy tracks plowing down his cheeks. Now he looked at John Mallory with those big eyes as if she had stabbed him with a hot poker.

When the donkey brayed, Lorenzo gave it a swift tug of the reins. The sack thumped to the ground and he grumbled as he leaned over to retrieve it.

"Why, Paco? Why?" she said, and then to Lorenzo, "What should we do about this?" Her voice was innocent and calm. "I'll take him into my charge and we'll have a good talking."

When he stood up, Lorenzo's eyes looked like he was boiling.

"You know nothing? Who gave him these coins?" Again, he shook the bag. "He refuses to tell me."

John Mallory started to speak up but found herself mute. She held her throat.

Paco trembled and turned toward the river. No doubt, he hoped a submarine would launch a missile in his defense. His baseball cap had slipped to the side, and she could see sweat beading in a fever on his forehead.

"The coins?" she said. A flash of scarlet rose in her cheeks, and she hid her nails behind her back, trying to look as if she were considering evidence. "Well," she said.

Paco had not begged her with his eyes, or even whimpered. She wanted to stay silent. But he kept staring at the river, his knees knocking so hard she had to open the door even if she knew there would be fire.

"I paid him."

"You paid him?"

"Yes, I paid him," she said again, this time with a little hip.

"You?" said Lorenzo. "Why?" But then he looked around and saw her empty basket turned upside down, used as a coffee table for a magazine, and the soft spots in the dirt where she had been sitting underneath the banana tree. "Aik! What do I tell his *abuela*? That her grandson is *perezoso*! Lazy! That he has learned lazy tricks from the lazy American girl?"

"You could tell her," she said as she snatched Paco's hand away from Lorenzo and pulled him to her side, "that her grandson is an entrepreneuring young man, and that the slave wages that he earns are never going to get him to a baseball game, much less buy him an education. Tell her that Paco did nothing wrong but set up a little side business. Is that not allowed? Are the laborers restricted from using their free will? Their brains? Maybe we could just toss him beans and rice until he can't think for himself anymore. Squash all his dreams! The boy wants to ride on airplanes, taste hot dogs, cotton candy and popcorn. He needs to learn." Her chest heaved. "That's why there are child labor laws."

Lorenzo's mouth fell open. He shook his head. "Coffee is our way of life," he said. "I thought you understood." His eyes were soft, and a little crease had formed above his nose. Although he still held the sack of coins, his knuckles had turned pale.

"I do," she whispered and held out her palms, but her skin betrayed her with red streaks from smeared fingernail polish. Lorenzo stared at her as if scarlet letters were emblazoned across her chest.

He said, "We do not need *mas* three-toed sloths. Hanging, sleeping, eating all day, pulling the leaves from the trees to their mouths. Even the pochote tree grew spikes on its bark to keep them away." He cocked his head and lowered his voice until she could barely hear him. "*Aquí*, we live together. We all work, for food, and it is not something we find in a box."

Then his fingers rose, as if he planned to continue, but maybe he felt the wind, because he sealed his lips. He walked to the donkey with his head down and tied the pouch with the coins onto the reins. Without lifting his eyes, he flicked his wrist over his head to signal for Paco. He startled the slumbering donkey. With his hands on the boy's hips, he lifted him onto the beast, and the only sound of the ride was from the bristle of the coffee branches and Lorenzo as he grumbled at the donkey to go back up the hill.

The sun didn't hiss, and the mountains didn't rumble, and John Mallory didn't cry when she collapsed to the ground like a dropped puppet. She watched Paco, his tiny hips sashaying back and forth with the gait of the donkey, the boots of his toes pointed to the east and west. And just before they disappeared over the horizon, Paco looked back at her. Afraid he must hate her, certain that his eyes would betray the shriveled apple of his soul, John Mallory was surprised to see him grin, and then he did the oddest thing. He lifted his tiny hand and pumped his finger at the backbone of the donkey, as if saying, "Look at me! I'm riding a donkey! I'm riding a *donkey*!" before he turned back around and disappeared over the hill.

Her mother often offered her tidbits of philosophy, pearls from her strings of wisdom, usually unsolicited. When she had an opinion, they all knew they'd hear it. She had always warned John Mallory that if she didn't work her mind, like a muscle, keep learning, and work her body, she would turn into an Empty Head and contract Empty Head Syndrome. Barbara Mallory had an entire dictionary of made-up diseases with complicated symptoms. She had once dreamed of going to nursing school but decided that her views were too far ahead of the century she lived in. Empty Heads, she said, sat on sofas watching TV until they turned into pillows. All the pillows in the world were former people who had contracted the Empty Head Syndrome. So, Barbara Mallory didn't seem the likely choice for John Mallory to call for guidance. But she couldn't tell her father, or her sisters with their megaphones straight back to God's ears. Knowing that her mother would be leaving for the Nelson Art gallery within the hour, John Mallory dialed the phone expecting brevity with common sense.

She had listened to John Mallory's story and then yawned. "They plowed over the graveyard next to McDonald's," her mother said. "No caretaker to see over it, all the relations gone."

John Mallory could see her with her silky hair pulled back in a barrette. She would be stretched out on the sofa in her black jeans and black jean jacket, the one with glitter sequins sewn in the shape of a hibiscus.

"And that boy who worked down at the gas station works there, at McDonald's. I haven't seen him in months. You know how optimistic I am. In my mind he had moved on, found a desk at Rockhurst College, finally enrolled in those classes I had encouraged him to take. But he has on this silly uniform, standing behind the counter at McDonald's. 'Hello, Mrs. M,' he says. 'I just walked out one day,' he tells me. 'Should have stayed, it's no better here.' I remind him about my wistful dreams for him—college, classes, learning about art—but all the while he has his eye on the white corvette in the parking lot, and an apartment with his buddy as soon as he turns eighteen. And he has no idea what happened to the cemetery. One day it was there, the next it was gone. Poof. He never even noticed. No tractor, no dump trucks, no weeping lovers. I heard we're getting another doctor's office. Or a bank."

"Mother? Did you hear a single word I said?"

"Your confession? What do you want me to do? Absolve you? You messed up. Royally."

"Give me some motherly advice. Tell me how to handle this. This family means a lot to me."

"What family? Your host family?"

"Yes, but…they're more than that."

"Really." She sighed and said, "I guess there really is no rest in peace after all. Not even next to McDonald's."

"Mother. Please."

"Church," she said.

"What?"

"Go to church. Everyone forgives a girl that sits in the front pew."

Sundays were a time for *siestas*, lighting candles, and saying the rosary. Not necessarily in that order. Most people in their town went to church, including Lorenzo and Juanita. Though Lorenzo had tried to talk her into it, John Mallory had not attended. She had never connected to organized religion, even though she had attended parochial school since the first grade. If she were going to be the first female Roastmaster, how could she support a religion that wouldn't even allow her to be an altar girl? In the Catholic Church, her gender was ignored. Neither girls nor women were allowed to hold positions with any power or authority. She couldn't support that. Her absence was her peaceful demonstration, like silently holding up a sign in the parking lot.

When she asked if she could go, Juanita jumped up and down, certain her prayers were being answered. Lorenzo glared at her, saying they may not have room in the boat, because they always took it to town on Sunday. The river was the quicker path. But Juanita slapped him on the shoulder and hugged John Mallory, rushing to help her comb her hair.

In Santa Maria, where the white steeple of the church, albeit modest, still rose higher than any other buildings, the faithful flocked from fields and farmhouses. In the distance, the steeple grew bigger as Lorenzo paddled down the river, with the bells calling them in. He had paused for only a brief moment to stare at the glittering sprays at the top of the waterfall, just a whisper away from the home of Machu.

John Mallory wore a lavender dress with a butterfly collar and clutched the green beads Juanita had given her. Juanita was seated at the bow of the boat. John Mallory sat at the stern, the aft-most part. Lorenzo had insisted. She knew that the rear was where they traditionally seated a mother-in-law, way in the back, hoping by some lucky chance a hungry crocodile would strike, and she could be its breakfast.

When the family, as Juanita so proudly referred to them now, pranced into church, John Mallory gave the desired illusion of a preacher's daughter. She was straight from the bush with her Bible and big dress, her straw hat with the silk ribbon, a thin slip dangling to her cheek. To secure her act of contrition, just like her mother suggested, she asked, "May we sit in the front pew?"

"Yes, yes!" Juanita said and proudly led the way.

"I pray for your soul," whispered Lorenzo as John Mallory brushed past him to take her seat. He smelled white and pure, but she knew he had bathed in smugness with the Ivory soap she had given him. John Mallory actually took his hissing as a good sign since these were the first words he had spoken to her since the incident with Paco.

In the front of the church, head to toe in black, a slight woman hunched over a row of votive candles. Her lips moved as she made the sign of the cross. Then she blew out a long wooden match and silver mist snaked through the air. Next to her, Paco looked around.

At first, John Mallory didn't recognize him without his baseball cap. With his hair spit-shined and parted, he wore black polished shoes that looked two sizes too big. They reminded her of the hand-me-downs from her sisters. Long ago, her mother had given her a pair of Abigail's orthopedics. John Mallory had tried them on and clopped down the black-and-white tiles in the front hall, but she tripped on the tassels on the oriental runner. She begged her mother not to make her wear them. They were heavy and inflexible. But her mother had told her to keep them in her closet. She said she'd grow into them someday. Eventually, she wore them to band concerts and church on Sunday. Whenever she had needed them, she shouted down the hall, "Have you seen Abigail's clown shoes? Where are Abigail's clown shoes?" long after Abigail had gone to college, graduated, and moved to a duplex across town.

Paco's leg jiggled as he waited for the woman to finish her pleas to God. She assumed she must be his grandmother. When Paco noticed John Mallory, he grinned. He had lost a tooth. The hunched woman turned, with her green eyes shining like apples. Her cheeks were sunken. John Mallory looked away. She concentrated on working her glass beads with her fingers. Since she had been in Costa Rica, she had seen the woman many times, in her dreams. Unforgettable, with her wrinkled gray skin, her bent body, and her penetrating eyes, she had always been telling her something, but when John Mallory woke she could never remember what. John Mallory thought she smelled fire, certain it was the odor of her burning ears.

Juanita wore the blue dress of *Domingo*. It had been wiped clean of kitchen spills, no beans or flour, or crystal beads. That morning she had wetted her hair with a dab of olive oil and sleeked it back in a bun. Unlike John Mallory's mother, with her striking patterns, Juanita dressed plainly. She would never crane her neck during church, either, to see what Beverly Hanson wore, or if Jane Smyth had made it on time. After church, there would never be whispers about the Taylor girl on the steps, and how she got in trouble with the Dougherty boy. Or exchanged glances when Victoria Cross never took communion. It's not that they were immune to gossiping, but here Juanita closed her eyes. Every now and then she kissed the closed hand that held her rosary.

Next to her, Lorenzo bent his head and closed his eyes, too. He wore jeans, work boots, and a clean shirt. His hands were folded and his eyebrows drawn together, but his lips didn't move.

A few rows back, Luis Alvarez did the same. And then there was Ramon, next to Rosa, whose belly had swollen to the size of a coffee bean sack. Based on countless hours of girl-talk on the porch, John Mallory had learned that Ramon had left his common-law wife Teresa and moved in with Rosa, even though he had three small children and his wife could not own his land. He still worked her land and Rosa's, and repaired both homes, and made sure that both women were taken care of. The men weren't sure what to do about it, but the women were. They devised plans that involved brooms. So wanting to be a bit more like Juanita (bottles of homemade black-banana vinegar) and a little less like her own mother (store-bought vinegar), John Mallory had to bite her tongue to keep from hissing at Ramon. Like most of the men in the church, he appeared to be praying. So did Rosa.

John Mallory turned her eyes back to the altar. That's the problem she had with religion. She felt some people used it as an okay for committing sins. After all, they could be absolved with a few Hail Marys. For all she knew, they all could be closing their eyes, confessing their sins, saying: "God help me. Forgive me my sticky fingers. Don't make me steal from the offering basket again. Lord, make me a good man. Don't make me cheat on my wife. Please forgive me..."

It scared her to see so many people sitting so quietly, squeezing shut their eyes. She never knew what the sinners were confessing.

She stared up at the whittled ceiling. Stained glass windows reenacted the Stations of the Cross in green, red, and gold. John Mallory tried to focus on her sins—she knew she shouldn't have paid Paco to pick her baskets. She had insulted Lorenzo and disrespected the Domingo family. Machu had laughed. He said it would blow over.

All she could think about was Machu. She knew she loved him, and he loved her, too. Consenting and unmarried, no matter what anyone thought or whispered, they didn't see anything wrong with loving each other.

As if she had conjured him from the confessional, right before Mass, Machu slipped into the pew next to her. Nerves rose like pigeons in her stomach, scattering in the sky from the Vatican square. Even with all the nights she had spent lying next to him, she still felt like a young girl at a school dance. His thigh pressed into hers. He didn't speak, but he touched her wrist, and then his fingers danced on her arm. He looked at her, like she'd looked at dresses in expensive boutiques. How she'd run her hands along the fine silk while no one was watching, just wishing she could buy one, if only she had the money.

"You are here," he whispered, as he made tiny crosses with his thumb on his forehead, and then to his mouth and chest, as if saying, "In my mind, on my lips, and in my heart." Just like Sister Rosetta had taught her to do.

She didn't dare squeeze his hand or utter a word. She was trying to appear virtuous.

Next to her, Juanita shifted in her seat, pressing her giant thighs into hers, too. John Mallory was sandwiched between mother and child. She found it curious how comfortable she felt. Typically, she would have desperately tried to wiggle some room. Yet, she wanted to stay there forever, with Machu and Juanita, her books ends, near Lorenzo, where it was warm. She snuggled down in the pew. Invited into this new world, it was as if she were a baby again, swaddled in her pink blanket, being swept up and carried from bedroom to kitchen. She dreamt of the day when she and Machu would have a daughter of their own, like they had planned. She would have his mocha skin and eyes, and her hair. Their little girl's breath would always have the sweetness of milk, coffee and cocoa. She would have to explain to her. *You were born of two worlds of coffee. Two worlds?* she would say. *Yes, of the United States, a land of great beginnings, of pioneers, of freedom, of great discoveries, and of here, the land of our love, where the birds sing you to sleep, and capuchin monkeys swing in branches outside your window, where the rainforest is your playground, where coffee is our way of life. Is that why we go to the United States? Yes, to see our family. And why can't our American family come here? Because...this is our home. And why isn't it their home? Just because... Don't they love coffee? Sí, they love café. Don't they love us? Sí, they love us. When will they come here? Maybe tomorrow. Sin café no hay mañana? Yes, my daughter, without coffee there is no tomorrow.*

The wave of incense from the altar overpowered John Mallory's senses. The priest spoke of Dios and amor, and John Mallory understood. All during Mass, she bit her lip and wished desperately to be part of this life. Here, in their herd, she was content to be a lamb. She also prayed if she couldn't be an obedient vessel, then she could somehow still be released of her guilt. She would love to wash away her sins with water and prayer. But with all her might, she couldn't stop smelling the warm wax that pooled in the bottom of the beaded glass of the votive candles. The golden goblet reeked of moisture, making her drunk with wine. She couldn't help yearn for a taste of fresh baked bread. She repeated the prayers, staring at the candles, but never could stop yearning to dance over their flames. Even in church, where love meant sacrifice and pain, she could only smell satisfaction. Every inch of sunlight came through in stained glass prisms, and John Mallory craved the taste of colors on her tongue.

So she pinched her nose and mouthed the words of the Hail Mary. She recited prayers for her father, her mother, her sisters, Juanita and Lorenzo, Paco and his grandmother, the farmers, the pickers, the townspeople, and finally for herself and Machu.

"*Perdón*," said the priest, speaking of forgiveness from the pulpit. With every ounce of desire, John Mallory wished for it. "*Perdón*," she said, as if she were questioning, begging. "*Sí, perdón*," Juanita said. She kicked Lorenzo with her shoe, and then he followed with a soft, "*Perdón, sí.*" He leaned forward and looked at John Mallory and stared ahead again.

That was when John Mallory felt the cool air. It breezed across her arms and ruffled her hair, moving her silk ribbon. She smelled the coffee trees. She turned around. Ramon tipped his head. She saw smiles from others. Even the old woman with Paco nodded. With her head bent, John Mallory lifted her pinky finger and held it against Machu.

She knew she had been forgiven.

After the priest ended Sunday Mass, Lorenzo stood and waited for Juanita to exit the pew. He cleared his throat and nodded at John Mallory. Their eyes locked and he nodded again. She passed by, smiling. Machu signaled to his father, then followed Lorenzo. Clustered, they walked down the aisle towards the carved doors. John Mallory moved her eyes through the congregation with renewal. And when she entered the bath of sunshine, she did not shield her face with her hand.

In the distance, she saw Paco and touched Machu's arm to signal that she planned to have a word with her friend. They walked together as if she were an old wife who didn't need words, and he was the dutiful husband who always followed her.

"Paco," she said, greeting the boy, her voice uneasy. She nodded to the woman. Paco introduced them, grinning and jiggling, eagerly looking at John Mallory and then his grandmother.

"*Una estrella*," said the woman. She kissed her cross, then covered her mouth with a handkerchief and coughed. Her nails were thick and yellow, her hands full of maps, veined blue roadways. Her Spanish was fast and soft, and John Mallory could only hear the whistles from the trees.

"*Mi abuela* says you are a star," said Paco.

"A star?" John Mallory blushed, just as Lorenzo joined them and pushed between Machu and her. Lorenzo's hands were clasped behind his back, but he released them and took the woman's hand in his. He bowed his head so he could hear her while she spoke.

"You are from the sky," said Paco. "You are of Sun and Moon, she says." He giggled.

"Yes, yes," said John Mallory. She smiled. Her first instinct had been to question the woman, ask her to explain, because she loved stories, particularly about myths, and the sun and moon. It took effort to stop herself. Instead, she tucked her hair behind her ear and shifted her feet. "A pleasure to meet you *doña*," she said. "*Lo siento de Paco*. I am sorry. I didn't mean harm. Paco, please tell her I didn't mean to do something that got you in trouble. I was wrong, and I'm sorry."

His grandmother leaned forward and stared into John Mallory's eyes, just inches from her face. Her breath had a tinny smell, of the stars and the depths of the ocean. She looked deeply at John Mallory as if she were searching a cupboard for the tiniest grain of rice. Then she patted her hand. She turned to Lorenzo. She spoke to him in Spanish, too fast and low for John Mallory to comprehend. With her bony fingers on Lorenzo's elbow, she looked at the sky. Again, the woman looked at John Mallory.

Lorenzo followed her gaze. Finally, he looked at the woman and nodded.

"*Sí, doña. Sí*," he said, softly.

She smiled and patted his arm. From the wind, John Mallory could smell the cherries of the coffee trees and the vanilla of the clouds. The old woman reached out and touched John Mallory's cheek and then her hair. Then the *abuela* turned and lightly laid a hand on Machu's breast, allowing it to stay there for a few heartbeats. Her green eyes had become watery. They swept across John Mallory and Machu one more time, and then she kissed her cross and hobbled away, singing a sad low song.

"What did she say?" John Mallory asked.

"It was nothing," said Lorenzo.

John Mallory looked to Machu. He was frowning, but then he shook his head and smiled. She watched Paco in the distance. She could still hear the beautiful ballad that his grandmother sang. John Mallory held her sides and laughed. Paco had to hop just to keep up with his grandmother in his clown shoes.

20

Security

A red-eye leaves in a couple of hours. At MCI airport in Kansas City, Mac and Capri book the late flight to Dallas. From there they can catch a flight out of the country. They don't talk to each other much while they wait. He makes a few calls, laughing and hooting with his buddies on his cellphone. She stares out the window and watches planes come and go. She watches a mother play with her little girl. Capri can smell the French roast coffee in the young mother's cup. She feeds her daughter Cheerios and apple juice. She reads her a book and changes her diaper. The mother's hair is a mess and there are splatters on her shirt, but she smiles at her baby.

Capri knows that is how her real mother would have been with her.

They board the plane and the woman and baby are already settled in seats behind theirs. Mac takes the window seat in front of them and leaves Capri the middle. As soon as they're settled and on their way to Dallas, she tells Mac she doesn't want to go to Mexico.

"Let's go to Costa Rica," she says.

"Costa Rica?" he says. "I don't want to go to Costa Rica. Come on, baby. Felix says he can get me a job in construction, in Cancun. I just got off the phone with him. He says he can do it. We can even crash at his place for a while. It's all set up."

"Felix? That guy we met at the bar?" Capri's wrapped in an airline blanket and it smells like dirty socks, like it hasn't been washed in a hundred years, if ever. She's starving. She doesn't know why she didn't eat at the airport, like Mac did.

A flight attendant wheels up offering sodas and peanuts. Capri asks for water, but it smells like lemon that has been rotting in an animal sack. Mac asks for a full can of Coke. He opens his bag of nuts and pours it in his mouth. He shoots two-fingers of Coke like it's tequila.

"Yeah, he said anytime. Anytime I want, he said, he can hook me up. We can live down there, drinking *cerveza*, going to the beach. You and me, babe. It's cheap." He covers his mouth with his fist trying to quiet a burp. "We don't need much. Five bucks a day, baby. Five bucks a day."

"What about high school? We're almost finished."

"To hell with high school," he says. "I'm done."

"What about your parents?" She feels a pit growing in her stomach. Maybe Trinka and her aunts really do matter. What about her granddaddy?

"No one will miss me."

"I can't leave my granddaddy," she says. "We'll have to come back for him."

He grabs her bag of peanuts and pours it in his mouth before she can stop him. Then he reclines, and the woman behind them has to hold her little girl to her chest.

"Mac," she says, "you're squishing a baby."

His eyes close. "Can't wait to be in Meh-ee-ko, baby," he says.

Capri smiles an apology at the woman through the crack of their seats, but she's busy feeding her baby a bottle. The little girl is covered by a pink blanket. Capri hears the baby sucking. The mother offers her index finger, and the little girl wraps her tiny baby fingers around it. The mother smiles, then hums, watching her baby's peach-colored face and her long black eyelashes.

It makes Capri feel envious, and she pushes back her seat.

She leans her head on Mac's shoulder and smells the onion he had in his sub sandwich. She lifts her head to breathe in his hair. It's thick, black and wavy. He uses mousse that mixes woodsy scents with citrus. He feels safe, rock solid, with his lean, muscular body, and she takes his hand. He rubs her knuckles with his thumb, and they fall asleep until the flight attendant wakes them.

It's the middle of the night when they arrive in Dallas to buy tickets for their next flight south. They're waiting in line at the ticket counter. Capri puffs out her lip and looks at Mac with big eyes.

She says, "Baby, I want to go to Costa Rica." While they move up in the line, she tells him all the things her mom said, correction, what Trinka said, and then what her Granddaddy said, too. "My mother is alive in Costa Rica, and I need to find her."

"You can't listen to Granddaddy," Mac says. "He's not all there." He does the twirling thing around his temple, like Capri does to Trinka, signaling to her that she thinks she's crazy. When he does it, though, it looks insensitive and wrong. His eyes point to the door. "Hey, baby, let's get hot and bothered in the bathroom. Join the mile-high club."

They're not even in the air, and she's already hot and bothered. She starts crying. It has just sunken in. She has no luggage, no clothes, not even a bra. Her nerves are shot. Her granddaddy is crazy, a prisoner in a mental institute, and her mom isn't her mom. Her real mom is alive in Costa Rica, and she's never even seen her. She may even have a daddy and family. Her Spanish isn't that great.

Mac says hush, and it kind of calms her. He kisses her eyelids and down her cheeks. "Baby, baby, don't worry," he says. "I still love you, don't worry. I know your family's crazy, but I still love you. I won't leave you, not like your daddy did."

Her mouth goes dry. She gets a strong whiff of votive candles, but they do not calm her. She gets out of line and leans against a wall. Mac has hit a nerve. Capri rarely talks about her father. When she told Mac about him, it was in a weak moment, one day when she was in a blue mood and they passed a Porsche. All she had been told about the guy is that he drove a luxury car and poured peanuts in his Coca-Cola. Capri hates Porsches and peanuts, but it doesn't mean she didn't want that bag of peanuts Mac ate. He didn't even ask her. Besides, she'd told him that in confidence. She didn't expect Mac to mention her father again. And now, with him labeling her family crazy, it makes her think Mac's either a jackass or an insensitive idiot. Neither one is good. She feels like he just sucker-punched her in the gut.

"What's the matter, baby?" he says, with his hand on his hip.

"What makes you think I'm worried about *you* leaving *me*?"

He pulls in his chin. She hates his weak chin. He has that blank look on his face, that one he always gets, like someone's sucked his brains through his nose. She hates that dumb look.

"I didn't mean anything," he says. "It's not like I think you're damaged goods."

"Damaged goods? Is that what you think?" Her heart falls to her stomach.

"No, I don't think—"

"Well, it's obvious you don't think. Just because my granddaddy is hospitalized."

"Listen," he says, "don't get mad at me. But you gotta admit, it was spooky. Him lying there in that bed, all bug-eyed and crazy. Man. The guy was strapped in. Did you hear that screaming down the hall? Jesus, I don't ever want to go back there. I just thank God my family's playing with a semi-full deck. That was heavy shit. It was like *One Flew Over the Cuckoo Nest*."

She smacks his arm hard. "You're lame," she says.

"What?" he looks around, half smiling at strangers.

"Mac, you're acting like an idiot. You have no idea what you're talking about."

"What?"

"Like you have room to talk. You could have been any one of those guys, shoveling mashed potatoes in your pie hole in the cafeteria. The way you drink beer and cuss. And now you're planning on dropping out of high school. You're just one step away from the front door. You're the crazy one!"

She huffs away, but he grabs her arm.

"Don't get pissed at me just because your gene pool's shaky."

"My gene pool? What about your parents? Didn't your mom change the locks while your dad slept with that chick from the Jiffy Lube? And your Uncle Lou, the one in prison for tax evasion, and what about your Aunt Edna, doesn't she live with like two hundred dogs?"

"Twenty-seven," he says, "and that's a rescue shelter."

"Yeah, right," she says, "some shelter. You can smell it two blocks away. Isn't the city trying to shut her down? So let's not start discussing family branches."

"Yeah, well," he says, as he walks away and heads for the men's bathroom, "just because yours are twisted." He looks at a couple of strangers and says, "Crazy!" and they look at Capri. Then he shouts over his shoulder, "You know what they say, the apple never falls far from the tree."

Even though she tries not to let it, her mouth falls open. "What's that supposed to mean?"

She runs after him and pushes him from behind. He turns around and grabs her. He flips her around and holds her in a clutch.

He says in her ear, "You're acting crazy, you know. Your mom, your aunts, dancing in the middle of the night. And then your mom," he says, spitting while he talks, "convincing you to shove lemons and coffee up your butt. And now you've got Granddad? You taking him that coffee, and him going woo-woo, thinking he's the sun or something. You were dancing with that guy with the soap. You ate those mashed potatoes. I saw you! You're crazy. Crazy!"

People walking by stop to stare. Mothers wheel away their babies.

Capri feels the blood rising in her neck and face. She can't catch her breath.

A piece of paper falls out of Mac's pocket. He lets her go so he can reach down to pick it up, then looks at it and starts smiling.

"What's so funny?" she says, but he isn't listening.

"Nothing," he says and starts to put the paper back in his pocket, but she snatches it and runs for the bathroom. In a stall, she reads it. It's directions to the party, in Tiffany's pink marker, along with two hearts. Tiffany had written, "Call me for a ride!" and added her phone number.

Mac's waiting outside the door when she comes out, and she throws it at him. "Why don't you just get it over with and call Tiffany."

"Come on, baby," he says. "She doesn't mean anything. You know that. Come on, baby. I'm sorry. I don't even know what I was saying. It's been a long night. Okay? Ignore me, will you? Come on. Let's go to Mexico. Me and you, baby." He wraps his arms around her, but she can't smell anything beyond the onions. "Don't be mad at me. You know I can't stand it."

Capri exhales. She always thought she was confident and sure. She thought her family acted weird, but when Mac said it, he called them crazy, he called her crazy, it sounded cruel and heartless. She has no idea what to do. "I want to go to Costa Rica," she says.

He inhales but then heads back for the line.

When it's their turn, he's smiling at her. The agent searches for flights. Capri tries to breathe in and smell Mac's musky scent but she can't, so she flares her nose breathing in the sweet seeds of fruits from Costa Rica. As soon as she finds them, she feels grounded again.

The agent finds them two seats on a flight to San Jose the next day. They can wait at the airport. Soon, Capri will be on her way to find her real mother, maybe even her dad.

The woman at the counter swipes the credit card, then pauses. Her face flushes. She scans their faces and smiles but picks up the phone and whispers, "Security. They're here."

Mac doesn't wait. He grabs Capri's arm and pulls her away. He sprints for the exit. He's five feet ahead of her, and she races after him. As she runs into the night, she looks up. The moon is following her. It illuminates her path with golden light. She is a blue star. She's free, and she soars from Earth, like she's riding in a basket, across the parking lot and up the steps, as if she were rising into the southern skies.

21

Café en Oro

The next morning, John Mallory followed Lorenzo to the east, with the rising red sun. Her toes were covered as he had directed her, wearing boots with thick hide. Her hair was tied into a ponytail, and she wore clothes that were tight, not blousy. She knew his commands that morning had been a form of restitution—no one would ever again speak of her error in judgment concerning young Paco—and instead of complaining about his hurried pace, she was thankful for his goodness.

As he walked, Lorenzo shook his head and clucked his tongue.

"Stay out of the way. Do not bother anyone. A *beneficio* is a busy place!" He glared at her and then tripped over a root. His eyes were large and questioning.

"I will," she said, almost unable to stop wiggling with excitement. She couldn't wait to see a real coffee processing plant, particularly *la cooperativa* that Gustavo Navariz and other prominent men of the community had formed when the private *beneficio* went kaput. However, if she were being completely honest (the coffee trees could easily tell, and even the strangler vine could see) then she would have admitted that her jitters were also jubilance because she would be closer to Machu. They would be forming their team, like they wanted.

"Do not speak to anyone!" he said. "You can do that? No men at the levers, or the water, no one carrying bags, or raking the beans. No one! *Posible* the worms. You will have time with the red worms of California. Watch their little mouths chew, listen to their stomachs be happy. Why do you need to speak with *los hombres*? They speak *poco* English, they do not need to be attracted."

"Distracted," she said. She had become accustomed to correcting his English.

"Distracted!"

"No, I won't distract them."

"And all that," he said, eyeing her, "hair! Keep it away from things."

"The men?"

"No, the machines. Yes! The men!"

Most believe that it was there, at *la cooperativa*, a drop in the bucket from punishment to salvation that John Mallory truly learned the secret of the bean. The *cafeteros* were whistling like coffee farmers will. The birds were humming, and even the coffee trees did a little shimmy. John Mallory would baptize her views, dip them in fermented waters, bake them in the sun, and digest them to make rich soil for future generations.

Yes, coffee had historically shaped desires of people. Some would say culturally, socially, politically, and even richly. Of course, John Mallory would add lustfully.

"Coffee is attractive to farmers because..." Lorenzo tried to educate her. He would bore her with his statistics about how easy coffee is to handle and store, how based on its weight its value is high, and that with its sure-footed feet it could grow on even the steepest slopes. "These slopes," he whispered, hoping that the mountains wouldn't hear him, "are no good for any other crop."

About then, Machu slipped up behind them, honked, and added, "Coffee is precocious." He winked.

"No!" Lorenzo said, even though he had no idea of the meaning of the word his son had used. Lorenzo stepped in front of him, pushed him away, and tried to edge his way to the lip of the tank where they watched the good cherries being separated from the bad by their buoyancy. Lorenzo had already explained to John Mallory the two methods of processing coffee: wet and dry. Although they didn't use the dry method at *la cooperativa*, he felt she should understand how some of his fellow farmers would not use water but would dry their cherries in the sun. And some would use mechanical driers. He assured her that the wet method, although more complicated and expensive, produced a better quality bean. Together, they watched the cherries being washed in large tanks, with their backs to Machu while John Mallory imagined her selfish mistakes were the dirt, leaves, and unripe cherries that floated to the top and were skimmed off.

Soon after, Lorenzo tried to lose Machu by darting in and out of paths. But it was never long before he reappeared. They were witnessing the washed cherries as they slid through the pulping machines, which removed the outer shell and most of the pulp.

"The beans are washed again. To remove the rest of the pulp, and then dried," Lorenzo said.

"Coffee is labor-intensive," Machu said, sneaking up behind them.

"No!" Lorenzo said, even though they all knew it was.

"Rather than capital intensive. That's what he means," said John Mallory.

"*Sí*, I know what he wants. *Pero* even if coffee is neglected, it can be rejuvenated with *poco* effort. It can be processed with little. It can be stored for long periods of time." By now, even Lorenzo knew he was repeating himself and that the naked and scrubbed cherries had fallen asleep in boredom.

He darted around a few of the men, down the back aisle, hoping Machu would stay put near the washing tanks. He could hear him honking, though, and it always made her laugh.

"Unroasted coffee is clean. Dried beans come from the center of the cherry. The beans are milled to remove the parchment. They leave green coffee to make the golden bean," Lorenzo said.

"Yes, yes. *Café en oro*," John Mallory said. He had told her a dozen times what they were called in Costa Rica.

His eyes wandered behind her, searching for Machu's shadow.

Lorenzo wove his way back through the building and stood at the open doors just as the farmers lined up outside to drop off their day's labor. Lorenzo felt certain that Machu would be far too busy to follow them around, like a dog, sniffing for a bitch in heat. Trucks were lined up. Engines were turned off.

"To make cherries not ferment, wet processing must happen before twenty-four hours after harvest," Lorenzo told her while she stared out at the waiting farmers. Certainly a longer delay would not render the beans totally useless, he said while he spit on the soil. "But fermentation does lower quality. Affects taste. *Mas o menos*." More or less.

He continued to beat the dead donkey of the importance of a timely harvesting. He reminded her how old cherries that had fallen from the trees and were collected from the ground days later would have already begun to ferment. On the other hand, he had added, young cherries, green and immature, were bitter when processed. Both yield inferior product. "You remember, *sí?*"

But for no reason apparent to Lorenzo, and without him noticing, John Mallory had jumped from the docks and was wandering through the aisles of the waiting farmers. He grunted, but the coffee cherries scolded Lorenzo, for even they knew, just like the chocolate trees could attest, John Mallory was a kinesthetic learner. Yet, they told him, he hadn't even tried to be interesting. How did he expect her to learn? Mother Bean decided to take over.

"*Buenos días*," John Mallory said to the farmers who swept their hats from their heads. They wiped the sweat from their brows with the back of their hands.

"*Buenos días*."

She peeked into a full sack, which made a farmer wince.

"They can be suspicious," Machu said behind her. "Because you are a stranger. They worry that you may be spying for the government, wanting to increase their taxes."

"Don't be silly," John Mallory said, flashing her best dimple. "I wouldn't work for the government."

"It has been mentioned in the village."

He spoke to them in fast Spanish, and they smiled at John Mallory, nodding.

Lorenzo struggled to jump down from the docks. He wanted to explain a few other things: how inelastic coffee is, because, after all, demand doesn't change much with price; the pruning required after harvest season; the California red worms—but the coffee cherries continued to harangue him. By the time he caught up with John Mallory, in between the trucks and mules, smiling at the farmers, she had stopped to toss a ball with the children.

"I love children," she said. "How soon do you think you'd want to have them?"

"Right away," Machu said, and winked. "I want many children. *Contigo*, my love."

She blushed.

The coffee cherries started perking. They were blustering, whispering and giggling, thrilled about the big ideas the two young lovers were brewing.

Forgiven, yes, but still, not all of John Mallory's ideas were accepted with open arms. Like when she tried suggesting that Lorenzo organize the trucks with a color-coding system, assigning times of the day farmers should arrive at *la cooperativa.*

"Blues could arrive at one o'clock, reds at two, and greens at three. Less waiting."

"No!" Lorenzo shouted. "No! No! No!"

She thought the farmers would appreciate the shorter lines and admire her efficiency. But he said they were used to gossiping around the trucks and mules, and the children spent the time playing and rejuvenating.

"We do not feel the need to use all our resources." Lorenzo told her. "You Americans are obsessed with efficacy."

"Efficiency," she said, correcting him.

"Yes, yes. Yes! Efficiency!"

Yet, even he couldn't deny that the farmers were interested. They listened to her, apparently hypnotized by the American woman with the long hair. They started buttoning their shirts and smoothing their hair. When she spoke, they even tipped back their hats. Later, at a meeting of the board of directors, Machu would report that business had picked up. A few more of the less-dedicated members of *la cooperativa* were making regular appearances now rather than going to competitors. He didn't admit what he knew. They all wanted to see her.

Word had flown on the lips of the wind. John Mallory was nicknamed *La Diosa,* although no one ever called her The Goddess in person. Somewhat of a celebrity with the men, she became an attraction for *la cooperativa.* Even Gustavo Navariz called her The Goddess. He was thrilled with the uptick in his business.

Yet, it was the coffee cherries that whispered to John Mallory in her dreams. They knew the truth: for the most part, the poor farmers lived on the edge of disaster. Mother Bean hoped that she could save John Mallory from the same fate.

"The farmers are foot draggers." John Mallory complained to Machu one evening by the river. "They listen to me but don't do anything."

"They are used to resisting control," he said.

"So when they feign ignorance, it isn't my imagination?"

"No," he said. "Tax evasion, pilfering, even slander are universal sports." He laughed.

In her dreams, Mother Bean encouraged John Mallory to go with Juanita to her monthly meeting of the fledgling Women's Group. One afternoon, she did. It was there that John Mallory learned of the home-based businesses some women had started, using their artisan skills to earn extra income. Mostly they knitted and cleaned houses. Artists painted local landscapes on coffee leaves that could be framed in glass.

"They're incredible," she said, staring closely at the intricate work, the patience it would take to paint a leaf. The women blushed. Through Juanita, she learned what the women were trying to accomplish, and how they were trying to create independent means. "These would be lovely logos for t-shirts. We could sell them to tourists in the gift shops. In San Jose."

John Mallory earned the respect of the ladies by suggesting new marketing ideas to sell their beaded necklaces to American tourists too. To compare products and discuss issues on a more regular basis, the women proposed that they move their meetings to every other week. John Mallory was invited.

It didn't please Lorenzo that Juanita was much busier. But even he couldn't conceal his pride when, before long, she was marketing her own hair combs and bead products outside the local market, and when John Mallory was by her side like a loyal daughter.

On top of that, John Mallory volunteered to serve on committees.

"The women have uncovered so many local issues," she told Machu. "We need things for the children. Computers and books and a new playground. A community center."

She volunteered to be on a task force with the local women to craft solutions. She was part of the team that lobbied *la cooperativa* for a medical clinic, as well as veterinary consulting services. Their first customer was the donkey Paco had ridden. They also wanted a credit service to help fund some of the women's investments. She formed a friendship with Rosa, possibly her first real girlfriend who wasn't one of her sisters, and cheered when Rosa was awarded money for home improvements for Ramon's blossoming compounds. The women didn't wait to be handed funds. Along with the local women, John Mallory helped persuade community residents to give of their time and labor. They led creative fund-raisers, raffles, and organized a festival with food and games, and dancing. They brought the merrymakers and their money to the saints. Even Father Ovares was delighted.

What made Lorenzo most proud, however, was John Mallory's approach. She wanted to help his people. It was her idea that *la cooperativa* negotiate with the Costa Rican government.

"We talked about it. It was a group think tank. Here's our idea. The government can acquire land for landless laborers. Give them ninety-nine year leases on small plots to grow coffee and other products that *la cooperativa* could process. Maybe macadamia nuts or avocados?"

"Maybe," he said. Sugarcane had been difficult, but the nuts would be good.

"We could also request land for your refuge. For the animals. The rainforest."

When she offered him this golden nugget, Lorenzo pretended to be studying the sky on his porch. But she could tell that he was pleased. His feet turned in, and he hooked his hands in the tops of his pants. His lips curled at the tips.

"*Dios te bendiga*," he said, pretending to talk to the coffee trees. But John Mallory knew. His *God bless you* was intended as a thank you to her.

Mother Bean clapped in delight.

And just like most things, once the women began to beat their breasts and join each other in support, the farmers took the lead. Even Lorenzo blushed when they referred to John Mallory as *La Diosa*. He puffed out his chest, like a proud father of a goddess.

Mother Bean wept with joy.

22

Ceilo de los Ceilos

John Mallory wandered away from the trail next to Pig River. She disappeared through the vibrant leaves, virgins to the cut of blades and stomp of feet, but Lorenzo had given up following her on her chases through the rainforest. It was early evening with little light, and he was tired. All day long, the coffee cherries had groaned like expectant mothers, swollen with exceeded due dates, heavy with red, eager to fulfill their destinies.

He stopped to rest on a rock. A collared redstart, a gregarious bird known as the "Amigo de Hombre," friend of man, stopped to whistle at him. With its golden face and blue cape, a tuft of red hair, its peppy nature put Lorenzo back in short pants. He remembered his father, a man with a penchant for small animals. In the distance, he could hear the piping call of the Great Tinamou—three short, powerful notes of the resident bird that John Mallory followed. She said it reminded her of the wild turkeys from her prairie plains. She, too, loved animals. In many ways, (he didn't want to admit) she ignited his love and devotion again.

She whiffed the air. "I swear I smell your jaguar. Besides," she said, teasing him about the Great Tinamou before she pushed through the brush, "I'd like to see a male that actually incubates and hatches the eggs."

Lorenzo grumbled. In his mind, the fowl was a sissy that sat at home while his mate prowled the forest searching for her next lover. Lorenzo had no interest in following him.

But suddenly he heard a high-pitched scream. His heart fell to his stomach and he hopped up. Without a thought for breaking branches, Lorenzo tore through the brush. He prayed while he ran that a jaguar hadn't found John Mallory.

As he drew closer, with his chest rising and falling, he saw her up ahead. She cradled something furry. It was a scrubby gray beast, with a small head and flat face and a snub nose. Its long bony arms and curving claws hooked over John Mallory's arms and grasped them like branches. It looked like it intended to spend its entire life suspended upside down from her limbs. Inching closer, its big eyes turned to Lorenzo. He recoiled from the smug grin of a baby three-toed sloth.

"No! Drop it!" he said. Lorenzo considered the sloth to be one of the ugliest animals on earth. The beast paid no attention to personal hygiene. Its shaggy fur would knot with algae and mold. That mess made an effective camouflage but a perpetual grazing ground for hordes of mites and beetles. It housed communities of parasitic moths that burrowed in its fur. "*No, perezoso.*"

Even its Spanish name meant lazy.

Her voice was soft. "I think it's hurt. It must have fallen from a tree."

But Lorenzo knew that the lazy creature, one that would spend up to eighteen hours a day sleeping, had been left behind.

No one knew why, but most times when a baby sloth tumbled from the branches, the mother would turn her back and continue munching on leaves. She would ignore its distress calls.

"You cannot keep it," he said. "If the mother leaves the baby it is because she does not want it."

"Abandoned? Oh no." John Mallory hugged the creature to her neck, and then tickled it where it should have had a chin. "How rude. Who could leave you?" she said cooing at the creature.

"It is their way to eliminate the weak. This one is not strong enough." He reached out for the baby sloth. He would place it on the ground, and they would walk away.

"You mean survival of the fittest?" John Mallory looked down and they both stared at the big eyes, the gentle face of the docile creature. "Well then, we'll just have to help it." She moved the baby closer to his outstretched hand as if he would want to pet it.

"No!" This time he stamped his feet and tried to snatch the animal. But realizing his intentions, she pointed her elbow to keep him back and protect it.

"We can't just leave it. How would it survive?"

Lorenzo knew its greatest predators: the eagle, the jaguar. Its only defense was disguise. He also knew that in four hours, at top speed, a sloth could not cover more than a mile. On the rainforest floor, even a grown sloth could barely crawl. A corpse made more movement during rigor mortis than a sloth. He spat on the ground. "We cannot cheat Mother Nature."

"Well, we certainly cannot abandon a baby. I know you wouldn't. After all, you were just explaining to me that the entire eco system in Costa Rica depends on families staying together. Isn't that right?"

It was true. He had told her that. He thought he had been so clever comparing his home to her farmlands of Kansas. He had explained to her about the domestic product of the family, and how it depended on the number of members in the household. He had explained how in Costa Rica whenever a boy was born, there was dancing in the streets. How daughters would marry to fortify their family.

"Marriages are meant to strengthen families," he had said. Matter of fact, the greatest threat to farmers, excluding age and illness, was their children migrating.

"It seems that farmers live in mortal fear of their children being attracted to outside influences. People and their things," she had said.

He had explained how farmers continually adjusted strategies according to the number of family members. He thought if he told her these facts, he would not have to deny her publicly. He wouldn't have to explain why she and his son could never marry.

But his cleverness had tripped him with its roots. He could tell by the look on her face that, once again, the communication styles of their cultures had clashed.

She said, "Just think if Ramon had abandoned his families. Or you yours." Then she tickled the beast. "What then? Thank goodness you're such a compassionate, welcoming man."

His cheeks began to flush. "Yes, but I also tell you," he slapped the back of his hand onto the palm of the other, "a history of friendship provides relief in hard times. In emergencies." He was thinking of the marriage deal he had made with Gustavo Navariz.

"Okay. So you think another sloth will come along and help this baby?"

He looked down at the hole in the fallen tree. A caterpillar with a thousand legs made its way up the trunk. He didn't dare look in her eyes.

"We must leave it."

"Everything depends upon loyalty. You told me," she said.

His lessons were boxing him in the ears. Just yesterday, he had diligently explained the way relationships worked in Costa Rica: large landowners, local merchants and political leaders provided cash loans, credit, important contacts and protection.

"You spoke of resources and social networks." She cuddled the sloth to her neck again. "Thank goodness for Costa Rican ways."

As he walked home with John Mallory, he could scarcely believe his predicament, her with a sloth riding on her shoulder, him with Mother Bean giggling until his ears burned. If this were a story he was telling on his front porch, it would be funny. Luis Alvarez would laugh so hard that his eyebrows would turn red. But instead, Lorenzo pursed his lips and swatted at the insects swarming at his neck. He couldn't help cursing the stars for attracting so many strays. Certainly only Mother Nature could find such humor in an old man's failed manipulations.

She named the baby sloth Daisy. She had never considered a daisy a marginal flower, even though its big button head was so heavy that its scruffy, thick neck would fold. She knew it also had bull's-eye potential to attract sunshine.

"I knew you would want us to keep her," John Mallory said, hugging Juanita.

Lorenzo groaned.

As John Mallory had expected, Juanita agreed to house the creature in need. She quickly got to work creating the sweetest concoctions for baby Daisy: fried mangoes and fried plantains, with a touch of vanilla and a pinch of sugar. Soon, baby Daisy was as much a part of the family as John Mallory. Juanita even beaded Daisy a necklace of pebbles from the garden. It had taken a grumbling Lorenzo all afternoon to drive holes through the center of the stones with steel.

Luis Alvarez watched him, laughing so hard he fell to the ground.

By this time, John Mallory's apprenticeship required that she spend most of her time in the roasting plant at *la cooperativa*. So she soon made it a habit of walking through the facility with Daisy riding on her shoulder. Aimless wandering through production facilities had always given her stronger connections to the products, more energy for her work. She had grown up around the rumblings of a packing plant, coffee cans jostling down a production line. The sound of pressurized air soothed her like a sweet breeze blown in her ear. Often, she had begged her father to take her on buildings tours that housed machines, big hungry contraptions that made things, converting one form into another. They had been to the Denver mint, two California wineries, even a prepared dough plant in Tennessee. She had studied crushers, bottlers, fryers and boxers. But she had always been fascinated by the people who stood next to the line: a woman that wore hot-pink butterfly barrettes, a man tapping his foot to music, the people at the machines who gave life to the products.

On that particular afternoon, everyone at *la cooperativa* was ready to go home. The guts of the building had started to turn gray and quiet, like a mouse inside a wall. John Mallory stood in the doorway smelling the coffee: brown from the soil of the mountains right outdoors, red of the Costa Rican sky, green of waxy leaves. She walked down the aisles with her hands in her pockets, wearing a woven hat that she'd bought from *Señora* Razanga, a fledging entrepreneur whom John Mallory adored. She hoped the sunhat would lend her an air of native friendliness. She shook her head. It didn't seem possible that already two months had passed. She knew that back home her sisters were still conducting their rituals, pitter-pattering to and from work, tucking little bits of themselves into coffee cans, the same mounds of hair arguing over nothing, but somehow John Mallory felt older and wiser, more peaceful here. She knew something had changed, but she didn't know what.

She had always marched up and down the aisles like a peacock at Early Mountain Coffee, proud of the fact that she had inherited authority. She knew her presence instilled a bit of skepticism, but she had also prided herself that she got along with employees, particularly the people on the front line. Here, she didn't crave the social distance. What she wanted was acceptance. Drawn to the loud Latin music they played, how they shouted back and forth across the floor in Spanish, she longed to be included in the playful teasing. But each time she entered their space at the roasting plant, they closed up like night-blooming flowers at dawn.

Her low-heeled espadrilles barely made a sound across the concrete floor.

She nodded and smiled, but their eyes didn't stay on hers for long, if at all.

On the other side of the room, she spied a fresh roast of dark beans as it spun around the cool-down fans. She walked over. John Mallory knew the beans would be too hot but she couldn't help herself, hypnotized by their dark, earthy scent. She thought she had waited long enough, just wanting to feel their warmth on her hands. She ran her fingers through the oily beans. But they were like embers, and she jerked her hand away and tossed them onto the cement floor. She howled and held her hands, jumping up and down on one foot. Daisy toppled back and forth, barely clinging to her cotton fabric.

Alonzo, the head roaster, ran for a cool towel. He pressed it against her palms. Faces appeared from behind the rows and peeked at her with sad brown eyes. A woman hurried towards her and rubbed something as cool as butter on her palm. It soothed and tickled, and John Mallory's eyes watered. She laughed. Then she heard a collective song of sighs.

One of the linemen, Rocco, an ill-reputed brawler with a buzz cut who bore half-Russian blood in his veins, jiggled from behind the crowd and imitated her with a howl. He hopped on one foot and spun in circles. Everyone froze. He went on for countless seconds. Once he finally settled down, there was bone silence.

Someone coughed.

Stunned, John Mallory clutched Daisy. Then, with an exaggerated thrust of her head, she craned her neck and howled back at him. Then she burst out, laughing, with a long musical sound that made everyone else giggle, too. (Later, they would compare her to a fire-breathing dragon that even Rocco claimed made him tremble.) It wasn't long before they were all in hysterics, giggling, hypnotized by her magical flute of laughter.

A woman inched in and petted Daisy.

"*Su perezoso?*"

"*Sí, mi perezosa,*" John Mallory said, and held out Daisy closer to the woman. "*Ella es muy perezosa!*" She is very lazy, she said, and they laughed.

Soon, all the women used Daisy as an excuse to get a little closer to John Mallory. The men hovered behind, peering over their shoulders. They, too, pretended to be interested in the hairy mammal that clutched her breasts.

From behind her, she smelled the familiar scent of Machu. He was panting. "Are you okay?"

"Yes," she said and smiled up at him. "I'm wonderful. My friends and I are just taking a little break."

"I heard you had been hurt." His eyes were large. Sweat had formed on his forehead.

"And you came running," she said, smiling. She didn't care who was watching. She kissed him on the lips. Someone catcalled and there were several laughs. He held her hand, inspecting it, when a harsh voice interrupted.

"Your father wants to speak with you," Lorenzo said, parting the crowd like the Red Sea. He led the way to the small office. With a sigh, he pointed to the phone that lay on the desk.

When she picked it up, her father's intentions were clear. "It's time for you to come home." His voice sounded weary but firm.

Each week, he had suggested she leave. She knew it wouldn't be long before he would insist.

"Why so soon?"

"It's been over two months. Long enough," he said. "It's almost spring. Remember? The magnolia trees and crab apples are blooming. Even the pear trees. The redbuds are incredible this year. You don't want to miss all this pink!"

"But there's so much to do," she said. "Here."

"I don't care," he said. "The redbuds are in bloom, and your mother wants you home for Easter."

They both knew that it wasn't her mother driving the demand. She would be busy with the spring show at the Nelson Art Gallery, watering the peace lilies at the church and cutting the crusts off of finger sandwiches for bridge club.

"My work here isn't finished," she said. "We're planning another fair. There's the raffle, and the children. I'm teaching English," she said. "Kids love me. I never knew—"

"You don't belong there, John Mallory. I've spoken to McCracken." She could hear him panting. "You can't stay, you must come home. They're busy, honey. It's been good, but your time is up. You're in the way."

"He said that?"

"In so many words."

"Then I'll have Lorenzo speak to him."

"No, it's time. Come home," her father said. "You've imposed long enough."

"Imposed?"

With Daisy nestled on her neck, she walked to the window and studied the sky. When she looked up into the heavens, she was blinded by the smells—sugar from fried plantains, the puppy breath of the three-toed sloth, chocolate growing in the rainforest. She thought she heard a splash. It was as if she had just slipped into Pig River. Her skin began to heat from the fierce sun. Her eyes were flat, and she looked away. In the distance, she could see the mountains, the rows of coffee trees, the stone walkway that led up to the terrace. She knew she had found home.

"I'm not ready yet," she said. "I need more time. There's so much to do, and I've just begun. This has all been so perfect, you were right—"

"You've learned enough," her father said. "A young girl can be seduced by knowledge. It'll interfere with life. Getting on with things. It's time that you got on with things."

But it seemed to John Mallory that she had learned how to get on with things, with life, *because* of seduction.

She had learned to seduce Machu with her eyes throughout the day when she walked past him at the wet mill. Even though they rarely spoke more than to say hello or *hola* in front of others, she could feel his dark eyes on her. If anyone were impatient it was her. In front of Machu, she would tell Lorenzo of her intentions to take a walk in the rainforest instead of eating lunch with him at the picnic table, so she could pick blackberries and wild herbs. Within minutes, Machu would follow.

Because of her love for Machu, she began to discern the taste of coffees she had grown up with all her life. She recognized the earthy taste of the Central American coffees of his home, the rich deep chocolate, the slightest hint of vanilla. She knew, without knowing how or why, she could identify any number of coffees now by their taste: the Kona coffee of Hawaii, single-origins from Guatemala and Sumatra, blends, and French Roast. More than just being able to tell when a bean was overripe or moldy (the easiest one to detect), she could tell Lorenzo which beans were not only a week old versus two weeks, but exactly which side of the farm they had been picked from. Her nose and palette had become so sensitized that she could identify the batch better than he could. And she finally understood the rituals of preparation: the specific roast by region, the importance of how it was brewed, the temperature of the water it brewed in, the critical length of time since brewing. She knew how to spit! She knew what it *took* to have coffee on a kitchen table.

She finally knew what it meant to serve others, and it didn't have anything to do with bone china.

"Life doesn't wait. It's impatient," her father said. He cleared his throat. "You're eighteen, and it's time for you to start taking some responsibilities. It's time for you to fulfill your destiny. This apprenticeship is only the steppingstone, a beginning."

"Maybe you need to be patient!" She had never spoken to her father in this manner, so it stunned them both to silence for several seconds.

"It's a man's prerogative to be impatient," he said with a laugh.

"I know that," she said, unable to keep the annoyance out of her voice, "now."

After all, she wanted to tell her father, sometimes her *novio* was impatient. The roasting room overlooked a garden in the back, and Machu would pretend to pick vegetables for dinner so she would see him. His tan, muscular shoulders arched, and his big and calloused hands would cradle a red pepper or eggplant, and he would point to the river. Always, he played in the dirt. One night when she overslept, missing their rendezvous, Machu snuck into the house and tiptoed to her small room in the back. He slipped inside her door. When she opened her eyes, his face hung over her bed like the moon. She had been dreaming that she was dancing and that Machu was watching her from the bushes. Now, because of his impatience, she would leave her window cracked after Lorenzo had gone to bed, her sign. He would slip inside and lie on the white sheets with her until almost sunrise. Sometimes, Juanita would tap on her door. They suspected she knew. He would bump into the table next to her bed, the only piece of furniture in her sparse room, and somersault out the open window. Juanita never said a word, but she always sang in the mornings now.

"Impatience is seductive in itself," John Mallory said.

"I know about your boyfriend," he said bluntly, stunning her. "I suppose it's perfectly natural for a girl to have," he paused, "interests. While she's away. Freedom. Away from home. It all adds to the excitement, but then we all know we have to go back home." He gave a laugh. "Where we belong. Get back to business. What about that Simpson boy?"

"Bobby Simpson? Since when did you give two toots about him?"

"He's not such a bad guy. Your mother's talked to him several times. He's very eager for you to come back. He misses you. Why, he's not so bad. He's going to be a lawyer."

"You always say we have enough lawyers in the world. You called him chubby. You said he has a big nose. Remember?"

"Well," he said, "no one is ever good enough for Daddy's Little Girl, but then again, no one's perfect."

She wanted to tell him that she also, finally, understood that, too. People who loved each other wore cherry-colored glasses. To others, Machu may not be handsome, but to her he was the most beautiful man on Earth. Smart, passionate, and kind, he saw her as the most beautiful and brilliant woman in any room. His complex ideas, dirty fingernails and scars were tattoos of his devotion to the earth. Although she kidded him that he spent too much time at work talking and too little time devising better ways to run the processing mill more efficiently, she admired his way with people. He made them laugh. He made them relax. She could see the admiration and respect for him reflected in their dark eyes. She wanted her father to know that even the old farmers took off their straw hats whenever they spoke to him. And to Machu, John Mallory was a blazing star. He told her that he found her enterprising ways invigorating. He never saw her as lazy, but charming and sweet, the way she hopped up on a table and sat idly for hours, sniffling and dangling her feet. How he swelled with pride whenever he saw her on the veranda for the coffee tastings, her mouth puckered, shaking her head. He had been used to hard-working women, women of the earth, but her smooth, flowered skin made his body shake. Looking at each other, they formed perfect reflections of light and darkness.

He said, "Your family needs you here. Your sisters. Me. You must come home."

She could hear desperation in his voice through the softness of his whisper. She held a blue sash that hung from the window and let the fabric run through her fingers until it rippled away. She knew all about domestic quotas, about the importance of families staying together. She also knew that it was the women who strengthened families, like golden linchpins.

What she *must* do? In her father's mind, she should adore only him and take her place seated at his right, maybe cross-legged at his feet. She didn't want to spend time refreshing their logo or fighting for more shelf space. She knew they needed people to work on attracting more consumers, but she could do that from here. She didn't want to cross-merchandise in the breakfast aisle, or in frozen foods, in front of the waffles. He meant she should taste the coffee—if it meant more sales and selling in bulk. She didn't deny his passion for innovation. She even supported his ideas for freeze-drying. But she belonged here, in the Earth, not hundreds of miles above it.

He'd tell her, she knew, "Just help your mother in the garden." Thing is, her mother never worked in the garden.

She could no longer be content to wait out winter with a sprinkle of cocoa from a packet, or a tin can. Her food should not come in boxes, her drinks should not come in cans, and her love would not be found in backseats.

She didn't want to find someone that her father thought was a good man. She didn't want him to find one for her, either.

Through heavy lashes she looked at the four corners of the sky. Within a few hours, the stars would dangle like beads in a rosary, tethered to the moon. It would be night, and she would meet her *novio*.

"Tonight there will be a full moon," she whispered.

"Ah, yes," her father said, his voice trembling, "but don't forget, the moon only reflects the light of the sun. It has none of its own."

"But what a vision it makes. Where would the tides be without it?"

He stayed silent.

"Here, the daughters of the farmers wear jeweled combs and dance in the moonlight. There's a myth they've told me about. Awakened by music, the moon comes down to kiss the cheek of the youngest girl. Then, all the other sisters turn to silver dust and float to the sky. They become stars. And stars provide their own light." With every ounce of courage she could muster, she said, "And stars can provide enough light for the coffee farmers to pick by, too, without burning them."

"You don't belong there!"

Yes, her skin was the color of wheat, and his was of coffee, but Machu Domingo believed it with his whole heart when he told her, "You illuminate the heavens, my love."

She believed him, for it was as if they were the only people in the world who had discovered otherworldly love.

For the first time in her life, she was certain what she must do.

23

Falling Stars

They're used to falling stars in Texas skies. Capri's ordeal is no more than a constellation of events. It doesn't take long for authorities to catch her and Mac. They have guns and handcuffs, but they don't use them. They say things like, "Stop. Don't make us run after you."

They take them into custody. Three guys escort them through the airport and to the police center for aviation security. There are more people there with guns and badges. They lead Mac to a separate room. He looks back at Capri, worried, but she can't tell any more if he's worried about her or only himself.

She sniffs, but they ignore it and put her in a room where they can watch her. Then they send in a woman with long arms. Dressed in a slick green pantsuit, she is round. Her cherry-red lipstick matches her blouse. Her lips are extra plump. Her dark eyes study Capri. Her hair pokes up, like the stem on a plant, and her skin is darker than the earth. When she speaks, Capri can smell the coffee on her breath. It is a rich blend, which makes her voice sound firm.

"You understand you've committed credit card fraud," she says. "Identity theft."

"It's my mom's card. Well, Trinka's. I'm related to her."

"Yes, we know. We were alerted by someone in your family. You weren't authorized to use it. That's theft." She spoke to Capri about imprisonment in a state correctional institution, jail time and fines. "It's a serious offense," she says.

She wants the story, but Capri cannot think. She always thought she knew what she was doing. But here, her nose is clogged. Her head spins. She tries to explain, but it comes out garbled. The woman hands her tissues and she blows her nose. She doesn't say much, and Capri realizes it's her strategy, to see if she'll crack. She wonders if Mac will be able to hold up under the pressure.

"This is big," the woman says.

Capri is small and shivering, sitting in a metal chair in a windowless room. The woman says they've screened her, looked her up in their system. It sounds painful the way she says it. "You've stolen," she says.

"It's my mom's. Well, my aunt's. She's either my aunt or my mom."

The woman raises her eyebrow. "This is a serious offense," she says.

"I know. I know. But if you check out my family, you'll see. We're just coffee people."

She gives her a look like Capri's on their computer screens.

"Do I get a phone call? May I have one, please? I want to call my mom."

The woman's face softens. She has an ancient look, like she may be a mother, too. Capri doesn't know if she's supposed to, but the woman lets her use the phone.

Aunt Lolly answers the phone. There are no jokes about Joe's Bar and Grill. It's quiet in the background. Capri asks for her mom, but Lolly says she's taking a bath.

"Get her, please," she says, but Aunt Lolly hands the phone to Aunt Abigail.

"Young lady," she says, "your mother is getting the first relaxation she's had since you ran off again. First time in years, probably. It's been a long night, and she didn't sleep a wink."

"I know, I know," Capri says. "And I'm so sorry. I can't tell you how sorry. But I need her. I *need* her. Please."

"She's taking a bath," she says.

"Please, Aunt Abigail. Please. They think I stole my mom's credit card."

"I know," she says.

Capri breathes in. She can see her mom in her mind's eyes. Her hair is up in bobby pins. She's chin-deep in a tub full of bubbles. The air is misty. It smells like lilac and honeysuckles. Her skin is turning rosy pink. Her head is resting behind her on the side of the tub. Her eyes are covered with cucumber slices.

Capri is the bucket of ice ready to shock her system.

"I'm sorry," she says. "I can't tell you how sorry, but I need her, Aunt Abigail. It's serious. Very serious. Please, please. Aunt Abigail. Please get my mom for me."

When her mother comes to the phone, her breath is full of worry. Capri can almost see water pooling at her feet. It has been over eighteen years since her mother has flown on an airplane, but Capri doesn't even hesitate to ask.

"Come! Come get me! Please. Help me. Oh, please. I'm so scared. I'm so scared, Mom. I'm sorry. I'm sorry for everything. Please, help me!" Capri cannot stop crying. She tries to explain to her mother, but all she can tell her is that she's being held captive by authorities in Dallas. "I don't belong here," she says. "I want to come home. Please. They're talking jail time. They're going to lock me up! Help me! Mom, please—"

"Oh, my god," her mother says, and starts yelling orders. "Celia, book me on the first flight to Dallas! Abigail, call Quicksilver! Quick, quick! Now! I need to go now!" Her mother rattles off commands like a drill sergeant. She is central station, and she's shooting at any flying creatures that come near her daughter's earth. She'll jump in any basket and risk the thundering skies. "Lolly, let me have some of those dog tranquilizers! Oh my god, a plane! Lolly? Please! It's Capri! She's in trouble! I've got to have them! I can't fly without them! I've got to save her! Damn it, Lolly, give them to me! I swear to God I'll kill you!"

"Mom!" Capri has never heard her mother so hysterical, her voice thick with terror.

"What did you say?" she shrieks. "You have got to be kidding me, Abigail. I'm going to kick your bony ass all the way from here to Dallas! You better not have turned my daughter in! You called who? I swear—"

Suddenly, Capri's nose unclogs. She can see everything clearly. All Trinka has ever wanted was to press Capri's fingerprint on her page. She's tried to warn her. She's tried to protect her, and she certainly does not deserve having mug shots of Capri from any police station for her scrapbook.

Capri cannot do this to her. Her mother deserves better. She breathes in while her mother shouts. It is about time she proves she can think of someone else besides herself.

"Mom, Mom. I'm okay," she says. "Don't worry. Please. Oh, Mom, don't cry. Please. I'm okay. I am. I can handle this. I can. Please, don't cry."

"No," she says, "I'm coming. Lolly, call that vet! He'll give them to you! Damn it! Fine! I'll go without them! Abigail, I swear. Go get your damn SUV warmed up and ready to drive like a bat out of hell! Get me to the airport! I'm warning you! Now! You're going to regret this! I swear!"

"Mom," she says, "no. I'm fine. Really. It's not her fault. Really. It's mine. I'll be fine. It'll work out. You'll see." With a calm voice, she tries to sooth her mother with her words. She tries to send her scents of salted crackers and raspberry tea under the moonlight.

"Things will work out?" Trinka says. "No! I'm coming! You called and I'm coming. They'll put you in jail. Some fat mama will use you for her love toy. Oh my god! Oh my god! My baby—"

Aunt Abigail takes the phone. "Capri?"

"Listen, Aunt Abigail. I'm fine. I know you reported me. You were right. I'm seventeen. I took my mom's card. I shouldn't have been using it. I'll figure this out. Take care of my mom, will you? I'll be okay, just take care of my mom. She's delicate. She's sensitive. She's not like other people. You know? Take care of her, will you? Please. I can take care of myself. Take care of my mom. I just want my mom to be okay."

"Capri, listen," she says. "Maybe I shouldn't have. Listen, I was wrong. Put someone on the phone. I'll take care of this."

She says, "No, thank you, Aunt Abigail. I mean it. I'll handle this and call you back later. As soon as they let me…" She hangs up the phone and hands it back to the woman.

The woman has been studying Capri as if she were watching a worker in the coffee fields. There's a two-way mirror, and Capri can see her pink hair. It makes her look like a garden fairy, lost in an endless sky.

"Listen, I know I've been stupid. I must sound like a spoiled brat to you. But I promise you, I don't do drugs, or smoke. I don't even like drinking, unless it's coffee. We're coffee people," she says, shrugging. "Just coffee people. And I've got this weird nose that smells too much. And there's this guy. I know it all sounds bad. And I have been thoughtless and immature and irresponsible. I haven't been grateful. Seems I've been spending too much time complaining about what I don't have, instead of being thankful. I even made a mess of my hair."

The woman leans back, placing her hands on her belly. "It's not so bad," she says. "You've got those honest blue eyes. You kind of look like a star with a hazy pink ring."

"A star," Capri says, sorting. "There are no stars in the sky tonight."

"Not true. There's a big bright moon and lots of stars." She exhales, then looks at Capri. "Did you know that astronauts say the moon smells like gunpowder?"

"I didn't know that."

The woman nods. "Sometimes, when you put two scents together, they can make interesting concoctions."

"Now that, I do know."

Without a word, the woman stands and walks out the door. Capri closes her eyes and inhales, then exhales loudly. She conjures up smells that remind her of home, and when the woman returns, she's carrying a cup. Capri can smell it before she reaches the door. It is an organic Costa Rican blend of coffee, fresh and oily, with hints of cocoa. She hands it to Capri.

"Thank you," Capri says, holding it, breathing it in. The woman hands her three packets of sugar, too, as if she's always known her. "Thank you so much. You don't know how much I appreciate this."

The woman nods, staring at her with her own cup.

Capri sips the coffee and lets it roll across her tongue. It is the richest, boldest cup of coffee she has ever tasted. It is sprightly and sharp. It tastes hand-picked, freshly roasted, and recently brewed. It fills the room with the sunshine of Earth.

"I was stupid," she says. "Just tell me where we go from here. I can't worry my mom any more. I was thoughtless. I swear, I don't even know why she puts up with me half the time. My goodness, where did you find this cup of coffee? It's heaven. Listen, please just tell me what I need to do to fix this. I don't want my mom to have to fly. You see, she's afraid of planes, and I don't want her to take some Great Dane's sleeping pills."

"This is a serious offense," the woman says.

"Yes, I know. I can't tell you how many serious offenses I've been putting my mom through. To be frank with you, I haven't been that good to her lately."

The woman brings her cup of coffee to her nose and whiffs, smiling as if someone has just opened the skies and turned on the sun. She gives Capri a knowing look. Then she slips out the door and talks to a guy in a dark suit. They look at Capri and the woman gives her a soulful look. Then they both nod and she comes back in.

"So? Where do we go?"

"I'm a mother," she tells her and Capri nods, then smiles. "I may be able to pull some strings."

"That's all I want," she says. "To go home and see my mom. I need to see my mom. You see, I've got to tell her... I love her. I don't tell her enough. And I haven't been the best daughter lately. But I can do better. I will do better. I just need another chance. You see, there's this guy, and things got a little crazy. You know, it's crazy. I've got to stop saying that word. But I need my mom. I'm only seventeen. I need my mom. Guess I'll probably always need her. You know, she'd fly to the end of the earth in a basket for me. She's like that. You know what I mean? You probably would for your kid, too. My family, well, we're different. My granddaddy. He gets lost in time because we lost someone we loved. We don't like to think she died. But it makes us different. Not like other people. It's a long story, but we have to stick together because they need me, too. I just need some time with them, with my family..."

"Time is a funny thing," she says. "We only think we understand it, but we don't."

Capri nods. "I know. Everything's been a swirl. I've been feeling a little messed up lately."

"You know," the woman says, leaning her fingertips on the table, "we don't really know what happens when someone dies. Maybe they're gone. Or maybe they're right here. All the time. Two stories can coexist. Maybe we just don't know it."

"That's interesting. I think that's kind of what my mom's been trying to tell me."

The woman tries not to smile. She takes Capri by the hand and leads her out the door and they stand in front of another guy. He's old, about Capri's height, with dark hair that falls over one eye. His skin is pocked and coffee-colored. He smells good, too, like he's been drinking that magical brew.

He has an accent, rolling his *r* when he calls Capri careless and lucky.

"I'm careless, that's for sure," she says.

"We're not in Kansas anymore," he says.

"I know," she says. "Believe me, I know."

It's the round woman who convinces him, telling him Capri's story. The whites of her eyes grow and shrink. She blows scents in the air, while her hands sway as if blowing in a southern breeze.

He finally looks at Capri and sighs, saying, "Go home."

Capri smiles at him. They take her credit card and she waits, drinking her coffee. They come back with tickets. They have booked Capri and Mac on a flight straight back to Kansas City the next morning. They charged them on her mom's card.

"What'd you say?" Mac asks her at the airport when they're out of ear shot.

"I told them we were thoughtless."

"That's what I tried to tell them," he says. "They weren't listening."

Mac watches over her while she sleeps in the airport, but when Capri boards the plane the next morning, Mac is two rows behind her. He falls sound asleep. But she doesn't care. The woman sent Capri on her way with another cup of the richest coffee, a Costa Rican blend from a saintly city. Even as she smells it, Capri can't get over the undertones of blackberries and plantains and cocoa. It has the slightest taste of chocolate. It lingers on her tongue as she flies north through the open skies.

24

Crepúsculo

One of the best things about sloths was that they were easy to find. All John Mallory had to do was look up into the green shrubbery to find Daisy nibbling on one of her favorite snacks. Daisy had proven so unadventurous that, most days, she could be found basking in the sun, a feigning bat upside down in the cecropia tree in front of the Domingos' home. Daisy needed the sun to warm her after a cold night, like a cold-blooded reptile, but John Mallory worried that she looked a bit too much like plump ripe bait for any eagle willing to swoop down and pluck her from the vine.

That Saturday morning, John Mallory dressed in a thin dress and cotton sweater. Overnight it had turned uncharacteristically chilly. She stood at the foot of the giant tree, banging on its trunk. Daisy wouldn't come down. Juanita had already left for market with the donkey, loaded down with beads, strings, and glass for Rosa's stained glass windows. With downcast eyes, Lorenzo had trailed behind them. He pretended not to pick up his shuffle just to keep up with Juanita, and John Mallory pretended not to notice. Besides, she was too busy trying to entice Daisy. She had promised Juanita that she would catch up with them at the neighbor's as soon as she collected her, but Daisy proved difficult to motivate. So she had just picked up two bananas and dangled them from her ears, then held them over her head and twirled in circles. She danced around pretending to be Miss Chiquita, a favorite character of Daisy's those rare times they watched television, and the Lady of Fruit who, back then, was still depicted as a banana instead of a woman.

When she heard the singsong voice coming from the front of the yard, she didn't recognize it. It seemed out of place. It was like the time her sister Trinka came to warn her that her father was on his way to a forbidden high school party. John Mallory had been deep in thought, smelling the odd party smells, underage and sipping a cold beer (which she hated), watching boys play pool (which was boring) when a ball of fiery red hair had blown in the door. The woman looked familiar. John Mallory knew she should know her, but she just couldn't put her finger on where from. It had taken her several minutes to collect her thoughts, even with Trinka frantically flapping her arms and shouting her name.

John Mallory had barely made it out of the driveway before the wheels of her father's Cadillac passed by the mailbox. So when she heard the voice shouting to her from the front of the yard, and she turned and saw the fluff of red hair, she experienced a bit of déjà vu. Matter of fact, it took her several seconds to recognize her sister.

"Have you lost your mind?" the voice said to John Mallory. "You've got two bananas and you're banging them together, dancing around a tree."

"So." John Mallory took a deep breath and closed her eyes. "I'm trying to get my sloth."

"Your what?"

"My sloth, of course."

"Oh, of course."

But John Mallory knew it sounded ridiculous. She closed her eyes and opened them again. Trinka still stood there. She wore wrinkled pink linen pants and a silk blouse with pearls. Her face was flushed, even though she hadn't even begun to experience the heat of Costa Rica. Her cream-colored pumps were completely unsuitable for her environment, and she clung to a purse that couldn't have held more than a comb and lipstick. "Trinka!"

"Surprise!" Trinka said. They hugged and twirled in a circle.

"What're you doing here?" John Mallory asked.

"I heard there were beaches."

"Right. Did you come alone?"

"You kidding?" Trinka said.

"I can't believe this. Daddy's here?"

"*I* can't believe this," Trinka said, looking around. "You've been living in that hovel?"

"Don't call it a hovel."

There was an awkward moment as they both stared at the Domingos' tin roof. Trinka craned her neck to peek at the back porch, but John Mallory knew she would never suspect that the rusty item she stared at was a tiny washing machine. When her voice sounded again, Trinka had less singsong and a little more melody.

"John Mallory, I ran ahead to warn you."

Just like before, Trinka might as well have been waving her arms, fanning smoke rings in the air. John Mallory knew her father would be hot on her trail, peeling into the yard at any moment.

"Where is he?" John Mallory said.

"We left our convertible at the edge of a cliff. That death-trap they call a road. We blew out a tire. Daddy panicked. No way was he driving any farther. It's just down the road, though. I was supposed to run here for help. In these!" She looked at the sole of her cream-colored pumps. "Right."

"Trinka, I can't go back, I belong here."

"Tell me what's going on," Trinka said, brushing off the tree stump and sitting down, trying to catch her breath. "Start with why you're dancing with bananas, and then explain that get-up you're wearing."

"This? Oh, it's my standard garb. You wouldn't last one minute in that."

"I wouldn't last one minute in that," Trinka said. Her eyes ran over the cotton dress that Juanita had made, the border of gold and turquoise ribbons sewn into the shape of a peacock to honor the many times John Mallory had entertained the Domingos with her stories about the fanciful birds from her childhood.

"Remember chasing peacocks?" John Mallory said.

"Don't tell me, you've cornered one up there."

John Mallory shook her head.

It was twilight and they were girls again, waiting for the peacocks on the Cahill's farm. The sisters were captivated by the birds' exotic Spanish looks: heavy eyeliner, sleek ultramarine hair gathered in a fan on the top of their heads, an array of rainbows in their trains. The birds fanned out their tails and called to them from the top of the roof, in the cold with steam puffing from their mouths. The girls would wait patiently on the ground, playing Candy Cane Lane on an old tree stump. Eventually the birds couldn't resist and they fluttered down, then strutted by. Close enough, the girls would promptly toss down their game pieces, spilling the board, and spring for the fowl. Then the peacocks would dart for the rusted truck behind the barn or try to fly back to the roof. But John Mallory and Trinka were runners, and they weren't afraid of a peck or two. *Help! Help!* the peacocks cried as the girls' chubby hands reached out and plucked a feather. But, John Mallory also remembered how sometimes the males would make the saddest dove coos when the sisters wore the feathered eyes in their hair.

"No, it's not a peacock," John Mallory said. "She's my sloth."

"Your what?"

"Daisy." Just then, Daisy tumbled from the tree like an overgrown melon and landed on John Mallory's shoulder.

Trinka jumped up and held her throat. "Actually, she thinks she's a parrot."

Trinka plugged her nose as she inched away, but John Mallory followed her.

"Listen," John Mallory said, "you've got to help me convince Daddy."

While she stroked Daisy, John Mallory spoke about her life. She told Trinka all about her work at *la cooperativa*. About the women and how she loved working alongside them.

John Mallory said, "They've helped me more than I ever could have helped them."

"Daddy says you've turned into a social worker. No money in that you know."

"We're going to get ninety-nine-year leases for farmers who don't own land. I'm helping create a refuge for wild animals. Restoring the rainforest."

"Yes, Daddy blames Lolly. He said if he hadn't funded her pet catering, none of this would have happened," Trinka said.

"You're kidding."

Trinka shook her head.

"Juanita loves me like a daughter. And Lorenzo, he pretends not to want me here, but I know he loves me, too."

"I'm not supposed to tell you, but Daddy just about blew a gasket when he called."

"Lorenzo? Lorenzo called Daddy?"

"Sure. The Roastmaster. He wants you to stay. He and Daddy got in an awful fight. That's why we're here."

"Really? I can't tell you how happy that makes me. You see, there's this guy..." She told Trinka about Machu Domingo. "He's the only man I could ever love. Romantically. You know what I mean."

"Is that all?" Trinka said. "You've always obsessed about love. You and your poetry. Machu? Is that his name?"

"Yes, and he loves me. He reads me poetry under the canopy of the rainforest." She raised her arms and pointed to the umbrella of trees.

"And Bobby used to send you flowers. But that stopped."

"It just kind of petered out." John Mallory bit her lip. "Seems like I've been chasing peacocks for too long."

"You probably have," Trinka said.

"Remember how they used to cry for help?" John Mallory petted Daisy, thinking about Machu. How he'd be there for her, how he has always been there for her. He still kissed her palms, then tapped his heart, as if he'd almost lost her when she burned her hands. Even Juanita had rushed to find her after she'd burned them. Lorenzo must have run all the way home to tell her about the accident. She had shown up, almost in tears, and insisted on using an entire jar of Vapo Rub on her hands. The greatest medical marvel in history, she had said, and she'd bought three more jars, so she could be ready anytime, in a pinch. She used so much, John Mallory could barely breathe.

"I just remember chasing peacocks—"

"Well, here everyone runs when someone cries. For everyone, not just me. But for me, Machu leads the way. For me! He'd follow me anywhere. Just to be with me. Even if I decided to fly in the sky in a basket—"

"I don't know why you'd be flying around in a basket."

"I'm just saying…he would. He loves me!"

The sisters stared at the ground. John Mallory's eyes were watery and still.

Trinka moved closer and craned her neck to study Daisy. She reached out, but when Daisy blinked she pulled her hand back.

"It's nothing more than a rug with eyes. Mangy thing, isn't it?" Then the translucence left Trinka's face. Desperation pinched her voice. "Oh God! Hide it! Here comes Daddy!"

"I won't hide her. Not anymore," John Mallory said.

"Suit yourself," Trinka said. "It's your funeral."

The sisters straightened their shoulders, both nibbling their lips. John Mallory looked at her sister, and for the first time she recognized the desperation in her eyes before she squeezed them shut.

Suddenly, she could feel the fear growing inside her. It dawned on John Mallory that she would have to tell her father. She became aware of his looming disappointment. Like a prodigal son, she would destroy the family's good name because of her lusty, spendthrift ways. She would be accused of being blinded by illicit love. No longer would she be considered a girl with promise.

How is it that the sun had grown so warm? In a matter of moments, it had passed the zenith, crossed the Caribbean Sea and the Yucatan Channel and was headed for the Gulf of Mexico. It singed her face. In the scheme of things, she knew she was insignificant—after all, only fourteen percent of the population lived in the Western Hemisphere—but why did they all *feel* so important? And why didn't everyone in the world speak the same language? A quarter of the world's people had no food or shelter. What did they do when the wind and rain came? Why weren't there wells to collect clean water for the children in Africa? Why had she waited so long to ask these questions?

Too late, she tried to smooth the wrinkles out of her dress. She straightened her shoulders, held up her chin, and looked straight ahead. She wanted to run inside and splash cold water on her face, emerge with blush rubbed on her cheeks. She desperately wanted him to be happy for her, slip his arm around her shoulder and say, "That's great, John Mallory." Yet, she couldn't ignore the familiar scent of someone desperately wanting to please: a French horn snapped inside its felt-lined case; a Girl Scout, ringing doorbells, loaded down with thin-mint cookies; coffee cake made from scratch. Tightness gripped her shoulders and pinched her neck. Pain swelled behind her eyes. A thousand pins pricked her feet. Her knees knocked so hard that Daisy vibrated and generated heat like a horrifying mink collar. She held her breath.

Up ahead, she thought she saw two figures, but they appeared as blinding lights.

So they came in pairs? A double vision of white blurs floated across the lawn.

She patted the curved claws of Daisy. Perhaps John Mallory was a fool.

Or perhaps, she thought for one brief moment, *I am magical.* She has a love story that travels beyond the boundaries of time.

"Did I mention," Trinka said, sucking air between her teeth, "he brought Bobby?"

"Bobby Simpson? Why would he do that?"

25

Roastmaster

The coffee cherries were nervous from the electricity in the air, like before a thunderstorm. They knew nothing of the men with the pasty skin but sensed a change and knew the infinity of change as well as they knew the taste of soil.

The strangers sat on the front porch as Juanita buzzed around them like a worker bee with too many queens to service. She poured coffee. She served muffins and fried plantains. She wrung her hands while Lorenzo perched on the edge of the porch like an eagle in its nest.

John Mallory spoke of the farmers, waving her arms to intensify her words.

"Wonderful people," she said. "People of the land. You'll love them, Daddy."

She spoke of the widening government, the shrinking labor, the growing organizations of people who banded together to support a world they believed in.

"We're doing big things here," she said. Their causes were deeper than the earth and complex as the crop. She spoke of hard work, of hunger, multiplied a thousand times. She flexed her muscles and promised that her mind had grown.

"I never knew how much I wanted to work," she said, "until I felt the ache beyond my own needs."

"What the heck does that mean?" Bobby said. She caught Trinka winking at him, as if she were an amused mother begging for him to play along.

"To grow something, to fill a need, to do something with your hands and mind that's important. Coffee is more than a beverage," John Mallory said. "It's a way of life."

"I just knew you'd understand," her father said, using his hands to push off his knees and stand up. "Valuable, valuable experience. I can't thank you enough Domingo," he said, extending a hand to Lorenzo. A gracious man, Lorenzo took it, and John slapped him on the back. "You have been so helpful, creating a desperately needed Roastmaster. I thank you. Early Mountain Coffee thanks you. Hell, the United States thanks you."

"But that's the thing, Daddy," John Mallory said. "We need to talk."

"About?"

John Mallory swallowed. She looked to Lorenzo, but his face stayed fixed on her father.

"I never knew," she said, "what it meant to have purpose." She explained how her own dark alleys of thought had squeezed her senses, deadened her taste buds and blinded her aspirations, until she had only smelled the simplest of scents. She had only scraped the surface. "It's like I had settled for a scratch-and-sniff world. I had no idea."

"It's hot here," her father said, unbuttoning his top button.

"Here, I've been filthy. In the dirt," she said, "and loving it."

"Well, that's great," her father said. "A little hard work, a little dirt under the nails, never hurt anyone. We're really proud of you, honey." Bobby swung his arm around her neck, pulling her hair. "Now you can pack up your bag of tools and take them back to a real challenge. Your sisters are going nuts. Leadership. That's what we need in the cupping room."

"About the cupping room," John Mallory said, wiggling away from Bobby. "Daddy, there are bigger worlds. Schools that need to be built, economic conditions that need to be stabilized, so many needs."

"Exactly," her father said. "And you are the answer, John Mallory."

"That's what I was hoping you'd say. I was so afraid you wouldn't understand—"

"Understand?" Her father squeezed her hand and grinned. "Understand what?" he asked.

"That I need to be here, that I'm staying." She glanced at Lorenzo, but his expression didn't change. His hands stayed folded in front of him.

"Come again?" Bobby said. Her father's eyes had locked on hers, even though he never dropped his smile.

"I think we'll have that minute now," her father said, holding up one finger, just as the sun moved behind the clouds.

***

John Mallory borrowed chairs from the porch and drug them into the yard. She wanted him to be close to the coffee trees, hoping Mother Bean would whisper in his ear.

The land needed her, she told him. Like a giant tractor she would turn the earth under her nimble fingers. It would be good. With his money, she could help people invest in the land, in the animals. Together, they could do their part to save the earth. After all, she said, shouldn't money be used to make the world a better place? Otherwise, the river between greed and need would be too wide. The oars too heavy.

"You're just one woman," he said. "They have hundreds of people, thousands to do their work. But it is *their* work. Don't get confused."

But she wouldn't budge. Her feet were hip-width apart, firmly on the soft ground. Both of her sit-bones were firmly pressed into the chair. With her mind clear, focused on her intentions, she took a deep breath. She could smell the fumes of the amanita mushroom, warning of toxicity. She could smell the hunger of the praying mantis, as it hunted amongst the bougainvillea. She knew that fungus beetles the size of ladybugs could cover an entire tree trunk in the rainforest, and she must defend herself. As a nighttime prowler, even the jaguar captured nesting birds. And like the deceptive quetzal that can vanish into the chaos of the rainforest canopy, so could she.

With more than twelve hundred species of orchids in Costa Rica to discover, she couldn't wait to find them.

"I'm in love, Daddy," she said, "with a man that I'm sure you'll love, too, if you just give him a chance. And he loves me. I plan to stay here with him. If he'll have me."

"If *he'll* have *you*? You're in love? You're not serious." He knew about this man, Lorenzo's son. He was absolutely unsuitable, but that didn't even begin to describe John's feelings. "He's Latino," he said, as if that said it all.

"And love crosses cultural boundaries," she said snippily. "Didn't you always teach us to be open-minded and accepting? Love one another? Don't judge. Isn't that a good Catholic?"

His heart stopped. She was serious. He peered at her in the dusk. The light in her sky-blue eyes made no impression on the gloom. "And Bobby? What about him?"

"Bobby? I have no interest in Bobby Simpson. None. Whatsoever. I can't believe you brought him."

He was silent for a moment and then sighed. "You're not staying here. Why? There's nothing here. No food, no Plaza. What do you intend to do with yourself in this godforsaken place? Let's pack up." He stood up and towered over her. "Big sale at Macy's this weekend. Let me buy you something. Anything your heart desires."

"Macy's, Daddy? Aren't you listening?" She stood up and faced him. "*This* is my heart's desire."

"I don't understand."

"Daddy, I'm trying to explain."

She held out her hand. In the distance, she could hear the singing of the pickers. She'd learned to listen for the rhythm and movement of their words. She could tell where they were by sniffing the air.

"Hear that?" she said. "They call them the songs of *milagro*. Miracle. Aren't they lovely?"

Their whimsical voices gave thanks in prayer. Soft clicking, so blissful, they plucked the red and golden cherries of burgeoning coffee trees and turned the earth back into the creation of a world.

"This guy? This Machu character? It's a fling. He won't do. He'll never be successful. Never make any money."

"Daddy, if I've learned one thing it's that love isn't something you can put in a safety deposit box. Drag it in and out to have a look at every now and then."

"I won't have it! You have so much potential, so much to do. Back home. I mean, that's what this was all about. Becoming a Roastmaster." He moved closer to her and rubbed her shoulder, then patted her. "You can't run out on your dreams now. When you're this close." With one eye shut, he held up his hand to show her less than an inch. "We've worked so hard. You can't give up. I didn't raise a quitter."

Her father had the look. His legs twitched as if trying to make sparks from two flints of stone. It seemed to her that he had always done that—thought *they* were winning the race even though a hundred girls raced past her. And if she didn't have the strength to cross the finish line, he would drag the blue ribbon to wherever she stood.

"You'll never make it without me. We can do it, but we've got to stick together. We're this close," he said, again with his fingers and one eye. "Don't give up on me now."

But she could no longer be the flailing girl tied to the train tracks of his disillusionment. She no longer wanted him to slide down the hill just in time to untie her.

"I'm not failing, Daddy. And if I am, it's not you failing with me. It's not your decision. It's not *your* life. It's mine. And I'll make mistakes. Let me. Let me trip and fall, maybe that's the only way I can see the sky."

"No. You'll get hurt, he'll break your heart, he'll leave you penniless. I won't have it I say—"

"I'm staying."

"I'll cut you out of my will. I won't give you one, red cent."

"I'm still staying," she said. "My mind is made up."

He stared at her, thinking how the sun had dried her skin. She had lost some of the plumpness that he had found so endearing. Her eyes were calmer, yet that pout on her mouth had turned slack. And where was her magical flute of a laugh? He hadn't heard it.

"I need a cold drink," he said. "Where can we get a drink? Something with a kick."

They fell into silence. The dark came, and even without looking up into the sky she knew that the stars were sharper and whiter than they had ever been before. She truly believed that they were all an extension of each other. Perhaps not. But then again, perhaps.

Someday, her father would understand. He would have to let her go, and being hopeful, she flared her nostrils to wait for the aroma of his blessing.

A few drops of water, a little bit of sunshine, and things eventually came to their senses. John had been through it all—World War, Depression, Fortune 500 acquisitions, and countless innovations: the introduction of modern electrical air conditioning, bar codes for retail use, and a man walking on the moon. He had become accustomed to twenty-five cent coupons meaning something. His expectations were large. Even though he wasn't certain whether a tree really made a sound when it fell in the forest if he wasn't there to hear it, he was certain of his ultimate influence upon his daughter. Like when she was a girl, he would wear John Mallory down with trips to the playground and too much fresh air, and promises of ponies.

For two days, his chubby feet took him through acres of rugged rainforests, coffee trees no taller than his head, and past rivers where Baird's tapir and jaguars roamed. Every time they went out, he expected a helicopter rescue, more than three dozen men searching the radius of his trail. Maybe he spent too much time envisioning heat-sensing equipment, volunteers searching through tangles of chest-high weeds. He could see his life unfolding, friends and colleagues making thousands of posters with his name and picture, putting them up in nearby towns, plastering paper across the United States and Costa Rica.

However, John Mallory wandered through the forest, oblivious to his pain, speaking of the coffee trees as if they were friends that her father should reacquaint himself with. She gave him no sympathy.

At night, he slept on a mattress stuffed with thick brush in a crackerjack home that she called quaint. She served him fried fruits and wore a rodent on her shoulder. He was frightened by the sound of birds and the possibility of coiled snakes in the tall grass, or dropping like fanged poison from the trees. He hated jumping spiders and startled easily.

Even worse, John had been completely unprepared for the site of his namesake's intended. But Bobby, the little buzzard, had not been able to conceal his mortification at the appearance of Machu Domingo—the round head, the brown skin, the long hairy arms. Everything about him rendered him speechless. After all, he said, how could he possibly fight someone he considered so utterly inferior?

"He's an anarchic freak, reminds me of a long-haired John Belushi," Bobby whispered to John with a wide-eyed expression. "Good-bye bed sheets, hello toga party." No one knew that Bobby's mind was playing scenes from *National Lampoon's Animal House,* a movie he had seen last week with a tight-sweatered sorority girl, a real hottie. They had necked in the back of the theatre for most of the film. "Not a guy you'd invite inside your house," he said.

"Bobby," John Mallory said, stunning in blue cottons that hugged her tightened figure, "would you like to take a walk?"

With a wink to her father, and a victory shrug to Machu Domingo, Bobby tromped down the steps. Machu would wait out the heat of the day on the porch, his arm raised like a white-faced capuchin, holding a branch of an almond tree. He pretended to listen to her father and sister argue about which one suffered the greatest discomfort. They would spend long minutes comparing blisters on their heels before he would slip away.

Always the city boy, Bobby dared not venture into the rainforest. He stopped at the edge of Pig River.

"I don't know why you're here, Bobby, so I'm just going to come straight out and tell you. I'm in love with Machu."

Bobby liked to imagine kissing strangers, so he could empathize with her desires.

She said, "I've never had a single ah-ha moment until I came here."

Bobby barely seemed to hear her. His eyes darted from the rocks to the leaves, to the rotted fruit on the ground. She knew he couldn't stand being surrounded by nature. He looked claustrophobic. Out of his element, blood vessels had burst on his face. He breathed fast and his pupils had dilated. She could tell his fight-or-flight response yearned to fly.

"So. You're really not going back?" he said with the kind of tone that said he was hypothesizing. His eyes were on the other side of the river. He jumped like he had seen something move. "I heard this guy has a girlfriend."

"No, he doesn't." Had someone told her father about Lorenzo's intentions to marry Machu to Tulipán Navariz? But, they had underestimated the lovers. It had been serendipitous actually. John Mallory had intended to hunt down the girl and threaten her with a meat cleaver, even though Machu said he could handle the situation peacefully. For weeks after he had told her about Tulipán, John Mallory practiced the evil eye in the mirror, as if she had the power to make heavy objects fly across the room, or drop poison in cups without lifting a finger. "Listen, sister," she had intended to say, "madness courses through my family veins." But just last week, the girl came to Rosa's booth at the market, with Carlos, batting her eyes, twirling a lock of her hair, exhibiting all the universal signs of madly-in-love. Both she and Machu had sighed in relief. Lorenzo had pretended not to notice the two teenage lovebirds.

"Bobby," John Mallory said, moving closer, as if she'd consider rubbing circles on his back, "I never meant to hurt you." She wouldn't even miss his lemon soft curls. "Please, try to understand."

"Yeah, babe." Something splashed in the water and his head snapped. His hands flew out in front of him. "What?" But when she didn't flinch, he steadied his legs. "You don't really plan to stay here, do you? This mosquito fest?" He slapped at his back as if bugs were digesting him. "Jeez, I'm dying for a burger. I don't know how you made it this long." His eyes moved back to her. "What? You want me to beg? Well, I would, but I'm not getting down on my knees in this swamp. Let's go." He grabbed her hand.

"Bobby, you don't want me."

"Sure, I do. We'll make a great team."

"Team?"

"Me, Chief Counsel. You, the Roastmaster."

She tried not to laugh. "Of course. He bribed you."

"No," he said, swallowing. "Of course not. I want you. Really." He gave her a peck on the cheek. "Now, let's go. Back to Kansas City."

Oddly enough, she realized that her happiness lived beyond the plains, deep in the rainforest where truth didn't have to crawl past the thorns and up the formidable spine of the zanthoxylum tree. Or fear its milky venom.

"I'm not," she said. "I'm not going back."

"Are you mad at me? Don't tell him I told you. He'll kill me if he finds out. Okay? Promise me? I get it. You've made your point, but why would you stay here? Come on—"

"Listen, I doubt you can understand, but I never thought I would stay here. Not when I came. I thought I was good. Everything was going as planned. I needed focus. My dad gave me an olive branch. A way out of my funk. Matter of fact, I thought I was finding my groove by coming here," she said, looking at him, "until I found out I was in a rut."

"A rut?" he said and swatted at his arm. "He told me you just like stirring things up."

"That's not true. Me? Did he say that? Well, maybe I do. But maybe I need to stir things up so I can settle down."

He moved closer to embrace her, grasping both of her shoulders. She flinched, and they heard rustling in the bushes. Bobby jumped and John Mallory had to hide her snicker behind her hand. She knew it was probably Machu.

"Well, if that's how you feel," he said, squeezing her and then letting go. He turned and quickly started back to the house, calling over his shoulder. "I'll take civilization."

Truth be known, his mind had already flown back to the hottie in the tight sweater in Lawrence. He would tell his friends that John Mallory had been bitten by a jungle bug. "She went granola," he would say. And about the job John had offered him, he'd tell everyone, "I never wanted that gig anyway."

With Machu's help, Bobby would be on his way to San Jose with a cash bonus from her father still burning a hole in his pocket, and he would spend two nights and days shooting shots of tequila. He would dance to Beatles songs in a bar with its only toilet a drain behind a curtain.

⁂

They gathered outside on the terrace. Lorenzo had set up porcelain cups for their cupping. Trinka shivered in her silk shawl. John Mallory stood next to her father, explaining the intricacies of tasting the Costa Rican coffees. Both she and her father could feel the weight of Machu's dark eyes on them as he leaned against the stone wall and crossed his arms.

"So you're a Roastmaster now," her father said. His hands were stuffed in his pleated pants. It was as if she had just received a certificate and all he needed to do was get a custom frame.

She swallowed and said, "In so many words."

She and Lorenzo were side-by-side again, ready to slurp their way down the line, as if this were her final exam.

At the first cup, she broke the crust with her spoon. She spat. She smelled and tasted vibrancy and brightness.

"Superb," she said. Her eyes were shining. "This one is huge. From the vines last week?" Lorenzo smiled and nodded. "It reminds me of my father's desk. It's too big for me!" She shook her head and backed away.

"What's that supposed to mean?" her father said, moving closer. He picked up the cup and took a sip.

"Oh, it's shop talk," she said with a hearty laugh and explained. "It's full of body. From the fruit of a massive tree, one solid block with short squatty legs. Just like your desk. Did I ever tell you that the movers wanted to saw off its legs to get it in the office door?" She turned to Machu and Lorenzo. "He set me up in this tiny office with this huge desk. It had already survived a fire, years ago, in its prior life. Amazing mortality. My father had it refinished, sanded and rubbed and stained. My father's desk," she said, her nostrils flaring, "has a drawer that smells of pipe tobacco. It's his scent of defiance against my mother's no-smoking rule."

Lorenzo and Machu laughed with her, while Trinka stood next to her father biting her tongue.

"My father's desk doesn't fit into an average room, so in the tiny office we turn it from the wall and face it in the middle, then squeeze around it like sand scattering in a jar of rocks. My father's desk," she said, her voice softer and slower now as she realized she would not be sitting at it again, "has gouges on its shins and ankles, bumps from his oversized chair. He gave me a leather chair, too. It has a broken back that threatens to let me topple over if I lean back too far. But the desk catches me before I do. Before I hurt myself."

"Sturdy and dependable," her father said and moved closer to her, taking her hand. "I'm sure they don't want to hear about our office furniture. But I'm impressed by your Roastmaster skills. You can tell all that from one sip of coffee?"

"Yes."

He patted her hand. "I knew you'd make a brilliant Roastmaster. You were always destined for greatness." His eyes twinkled at her and she smiled.

From the shadows, Lorenzo shifted down the line of porcelain cups.

"You still have *mucho* to learn," he said.

"I do?"

"Yes," he said, shaking his head.

He thought about how every time he stumbled across a rock now, he would inspect it with her eyes for its potential to make a necklace. He wondered if he could drill a hole in it, so she and his wife could dangle it from a string with beads. And even though he cursed her persistence, he loved her passion, her awkward strangeness. After all, she had coached Juanita to add chopped parchment to his diet for roughage and cured his stomach ails. He even pretended he didn't notice it in his rice and beans. And when she created a facial mask made of fermented coffee cherry juice and bottled it for the women, (besides Rosa, who broke out hives and pimples) the women's skin really did appear to glow.

"There is magic in life," Lorenzo said leaning over the cup. "You drink coffee at *medianoche*. Watch stars come and go." He slurped and spat, and then handed her his spoon, hoping she would smell the sweet nectar of fruits and the rainforest at midnight. "Even if you know you may have *loco* relatives," he said and winked.

Her father bristled, but John Mallory knew Lorenzo was referring to himself.

She smiled and sipped the coffee, then spat. "Yes, I understand. Love when it's hard, not just when it's convenient." Her father stood closer to her, and she turned to him and said, "This one is certainly too young."

Lorenzo had moved to the next cup.

"Learn and grow," Lorenzo said. "We all have successes and failures. Know the difference." John Mallory picked up Daisy and cradled her on her chest. "And, yes," he added, "be thankful for blessings. Even ugly furry animals. And girls who tell stories about birds with eyes in their feathers, even if the girl has too much hair."

She laughed, but her father frowned.

"Stretch," she said, and then added, "for your own cherries."

Machu laughed. Trinka did, too, but for no apparent reason.

"There's nothing here," John said, sipping the coffee. "This is bitter."

At the next cup, as if he didn't hear her father, Lorenzo turned to her and said, "To acquire anything you must be rich."

"That's what I tried to tell her—" her father said.

"You know Mother Bean. She knows you," Lorenzo said. "Can you smell the riches of a coffee tree? Appreciate her ways? Do you know the laugh of the toucan? Joy of chocolate? Quiet peace of the mountains? Do you know it now?"

She took the spoon from him, her eyes watery and fixed. With the help of her nose, she chose a cup. It was in the second row, near the end. She leaned over it, slurped and spat.

"This is coffee of boundless energy, beauty and peace. It's a peaberry. It's so important," she said to her father and then looked at Trinka, "to recognize when you have something wonderful, like this smooth bean in your pocket. Or a chance to fail. Many people consider the peaberry to be flawed. Only one bean found inside the fruit instead of two. Yet, isn't it funny how some people, many of us, consider the peaberry the most delectable taste? Because it's more concentrated, because its soil lacks sufficient boron. Some people love it. They pay more for it."

They were all silent, looking at her.

"It is the taste of a divided heart," Lorenzo said quietly. "Patience, *hija*. Ask, and Mother Bean answers."

She blushed.

"John Mallory, do you need some water?" Her father looked to Trinka for confirmation, judge to jury. Trinka nodded.

Lorenzo stepped away from the table. "To use your gifts," he said, "you must know them. Appreciate them. To be an inspiration, you must be an enlightened teacher *and* student." He nodded.

She touched her heart and smiled at him.

"What more do you smell?" he asked.

She turned her nose in the air and then picked up a cup. She inhaled deeply.

"This is slightly moldy," she said and smiled at Lorenzo. "It is the smell of pity. Fear. Scarcity withered on a branch." She extended her hand with an open palm to Lorenzo. He handed her a spoon. She broke the crust, tasted, and spat. Then she nodded. "Mother Bean taught me to listen with an open heart. When there is no food or drink, only emptiness, there is still hope. She showed me the abundance of coffee. You did, too. To drink nectar and bask in the world's magic." She nodded her head. "No doubt. It's moldy."

He smiled and nodded for her to continue.

She lifted her chin and inhaled deeply. Then she walked to the furthest porcelain cup on the other side and broke the crust. She slurped and spat.

"Wow, it's flawless. This is the most incredible creation! Taste Costa Rica, Daddy! Trinka!" She stepped back so they could move closer. "Broad strokes of chocolate, tinctures of blackberry and plantain, big fat dollops of vanilla. There's even a touch of avocado. Animals, birds. It's eternity! Oh, Lorenzo! It's the footprint of our land. It's our family. You have created it," she said.

"*You* have created it," he said. His eyes were watery. "You manifest, yes? You give it away."

"Give it away?" She shook her head, searching for the right word for him.

Trinka leaned over and sipped the coffee, but her father stared at Lorenzo.

Lorenzo repeated himself. "You must give yourself away." Then he softened his voice. His eyes were large round pools of chocolate. He spoke from his heart but as if he had rehearsed it a thousand times in his head. "We were created whole, *hija*, like the bean. When a man and a woman join, it is a union of dance. Two parts create one. It is a dance of attraction. There is a mutual knowing. Unfolding. The force that created you also created the magic of Mother Bean. That same force is alive today. It is known to you. Like the red and golden cherries that hang from the coffee tree. If you look into the sky, you see the embryo of mankind. It is the same image. That of the cosmos. That of the coffee cherry. Like Mother Bean. We are an inspiration of life." He held up his cupped hand and blew into it, opening his fingers as he did.

"We are the breath of life. You are Mother Bean, and she is you."

John Mallory shook her head. Her eyes were moist.

Lorenzo turned to Machu. He walked to his son and pulled him out of the shadows. He led him to John Mallory. He grabbed his son's hand and hers, and pushed them together.

Lorenzo said, "He who teaches, he teaches what he most needs to learn. Our hearts were created in our bodies before our brains. In the fetus. Did you know? Because sometimes I forget, too."

He nodded at Machu.

Machu stroked John Mallory's fingers, interlocking them. He swallowed as if he too recited from his heart. As if he knew it was after midnight. He knelt before her and said, "Live with me in a castle, with our colors of people. Full of children and love. Farmers of life. With plenty of rooms. We need nothing. Our stories come from the rainforest. Our pens from the branches of the giant jabillo tree. It is not our path to be blind. Our lives are of the sloth and monkeys. We are two peacocks breathing fire in our yard. There is shade underneath the canopy. There are patches of sunshine to kiss your face and moonlight to light your path. Please, stay and be my wife."

"No!" her father said. He clamored towards John Mallory. "I forbid it—"

But Lorenzo's hand gripped his arm. "It is *el verdad*," Lorenzo said. "Life is *un milagro*. A miracle. We are all observers. And this is truth."

Before John could step between Machu and John Mallory, Lorenzo joined the breath of the Costa Rican winds, and the power of the great green mountains, to the dance of Mother Bean.

"Your love is your legend. You are coffee," he said.

26

Estar en Casa

It was really because of the phone call from her mother that John Mallory finally agreed to go back to Kansas City at all. Only for a few weeks, a month at most, she had told Machu, Lorenzo and Juanita. With all of her father's manipulations and tactics—pointing out scarcity of packaged goods in Costa Rica, abundance of disease, and trying to create general doubt about multicultural relationships—he had failed.

When the call came on Sunday night, John was fuming in *la cooperativa*. He despised the fact that his daughter felt free to make her own decisions. Flex her own free will and put down her own foot. The foot *he* had created. To prove it, he poked holes with a pencil in the Costa Rican map that hung on the wall.

He was miles from home. Yet, he had only been gone seventy-two hours and twenty-three minutes. He was losing his daughter, and he had already been treated for sunburn, dehydration, minor cuts and insect bites.

"I really don't believe this," he said when Barbara called.

Little did he know that his out-clause, the ordeal, began the night before when Barbara Mallory and some friends from her bridge club attended a benefit at a local hotel. John had been quite happy to miss it. There would be dancing and idle chitchat, two things he had no interest in. About one thousand people would gather in an atrium, dozens packed in front of tables with skimpy hors d'oeuvres and watered-down drinks, two blocks away from Early Mountain Coffee.

Barbara had not been there long, possibly only thirty minutes. The hotel was probably packed, just like he suspected, full of socialites in party dresses and tuxedos, middle-aged and middle income. All of the Mallory daughters had planned to attend, but Celia was running late. An hour later, when they arrived, it would be to collect Barbara. By the time she got to the Early Mountain building, there was a blaze of lights and fine mist in the air.

Kansas City had been no stranger to heartbreaking blows—the Brush Creek flood in 1978, the roof collapse at Kemper Arena the next year, a major flaw design involving inefficient nuts and bolts that would cause a catwalk to collapse in a plush downtown hotel in 1981. That tragedy would kill one hundred and fourteen, and injure over two hundred friends and acquaintances, parents of children in their community.

The partial demise of Early Mountain Coffee would not serve as a major catastrophe. It made no sizzles on national news.

As John listened to his wife, he realized that his greatest disappointment wasn't losing part of the building in what sounded like nothing more than a hiss-fire, but that he wasn't there to hype the loss with the media. He would have collected at least thirty minutes of fame.

"I'm glad no one was injured, but were people wandering around like zombies in the streets?" he asked.

"Not really," Barbara Mallory answered. "The roof of the building just kind of deflated, like one of those blowup dolls hit with a dart gun."

"Any clothes covered in soot?"

"John! Bless your lucky stars no one was hurt!"

He sighed. He was glad, but a little part of him felt disappointed. There would be no news clips of women frantically searching for their men. No firemen or policemen holding them back. There would be no need to search the wreckage. Early Mountain Coffee went down without a fuss.

"It was that old roaster," Barbara told him. "If you hadn't been so cheap, the girls would've replaced it like they wanted to."

"Oh, God," he said with an overwhelming urge to get home and plant evidence. If it wasn't too late, he could post rewards for any information leading to——. Certainly he could get some press.

"Isn't there any chance," John Mallory asked his wife, "that someone saw something suspicious? Did you take any pictures? No one cried outside the building? How about Abigail? Never mind. If only Trinka were there, she would have cried up a waterfall—"

He heard his wife sigh. Then it occurred to him that he could use this. After all, he was the original spin doctor. Certainly he still had a little spring for a dance. He must find John Mallory.

Stained glass in flight
　　a few candle stubs...
　　　　pews covered in dust...

Why would Sun
ever give up
Seventh Daughter?

Jeweled combs
in her hair
dancing
in moonlight
to flute and drum.

Why leave only six
blue stars,
a gaping hole
in the sky
Forever?

27

Fuego

John Mallory and Trinka were still on the terrace when their father came to tell them the news about the fire at Early Mountain Coffee. They were cupping a sample of Kona coffee, something Lorenzo Domingo mocked with, "Hawaiian coffee? Do they harvest in hula skirts?"

John Mallory had just spat, in a grace Lorenzo could be proud of, and she mentioned the trace of pineapple. Then, she stopped to sniff the atmosphere, listening to the coffee cherries. She noted the gamey hint of a jaguar.

As her father trotted towards them, his head up, mumbling, she thought of the years ahead without his pipe tobacco and its blue cloud of sweet aroma filling the air. She would miss seeing him tilted in his chair on the back porch, his voice a bagpipe, singing *Amazing Grace*. The irony didn't escape her, how it had been her father who had helped her stretch to touch the sky. He taught her to be ready to believe in the magical light of the moon.

But his eyes were on the sky, as if he was searching for something. Then he looked at her and explained carefully. "They burned the building last night."

"Who?" John Mallory and Trinka rushed to his side. "What's happened?" she said.

He shrugged. He had whipped himself into a shield of armor and armed himself with guns, gas, and clubs.

"Vandals?" Trinka said. "It couldn't be a disgruntled employee."

"FBI doesn't know yet," he said.

"FBI?" John Mallory looked from her father to Machu. "Why are they involved?"

"They aren't yet, but they're on their way. Arson. Maybe connected to a string of events. In the four-state area. I'm not sure."

"Was anyone hurt?" John Mallory asked.

He shook his head.

"Thank God," she said.

"And we weren't even there to stand by and see it all go up in flames." John appeared to collapse, his knees buckling. He had to grab the corner of the table for balance. While Trinka ran for a washcloth, John Mallory petted his arm. He stared at his dusty shoes. Then he said the words that would transform John Mallory back to her days of pigtails and bare feet. They were his best defense. "You must come home with me," her father said. "You understand," he said to Machu and then Lorenzo. "Her family needs her."

Those words took John Mallory back to early in summer when she was ten years old. The air filled with late spring, misty and green. She balanced on the top bar of the swing set, clutching a vine of the weeping willow tree. For what seemed like hours, she had tried to persuade herself to jump. Already she had climbed the silver ladder, but each time she had chickened out. From the screened porch, her father called to her. On her tiptoes, she could see inside: Trinka sat on the top of the homemade ice cream maker, clutching the wooden barrel; her body jerked while her father turned the crank; beads of sweat glittered on his temples. Trinka wanted off, and her sisters were arguing over whose turn it was to sit on the bucket. The same spats of revolution, power versus age.

"Lolly," Abigail said. "It's your turn. You're the next Little Girl."

So her father had called to John Mallory to settle their disagreeable stomachs.

"Come here, John Mallory! She'll do it," he said, hissing at her sisters. "She *loves* her father." His voice grew soft. "John Mallory never complains. Come here, honey. Let's make something special. Come here, John Mallory! I need you!"

"Yes, come here, John Mallory," Bess said. Her other sisters joined in.

Back then, for a brief moment, John Mallory had paused. She still wanted to swing. But her back was burned from a day in the sun. Her tender skin was strips of red and white. She tried to move forward, balance her body as it swayed. Looking down through the rusted gullet of the teeter-totter she could only see chains. Twisted branches lay on the ground. Yet, she heard the soft breath of the willow; the leaves of the vine had turned to whispers. *You are the falcon, John Mallory! Swing from our branches and fly through the wind.* Perhaps, she thought, she might hit the tree. *Or, perhaps*, they told her, *she wouldn't.*

"John! She's on top of the swing set again!" Her mother stood in the doorway of the screened porch with her hand to her forehead.

"John Mallory! Don't you dare!" Her father's voice was full of thunder. "Get down right now! You'll break your neck!"

With a tiny whimper, she dropped the vine and followed her father's voice. As she slid down the slide, the metal burned her legs. A locust pierced the sole of her foot as she crossed the yard. Even a hornet sunk its teeth into her shoulder. Still, she obeyed. When she got closer, she could see them clearly. Her mother had her hands on her hips. Her sisters were huddled together, tapping their feet. But her father's eyes were cast down at the shadow, the empty spot on the bucket that Trinka had left behind. His eyes were focused on the prospects of ice cream.

28

Red and Blue Clusters

Capri's strength comes in clusters, like the rich red cherries that hang from the coffee tree branches. The trees root to the ground while reaching for the heavens. As soon as Capri exits the plane in Kansas City, she sees her mother and aunts through the plexiglass. They cluster in bunches, like bright blue stars standing on rich soil.

Her mother's hair is up in bobby pins. She has on a pair of navy-blue sweat pants Capri knows she never wears outside the house. Aunt Abigail and Aunt Lolly are at her side, like wings pinned to her arms. Aunt Diana is there, too. Aunt Celia looks around as if scouting out their exit path. Aunt Bess presses closer, breathing down the back of the man at the checkpoint. He turns around and tells her to back up.

They search the crowd, looking from face to face. Her mother sees Capri first and her face melts. Aunt Bess points. When Capri runs through security, they circle her.

"Mom, I'm so sorry. I'm so sorry…"

"You're safe," her mother says. Her lips tremble. "That's all that matters."

"I was so scared," Capri says.

"But you did it," says Aunt Abigail. "You did it all by yourself. You made it back."

Her mother kisses her forehead and looks at the sky.

"Mom," she says, "you were right. You were right about everything. I'm so sorry. I'm so sorry I worried you."

"No, no. Hush," she says. "Hush. No one's right about everything. Even mothers."

Capri's nose runs and Aunt Bess hands her a tissue. She shivers and Aunt Lolly gives her a sweater. It smells like kittens and puppies and butter cookies. Capri has never been so glad to smell the black Kansas soil in the air. Her aunts rub her back and touch her hair. They would have stayed that way for hours, but the checkpoint man asks them if they could please move to the side. They're blocking traffic.

"Back off, buddy," her Aunt Abigail says, but they break apart. That's when Capri sees Mac. He looks small and lost. Nobody's there for him, but she know he has his Mustang.

"I'm going to ride with them," Capri says and points with her chin to her mother and aunts.

"Sure," he says. He cringes under her aunts' glares.

"Let me talk to him," Capri says to her mother, "just for a minute."

As she walks towards him, butterflies fill Capri's stomach. She and Mac stand near the bathrooms, close to the exit. She can smell the sweat of his discomfort.

"No mile-highs for me for a while," Capri says, pointing to the ladies' bathroom, and they kind of laugh.

She always wanted to travel the world, be where the weather is hot and the food is spicy. And she desperately wanted to be a girl in love. But she is older now, and she realizes she's not as confident and comfortable in her own skin as she thought she was. What she does know is that scents come in pairs. Whether father or mother, daughter or son, two lovers or friends. An incredible gift, love is an exchange of breath, breathing in and breathing out. It's okay if she has no-nonsense ideas about love, because she is rooted and down-to-earth.

"I saw some ugly sides of myself," Capri says.

"Me, too," he says. "Me, I mean." And then, "I'm sorry."

She says she's sorry, too.

"You're not going with me, right?" His hand rests on her hip. They both know he doesn't mean in his car. He still has hope for Mexico.

"No," she says, "I think I'll stay with them." Because with them, her mom and aunts and granddaddy, she can learn about herself. Be with herself. She needs to learn things only they can teach her. She needs to figure things out. She's got to learn to love herself before she can love anyone else, and she can't give herself away until she knows who she is.

She sniffs, then says, "I'm kind of stuffed up."

"Gotch ya," he says, but his eyes are moist. He clears his throat. "Well, I'd better head home. Call you later?"

She shakes her head. "I probably need some time alone."

He swallows. "I can be what you want. I promise, I could be your hero if you'd let me."

"I know you could," she says. She smiles and tilts her head. As he turns, she reaches for him. "Mac, maybe...Maybe someday. You never know."

"You never know," he says, trying to smile. His thumb is tucked into his belt and his eyes are down on his boots. "Because, baby, you know what?" he says, looking up. "You're worth waiting for," he says.

Then he leans over and steals a kiss. He shakes his head as if he can taste the baby powder disappearing from his lips. He looks up at the ceiling, like he can see a blue morpho butterfly flittering away.

~

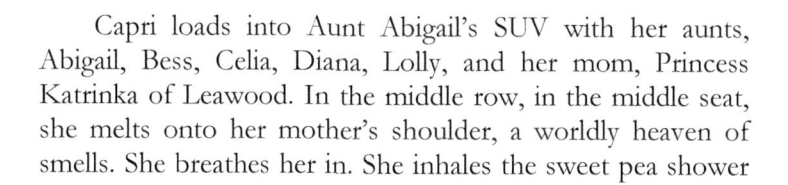

Capri loads into Aunt Abigail's SUV with her aunts, Abigail, Bess, Celia, Diana, Lolly, and her mom, Princess Katrinka of Leawood. In the middle row, in the middle seat, she melts onto her mother's shoulder, a worldly heaven of smells. She breathes her in. She inhales the sweet pea shower gel still lingering on her skin, the tea tree shampoo in her hair, and cinnamon gum on her breath.

Now she sees the absurdity. Her world cannot just be about guys and girls who try to steal her guys. Which guy calls her, which one holds her gaze, and which one looks away. She's spent too much time noticing who makes a point of talking to her and who doesn't. Who responds to her with long funny remarks, and who gives her two-word answers. Who smiles at her, who acts annoyed, and who doesn't notice her at all. It doesn't really matter who talks to her but keeps walking. She knows who responds to her. Who cares deeply about her. Who loves her even when she feels she may not be worthy of their love.

Some people may have to fly out of the flatlands and beyond the Gulf of Mexico to figure things out. It may take a few days longer than it should, to understand what love really means. But some... She knows. Some are willing to soar through the skies in a basket, just for her.

This is the only circle Capri needs to be in right now.

"A golden retriever adopted three tiger cubs at the zoo," her mom says. "They were abandoned by their mother." She strokes her daughter's hair. "It was in the papers."

"You're not abandoning me, are you?" Capri asks.

"Oh, no. Never," she says. "I just wanted you to know there are always other options."

Capri blinks. Then they both giggle.

"I suppose you're going to lock me in my room again," Capri says.

"I suppose I am," her mother says and then squeezes her knee.

As they pull away from the curb, Aunt Bess says, "Who cut the cheese?"

"Oh, come on," Aunt Abigail says, "let's not rile Daddy. Anyway, it's supposed to be a sunny day."

In a split-second they all start laughing. Capri finally gets it. Finally, she understands the inside jokes. Maybe Aunt Abigail does have a sense of humor after all.

Aunt Lolly starts singing "Here Comes the Sun."

They sing, but no one knows all the words. Her mother chair dances, swaying her hips and shimmying her shoulders, as if she were dressed in red, dancing beside a bull. With a jeweled comb in her hair, Capri reaches up to touch it. She breathes in her mother's perfume. Capri laughs, trying to keep rhythm with her mom as they dance. They are seven winking lights flying down Interstate 35, speeding towards Rainbow Boulevard.

29

Medianoche

On this hot and moon-filled night, Capri sits at the kitchen table at Rainbow Boulevard. She smells the torment she knows her mother feels, like gunpowder in the air. Yet Capri can also smell the sweet perfume of coffee. Since John Mallory's death, her mother must have told the story a million times in her head. As if she could catch up to her sister and push her onto another path, she could change her ending. But she can't change the story, no more than coffee cherries can stop whispering John Mallory's tale to songbirds in shade trees.

"I've never told anyone the whole story about how John Mallory died," her mother says. Capri sits at the kitchen table drinking a cup of Costa Rican coffee. Her aunts listen, too. "Because it's always been too painful. I've been torn all these years. One minute I feel sad, another minute I'm angry. I wonder if I couldn't have stopped her. Or maybe I could have saved her. Helped her. And then sometimes I'm mad because her death has completely defined my life. All of our lives."

Capri holds her mother's hand. Aunt Diana rubs her shoulder, saying, "Yes."

"I bet we all feel that way," Aunt Lolly says. "We all feel like it was our fault."

They give each other knowing looks.

"I sent her off with a paper ticket and pocket money," Aunt Abigail says, looking down, "as if that were enough…I was jealous she got to go."

Aunt Bess whispers, "I was jealous she got new clothes."

Trinka says, "But I could have stopped her. I was there."

"No," Aunt Abigail says. "It wasn't your fault."

"It was just John Mallory's destiny to stay a Little Girl forever," Aunt Lolly says.

On the shore of Pig River, John shook Lorenzo's hand and thanked him for handling the rental car. He had arranged for a prop plane to meet them in Santa Maria and take them to San Jose. Headed for the white church steeple, they borrowed Lorenzo's boat so they could cross the river. It was the fastest path. Soon, they would be on their way back to Kansas City.

Perched in the bow of the boat, her father stood ready to thrust a long spear down the throat of any giant that tried to stop them. Behind him, Trinka sat in stillness, a nymph in linen with her hair fluttering in the wind. Her eyes were straight ahead, intent on open waters.

From the back of the boat, John Mallory stared at Machu Domingo, and then her empty hands that rested in her lap.

"I am a simple man," Machu said, leaning over to her, "in love with a Goddess."

"I'll be back," she said. "Before the next full moon."

He nodded, then kissed her lips, but his kiss tasted sad and lonely.

He pushed the boat, grimacing, then stood at the riverbank as if he represented humankind, present for over fifty thousand years, a hunter-gatherer who lived off the land.

It was before the Pleiades shone from the sky, but in the air John Mallory could smell the mystery of the lunar cycle.

As Machu stood on the shore, she saw only his shining face, big, round, and white, becoming paler and ghostlier the farther she drifted away. Finally, with the sun in her eyes, she saw only half his face, until it became a crescent moon, and then she turned around.

Lorenzo Domingo had turned away from the boat. His feet left heavy tracks in the mud. He doubled over with grief. He knew his wife was home crying, too. But as he stared at the ground, he noticed a set of fresh paw prints next to his own. They were clear and large, well-formed, fresh and sharp, and heavy with scent. His brow furrowed with confusion as he stared at the back of John Mallory's head, and then ahead at the trail. He knew they were the impressions of the jaguar. He had finally attracted one! But why hadn't she smelled it?

With his eyes, he followed the trail as it veered to the left toward the waterfall. The cat must have hurried. The prints increased, as if it had skipped and leapt, pacing its game. The trail stopped at the rainforest edge, before a large rock small enough to be hurdled. Curious and overcome with joy, Lorenzo ran to it, and stopped to ponder at the scruffy prints at the base of the rock. Suddenly, an overwhelming image took his breath as the creature lay in front of him like a spotted ghost. Crouched behind the rock, the massive feline kneaded the ground and flexed its claws. It peered ahead through the underbrush.

Powerful and secretive, what did it watch? He wanted to shout, but he didn't want to scare it away. And he didn't want it to turn around.

Slowly, Lorenzo backed away. He knew the wagging of the spotted tail would be its last act before attack. But its cannon of a body and green eyes pointed to the west. It hunted another. As its front paws poised for the lunge, Lorenzo's eyes followed the creature's trail.

Further down the bank, he saw the raccoon-sized sloth creep out onto the rocks. Behind Daisy, followed the small child, Paco.

Lorenzo tried to scream, but his breath caught in his throat. Before he could shout a warning, the creature lunged.

John Mallory detected every juicy drip of life. With the sprightliest sense of smell, no aroma ever swept by her nose without her flaring her nostrils. That was how she knew she was destined for storybook greatness.

She had been born of coffee. Nestled in a rowboat, she no longer feared the blinding sun. With her breath the sweetness of coffee and cocoa, she was raised on coffee—by coffee—for coffee. She looked ahead.

From the deepest power that lay like a sleeping falcon within her, she could again see the rusted chains of the swing, but not as manacles of her soul, but rather the limitations to her flying. The ageless murmur resonated from the lips of the kaleidoscope mountains: *The thrill of flying begins with the fear of the fall.*

But before she heard the weeping willow cry or the screech from the falcon, before the coffee cherries rustled and shouted in unison, John Mallory smelled the jaguar.

She turned around.

Lorenzo stood with his back to her, frozen in fear. Machu watched her with longing eyes. She could see through the sun. Inside the bushes, she knew the jaguar crouched. Her nose recognized the pairs of scents, hunger mixed with innocence and love. Her eyes landed on Paco and Daisy at the edge of the river. They had come to tell her good-bye. Good-bye.

With her toes spread and the four corners of her feet firmly planted in the stern of the boat, like a captive falcon, she tore off the helmet of tassels and ribbons that had kept her blind.

She knew that the greatest gift she could give to herself would be a push from the nest.

"I called her name. John Mallory! Don't!" Trinka says. Aunt Lolly hands her a tissue and she blows her nose. "It wasn't until Daddy heard the splash that he turned around, but John Mallory's seat was already empty."

Capri squeezes her mother's hand.

"Daddy's face was ashen white. He clutched his chest. I had to jump up and grab him before he toppled over. That was when we saw John Mallory's face disappear under the water." She looks around the table at her sisters, then at Capri. She gently touches her fingers to her daughter's cheeks and closes her eyes, as if she were feeling her sister's face. "John Mallory's face was like the moon vanishing behind the clouds," she says.

Her sisters reach out to touch her.

"Time seemed to stand still and speed up. I still don't understand it. It seemed like moments later, John Mallory rose from the water headed for the shore. A white light surrounded her. She was raw power. It's the only way I can describe it. She swept past Lorenzo and headed for the beast. Machu screamed after her, 'No! My love!' I can still hear him screaming. It's as if he were in this room," she whispers and wipes her nose. "I should have swum after her," she says, crying. "I tried to step out. I tried to jump in the water, but I couldn't move. My feet were cemented to the bottom of the boat."

Capri wipes her own eyes with a tissue.

"But she was *medianoche*. Half night. A wild thing, she was ready to fight any creature. John Mallory was a madwoman. She waved her arms. She made awful, inhuman sounds. She bared her teeth and clawed at the air. I could see the animal now, too. The jaguar crouched, ready to jump. But she was fearless. John Mallory didn't stop. She kept pressing it, squeezing it, but the jaguar didn't back away. The beast pounced. And then...and then they tumbled. I saw the cat's fangs sink into her neck, but she didn't scream. I'll always remember that, how she didn't even scream. Her arms were around its back, like she embraced it. Her hands were gripping its fur. They rolled and rolled, as if they had become one, one wild mad animal, together in time, and when they splashed into the water, they disappeared. Machu dove in after them. They all went over the waterfall."

"So she's dead? You're sure?" Capri says. "You didn't find a body—"

"Yes, she's dead," her mother says. "We never found her. Everyone in the village searched for weeks. No one could have survived that fall. And I'm ashamed. Because I was…I was a coward. You see, I hadn't told anyone yet, but I was pregnant with you. Still, I could have…"

Capri breathes in short breaths. "You were pregnant?"

Her aunts don't say a word.

"Yes, and I hadn't told Daddy, and I probably shouldn't have gone to Costa Rica, I know. But I wanted to tell my little sister. I wanted to tell her first. She and I were like twins, but she never knew. I never got to tell her." She wipes her eyes with a new tissue. "And, believe me, I worried about taking that trip the entire time I was carrying you. And frankly, with John Mallory dead, we were all so sad. But you," she says, and looks into Capri's eyes, "you were the only thing that kept your granddaddy from going completely mad. I think he tries to keep it together as much as he can, just for you. He sees her in you. He always loved to dance with her."

Her aunts nod.

"So who is my dad?" Capri asks.

"Like I said," she says, waving away the thought with her tissue, "some pretty boy with a fast car. A two-seater. He was a stock broker and didn't want a baby. He moved to New York."

When Capri's face sinks and she pokes her coffee with her spoon, her mother adds, "Oh, I'm sure he would have wanted you, honey. If he had ever met you."

"That's right," her aunts' voices echo around the table. "He would have."

"You know," says her mother and squeezes Capri's arm, "we could find him, I'm sure, if it's important to you. Heck, we could probably trace him through the Porsche registry."

"No," Capri says, "I don't think so." She looks around the table. "I've got you and you and you and you and you... and Granddaddy."

"Never forget Granddaddy," her mother says and laughs.

Aunt Abigail adds, "Like the sun would ever let the stars forget."

Capri says, "He does provide the light," and then she smiles.

"Natives claim that the coffee cherries still whisper the story of the two lovers," her mother says. "They say they see John Mallory and Machu Domingo at the foot of the waterfall. Bathing with the Baird's tapir. John Mallory is holding a three-toed sloth. Some Costa Ricans even claim a jaguar rests near that spot. There's a refuge there, not far. It's called *Un Sendero de Paraíso*, a path of paradise that connects the forests." She hesitates and looks away from Capri, focusing on the coffee pot. "Part of it's mine. I've never told my sisters or Granddaddy." Capri hears her aunts gasp, but she can't take her eyes off her mother. "I bought into an investment group with my own money, under a corporate umbrella. They don't know anything about me, but they don't need to know everything."

"What happened to them? Lorenzo and Juanita. How about Paco? Are any of them alive?"

"I don't know, honey," her mother says. "For all I know, they live on the land. I don't know though. Being part of it, it's my way of keeping close to Costa Rica and her, without breaking my heart. I like to think John Mallory's work continues, with them. I still love those people, because of her, but I don't know about them. I had to let them go. Because it would break our hearts if we had to deal with it."

"Maybe we can go there someday," Capri says, "When you think you're ready."

Her mother is smiling because she knows she means with her.

"We all have two stories," Capri says, looking down at her cup.

"Myth and reality can be one in the same perception," Aunt Abigail says. She's been pretending to read the newspaper at the other side of the table.

Her mother says, "It's said that the moon escaped Earth eons ago. There was a fight, an explosion, and the moon took its solace in the sky. The sun and the moon split the world in half. They created *medianoche*. One would bring light to the darkness, and one would reflect darkness to the light. Some say the argument was over the seventh daughter. Personally, I think the moon is a woman."

"I like that," Capri says. "They bring light and darkness to each other."

"I like it, too," her mother says.

"John Mallory isn't just a Little Girl," Capri says to Aunt Lolly. "She's a legend."

"You're right, honey," her mother says. "I guess I never really realized it until now, but the truth is, John Mallory found her own path in Costa Rica. She had to go away to become the person she was meant to be." She shakes her head and looks at her sisters. "John Mallory was no Little Girl when I saw her. She became everything she wanted. The work she did, the life she created. She touched so many people's hearts. It's no wonder we can't let her go." Trinka looks at Capri and smiles. "John Mallory didn't need any of us to tell her what to do. She figured it out on her own. Just like you did," she says. "You're like her that way, honey. That way, too."

Capri smiles and closes her eyes. She breathes deeply and smells the coffee.

She may be a child in a world of brainwashed souls, with instant gratification shocking her olfactory senses. Hers is a life of consumption: greasy fast foods and scented laundry, gas logs not crackling in the fireplace. She lives where drugs come in cartoon characters. It's a place where people speed read news, if they read at all. People become human bombs. They kill in the name of God. But they are also people who dance. Sometimes to music with angry lyrics, and sometimes in high-heeled sneakers, and they laugh and cry and hurt and heal. They create messes. That's life. *Pura vida.* They always have the ability to grow and love.

Capri's creaseless face is protected from the sun with SPF 30, but she can still feel the sunshine. She can dance in the moonlight. And she can smell the sugar of the soil from faraway lands in a cup of Costa Rican coffee.

Because, sometimes, when she smells the coffee, she can feel the dirt between her toes. She can breathe the cool cloud forest, and for that second, that one moment in time, she tastes a bit of chocolate. And maybe, she thinks, maybe coffee trees do have eyes, they can tell stories. The canopy of the rainforest can be her shade. And she wishes, she wishes that sometimes she lived just a little farther south, across the river, over the sea.

Even Capri can convince herself that John Mallory just floated away in a basket.

She'll be back.

When they dance with her, she is.

And then she can convince herself that the moon is more than the reflection of the sun's light. It becomes her light.

Capri looks down at her coffee cup and says, "*Sin café no hay mañana.*"

They speak of love, but not just as wings lured to the sun or the veil of the moon. At seventeen, Capri knows the spicy scent of desire and the sweet warmth of love, too.

Though Capri can barely see through the crystals on her eyelashes, she sees her mother stand and reach for the pot of coffee. It smells young and bold and sprightly. It takes Capri back underneath the stars in a moonlit night, with her in her blue-green dress that matches her eyes, with Granddaddy in his red cowboy boots. They are twirling and spinning, and when her mother joins them, and Capri looks in her eyes, they hold her like fancy green diamonds. She can see herself in them.

SPACE

You sleep in my bed, hot with fever.

When I rub your back
in the moonlight, and stars dance in your hair,
I kiss your forehead, and you curl next to me
tight,
sighing, as if your breath with mine means
we could be saved. I think
you think
I will live forever, I think
to you I am earth and trees
even though
my sap is the blood in your veins,
your tears should not be my dew.

When you hurt, if I could, I would make from my limbs
a Murphy bed, and fold you
into my walls where you would stay
hidden,
tucked away, as if
I could keep you,
safe buried in my soil.

But I am nothing more than the scientist who watches the sky
hoping to discover shooting comets
20 or 30 years before they hit your Earth
felling millions of trees. I will find them,
to nudge them,
to slow them down just a millimeter per second
pushing them into the ocean,
or empty areas where they can
explode over desolate regions.

JANICE LIERZ

When together we lie in our dreams
we spring as two saplings
scratching out time in dirt and rings,
like diamonds in the sky
like shooting stars already home.

30

Dance of the Goddess

Madness smells like a predator. It obeys no one. With wild eyes, it explodes, fiery and hot, yelling and spitting from the river. It sends jaguar racing for the underbrush. Its aroma is smoky. Dynamite, dropped down a dried up hole, it has no other course than to fall into the darkness. Yet, no matter how unpredictable and uncontrollable, it can be coaxed, like a hesitant lover, soothed with fragrant oils and dark chocolate.

There must be offerings.

Capri watches as her mother pours the coffee in a carafe, then hides it in her leather bag. She's humming. Her aunts are drinking the exotic Costa Rican blend at the kitchen table. They're chit-chatting about green coffee prices, the stock market, and the soaring price of gas.

Capri has slipped off the ring from her finger and clasped the stone around her neck. She has changed into her long flowery blue frock, the one with blue stars that her Granddaddy calls her Pleiades robe.

"Where are you going?" she says to Trinka.

"To see Granddaddy," her mother answers, zipping shut her bag and heading for the front hall. Capri follows her.

When her mother flings open the door, the stars are glittering, whispering, showering, spritzing, sprinkling, and dizzying Capri with their scents. Her senses open up. She can smell the river next to the old trail where years ago her Great Great Granddaddy drove corn-fed cows to market. She can see Great Granddaddy's bucket and Granddaddy's footpath. She can smell the sweet scent of her grandmothers and mothers and aunts standing in doorways with pitchforks. She smells a waterfall where the hurried paddled across the river, for a shortcut, and she can see the longer path, past jagged rocks. Capri's walk may have taken a little more time, but she can breathe in the baby powder along with the jungle coffee.

Moonlight shines into Rainbow Boulevard.

She grabs her purse and runs outside, calling to her mother, "I want to go, too."

Her aunts scatter from their chairs like fairy dust. Her mother stops and turns around. She stares at Capri. "Capri and I are going to see Granddaddy," she says to her sisters.

Their mouths fall open.

"Trinka," Abigail says, "we've agreed that it's no place for the children."

"Daddy wants the grandkids to stay away," Aunt Bess says.

"I know it was our agreement, but my daughter wants to see her granddaddy." She touches Capri's hair as if she's touching a bubble. "And I'm taking her," she says.

Capri races to keep up with her mother as she heads down the brick sidewalk.

"There are some things we don't like," her mother says, "and some things we'll never understand. Still, they are the truth, and the truth is our story. And no one can take our story away from us."

Outside, Capri gazes up into the sky. Only the brightest stars attract her attention. It is drizzling. She and her mother have no umbrella. As Capri's eyes adjust to the thousands of twinkling lights, she can smell the rainbow of blue stars in the ink of the night. Along with gold and silver, there is a kaleidoscope of green and cherry-red that opens up the sky to the tiny earth. Wind takes a message to the stars, and they twinkle at the moon.

Capri feels the receptionist watching them through the door, a white dress that smiles from an artificial tan.

"Let's go, honey," her mother says and gently nudges her daughter towards the entrance.

Inside, they stomp off the moisture and her mother complains to the girl behind the desk about the drizzle. Bundled under layers of cotton, buttons and straps, pink raindrops stick to Capri's hair and eyelashes but vanish before she reaches the desk.

"Oh, Brandy, it's such a messy night, isn't it?" her mother says.

"It is," the receptionist answers, "but it's good to see you, Ms. Mallory."

Brandy pretends she doesn't recognize Capri, but Capri knows she does. She gives Capri an understanding smile. When Brandy slips the plastic badges on the counter, she asks about traffic on Prospect Avenue, her way home. While her mother signs the log, she uses her best motherly tone and tells her to be careful, that the streets are slick.

Brandy buzzes them in and they step forward. They are all virgins at the mouths of volcanoes.

Shiny hallways picket orderly rooms, yet everything reeks of fright: antiseptics and soiled sheets, the cold terror when a face appears at a darkened window. Someone screams. No one slows down or gives a quizzical look. Nurses and orderlies nod their heads as Capri and her mother pass, like they are old friends who have come for dinner.

Around the corner, her mother presses the button on the wall.

"Oh good, Pat's here. She's my favorite," her mother says. Pat lets them in, with her keys jingling from her belt loop. She is the cowgirl nurse, wearing the same electric-blue boots that match her shirts and pants, and Capri can't help but think of her as a girl in search of her own basket in the sky.

Pat crinkles her nose and playfully nudges Trinka. Her mother smiles and swats at her. Pat nods at Capri and smiles.

"Hello, Elizabeth," her mother says, and the woman behind the desk looks up from her computer. Her eyes are hallowed. Her mother asks about her hip treatment, if the cortisone has helped. Elizabeth thinks it has, somewhat. But she says she still limps and it hurts.

"Hello, Reverend," her mother says.

The reverend shuffles by, and Capri greets him, too. He tilts up his face, a wide expanse of wrinkles, spots and glasses. He searches Capri's eyes. Finally, he smiles. He asks her where he can find a train. Capri is flustered and tells him she doesn't know, but her mother holds his hand and points to the dayroom.

"If you wait there," she tells the reverend, "one will come soon."

He almost slips as he hurries for a seat.

Down the linoleum, in room eleven, Capri and her mother find Granddaddy in bed. Even with the bedside light on, darkness takes the room. Stars cannot squeeze between the slats of the shades. Under the sheets, he is tucked into a ball. They are still at his foot when a man in a white coat appears. He reports that her granddaddy is doing better. Still some cognitive dysfunction, he says, but he's effectively better.

But what Capri still wants to know is: *Where does he go? Where is he when we can't reach him?*

Pat bobs behind the doctor in her cowgirl boots, flashing her black eyes and white smile, clicking on the linoleum. She's making kissy faces in the air behind the doctor's head. Capri's mother reprimands her with her eyes and swats her away behind the doctor's back.

When they leave, her mother turns to Capri. "Madness knits families of strangers," she says. Her mother looks down the hallway. Certain they are gone, she pulls a Styrofoam cup and the coffee carafe from her purse. She pours Granddaddy a cup of coffee and positions it on the bedside table. She pops the lid of the carafe and fans the air, hoping the smell will wake him.

The room fills with the sweetest scent, a magical brew of Costa Rican coffee.

Mr. White is asleep in his bed, and Capri wonders if he dreams about dancing, like some people dream in songs and sounds. His foot moves a little.

As soon as Capri and her mother settle into chairs, Capri hears slippers in the hallway. A woman stands in the doorway wearing turquoise silk pajamas, holding her arm at a ninety-degree angle. She is regal, with a long neck and sculptured hair.

"Poor Francis would be horrified if she knew," her mother whispers. "This is not your room, Francis," she tells the woman. "Your room is next door, Francis," she says, gently, and smiles at her.

Francis leaves, but Capri has a feeling she'll be back.

"Francis jumps into other people's beds," her mother says, "but then the orderlies have to change the sheets. Too much work."

Granddaddy's eyes snap open. They are dark, droopy clouds that rest on the topaz necklace around Capri's neck. It's a lasting treasure, the stone he had cut for her at Silver Dollar City.

"Please," he whispers. "Dance with me." His eyes remain hazy, but they're fixed on Capri, not her mother.

Her mother taps Capri's arm and says, "I'll dance for you, Daddy." She stands up and moves away her chair.

"John Mallory? John Mallory," he says still staring at Capri. "Please."

"No, honey, don't worry," she whispers to Capri. "Look, Daddy, look. I'm dancing." Her mother begins to move her hips.

"John Mallory, why can't we dance? Honey. John Mallory? Please. Please, forgive me. Dance with me, John Mallory."

"Look, Daddy. Look at me." Her mother moves in between them. She is swiveling her hips and spinning around.

Capri takes a deep breath. She is not a little girl. She doesn't stand up for causes she believes in. She doesn't clean up the environment to protect animals. She volunteers in the community when she's trying to rack up service hours for honor societies. She may never save the world, or children, or animals, not yet at least, but maybe she can save someone. Maybe she can save her granddaddy. And, right now, that's good enough.

Capri knows about love.

"I'm here," Capri says, standing up. She holds his hand. Her voice is strong and foreign and exotic. "It's John Mallory," she says. "I'm here. I've come to dance with you. Don't worry, I'm always here. With you, Daddy."

She leans over to whisper the hush of the greatest star. He looks at her, and her eyes flutter like the blue morpho butterfly.

She is a girl stepping out of a basket.

She looks at her mother and smiles. She knows scents come in pairs, yet she doesn't have to choose. Capri moves away the chair, and reaches up to her fading pink hair. She knows how her granddaddy sees her. In his eyes, her hair is tumbling until it flows down her back. Sun-drenched, she raises her arm to the window so any little bird can land on her wrist.

Then, slowly, she spins and fans out her robe. With her mother beside her, Capri dances. She twirls, laughing, her voice the sound of a musical fruit.

She is the scent of Mother Bean.

In the sprinkle of moonlight, barefoot in a field of cocoa and vanilla, they are deep in the cool cloud forest of plantain and banana. Their fragrance perfumes and mists through the canopy of kapok trees. Nearby, under the eyes of the sun, birds rise from nesting in shade trees. Capuchin monkeys swing high in the branches. Sun-soaked flowers burst on the vine and turn into pomegranate. They are the rhythm of flute and drum. Migrant Indians and farmers. Heavenly children, they roam the kaleidoscope mountains with jaguar. They are the smell of the red and golden cherries on the coffee trees, of yesterday, today, and tomorrow. Always. They are coffee.

Sín café no hay mañana. Without love there is no tomorrow.

This is their story.

They are the Seven Sisters. Some say it was Sun's fault, but others claim it was a man. Throughout the mountains of Costa Rica, John Mallory walks, where they say she is a river, her breath the rise and flood, the fertilizer for the soil of her beloved coffee. People of the land still sing of the young lovers. Coffee cherries whisper the ballad of the Roastmaster, of the man with the large round moon face, of Mother Bean, of the sweet nectars of life.

The blue stars brighten, and the scent of the moon slips into the room and blends with the organic brew. Capri breathes in, and her mother breathes out. Granddaddy inhales deeply.

Capri understands why seven sisters dance. Why they travel the northern skies in a basket. And she can unveil her shape in front of any mirror and point to faded tattoos and timely battle scars. She can smell the coffee cherries beneath her fading pink hair and feel the blue stars sparkling in her eyes.

She knows magic can be found in the bean of a fruit.

Acknowledgements

This novel found its way into the physical world thanks to an abundance of encouragement and assistance from many people. It certainly spent too many years languishing in crowded offices. Yet all things happen for a reason. My heartfelt appreciation and gratitude goes to the following individuals and organizations: to my husband, Dan, and our three children, Sydney, Jonah, and Oliver, for being my brilliant stars, for their love and support; to my writing partners Susan Hasler and Nancy Collins, talented writers who have been thoughtful readers, editors, and die-hard nudgers; to my many writing teachers but especially Dr. Barbara Kidneigh, Natalie Goldberg, Ann Hood, and Ron Rash; to Novello Festival Press, publisher Amy Rogers, and *Charlotte ViewPoint* and editor Jeff Jackson, where an excerpt of this novel appeared, and for recognizing *Roastmaster* as a Finalist for the Novello Literary Award; to the many literary institutions where I continue to hone my craft but especially Bread Loaf and Wildacres; to the literary publications where my work has appeared with a special thanks to *Hiram Poetry Review* who first published the poem "Space" and early supporters *Asheville Poetry Review, Del Sol Review, Tar River Poetry, The Evansville Review, The Louisville Review, Quercus Review, Tightrope, Eclipse and Wisconsin Review*; to the dedicated coffee farmers, harvesters, marketers and lovers of the bean, everywhere, especially those at the coffee farm in Costa Rica where I was inspired to write this novel and to my friends and former colleagues in the coffee industry; to my fellow writers and poets, friends and enthusiasts who know what it is like to bare your soul on the page; and finally, to those readers who connect to my writing, for helping me close the loop to my creative process. Thank you, one and all. May you always enjoy a good cup of coffee.

About Janice Lierz

Janice Lierz is a former Fortune 500 executive and an award-winning writer and poet whose work has appeared in literary journals, magazines and anthologies. Before turning to writing, she spent decades climbing corporate ladders at Johnson & Johnson/McNeil CPC, Heublein, Frito-Lay/PepsiCo, and Whole Foods Market, where she was the president of several subsidiaries, including a coffee company.

She has a long family history with coffee and was inspired to write this novel while on a visit to a coffee farm in Costa Rica. She lives in the Blue Ridge Mountains in North Carolina with her family and pets, where she is working on her next novel.

Please visit Janice at www.JaniceLierz.com

Printed in Great Britain
by Amazon